U0025421

聚焦英語演說

56篇偉大演講 新增二版

經典暢銷書
榮獲
好書大家讀

編者 _ Cosmos Language Workshop

Part 1
遇見偉大的聲音

01/

I Have a Dream

金恩博士：
我有一個夢想

......14

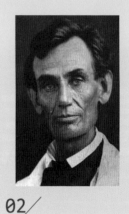

02/

Gettysburg Address

林肯總統：
蓋茨堡宣言

......22

03/

John Brown's Address to the Court After His Conviction

約翰・布朗判刑後
的發言：猶如自己
也同樣受縛

......26

04/

The Four Freedoms

小羅斯福總統：
四大自由

......34

05

Chief Seattle's Treaty Oration

西雅圖酋長宣言

......40

06

Chief Red Eagle: Address to General Andrew Jackson

紅鷹酋長投降宣言：
我無懼於任何人

......48

07

Black Hawk: Surrender Speech

黑鷹酋長投降宣言：
我不曾做過令族人
蒙羞的事

......52

08

Blood, Toil, Tears and Sweat

邱吉爾開戰宣言：
熱血、辛勞、眼淚
和汗水

......56

09

Ich bin ein Berliner

約翰・甘迺迪：
我是柏林人

......62

10

The Great Dictator

卓別林：
《大獨裁者》
演講片段

......68

11/
Non-Violence: The Doctrine of the Sword
印度聖雄甘地：
非暴力，武力的
法則

……76

12/
Our March to Freedom Is Irreversible
曼德拉出獄演講：
邁向民主的腳步
不會倒退

……84

13/
Old Soldiers Never Die
麥克阿瑟國會告別
演說：老兵不死，
只是凋零

……92

14/
Arms Can Bring No Security
愛因斯坦：
武器捍衛不了國土

……98

15/
Shall We Choose Death?
英國哲學家羅素：
我們該選擇死亡
嗎？

……104

16/
Strike Against War
海倫‧凱勒：
不要順從於毀滅者

……112

17/
The Perils of Indifference
集中營倖存者維瑟
爾：冷漠的危險

·······118

18/
On Charity and Humor
英國文學家薩克
雷：論慈善與幽默

·······124

19/
Truths of the Heart
福克納諾貝爾得獎
感言：心靈的真諦

·······130

20/
Our Family Creed
洛克斐勒家訓：讓
生命有意義的方法

·······136

21/
Lou Gehrig's Farewell Speech
洋基鐵馬賈里格告
別演說：我是世界
上最幸運的人

·······142

22/
Courage
馬克·吐溫：
勇氣

·······148

23/ **Tribute to a Dog**
為老鼓忠犬辯護：
忠犬禮讚
　　　……152

24/ **To Temper Justice With Mercy**
丹諾律師為少年請
纓：用仁慈之心行
正義之事
　　　……156

25/ **Nothing Is Impossible**
「超人」李維演說：
沒有不可能的事情
　　　……162

26/ **The Audacity of Hope**
歐巴馬基調演說：
無畏的希望
　　　……170

Part 2
感動世界的聲音

27/

**United States
Declaration of
Independence**

美國獨立宣言

‧‧‧‧‧‧180

28/

**Give Me Liberty
or Give Me Death**

不自由，毋寧死

‧‧‧‧‧‧186

29/

**Thomas Jefferson:
The Creed of Our
Political Faith**

傑佛遜第一次就職演
說：我們的政治信
念

‧‧‧‧‧‧194

30/

**Abraham Lincoln:
Second Inaugural
Address**

林肯第二次就職演
說：我們禱告的是同
一個上帝

‧‧‧‧‧‧200

31/

Franklin D.
Roosevelt: First
Inaugural Address

小羅斯福第一次就
職演說：我們唯一
要害怕的，是恐懼
本身

……206

32/

John F. Kennedy:
Inaugural Address

甘迺迪就職演說：
火炬已經傳給新一
代的美國人

……212

33/ song

We Shall
Overcome

詹森總統：我們
終將克服難關

……220

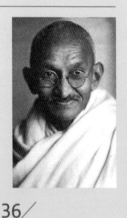

34/

Duty, Honor,
Country

麥帥西點軍校告別
演說：責任、榮耀
和國家

……228

35/

Edward VIII:
Farewell Address

只愛美人不愛江
山：愛德華八世退
位宣言

……232

36/

Appeal to
American

印度聖雄甘地：
向美國呼籲

……238

37

I've Been to the Mountaintop

金恩博士最後的演講：我已踏上山頂

······242

38

On the Death of Martin Luther King

羅伯特‧甘迺迪：金恩博士之死

······250

39

Eulogy for John F. Kennedy

約翰‧甘迺迪總統哀悼文

······256

40

Eulogy for Robert F. Kennedy

羅伯特‧甘迺迪哀悼文

······262

41

The Ballot or the Bullets

麥爾坎‧X：是選票還是子彈？

······268

42

Nelson Mandela: Inaugural Address

曼德拉總統就職演說

······278

43/

Who Will Speak for the Common Good?

女性黑人議員基調演
說：誰能代表共同的
利益？

······284

44/

Science and Art

生物學家赫胥黎：
科學與藝術

······292

45/

The Road to Business Success

卡內基給年輕人的
話：事業成功之道

······298

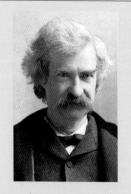

46/

Seventieth Birthday

馬克・吐溫：
七十大壽謝辭

······302

47/

Mother Teresa: Nobel Lecture

德蕾莎修女諾貝爾
獎謝辭：毀滅和平
的最大兇手

······306

48/

Helen Keller: Knights of the Blind

海倫・凱勒：
盲人的騎士

······314

49/
Show Me What You're Doing on HIV
民主黨全國大會演說：為愛滋請命
⋯⋯320

50/
For America
911 恐怖攻擊追悼詩：給美國
⋯⋯328

51/
The BioTech Century
生物科技的世紀：生命的大哉問
⋯⋯332

52/
Barack Obama: Inaugural Address
歐巴馬就職演說：這一代的美國人也要這樣走下去
⋯⋯340

Part 3
時代脈動的聲音

53/

Aung San Suu Kyi: Nobel Lecture

翁山蘇姬諾貝爾獎謝辭：我們不會被遺忘

......346

54/

Malala Yousafzai's Speech to the UN General Assembly

馬拉拉聯合國大會演說：書本和筆才是最強大的武器

......356

55/

Haruki Murakami's Jerusalem Prize Acceptance Speech

村上春樹耶路撒冷獎得獎感言：牆與蛋

......364

56/

Gerhard Schröder Speech: I Express My Shame

德國總理施羅德道歉演說：我深表羞愧

......374

All the great things are simple,
And many can be expressed in a single word:

Freedom
Justice
Honor
Duty
Mercy
Hope

—Winston Churchill

I Have a Dream

馬丁·路德·金恩是美國歷史上最重要的黑人民權運動領袖,他是 1964 年諾貝爾和平獎的得主,常被稱為金恩博士或金恩牧師。

金恩博士為黑人民權奔走的結果,迫使美國國會在 1964 年 4 月通過《民權法案》,宣佈種族隔離和歧視政策為非法政策。1968 年 4 月 4 日,金恩博士在支持田納西州孟菲斯市清潔工人的罷工活動中,被種族主義分子暗殺,享年 39 歲,而他的遇害也引發了美國史上前所未見的黑人抗暴浪潮。

金恩博士的演講被喻為「充滿林肯和甘地精神的象徵,以及聖經的韻律」,而在他所有的演講中,又以《我有一個夢想》最為知名。這篇演講至今仍發揮著極大的影響力,2008 年英國《每日電訊報》評選出 20–21 世紀最重要的 25 場政治演說,這篇演講選入其中。

他在去世之後,1977 年被追頒「總統自由勳章」(Presidential Medal of Freedom),2004 年被追頒「國會金質獎章」(Congressional Gold Medal),這兩項榮譽並列為美國最高的平民榮譽。

2009 年,諾貝爾基金會評選出「諾貝爾獎百餘年來最受尊崇的三位獲獎者」,金恩博士名列首位,其餘兩人分別是 1921 年物理學獎得主愛因斯坦,以及 1979 年和平獎得主德蕾莎修女。

Martin Luther King, Jr. acknowledges the crowd at the Lincoln Memorial for his "I Have a Dream" speech during the March on Washington, D.C., on August 28, 1963.

Speaker 美國牧師兼黑人民權運動領袖馬丁‧路德‧金恩
（Martin Luther King, 1929–1968.4.4）

Time 1963 年 8 月 28 日

Place 美國華盛頓特區林肯紀念堂（Lincoln Memorial）

☉ 原音重現　☉ 擷選

I am happy to join with you today in what will go down in history as the greatest demonstration for freedom in the history of our nation.

Five score[1] years ago, a great American, in whose symbolic shadow we stand today, signed the Emancipation Proclamation[2]. This momentous decree[3] came as a great beacon light of hope to millions of Negro slaves who had been seared[4] in the flames of withering injustice. It came as a joyous daybreak to end the long night of their captivity.

But one hundred years later, the Negro still is not free. One hundred years later, the life of the Negro is still sadly crippled by the manacles[5] of segregation[6] and the chains of discrimination. One hundred years later, the Negro lives on a lonely island of poverty in the midst of a vast ocean of material prosperity. One hundred years later, the Negro is still languished in the corners of American society and finds himself an exile in his own land. And so we've come here today to dramatize a shameful condition.

In a sense we've come to our nation's capital to cash a check. When the architects of our republic wrote the magnificent words of the Constitution and the Declaration of Independence, they were signing a promissory note[7] to which every American was to fall heir. This note was a promise that all men, yes, black men as well as white men, would be guaranteed the "unalienable Rights" of "Life, Liberty and the pursuit of Happiness."

It is obvious today that America has defaulted on this promissory note, insofar as her citizens of color are concerned. Instead of honoring this sacred obligation, America has given the Negro people a bad check, a check which has come back marked "insufficient funds."

But we refuse to believe that the bank of justice is bankrupt. We refuse to believe that there are insufficient funds in the great vaults of opportunity of this nation. And so, we've come to cash this check, a check that will give us upon demand the riches of freedom and the security of justice. →

我很高興今天能和你們站在一起，在我們國家歷史上，這是最偉大的一次爭取自由的運動，我們將寫出我們的歷史。

一百年前，一個偉大的美國人簽署了《解放黑奴宣言》，我們現在就站在這個偉人的雕像前面集會。這個劃時代的法令，是一道明亮的希望之光，照亮了數百萬名黑奴，他們一直深受著不公不義的烈火所煎熬。這是一道充滿喜悅的曙光，驅走了他們慘遭奴役的漫漫長夜。

然而，一百年後，黑人並未真正自由。一百年後的今天，種族隔離的腳鐐和種族歧視的枷鎖，將黑人拘禁在悲慘的生活裡。一百年後的今天，黑人居住在一座貧窮的孤島上，島的四周是一片物質充裕的海洋。一百年後的今天，黑人仍舊受困在美國社會的角落裡，被自己的國家所驅逐。所以，我們今天來到這裡，就要把這種可恥的情況公諸於世。

就某種意義上來說，我們今天來到我們國家的首都，就是來要求兌現承諾。我們這個共和國的締造者們，當他們在《憲法》和《獨立宣言》上寫下了偉大的宣言時，他們就如同簽署了一份每一位美國人民都有權要求兌現的承諾書。這份承諾是給予所有人的，是的，不分黑人還是白人，每一個人的「生存、自由和追求幸福」的「權利」，都是「不可剝奪的」。

很顯然地，就有色公民來說，美國並未兌現這份承諾。政府不但沒有履行神聖的義務，相反地，它向黑人開出的是一張被退回的空頭支票，上面寫著「資金不足」。

然而，我們決不相信「正義銀行」會破產。我們決不相信這個國家庫存滿滿的「機會庫房」，會資金不足。所以，我們來這裡要求兌換支票，要求兌換一張將給予我們寶貴自由和正義保障的支票。

the statue memorial for Martin Luther King Jr. in West Potomac Park, Washington D.C.

Martin Luther King (1929–1968)

1. score [skɔːr] (n.) a set of twenty members
   二十（單複數同形）

2. Emancipation Proclamation: declaration of freedom for enslaved people in Confederacy《解放黑奴宣言》

3. decree [dɪˈkriː] (n.) an official order 法令

4. sear [sɪr] (v.) to make very hot and dry 焦灼

5. manacle [ˈmænəkəl] (n.) ring around a prisoner's wrist 手銬；腳鐐

6. segregation [ˌsegrɪˈɡeɪʃən] (n.) enforced separation of groups 種族隔離

7. promissory note: a signed document containing a written promise to pay a stated sum 本票

We have also come to this hallowed spot to remind America of the fierce urgency of Now. This is no time to engage in the luxury of cooling off or to take the tranquilizing drug of gradualism[8]. Now is the time to make real the promises of democracy. Now is the time to rise from the dark and desolate valley of segregation to the sunlit path of racial justice. Now is the time to lift our nation from the quicksands of racial injustice to the solid rock of brotherhood. Now is the time to make justice a reality for all of God's children.

It would be fatal for the nation to overlook the urgency of the moment. This sweltering[9] summer of the

Negro's legitimate discontent will not pass until there is an invigorating[10] autumn of freedom and equality. 1963 is not an end, but a beginning. And those who hope that the Negro needed to blow off steam and will now be content will have a rude awakening if the nation returns to business as usual. And there will be neither rest nor tranquility in America until the Negro is granted his citizenship rights. The whirlwinds of revolt will continue to shake the foundations of our nation until the bright day of justice emerges.

There are those who are asking the devotees of civil rights, "When will you be satisfied?" We can never be satisfied as long as the Negro is the victim of the unspeakable horrors of police brutality. We can never be satisfied as long as our bodies, heavy with the fatigue of travel, cannot gain lodging in the motels of the highways and the hotels of the cities. We cannot be satisfied as long as a Negro in Mississippi cannot vote and a Negro in New York believes he has nothing for which to vote. No, no, we are not satisfied, and we will not be satisfied until "justice rolls down like waters, and righteousness like a mighty stream[11]." →

我們今天來到這個聖地，也是要提醒美國了解到事態的緊迫。現在不是要求冷靜或採取緩進主義的時候。此時此刻，就是要真正實現民主承諾的時刻。此時此刻，就是要走出種族隔離黑暗荒涼的山谷、迎向種族平等的日光大道的時候。此時此刻，就是將國家從種族不平等的流沙中拯救出來、移到充滿同胞愛的磐石上的時候。此時此刻，就是為所有上帝的子民實現公義的時候。

政府如果忽視這種急迫性，後果將不堪設想。自由與平等的舒爽涼秋如果不到來，黑人義憤填膺的酷暑就不會過去。1963 年決不是一個終點，而是一個起點。有些人以為，黑人只是想要發洩一下，鬧一鬧就沒事了，但是政府如果依舊我行我素，那他們一定會被驚醒。只要黑人尚未取得公民權利，美國安寧祥和的日子就不會到來。只要正義的光明一天不到來，革命的浪潮就會繼續動搖這個國家的基礎。

有人問這些獻身於公民權運動的人說：「你們要爭取到什麼地步才會滿意？」只要黑人仍遭受警察粗暴不堪的對待，我們就不會滿意；只要我們在外奔波的疲憊身體，不能在公路旁的汽車旅館或是鎮上的飯店中投宿，我們就不會滿意；只要密西西比州還有一個黑人沒有投票權，或是紐約還有一個黑人認為自己的選票無濟於事，那我們就不會滿意。不會，不會，我們不會滿意的，我們始終都不會滿意的，除非「公平如大水滾滾，公義如江河滔滔」。

8. gradualism [ˈɡrædʒuəlɪzm] (n.) the policy of advancing toward a goal by gradual stages 緩進主義

9. sweltering [ˈsweltərɪŋ] (a.) excessively hot and humid 悶熱的

10. invigorating [ɪnˈvɪɡəreɪtɪŋ] (a.) giving strength, energy, and vitality 舒爽的

11. An extract from *Amos* 5:24. "But let judgment run down as waters, and righteousness as a mighty stream."
出自《聖經‧阿摩司書》第 5 章第 24 節：「惟願公平如大水滾滾，使公義如江河滔滔。」

Let us not wallow[12] in the valley of despair, I say to you today, my friends. And so even though we face the difficulties of today and tomorrow, I still have a dream. It is a dream deeply rooted in the American dream.

I have a dream that one day this nation will rise up and live out the true meaning of its creed: "We hold these truths to be self-evident, that all men are created equal."[13]

I have a dream that one day on the red hills of Georgia, the sons of former slaves and the sons of former slave owners will be able to sit down together at the table of brotherhood.

I have a dream that one day even the state of Mississippi, a state sweltering with the heat of injustice, sweltering with the heat of oppression, will be transformed into an oasis of freedom and justice.

I have a dream that my four little children will one day live in a nation where they will not be judged by the color of their skin but by the content of their character.

I have a dream today!

I have a dream that one day, down in Alabama, with its vicious racists, with its governor having his lips dripping with the words of "interposition" and "nullification"[14]—one day right there in Alabama little black boys and black girls will be able to join hands with little white boys and white girls as sisters and brothers.

I have a dream today!

I have a dream that one day every valley shall be exalted, and every hill and mountain shall be made low, the rough places will be made plain, and the crooked places will be made straight;[15] "and the glory of the Lord shall be revealed and all flesh shall see it together[16]."

This is our hope, and this is the faith that I go back to the South with. With this faith, we will be able to hew out of the mountain of despair a stone of hope. With this faith, we will be able to transform the jangling discords of our nation into a beautiful symphony of brotherhood. With this faith, we will be able to work together, to pray together, to struggle together, to go to jail together, to stand up for freedom together, knowing that we will be free one day.

朋友們，今天我要跟你們説，我們不應該在絕望的谷底打滾。儘管現在和未來有重重的困難橫在我們眼前，但我仍然懷有一個夢想，這個夢想深植於美國夢之中。

我有一個夢想：期待有一天，這個國家會站起來實踐宣言的真諦：「這個真理是不言而喻的，那就是，人人生而平等。」

我有一個夢想：期待有一天，在喬治亞州的紅土山丘上，昔日的奴隸之子和蓄奴者之子，能夠並肩而坐，親如手足。

我有一個夢想：期待有一天，即使是深受不義與壓迫之火所煎熬的密西西比州，也能夠變成一塊自由與正義的綠洲。

我有一個夢想：期待有一天，在我的四個小孩所住的國家裡，人們是以品性而不是膚色來評斷人。

我今天有這麼一個夢想！

我有一個夢想：期待有一天，在種族歧視最嚴重的阿拉巴馬州，州長目前仍然持異議，拒絕承認聯邦法令——期待有一天，就在阿拉巴馬州裡，黑人與白人的小孩們能夠像兄弟姐妹那樣牽手。

我今天有這麼一個夢想！

我有一個夢想：期待有一天，每一個山谷都能被填平，每一座山岳丘陵都能被削平，崎嶇不平的地方能變成平原，曲折的彎路能變成筆直的道路，「上帝的榮耀必然顯現，凡有血氣的，必一同看見。」

這就是我們的願望，我就是帶著這個信念回到南方的。有了這個信念，我們就能夠在絕望的山中挖出希望之石。有了這個信念，我們就可以把國家內部各種不和的聲音，變成一首歌頌手足之情的美麗交響曲。有了這個信念，我們就能夠一起工作，一起祈禱，一起奮鬥，一起入獄，一起共同捍衛自由。我們知道，終有一天，我們會是自由的。

12. wallow ['wɑːloʊ] (v.) to roll around 打滾

13. An extract from the *United States Declaration of Independence* 出自《美國獨立宣言》

14. nullification [ˌnʌlɪfɪ'keɪʃən] (n.) refusal or failure of a U.S. state to recognize or enforce a federal law within its boundaries 州對聯邦法令的拒絕執行或承認

15. An extract from *Isaiah* 40:4. "Every valley shall be exalted, and every mountain and hill shall be made low: and the crooked shall be made straight, and the rough places plain." 出自《聖經‧以賽亞書》第 40 章第 4 節：「一切山窪都要填滿，大小山岡都要削平；高高低低的要改為平坦，崎崎嶇嶇的必成為平原。」

16. An extract from *Isaiah* 40:5. "And the glory of the LORD shall be revealed, and all flesh shall see it together: for the mouth of the LORD hath spoken it." 出自《聖經‧以賽亞書》第 40 章第 5 節：「耶和華的榮耀必然顯現；凡有血氣的必一同看見；因為這是耶和華親口説的。」

Gettysburg Address

林肯總統：
蓋茨堡宣言

1861 年，美國爆發了南北戰爭（American Civil War, 1861 年 4 月 12 日至 1865 年 4 月 9 日）。美國南北戰爭的爆發和結束，都在林肯的總統任期內，戰爭持續了四年。

在 1863 年六、七月期間所發生的一連串戰役，統稱為「蓋茨堡戰役」（Gettysburg Campaign），而在這一連串戰役當中，又以持續了三天的「蓋茨堡之役」（Battle of Gettysburg，1863 年 7 月 1 日至 7 月 3 日）最為關鍵。

「蓋茨堡之役」在三天內死傷超過五萬人，是美國內戰中最慘烈的一戰，但也是個轉捩點。在這場戰役中，南方的李將軍（Robert Edward Lee, 1807–1870）於 7 月 3 日美國國慶日當天敗退，四個半月之後，在同年的 11 月 19 日，林肯在賓州蓋茨堡的蓋茨堡國家公墓落成典禮上，發表了這場著名的《蓋茨堡宣言》，哀悼陣亡的將士。

《蓋茨堡宣言》是林肯最著名的演說，也是美國歷史上被引用最多的政治性演說。這篇演講雖然簡短，但在現代民主政治中，卻是最具代表性的。演講中所強調的「自由」、「平等」和「民有、民治、民享的政府」，一直是現代民主社會所追求的目標。

美國第 44 任總統歐巴馬在 2009 年的就職演說中，還模仿了林肯這篇演說的語句結構和修辭，其影響力可見一斑。

Pennsylvania State Memorial at Gettysburg

Speaker 美國第 16 任總統亞伯拉罕・林肯
（Abraham Lincoln, 1809-1865）

Time 1863 年 11 月 19 日

Place 賓州蓋茨堡的蓋茨堡國家公墓落成典禮
（Gettysburg National Cemetery）

◉ Jeff Daniels 讀誦　◉ 全文收錄

Fourscore and seven years ago our fathers brought forth on this continent a new nation, conceived[1] in liberty, and dedicated to the proposition that all men are created equal[2].

Now we are engaged in a great civil war, testing whether that nation, or any nation so conceived and so dedicated, can long endure. We are met on a great battlefield of that war. We have come to dedicate a portion of that field as a final resting place for those who here gave their lives that that nation might live. It is altogether fitting and proper that we should do this.

But, in a larger sense, we cannot dedicate—we cannot consecrate[3]— we cannot hallow—this ground. The brave men, living and dead, who struggled here, have consecrated it far above our poor power to add or detract[4]. The world will little note nor long remember what we say here, but it can never forget what they did here. It is for us, the living, rather, to be dedicated here to the unfinished work which they who fought here have thus far so nobly advanced.

It is rather for us to be here dedicated to the great task remaining before us—that from these honored dead we take increased devotion to that cause for which they gave the last full measure of devotion; that we here highly resolve that these dead shall not have died in vain; that this nation, under God, shall have a new birth of freedom; and that government of the people, by the people, for the people, shall not perish from the earth.

八十七年前，我們的先人在這片大陸上建立了這個新的國家。這個國家在自由中孕育，奉行人人生而平等的原則。

現在，我們投入這場偉大的內戰，考驗著這個國家、像這樣一個在自由中孕育、奉行上述原則的國家，是否能夠長久生存下去。我們在這場戰爭的偉大戰場上聚集在一起，是為了要在這塊戰場上，為那些為國家捐軀的烈士們覓得一塊安息之地。這是我們義不容辭、應該要做的事。

然而，從更深刻的意義來說，我們無法奉獻——無法神化——無法聖化——這塊土地。那些曾經在這一塊土地上奮鬥的勇者們，不論是生者或逝者，他們已經讓這塊土地變得神聖了，我們微薄的力量遠遠無法再增添什麼，但也無法去玷污它。我們今天在這裡所說的，微不足道，很快就會被遺忘，但人們永遠會記得那些勇者們曾經在這裡做過的奉獻。對我們這些生者來說，我們在這裡要獻身的，是去完成尚未完成的大業，那是勇者們在此奮戰、以崇高精神向前邁進的大業。

我們這些站在這裡的人，應該獻身於眼前尚未完成的事業——我們應該繼承這些光榮先烈的遺志，他們已經完全奉獻出自己，我們應該對此做出更進一步的貢獻。在這裡，我們下了最大的決心，決不讓先烈的鮮血白流。這個國家，蒙上帝之恩，即將破繭成為一個嶄新的自由國家。我們要讓這個民有、民治、民享的政府，永世長存。

1. conceive [kən'siːv] (v.) to begin or originate in a specific way 孕育

2. An extract from the *United States Declaration of Independence*
出自《美國獨立宣言》

3. consecrate ['kɑːnsɪkreɪt] (v.) to make sacred 使神聖

4. detract [dɪ'trækt] (v.) to diminish or take away 降低；減損

John Brown's Address to the Court After His Conviction

約翰‧布朗判刑後的發言：
猶如自己也同樣受縛

約翰‧布朗（John Brown, 1800–1859）為美國白人，他承續父親反對蓄奴的精神，最後成為一位激進的廢奴主義者。他為解放黑奴，不惜訴諸武力，他認為不透過激烈的手段，無法改變這種蓄奴的惡風。

1859 年 10 月 16 日深夜，約翰‧布朗帶著 21 名武裝夥伴潛入維吉尼亞州一座名為哈普斯渡口（Harpers Ferry）的小鎮，抓了 60 位當地的重要人物當人質，並佔領鎮上的軍火庫和槍枝製造廠。第三天，名將李將軍（Robert E. Lee）的軍隊攻入，逮捕了約翰‧布朗。約翰‧布朗在這場起義中不但失去了兩個兒子，自己也遭到逮捕，並處以死刑。

同年 11 月 2 日，他被判處極刑的罪名包括叛國罪、謀殺罪和煽動叛亂罪，以下收錄的法庭上的陳述，就是他在聽完判決之後所做的聲明，隔天他的這篇言論登上了《紐約先驅報》。一個月後，在他伏法的那一天，北方人民將之視為英雄烈士，教堂的鐘聲和致哀禮炮四處響起，並且為他建立了紀念碑。他在受刑前的最後一刻，留下了最後的話：

I, John Brown, am now quite certain that the crimes of this guilty land can never be purged away but with blood.
我，約翰‧布朗，我此刻甚為確定：這一塊罪惡之地上的罪行，只能用鮮血來蹓滌。

約翰‧布朗被視為「美國 19 世紀最具爭議性的人物」，林肯總統稱他為「誤入歧途的狂熱者」（misguided fanatic），但愛默生和梭羅對他持肯定、讚許的態度。歷史學家則皆認為，約翰‧布朗的事件是引爆美國內戰的重要原因之一。

美國內戰時期最知名的愛國歌曲《約翰‧布朗的軀體》（John Brown's Body），被傳唱的程度不下於美國國歌《星條旗》（The Star-Spangled Banner），或是《天佑美國》（God Bless America）。原版《約翰‧布朗的軀體》中的「約翰‧布朗」最初雖然不是指這位廢奴主義者，但當時候人人都把這首歌當成是紀念他的歌曲，並且由此而編出歌詞，唱出內戰的光榮目標。這首歌傳唱甚廣，歌詞有諸多版本，以下是其中一個常見的版本。→

Speaker 美國激進廢奴主義者約翰‧布朗
（John Brown, 1800–1859）

Time 1859 年 11 月 2 日

Place 美國維吉尼亞法庭（Virginia Court）

▣ 錄音　▣ 全文收錄

John Brown's Body

John Brown's body lies a-mouldering in the grave; *
His soul's marching on!

Glory, glory, hallelujah! *
His soul's marching on!

He's gone to be a soldier in the army of the Lord! *
His soul's marching on!

John Brown's knapsack is strapped upon his back! *
His soul's marching on!

His pet lambs will meet him on the way; *
They go marching on!

They will hang Jeff Davis** to a sour apple tree! *
As they march along!

Now, three rousing cheers for the Union; *
As we are marching on!

03

猶如自己也同樣受縛

約翰·布朗的軀體（歌曲演唱）

約翰·布朗的軀體躺在墳墓裡腐爛，*
他的英魂正在前進著！

光榮！光榮，哈利路亞！*
他的英魂正在前進著！

他已經是上帝軍隊裡的一個士兵，*
他的英魂正在前進著！

約翰·布朗的背包綑緊在他的背上，*
他的英魂正在前進著！

他寵愛的羔羊將在路上迎接他，*
牠們將跟著前進著！

他們將把傑夫·戴維斯吊死在酸蘋果樹上，*
他們正在前進著！

現在，響起對合眾國的歡呼聲，*
因為我們正在前進著！

* repeat three times
** Jefferson Hamilton
   Davis（1808–1889），
   美國內戰期間擔任南
   方主張蓄奴的「美利
   堅聯盟國」的總統。

I have, may it please the court, a few words to say. In the first place, I deny everything but what I have all along admitted—the design on my part to free the slaves. I intended certainly to have made a clean thing of that matter, as I did last winter when I went into Missouri and there took slaves without the snapping of a gun on either side, moved them through the country, and finally left them in Canada. I designed to have done the same thing again on a larger scale. That was all I intended. I never did intend murder, or treason, or the destruction of property, or to excite or incite[1] slaves to rebellion, or to make insurrection[2].

I have another objection; and that is, it is unjust that I should suffer such a penalty.

Had I interfered in the manner which I admit, and which I admit has been fairly proved (for I admire the truthfulness and candor[3] of the greater portion of the witnesses who have testified in this case)—had I so interfered in behalf of the rich, the powerful, the intelligent, the so-called great, or in behalf of any of their friends—either father, mother, brother, sister, wife, or children, or any of that class—and suffered and sacrificed what I have in this interference, it would have been all right; and every man in this court would have deemed it an act worthy of reward rather than punishment.

This court acknowledges, as I suppose, the validity of the law of God. I see a book kissed here which I suppose to be the *Bible*, or at least the *New Testament*. That teaches me that all things whatsoever I would that men should do to me, I should do even so to them. It teaches me, further, to "remember them that are in bonds, as bound with them.[4]"

I endeavored to act up to that instruction. I say I am yet too young to understand that God is any respecter of persons. I believe that to have interfered as I have done—as I have always freely admitted I have done—in behalf of His despised poor was not wrong, but right.

Now, if it is deemed necessary that I should forfeit[5] my life for the furtherance of the ends of justice, and mingle my blood further with the blood of my children and with the blood of millions in this slave country whose rights are disregarded by wicked, cruel, and unjust enactments—I submit; so let it be done! →

我想請法庭讓我説幾句話。首先，除了我向來供認不諱的解放黑奴的計畫，我不承認所指控的一切。我確實很想像去年冬天那樣，可以痛痛快快地解決問題，當時我去密蘇里州，在雙方一槍都沒有打的情況下，就把黑奴帶走，帶他們穿越美國，最後將他們留在加拿大。我計畫如法泡製，再進行一次更大規模的行動，我想做的事就只是這樣！我從來無意去殺人或是進行叛亂，也無意毀壞別人的財物，或是煽動黑奴起來反抗或進行暴動。

還有一點我也要提出異議，那就是：對我的這項懲處，是有失公正的！

我承認我的所作所為，而我所承認的事，也經過了相當的證實（我敬佩本案大部分作證者的真誠公正）——但假設我的所作所為，是為了有錢有勢的人，或是為了菁英分子、為了所謂的大人物，或是為了這些人的朋友、父母、兄弟姐妹、妻兒等等的——那麼，我在事件中所遭遇的、所犧牲的，就會被認為是正當的，法庭中在場的所有人，都會認為這是一件值得嘉獎的懿行，而不應該受到懲治。

我想，本法庭也認可上帝律法的正當性。我在法庭裡看到大家會親吻一本書，我猜想那一本是《聖經》，或起碼是《新約聖經》。《聖經》教導我，不論是什麼事，如果我希望人們怎麼對待我，我就要先怎麼對待別人。《聖經》還教誨我，「你們要記著受縛的人們，猶如自己也同樣受縛。」

我為此一教誨努力奮鬥。我想我還太年輕，無法了解人們是如何來崇敬上帝的。我相信，如我所行之事——我一向敢做敢當——為上帝那些受到欺負的子民做事情並沒有錯，而這是正當的行為。

現在，如果認為取我的性命是必要的，以便加快讓正義走向終點，那麼，就把我的鮮血，和我孩子們的鮮血，連同這個奴隸國家裡那些遭受殘酷、惡劣、不公平對待的無數黑奴的鮮血，都混合在一起吧！我建議這樣做，就這樣執行吧！

---

1. incite [ɪnˈsaɪt] (v.) to provoke or stir up 煽動
2. insurrection [ˌɪnsəˈrekʃən] (n.) a rebellion against the government or rulers of a country, often involving armed conflict 起義；暴動
3. candor [ˈkændɚ] (n.) honesty, even when the truth is not pleasant 公正；真誠
4. An extract from *Hebrews* 13:3. "Remember them that are in bonds, as bound with them." 出自《聖經・希伯來書》第 13 章第 3 節：「你們要記著受縛的人們，猶如自己也同樣受縛。」
5. forfeit [ˈfɔːrfɪt] (v.) to lose something or have something taken away as punishment for a mistake（因犯罪等）而喪失（名譽、生命等）

John Brown Going to
His Hanging
(by Horace Pippin)

Let me say one word further.

I feel entirely satisfied with the treatment I have received on my trial. Considering all the circumstances it has been more generous than I expected. But I feel no consciousness of guilt. I have stated that from the first what was my intention and what was not. I never had any design against the life of any person, nor any disposition to commit treason, or excite slaves to rebel, or make any general insurrection. I never encouraged any man to do so, but always discouraged any idea of that kind.

Let me say also a word in regard to the statements made by some of those connected with me. I hear it has been stated by some of them that I have induced them to join me. But the contrary is true. I do not say this to injure them, but as regretting their weakness. There is not one of them but joined me of his own accord, and the greater part of them at their own expense. A number of them I never saw, and never had a word of conversation with till the day they came to me; and that was for the purpose I have stated.

Now I have done. ◀

03

猶
如
自
己
也
同
樣
受
縛

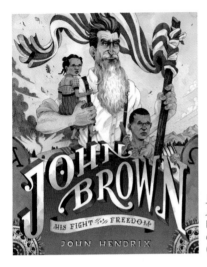

John Hendrix's book
John Brown: His Fight for Freedom
has been picked as one of the best
children's books of 2009.
(Publisher: Abrams Books for Young Readers)

讓我再説幾句話。

法庭對我所做的懲處，我欣然接受。整體的情況考慮起來，這個判決比我預想的還寬容。然而，我並不認為自己有罪。我在前面一開始已經陳述過什麼是我的意圖、什麼不是我的意圖。我從來就不曾計畫要謀取任何人的性命，或是背叛國家、煽動黑奴起來反抗，或是發動全面的起義。我不曾唆使任何人去做這些事，我反而都勸他們放棄這種想法。

那些和我有關的人，對於他們所做的陳述，我也有幾句話想講。我聽他們當中有些人陳述説是我慫恿他們加入的，然而事實正好相反。我提出這一點，並不是要傷害他們，而是為他們的軟弱感到遺憾。他們每一個人都是自願加入的，而且他們多數人都還得負擔自己的生活開銷。有一些是我素未謀面、不曾交談過的人，他們都是來到我這裡之後才和我認識的，而他們為何而來，其目的我上面已經陳述過了。

現在我説完了。

The Four Freedoms

小羅斯福總統：
四大自由

相對於第 26 任總統西奧多·羅斯福（Theodore Roosevelt, 1858–1919），第 32 任總統富蘭克林·羅斯福又被稱為「小羅斯福」。小羅斯福曾連續出任四屆總統（1933–1945 年），是美國歷史上唯一連任超過兩屆的總統。此後根據 1951 年通過的憲法第 22 條修正案，總統任期不得超過兩次。

在美國歷史上，羅斯福是公認最偉大的美國總統之一。小羅斯福任內遭遇到了兩件歷史大事：1929–1940 年期間的經濟大蕭條危機，和第二次世界大戰。

這篇演說是 1941 年 1 月 6 日的國情咨文，在這次的咨文中，他提出《租借法案》（Lend-Lease Program），目的是讓美國在不捲入世界大戰的情形下，可以把軍事武器和戰爭物資提供給盟國。《租借法案》後來於 3 月 11 日簽署通過。同年 12 月 7 日，發生珍珠港事變，隔天國會通過對日本的宣戰，羅斯福總統簽署宣戰書，正式加入第二次世界大戰。

在發表這篇國情咨文之際，世界大戰正打得如火如荼，小羅斯福在咨文中，提出了四項「人類的基本自由」，這被視為是美國為自由而戰的簡要原則聲明。這四大基本自由，也就是現在公認的自由國家所需具備的基本條件——

言論的自由，信仰的自由，
免於匱乏的自由，以及免於恐懼的自由。

Speaker	美國第 32 任總統富蘭克林·羅斯福（Franklin Delano Roosevelt, 1882–1945）
Time	1941 年 1 月 6 日
Place	美國國會國情咨文

▣ 原音重現　▣ 擷選

Franklin D. Roosevelt (1945)

8

I have called for personal sacrifice, and I am assured of the willingness of almost all Americans to respond to that call. A part of the sacrifice means the payment of more money in taxes. In my budget message I will recommend that a greater portion of this great defense program be paid for from taxation than we are paying for today. No person should try, or be allowed to get rich out of the program, and the principle of tax payments in accordance with ability to pay should be constantly before our eyes to guide our legislation. If the Congress maintains these principles the voters, putting patriotism ahead pocketbooks, will give you their applause.

In the future days, which we seek to make secure, we look forward to a world founded upon four essential human freedoms.

The first is freedom of speech and expression—everywhere in the world.

The second is freedom of every person to worship God in his own way—everywhere in the world.

The third is freedom from want, which, translated into world terms, means economic understandings which will secure to every nation a healthy peacetime life for its inhabitants—everywhere in the world.

The fourth is freedom from fear, which, translated into world terms, means a world-wide reduction of armaments to such a point and in such a thorough fashion that no nation will be in a position to commit an act of physical aggression against any neighbor—anywhere in the world.

That is no vision of a distant millennium. It is a definite basis for a kind of world attainable in our own time and generation. →

我曾號召大家作出個人的犧牲，我確信幾乎每一個美國人願意響應。其中一部分的犧牲，是指多繳納一些稅。在我的預算咨文中，我建議能提高稅收來支付更大比例的國防計畫。這項計畫決不會讓任何人從中得到私利，我們會嚴加監督立法，讓納稅辦法務必要與納稅人的能力相稱。如果國會能謹守這些原則，願意為國捐獻的選民會給你們掌聲。

對於我們力求安定的未來，我們期待的世界是建立在人類的基本四大自由之上。

第一是發表言論與表達意見的自由——這是舉世皆然的自由。

第二是擁有個人信仰的自由——這是舉世皆然的自由。

第三是免於匱乏的自由，也就是說，經濟上能互通，以確保每一個國家的人民都能擁有健康和平的生活——這是舉世皆然的自由。

第四是免於恐懼的自由，也就是說，世界各國要全面徹底裁減軍備到一定的程度，使任一國家不具有足以侵犯鄰國的武力——這是舉世皆然的自由。

這並非是在憧憬一個虛無縹緲的千禧年天堂，而是在我們這個時代，我們這一代人就可以實現的一個堅實的世界基礎。

9

That kind of world is the very antithesis[1] of the so-called "new order" of tyranny which the dictators[2] seek to create with the crash of a bomb. To that new order we oppose the greater conception—the moral order. A good society is able to face schemes of world domination and foreign revolutions alike without fear.

Since the beginning of our American history we have been engaged in change, in a perpetual, peaceful revolution, a revolution which goes on steadily, quietly, adjusting itself to changing conditions without the concentration camp or the quicklime[3] in the ditch. The world order which we seek is the cooperation of free countries, working together in a friendly, civilized society.

This nation has placed its destiny in the hands and heads and hearts of its millions of free men and women, and its faith in freedom under the guidance of God. Freedom means the supremacy of human rights everywhere. Our support goes to those who struggle to gain those rights and keep them. Our strength is our unity of purpose.

To that high concept there can be no end save victory. ◀

Lincoln Memorial Reflecting Pool, Washington, D.C.

這個新世界和獨裁暴政用武力征服的所謂「新秩序」，是截然相反的。相對於獨裁暴政的新秩序，我們採取的是一種偉大的理念——道德秩序。一個良好的社會，能夠無畏地面對各種陰謀，像是企圖征服世界或是在海外掀起革命等等的陰謀。

從我們美國開國以來，我們就一直在從事改革，那是一種永久且和平的改革。這個改革穩定而溫和，改革的腳步配合局勢的變化而調整，而不用透過集中營或萬人塚來達成目標。我們所追求的世界秩序，是自由國家能夠彼此通力合作，在友好的文明社會中共同努力。

這個國家已經把命運託付給千百萬的自由人民，把命運交到了他們的手裡頭、心裡頭，並把對自由的信仰，交由上帝來引導。自由，意謂著在任何地方，人權都是至上的。凡是為爭取或保有這種權利而奮鬥的人，我們都予以支持。我們的力量，來自於我們目標的一致。

為了實現此一崇高理想，我們在未達到勝利之前，決不休止。

1. antithesis [æn'tɪθɪsɪs] (n.) exact opposite 對照
2. dictator ['dɪkteɪtər] (n.) an absolute ruler; a tyrant 獨裁者
3. quicklime ['kwɪklaɪm] (n.) a white crystalline powder 生石灰

Chief Seattle's Treaty Oration

西雅圖酋長宣言

（Henry Smith 版本）

西雅圖酋長的部落位於現今的美國華盛頓州。他早年受法國傳教士的影響，信仰天主教。他與白人維持友好關係，白人為了感謝西雅圖酋長的支持，還將地名取為西雅圖。但隨著白人的擴張，雙方的衝突增加。

白人想以 15 萬美元買下位於現今華盛頓州普吉灣（Puget Sound）的兩百萬英畝土地，然後將印地安部落遷入保留區，西雅圖酋長當時於是發表了這篇感人的宣言。1855 年，按白人所提出的計畫，西雅圖酋長與白人簽訂《伊利奧特條約》（Point Elliott Treaty），出讓印第安土地，並建立印第安保留區。

雖然這篇宣言內容的真實性有爭議，但絲毫不減它撼動人心的力量，也無損於其所提出的生命哲學。尤其在物質發達、心靈空虛的現代社會裡，它強調的人與大自然的完整關係，感動了全世界的讀者。在重視環保的今日，它更成了環境保育上公認極為重要的一份聲明。

這個詞藻華麗的版本，出自亨利‧史密斯（Henry A. Smith, 1830–1915）之手，首次刊登於 1887 年 10 月 29 日的《西雅圖週日之星》（Seattle Sunday Star）。亨利曾親聆西雅圖酋長的宣言，但離出版時間隔了三十餘年之久。

另一個比較白話的常見版本是「你如何能夠買賣天空、買賣溫暖的大地？」（How can you buy or sell the sky, the warmth of the land?），這是編劇家泰德‧派瑞（Ted Perry）的自由創作版本，這是 1974 年在華盛頓州某一博覽會中，出現在一部紀錄片上的旁白。

Speaker 印第安人西雅圖酋長（Chief Seattle, 1786–1866）

Time 1854 年 12 月

Place 美國華盛頓州西雅圖
（Seattle, Washington, USA）

◙ 錄音　◙ 擷錄

10

Yonder sky that has wept tears of compassion upon my people for centuries untold, and which to us appears changeless and eternal, may change. Today is fair. Tomorrow it may be overcast with clouds. My words are like the stars that never change. Whatever Seattle says, the great chief at Washington can rely upon with as much certainty as he can upon the return of the sun or the seasons.

To us the ashes of our ancestors are sacred and their resting place is hallowed ground. You wander far from the graves of your ancestors and seemingly without regret. Your religion was written upon tablets of stone by the iron finger of your God so that you could not forget. The Red Man could never comprehend or remember it. Our religion is the traditions of our ancestors—the dreams of our old men, given them in solemn hours of the night by the Great Spirit; and the visions of our sachems, and is written in the hearts of our people.

Your dead cease to love you and the land of their nativity as soon as they pass the portals of the tomb and wander away beyond the stars. They are soon forgotten and never return. Our dead never forget this beautiful world that gave them being. They still love its verdant valleys, its murmuring rivers, its magnificent mountains, sequestered vales and verdant lined lakes and bays, and ever yearn in tender fond affection over the lonely hearted living, and often return from the happy hunting ground to visit, guide, console, and comfort them.

Day and night cannot dwell together. The Red Man has ever fled the approach of the White Man, as the morning mist flees before the morning sun. However, your proposition seems fair and I think that my people will accept it and will retire to the reservation you offer them. Then we will dwell apart in peace, for the words of the Great White Chief seem to be the words of nature speaking to my people out of dense darkness. →

不知多少世紀以來，蒼天為我的族人流下了多少憐憫之淚，看似亙久不變的穹蒼，實則變化不定。今天晴空萬里，明日卻可能烏雲密佈，然而，我的這番話，將如星辰，永不墜落。就像日出日落、春去冬來那般地不容置疑，對於這位西雅圖酋長所說的一切，華盛頓的大長官同樣毋須置疑。

　　對我們而言，我們祖先的骨灰是不可侵犯的，而他們長眠的大地也是很神聖的。你們遠遠地避開你們祖先的墳墓，而且不會感到遺憾。你們的上帝，用祂堅硬的手指，把你們的信仰寫在石板上，以免你們遺忘。這一點是我們紅人所無法理解的，而且這種方式我們也銘記不了。我們的信仰就是祖靈的傳統——那是偉大神靈在夜晚肅穆時刻傳達給長者的夢，那是酋長的靈視。這些，都寫在我們族人的心中。

　　你們的死者，在進入墳墓之後就會立刻離開，到星辰之外的地方去。他們將不再愛護你們，不再愛護這一塊他們曾經誕生的土地。他們很快就會被遺忘，不再回來。而我們的死者，他們從不會忘記這個曾經孕育他們生命的美麗世界。他們仍深愛著翠綠的山谷、潺潺的流水、巍峨的山嶽、幽靜的溪谷、被綠野所環抱的湖泊海灣。甚者，對於生者孤獨的心靈，他們仍渴望能給予溫暖的呵護。他們常常會從彼岸極樂的狩獵天堂回來探視生者，給予指導、慰問和撫慰。

　　白天與黑夜，如同參與商。紅人在白人來到之前逃逸而去，猶如晨霧在日出之前消退一樣。不過，你們的提議看起來還算公平，我們的族人或許可以接受，並且遷入你們所規畫的保留區。如此，我們就可以各居一方，相安無事。那位白人大首領的話，無異於大自然在漆黑夜裡對我們族人所說的話。

Indian Dream Catcher

43

11

It matters little where we pass the remnant[1] of our days. They will not be many. The Indian's night promises to be dark. Not a single star of hope hovers above his horizon. Sad-voiced winds moan in the distance. Grim fate seems to be on the Red Man's trail, and wherever he will hear the approaching footsteps of his fell destroyer and prepare stolidly to meet his doom, as does the wounded doe that hears the approaching footsteps of the hunter.

We will ponder your proposition and when we decide we will let you know. But should we accept it, I here and now make this condition that we will not be denied the privilege without molestation of visiting at any time the tombs of our ancestors, friends, and children. Every part of this soil is sacred in the estimation of my people. Every hillside, every valley, every plain and grove, has been hallowed by some sad or happy event in days long vanished.

Even the rocks, which seem to be dumb and dead as the swelter[2] in the sun along the silent shore, thrill with memories of stirring events connected with the lives of my people, and the very dust upon which you now stand responds more lovingly to their footsteps than yours, because it is rich with the blood of our ancestors, and our bare feet are conscious of the sympathetic touch. →

　　我們要在哪裡度過我們的餘生，並不是很重要，我們所剩的時日不多了。印地安人的夜晚一片漆黑，天際上看不到一絲絲希望之星的光芒，遠處呼嘯著悲切嗚咽的風聲。悲慘的命運緊跟著紅人的腳步，他們無時無地都能聽到毀滅者逼近的腳步聲。他們已經準備好迎接命運，他們的心已經麻痺，猶如一頭受傷的母鹿，聽著獵人步步逼近的腳步聲。

　　我們會考慮你們的提議，等我們做好決定，就會通知你們。但對於我們是否應該接受提議，我現在在這裡開出條件：我們有權在任何時刻回去探望我們的祖先、友人或孩子的墳墓，而不會受到任何的阻撓。在我們族人的心裡，這塊土地的每一分、每一寸都是神聖的。每一塊山坡地，每一座山谷，每一片平原，每一座樹林，都因為久遠以來各種或喜或悲的事跡而顯得神聖。

　　即使是那些躺在靜謐岸邊、遭受烈日曝曬的生硬頑石，也都因為見證過族人那些激動人心的往事，而顯得令人肅然起敬。甚至是你們腳底下的塵土，對我們來說也是富含著感情，因為那裡曾經留著我們祖先的鮮血，我們赤裸的雙足可以感受到祖先對我們充滿憐惜的輕撫。

1. remnant ['rεmnənt] (n.) a small part of something that remains after the rest has gone 殘餘
2. swelter ['swεltər] (n.) a state of oppressive heat 熱得難受

12

Our departed braves, fond mothers, glad, happy hearted maidens, and even the little children who lived here and rejoiced here for a brief season, will love these somber solitudes and at eventide they greet shadowy returning spirits.

And when the last Red Man shall have perished, and the memory of my tribe shall have become a myth among the White Men, these shores will swarm with the invisible dead of my tribe, and when your children's children think themselves alone in the field, the store, the shop, upon the highway, or in the silence of the pathless woods, they will not be alone.

In all the earth there is no place dedicated to solitude. At night when the streets of your cities and villages are silent and you think them deserted, they will throng with the returning hosts that once filled them and still love this beautiful land. The White Man will never be alone.

Let him be just and deal kindly with my people, for the dead are not powerless. Dead, did I say? There is no death, only a change of worlds.

我們去世的勇士、溫柔的母親、輕盈快樂的少女，甚至是曾在這裡短暫生活與嬉笑的孩子們，都熱愛著這一片荒涼的孤寂之地，並且在日暮時分，迎接著歸來的幽幽祖靈。

　　有朝一日，當最後一位紅人撒手人寰之後，與我們族人有關的回憶，就會變成神話，然後在白人之間流傳。這些河岸會充滿我們族人無形的靈魂，當你們的後代子孫隻身站在田野、倉庫、商店、公路上，或是走進人跡罕至的森林裡時，他們其實不是孤獨一個人的。

　　在這個世界上，沒有任何地方是真正孤寂的。夜裡，當你們城鎮上的街道闃寂無聲時，你們以為路上一個人都沒有，但其實，街道上擠滿了昔日的故人，他們的靈魂歸來，仍舊深愛著這片美麗的土地。白人們將永遠不會是孤獨的。

　　但願白人能公正地善待我們的族人，死者並非是無能為力的。死者，我是這麼說的嗎？世上是沒有死亡的，只是換了一個世界。

Chief Red Eagle: Address to General Andrew Jackson

紅鷹酋長投降宣言：
我無懼於任何人

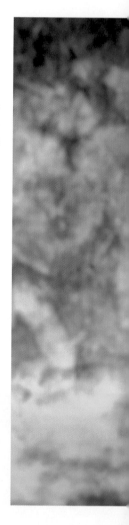

克里克印地安人紅鷹酋長（Chief Red Eagle）曾帶領族人對抗美國政府，參與過克里克戰爭（Creek War）。紅鷹酋長的父親為蘇格蘭人，所以他有個正規的英文名字 William Weatherford，又因為其母親也是多族系的混血，所以他實際上只擁有八分之一的克里克印地安人血統，「紅鷹」則是他克里克語的戰名。

後來成為美國第七任總統（任期 1829–1837 年）的傑克森（Andrew Jackson, 1767–1845），曾在克里克戰爭時期擔任將軍。1812 年，傑克森將軍在一場戰役中，成功擊敗了一個反白人的克里克人組織「紅棍」（Red Sticks），而紅鷹酋長就是組織中的一員。

1813 年 8 月 30 日，「紅棍」展開「閔士堡大屠殺」（Fort Mims Massacre），殺害了數百位白人移民和白紅混血兒。紅鷹酋長被懷疑是參與者之一，但這件事情缺乏史料上的證明。當時他也曾力阻慘案的發生，而且在閔士堡還有他的親戚。

1814 年 3 月 27 日，在「馬蹄彎之役」（Battle of Horseshoe Bend）中，「紅棍」成員潰逃，但紅鷹酋長後來卻自動回到傑克森堡。後來，傑克森將軍赦免他，並授命他號召克里克族簽署合約。下面這篇演說，就是紅鷹酋長於 1814 年向傑克森將軍所做的宣言。

1814 年 8 月 9 日，傑克森將軍強迫克里克族簽署《傑克森堡條約》（Treaty of Fort Jackson），從克里克部落奪走兩千萬平方英哩的土地。美國印地安人為傑克森取了「長刀」（Long Knife）的外號，因為他在 1814 年的克里克戰爭中曾殘酷地殺害了印第安人。

↘ Native American's dreamcatcher

Speaker 美國克里克族印第安人紅鷹酋長
（Chief Red Eagle, 1781-1824）

Time 1814 年

Place 傑克森堡（Fort Jackson），位於今日美國阿拉巴馬州

▣ Vine Deloria, Jr. 讀誦　　▣ 全篇收錄

13

General Jackson,

I am not afraid of you. I fear no man, for I am a Creek warrior. I have nothing to request in behalf of myself; you can kill me, if you desire. But I come to beg you to send for the women and children of the war party who are now starving in the woods. Their fields and cribs have been destroyed by your people, who have driven them to the woods without an ear of corn. I hope that you will send out parties who will safely conduct them here in order that they may be fed.

I exerted myself in vain to prevent the massacre of the women and children at Fort Mims. I am now done fighting. The Red Sticks are nearly all killed.

I have done the white people all the harm I could. I have fought them, and fought them bravely. If I had an army I would yet fight, and contend to the last. But I have none. My people are all gone. I can now do no more than weep over the misfortunes of my Nation.

There was a time when I had a choice and could have answered you; I have none now. Even hope has ended. Once I could animate my warriors to battle, but I cannot animate the dead. My warriors can no longer hear my voice. Their bones are at Talladega, Tallashatchie, Emunckfow and Tohopeka.

If I had been left to contend with the Georgia Army, I would have raised corn on one bank of the river and fought them on the other. But your people have destroyed my Nation. I rely on your generosity. ◖

傑克森將軍：

我並不害怕你，我無懼於任何人，因為我是一名克里克的戰士。關於我個人的部分，我無絲毫的懇求之處；如果你想取我的性命，悉聽尊便。我來這裡，是為了懇請你去接回敵方的婦女與兒童，他們此時正在樹林裡受著飢餓之苦。他們的田地和儲糧被你的軍隊摧毀殆盡，你的手下把他們驅趕進樹林裡，身上沒有帶上半點糧食。我希望你能派人安全地把他們帶回來，好讓他們得到溫飽。

我一度力圖阻止閔士堡的婦孺屠殺慘案，但我無功而返。現在，我一身戰後的疲憊，「紅棍」的成員幾乎無一倖存。

我曾經盡其所能地攻擊白人，我向白人開戰，無所畏懼地抵抗白人。如果我還有一兵一卒，我會繼續戰鬥，奮戰到底。但現在，只剩下我一個人，我的人馬一無所剩。如今，我唯一能做的，就是為族人的悲慘命運哀泣。

曾有一段時間，我擁有選擇的籌碼，可以和你相對抗。但現在，我萬般皆休，即使是一絲絲的希望，也不可求。以前，我可以激勵我的戰士投身奮戰，但我無法令死者振作起來。我的戰士們，他們再也聽聞不到我的聲音了，他們的屍骨遍在各地。

如果我被留下來對抗喬治亞軍隊，我會在河的這一岸繼續耕作玉米，在河的另一岸繼續堅勇奮戰下去。然而，你的軍隊已經殲滅了我的族人，所以，我祈求你的寬宏大量。

Black Hawk:
Surrender Speech

黑鷹酋長投降宣言：
我不曾做過令族人蒙羞的事

在美國獨立革命之前，白人逐漸迫使印地安人西移。1830 年，美國國會通過《印地安人移居法》（Indian Removal Act），並撥款 50 萬美金來完成此一目標。

在美國政府的壓力下，有一些部落自願西遷，然而，在 1832 年 4 月到 8 月之間，索克族印第安人黑鷹酋長（Chief Black Hawk, 1767–1838）領導索克族（Sauk）和福克斯族（Fox），企圖重新佔領舊有的領土，取回玉米耕作地。後來白人將他們逼臨密西西比河時，對部落的婦幼展開屠殺。最後，黑鷹酋長別無選擇，只好投降。

在這篇投降宣言中，黑鷹酋長無畏地指責白人的欺騙行為，表現出慷慨赴義的高貴情操。之後，他與兒子迅雷（Whirling Thunder）被捕，四處被公開示眾，然而父子倆卻展現了無比的骨氣與尊嚴，博得了大眾的尊敬。

Speaker 美國索克族印第安人黑鷹酋長
（Chief Black Hawk, 1767–1838）

Time 1832 年

▣ 錄音　▣ 全篇收錄

Black-hawk is an Indian. He has done nothing for which an Indian ought to be ashamed. He has fought for his countrymen, the squaws and papooses, against white men, who came, year after year, to cheat them and take away their lands. You know the cause of our making war. It is known to all white men. They ought to be ashamed of it.

The white men despise the Indians, and drive them from their homes. But the Indians are not deceitful. The white men speak bad of the Indian, and look at him spitefully. But the Indian does not tell lies; Indians do not steal.

An Indian, who is as bad as the white men, could not live in our nation; he would be put to death, and eat up by the wolves. The white men are bad schoolmasters; they carry false looks, and deal in false actions; they smile in the face of the poor Indian to cheat him; they shake them by the hand to gain their confidence, to make them drunk, to deceive them, and ruin our wives.

We told them to let us alone, and keep away from us; but they followed on, and beset our paths, and they coiled themselves among us, like the snake. They poisoned us by their touch. We were not safe. We lived in danger. We were becoming like them, hypocrites and liars, adulterers, lazy drones, all talkers, and no workers.

We looked up to the Great Spirit. We went to our great father. We were encouraged. His great council gave us fair words and big promises; but we got no satisfaction. Things were growing worse. There were no deer in the forest. The opossum and beaver were fled; the springs were drying up, and our squaws and papooses without victuals to keep them from starving; we called a great council, and built a large fire.

The spirit of our fathers arose and spoke to us to avenge our wrongs or die. We all spoke before the council fire. It was warm and pleasant. We set up the war-whoop, and dug up the toma-hawk; our knives were ready, and the heart of Black-hawk swelled high in his bosom, when he led his warriors to battle. He is satisfied. He will go to the world of spirits contented. He has done his duty. His father will meet him there, and commend him. ◖

黑鷹是一個印地安人，他不曾做過任何令族人蒙羞的事情。他為他的族人、為部落的婦孺，與白人奮戰。白人欺騙了他們，奪走了他們的土地。你們很明白，我們是為何而戰，這一點所有的白人都心知肚明，他們應該深感羞愧的。

白人歧視印地安人，並且將他們趕出了他們的家園。印地安人是誠實不欺的，白人卻妄加詆毀，而且不懷好意。事實上，印地安人是不打妄語、不偷不搶的。

要是有印地安人的品性和白人一樣那麼差，那他在部落裡是毫無立足之地的，他會被處以極刑，扔去餵野狼。白人就像是心懷不軌的師長，他們道貌岸然，卻是壞事做盡。他們對可憐的印地安人笑裡藏刀，他們跟印地安人握手，騙取信任；他們用酒把印地安人灌醉，騙取他們的東西，還玷污了印地安的婦女。

我們要白人離開，離我們遠一點，但他們緊跟著不走，在我們的部落裡四處蹓躂，像蛇一樣蜷伏在我們的族人當中，只要一跟他們接觸，我們就會受到毒害。我們的處境一點也不安全，我們生活在危機四伏的環境中。我們逐漸變得愈來愈像白人：虛偽矯情，滿口謊言，私生活不檢點，好吃懶做，好說大話，不願腳踏實地的工作。

我們崇敬偉大的神靈，我們敬拜祖先，祂們給予我們勇氣。在祈神會上，上天賜與我們美好的祝福、光明的遠景。然而，事實卻與之相違。現在的局勢，每況愈下。樹林裡再也看不到鹿，負鼠和河狸也都消聲匿跡；河泉日漸乾涸，我們的妻兒沒有食物可以填飽肚子。為此，我們再度築營火、召開祈神會。

我們的祖靈出來告訴我們，我們必須為我們已受的冤屈而戰，否則會走上滅亡之路。在祈神會的營火前，我們作出宣誓，這令我們感到溫暖而愉悅。我們高喊戰爭的口號，並且挖出戰斧，備妥刀槍。當黑鷹領著他的戰士們投奔戰場時，他的胸膛如此澎湃地鼓動著。他感到無比的滿足，他終將前往充滿神靈的世界。他此生的責任已了，他的父親會在彼岸迎接他，並且好好稱讚他一番。

Blood, Toil, Tears and Sweat

邱吉爾開戰宣言：
熱血、辛勞、眼淚和汗水

英國首相邱吉爾是在第二次世界大戰期間，帶領英國人民取得勝利的民族英雄。此外，他也是著作等身的作家、辯才無礙的演說家。他一生中寫出了 43 部共 72 卷的專著，1953 年，還得過諾貝爾文學獎。

邱吉爾出身顯赫的貴族家庭，他的祖先是英國歷史上的著名軍事統帥，父親是 19 世紀末英國的傑出政治家。邱吉爾於 1940 年至 1945 年出任英國首相，並於 1951 年至 1955 年再度出任英國首相。

第二次世界大戰（1939 年 9 月 1 日至 1945 年 9 月 2 日）爆發後的數小時，前任首相張伯倫召見邱吉爾，邀請他加入戰時內閣。1940 年 5 月，下院議員對張伯倫政府提出不信任動議，5 月 8 日，張伯倫內閣僅以 81 票的多數獲得信任案，張伯倫感覺到自己無法繼續執政，因此準備組建聯合政府，並辭去首相職務。

後來經過三大黨派的磋商，張伯倫最後決定請邱吉爾接任首相，於是他向國王喬治六世提出辭呈，並建議由邱吉爾組織聯合內閣。5 月 10 日，國王基於共識而召見邱吉爾，並請他組閣。三天後，邱吉爾首次以首相身分出席下議院會議，發表了《熱血、辛勞、眼淚和汗水》這篇著名的演說。在演說中，邱吉爾把英國的存亡繫於和納粹作戰的成敗上，是歷史上一篇精彩的戰爭宣言。

邱吉爾是 20 世紀最重要的政治領袖之一，對英國乃至於世界都有深遠的影響。2002 年，BBC 舉行了一個名為「最偉大的 100 名英國人」的調查，結果邱吉爾榮登榜首。

Speaker 英國首相邱吉爾（Winston Churchill, 1874–1965）

Place 英國下議院（House of Commons, UK）

Time 1940 年 5 月 13 日

▣ 原音重現　▣ 全篇收錄

15

On Friday evening last I received His Majesty's commission to form a new Administration. It was the evident wish and will of Parliament and the nation that this should be conceived on the broadest possible basis and that it should include all parties, both those who supported the late Government and also the parties of the Opposition.

I have completed the most important part of this task. A War Cabinet has been formed of five Members, representing, with the Liberal Opposition, the unity of the nation. The three party Leaders have agreed to serve, either in the War Cabinet or in high executive office. The three Fighting Services[1] have been filled. It was necessary that this should be done in one single day, on account of the extreme urgency and rigor of events.

A number of other key positions were filled yesterday, and I am submitting a further list to His Majesty tonight. I hope to complete the appointment of the principal Ministers during tomorrow. The appointment of the other Ministers usually takes a little longer, but I trust that, when Parliament meets again, this part of my task will be completed, and that the Administration will be complete in all respects.

Sir, I considered it in the public interest to suggest that the House should be summoned to meet today. Mr. Speaker agreed and took the necessary steps, in accordance with the powers conferred upon him by the Resolution of the House. At the end of the proceedings today, the Adjournment of the House will be proposed until Tuesday, the 21st May, with, of course, provision for earlier meeting, if need be. The business to be considered during that week will be notified to Members at the earliest opportunity.

I now invite the House, by the Resolution which stands in my name, to record its approval of the steps taken and to declare its confidence in the new Government. →

上週五晚上，我奉陛下之命，組織了新政府。國會和國民顯然的共同希望是，新政府應該建立在最廣泛的基礎上，應該容納所有的政黨，包括支持前政府的政黨或各個反對黨。

此一任務的最主要部分，我已經完成。戰時內閣由五人所組成，包括自由派反對黨，這體現了國家的團結。不論是戰時內閣或政府高層的運作，三個政黨的領導人都同意為國效命。陸海空三軍也已經準備就緒。因為目前情勢緊迫，新內閣須於一天之內組成。

昨天我們已經任命了幾個主要的內閣，今晚我還會再向陛下呈報其他的人員名單，希望明天就能完成主要大臣的任命工作。剩下的人員任命需要再多一點的時間，但我相信，在下一次召開國會時，這個部份的事務就會全部完成，新政府將完全成立完畢。

諸位，為了政務著想，我建議今天就召開議會。發言人基於國會決議的授權，同意採取必要的步驟。在今天的議程結束時，會建議休會到 5 月 21 日，但如有必要，會提前召開會議。相關事項會及早通知各位議員。此後一週的事務都會在第一時間通知議員。

現在我請求國會作出決議，批准和記錄我所採取的各項步驟，並聲明信任新政府。

Statue of Winston Churchill in Parliament Square, London

Winston Churchill (1874–1965)

1. Fighting Services: the army, navy, and air force; the armed services 陸海空三軍

16

Sir, to form an Administration of this scale and complexity is a serious undertaking in itself, but it must be remembered that we are in the preliminary stage of one of the greatest battles in history, that we are in action at many points in Norway and in Holland, that we have to be prepared in the Mediterranean, that the air battle is continuous and that many preparations have to be made here at home.

In this crisis I hope I may be pardoned if I do not address the House at any length today. I hope that any of my friends and colleagues, or former colleagues, who are affected by the political reconstruction, will make all allowances for any lack of ceremony with which it has been necessary to act.

I would say to the House, as I said to those who've joined this government: "I have nothing to offer but blood, toil, tears and sweat."

We have before us an ordeal of the most grievous kind. We have before us many, many long months of struggle and of suffering. You ask, what is our policy? I will say: It is to wage war, by sea, land and air, with all our might and with all the strength that God can give us; to wage war against a monstrous tyranny, never surpassed in the dark and lamentable catalogue of human crime. That is our policy.

You ask, what is our aim? I can answer in one word: victory.

Victory at all costs, victory in spite of all terror, victory, however long and hard the road may be; for without victory, there is no survival. Let that be realized; no survival for the British Empire, no survival for all that the British Empire has stood for, no survival for the urge and impulse of the ages, that mankind will move forward towards its goal.

But I take up my task with buoyancy[2] and hope. I feel sure that our cause will not be suffered to fail among men. At this time I feel entitled to claim the aid of all, and I say, "Come then, let us go forward together with our united strength."

諸位，組織這樣一個大規模且複雜的政府，是很重大的一項任務，但不能忘記的是，我們正處在歷史上最大一場戰爭的開戰階段，我們在挪威和荷蘭的許多地點都已經部署完畢，另外也要在地中海部署軍隊，空戰持續在進行，我們還需要在後方國土做很多的備戰工作。

在這個危急的時刻，請大家見諒我今天無法對議院做長篇談話。我希望在這次政府改組中受到影響的友人和同仁，還有前任同僚，對必要儀式的不周之處，都能予以包容。

我向議會表明，一如我向新內閣成員所說過的：「我唯一能奉獻的，只有熱血、辛勞、眼淚和汗水。」

我們所面臨的，將是一場最嚴峻的考驗。在未來的日子裡，將是曠日經久的奮鬥和磨難。如果你們問，我們所持的政策到底是什麼？我會說：那就是開戰！海戰，陸戰，空戰，用我們所有的能力，和上帝所給予我們的力量，全面開戰！向人類罪惡史上最黑暗、最不堪的殘酷暴政開戰，這就是我們的政策！

如果你們問：我們的目標又在哪裡？那我可以用一個字來回答，那就是：勝利！

我們要不惜一切代價來獲得勝利。不管會遭遇任何的恐怖，不管未來的路會如何的漫長艱辛，我們都要打贏這場戰爭！我們不成功，便成仁，我們一定要認清這一點：不成功，就不會再有大英帝國，大英帝國所代表的一切都將消失殆盡，推動人類歷史不斷前進的驅策力也將蕩然無存。

但我充滿樂觀與希望的肩負起我的職責，我確信，靠著我們大家的努力，我們的理想目標決不可能有機會失敗的。在這個時刻，我要請求你們所有人的支持，我要說：「來吧，讓我們團結一致，一起向前邁進！」

Big Ben and Houses of Parliament, London

2. buoyancy [ˈbɔɪənsɪ]
(n.) cheerfulness or optimism
輕鬆而自信的心情

Ich bin ein Berliner

"I am a 'Berliner'"

約翰·甘迺迪：
我是柏林人

1961 年 8 月 12–13 日夜間，東德政府築起了柏林圍牆（Berlin Wall），把柏林分成東西兩半。一開始，柏林圍牆只是一道鐵絲網屏障，用來防止東德人逃往西德；不久，鐵絲網便被水泥牆所取代，並派哨兵巡邏警戒。整道柏林圍牆長約 155 公里，高約 3 至 4 公尺。

1962 年 8 月 17 日，18 歲的東德人彼得·費赫特（Peter Fechter）企圖翻越圍牆，結果被東德士兵開槍射殺，這是第一位喪命於柏林圍牆的人。

在德國官方的柏林圍牆網站上，估計有十萬名東德人民企圖翻越圍牆，其中有數百名被東德士兵擊斃，或是死於逃亡的艱險過程中，但確切的統計數字尚不可得。2005 年，一些單位開始調查柏林圍牆的罹難者，但尚未得出結果。

柏林圍牆的建立，是第二次世界大戰後美蘇兩大陣營冷戰的重要象徵。1963 年，甘迺迪總統訪問歐洲，6 月 26 日這一天是他此行的高潮，他在柏林圍牆前發表了這場著名的演講。

1989 年 11 月 9 日，屹立了 28 年柏林牆終於倒塌。

在英國《每日電訊報》2008 年評選出 20–21 世紀最重要的 25 場政治演說中，這一篇被排名在第二位。

Speaker 美國第 35 屆總統約翰・甘迺迪
（John Fitzgerald Kennedy, 1917–1963.11.22）

Place 德國西柏林（West Berlin, Germany）

Time 1963 年 6 月 26 日

☑ 原音重現　☑ 全篇收錄

17

I am proud to come to this city as the guest of your distinguished Mayor, who has symbolized throughout the world the fighting spirit of West Berlin. And I am proud to visit the Federal Republic[1] with your distinguished Chancellor[2] who for so many years has committed Germany to democracy and freedom and progress, and to come here in the company of my fellow American, General Clay, who has been in this city during its great moments of crisis and will come again if ever needed.

Two thousand years ago the proudest boast was "civis Romanus sum."[3] Today, in the world of freedom, the proudest boast is "Ich bin ein Berliner."[4] I appreciate my interpreter translating my German!

There are many people in the world who really don't understand, or say they don't, what is the great issue between the free world and the Communist world. Let them come to Berlin. There are some who say that communism is the wave of the future. Let them come to Berlin. And there are some who say in Europe and elsewhere we can work with the Communists. Let them come to Berlin. And there are even a few who say that it is true that communism is an evil system, but it permits us to make economic progress. Lass' sie nach Berlin kommen.[5] Let them come to Berlin.

Freedom has many difficulties and democracy is not perfect, but we have never had to put a wall up to keep our people in, to prevent them from leaving us. I want to say, on behalf of my countrymen, who live many miles away on the other side of the Atlantic, who are far distant from you, that they take the greatest pride that they have been able to share with you, even from a distance, the story of the last 18 years. I know of no town, no city, that has been besieged for 18 years that still lives with the vitality and the force, and the hope and the determination of the city of West Berlin. →

我很榮幸能接受你們傑出市長的邀請來貴市作客，市長在世界上象徵了西柏林的奮戰精神。我也很榮幸你們優秀的總理帶我參訪了西德，總理多年來致力於德國的民主、自由和進步；還有，陪同我一起來的美國同胞克雷將軍，他在這個城市危機的重大時刻來到了這裡，只要一有需要，他就會再回來。

兩千年前，最神氣的一句話是：「我是羅馬公民。」今天，在自由世界裡，最神氣的一句話則是：「Ich bin ein Berliner!」（德語：我是柏林人！）我很感謝我的翻譯人員教我如何講這一句德語。

在這個世界上，還有很多人不瞭解，或者說他們不明白自由世界與共產國家之間的根本分歧。那麼，就讓那些人來一趟柏林吧！對於那些主張共產主義是未來潮流的人，就讓他們來柏林瞧一瞧吧！對於那些在歐洲或其他各地主張和共產國家合作的人，也讓他們來一趟柏林吧！還有一些少數的人說，共產主義是邪惡的制度，但和他們合作還是有利於經濟發展，那麼，「Lass' sie nach Berlin kommen!」（德語：讓他們來柏林吧！）都讓這些人來柏林看一看吧！

自由，會讓我們面臨許多困難；民主，也不是最完美的，但我們再怎麼樣也不會高築城牆將人民圍起來，不准他們離開。我想說的是，我代表我的同胞，他們居住在大西洋千里之外的另一邊，與你們遙遙相望，但即使和你們隔著距離，但對於能與你們一起走過這十八年，他們身感無比的驕傲。我沒見過任何一個城市，能夠在被圍困了十八年之後，還能像西柏林一樣保留這樣的生機、力量、希望和決心。

Berlin Wall

1. Federal Republic: Federal Republic of Germany 德意志聯邦共和國

2. chancellor ['tʃænsələr] (n.) the chief minister of state in some European countries 德奧等國的總理

3. 「我是羅馬公民。」（I am a Roman citizen.）的拉丁語

4. 「我是柏林人。」（I am a Berliner.）的德語

5. 「讓他們來柏林吧。」（Let them come to Berlin.）的德語

18

While the wall is the most obvious and vivid demonstration of the failures of the Communist system, for all the world to see, we take no satisfaction in it, for it is, as your Mayor has said, an offense not only against history but an offense against humanity, separating families, dividing husbands and wives and brothers and sisters, and dividing a people who wish to be joined together.

What is true of this city is true of Germany—real, lasting peace in Europe can never be assured as long as one German out of four is denied the elementary right of free men, and that is to make a free choice.

In 18 years of peace and good faith, this generation of Germans has earned the right to be free, including the right to unite their families and their nation in lasting peace, with good will to all people. You live in a defended island of freedom, but your life is part of the main.

So let me ask you as I close, to lift your eyes beyond the dangers of today, to the hopes of tomorrow, beyond the freedom merely of this city of Berlin, or your country of Germany, to the advance of freedom everywhere, beyond the wall to the day of peace with justice, beyond yourselves and ourselves to all mankind.

Freedom is indivisible, and when one man is enslaved, all are not free. When all are free, then we can look forward to that day when this city will be joined as one and this country and this great Continent of Europe in a peaceful and hopeful globe. When that day finally comes, as it will, the people of West Berlin can take sober satisfaction in the fact that they were in the front lines for almost two decades.

All free men, wherever they may live, are citizens of Berlin, and, therefore, as a free man, I take pride in the words "Ich bin ein Berliner." ◀

這一道牆，就是共產制度挫敗最活生生的例子，這是全世界的人都有目共睹的，但我們並不因此而感到稱心如意，因為，就如你們市長所說的，這不只是在歷史上倒行逆施，而且更是違反了人性，它拆散家庭，讓夫妻、兄弟姐妹骨肉分離，硬生生地將希冀相連在一起的民族分成兩半。

這個城市的情況，就是整個德國的縮影——只要四個德國人當中有一個被剝奪了自由人類的基本權利，也就是說，他連自主權都沒有的話，那麼，歐洲就不可能擁有真正且永久的和平。

經過了這十八年的和平和善意，在與世界和平共處之後，這一代的德國人終於贏得了自由的權利，包括和家人團圓、國家和平統一的權利，你們住在一個受到保護的自由之島上，但你們的生活是整片海洋的一部分。

所以，在演講的最後，我想請求你們將眼光放得更遠，不要只是看到今日的危機，更要看到明天的希望；不要只是看到柏林市的自由，或是德國的自由，更要看到每一個地方自由的發展。我們要把眼光越過圍牆，超越自己，看到全人類和平正義的日子來臨的那一天。

自由是不能分割的，只要有一個人受到奴役，其他所有人就不能說是自由的。等到人人都自由了，那我們就可以期待這一天的到來——在和平、充滿希望的地球上，這個城市統一了，德國統一了，歐洲大陸統一了。當這一天終於到來時，總有那麼一天的，西柏林的市民將會萬分欣慰，因為將近二十年來，他們一直就是站在這個前線上的。

所有自由的人類，無論他是居住在什麼地方，他也都是一個柏林公民。身為自由的人們，我可以驕傲地說：「Ich bin ein Berliner!」（德語：我是柏林人！）

10

The Great Dictator

卓別林：
《大獨裁者》演講片段

卓別林是英國的喜劇泰斗，同時身兼演員和導演。他也是一位反戰人士，充滿人道關懷，他的作品流露出悲天憫人的胸懷，是一位偉大的藝人。

《大獨裁者》是卓別林自導自演的第一部有聲電影，片中尖銳地諷刺了希特勒和納粹。這部電影上映時，美國仍未加入第二次世界大戰，且與德國納粹關係良好，全球還未陷入對法西斯主義的恐慌之中。喜歡看電影的希特勒，還看了這部電影兩次。

據說這篇演講是卓別林臨時加入的即興演出，這段慷慨激昂的演說是對德國納粹的控訴，體現了卓別林的道德勇氣。這段演講如此迴盪人心，卓別林還曾在全國性的廣播電臺上被要求重述演說。

時至今日，他在這場電影演講中的訴求，仍是人們心中渴望的夢想，以至於有人甚至拿這段演講與馬丁‧路德‧金恩的《我有一個夢想》相提並論。

卓別林兩次獲得奧斯卡榮譽獎，他也曾因為《大獨裁者》被提名最佳電影、最佳男主角和最佳原創劇本。1977 年聖誕節卓別林在瑞士逝世，享年 88 歲。

Film "The Great Dictator"

Speaker   英國演員及導演查理・卓別林
（Charles Chaplin, 1889–1977）

Movie   1940 年 10 月 15 日美國紐約首映

▣ 電影片段原音重現　▣ 整段收錄

69

19

I'm sorry. I don't want to be an Emperor, that's not my business. I don't want to rule or conquer anyone. I should like to help everyone if possible.

Jew, Gentile[1], Black man, White—we all want to help one another, human beings are like that. We want to live by each other's happiness not by each other's misery; we don't want to hate and despise one another.

In this world there's room for everyone. This good earth is rich and can provide for everyone a way of life to be free and beautiful.

But we have lost the way, greed has poisoned men's souls, has barricaded[2] the world with hate, has goose-stepped us into misery and bloodshed. We have developed speed, but we have shut ourselves in.

Machinery that gives abundance has left us in want. Our knowledge has made us cynical[3], our cleverness hard and unkind. We think too much, and we feel too little.

More than machinery we need humanity. More than cleverness we need kindness and gentleness. Without these qualities life will be violent, and all will be lost.

The aeroplane and the radio have brought us closer together. The very nature of these inventions cries out for the goodness in men, cries out for universal brotherhood, for the unity of us all.

Even now my voice is reaching millions throughout the world, millions of despairing men, women and little children, victims of a system that makes men torture, and imprison innocent people. →

很抱歉，我並不想當什麼皇帝的，而且這方面我一點也不在行。我才不想統治或征服任何人，我比較想要的是能夠盡量幫助別人。

我們不論是猶太人、非猶太人，或是黑人、白人——我們都想要互相幫助彼此，這才是人類的本性。我們的生活是要建立在彼此的幸福上，而不是痛苦上。我們不想要彼此憎恨或鄙視。

天下之大，豈無容身之處。這個美好的世界物產豐饒，每一個人都可以過自己逍遙自在的生活。

可是，我們走偏了，貪婪之心囚禁了人們的靈魂，仇恨的城牆林立，驅使我們走入痛苦和血泊之中。人類發明了讓速度加快的方法，結果是加速把自己困入愁城。

機器的發明帶來了富庶，卻讓我們更加陷入窮困。知識的發展讓我們變得憤世嫉俗，我們的心智變得又冷又硬。我們想得很多，卻缺乏同理心。

我們更需要的是人性，而不是機器；我們所欠缺的是仁慈與善心，而不是聰明才智。少了這些，生活會充斥著暴力，到最後一無所剩。

飛機和廣播，拉近了我們彼此的距離。這些發明的本意是為了要喚醒人類的善良，喚醒四海之內皆兄弟的胸懷，喚醒一個大同世界。

此時此刻，我的聲音傳到了全世界數百萬人們的耳裡，他們是數百萬陷於絕望之中的男女老少。他們在一個專門荼毒人類的體制下成為受害者，是一群被囚禁的無辜人們。

the statue of Charles Chaplin

Charles Chaplin (1889–1977)

1. Gentile [ˈdʒɛntaɪl] (n.) a person who is not Jewish 非猶太人

2. barricade [ˌbærɪˈkeɪd] (v.) to shut in or keep out with a barrier that protects defenders or blocks a route 築柵防禦

3. cynical [ˈsɪnɪkəl] (a.) believing the worst of human nature and motives 憤世嫉俗的

Film "Shoulder Arms" (1918)

For those who can hear me, I say, do not despair. The misery that is now upon us is but the passing of greed, the bitterness of men who fear the way of human progress.

The hate of men will pass and dictators die, and the power they took from the people will return to the people, and so long as men die, liberty will never perish.

Soldiers, don't give yourselves to brutes, men who despise you and enslave you, who regiment your lives, tell you what to do, what to think and what to feel; who drill you, diet you, treat you like cattle, use you as cannon fodder.

Don't give yourselves to these unnatural men, machine men with machine minds and machine hearts.

You are not machines, you are not cattle, you are men. You have the love of humanity in your hearts, you don't hate. Only the unloved hate, the unloved and the unnatural.

Soldiers, don't fight for slavery, fight for liberty. →

對於這些能聽得到我的聲音的人,我要對你們說,千萬不要絕望。現在降臨到我們頭上的災難,是一時的貪婪所致,是一些人唯恐人類會進步的怨恨所致。

人類的仇恨終將會消失,獨裁者終將會死去。他們從人民手中所奪去的權力,終將會歸回人民所有。只要前仆後繼,自由就不會被消滅。

士兵們,不要屈服於那些殘暴者;他們鄙視你們,奴役你們;他們嚴格控制你們的生活,規定你們要有什麼樣的行為、思想和情感;他們壓榨你們,讓你們餓肚子,把你們當牛馬使喚,要你們去當炮灰。

不要屈服於這些沒有人性、無血無淚、毫無感情的人。

你們不是機器人,不是牛馬,你們是人。你們有一顆人類慈愛的心,你們沒有恨。只有不被人愛的人、不正常的人,才會滿懷恨意。

士兵們,不要當奴役者的走狗,而是要為自由而奮戰。

In the 17th chapter of St Luke, it is written the Kingdom of God is within men, not one man nor a group of men but in all men, in you[4].

You the people have the power, the power to create machines, the power to create happiness. You the people have the power to make this life free and beautiful, to make this life a wonderful adventure.

Then in the name of democracy let us use that power, let us all unite. Let us fight for a new world, a decent world that will give men a chance to work, that will give you the future, and old age a security.

GEORGE GROSZ
DAS GESICHT DER
HERRSCHENDEN KLASSE
DER MALIK-VERLAG / BERLIN-HALENSEE

By the promise of these things brutes have risen to power. But they lie, they do not fulfil that promise, they never will. Dictators free themselves but they enslave the people.

Now, let us fight to fulfil that promise, let us fight to free the world, to do away with national barriers, to do away with greed, [do away] with hate and intolerance.

Let us fight for a world of reason, a world where science and progress will lead to all men's happiness. Soldiers, in the name of democracy, let us all unite! ◀

Charles Chaplin and Mohandas Gandhi

〈路加福音〉第 17 章寫道：神的國，就在你們心裡。不是在某一個人的心裡，不是在某一群人的心裡，而是在所有人的心裡，就在你們的心裡！

你們是那些擁有能力的人，你們有能力製造機器，也有能力創造幸福。你們是有能力的人，可以讓生活變得自由美好，創造精彩的一生。

那麼，就讓我們以民主之名，運用這種能力來讓所有人都團結起來。讓我們一起為一個嶄新美好的世界而奮鬥。在美好的世界裡，我們都擁有工作機會，擁有未來，而老年人也都擁有保障。

那些殘暴者就是靠這些承諾奪取了權力，但他們是騙子，他們不會兌現承諾，永遠都不會。獨裁者將自己解放，卻將人民奴役起來。

現在，讓我們為實現這個承諾而戰，我們要為自由世界而戰。我們要突破國與國之間的藩籬，除去人類的貪婪，消弭仇恨與偏狹的心。

讓我們為一個理性的世界而戰，科學和進步將帶領我們所有人走向幸福。士兵們，以民主的名義，讓我們團結起來！

4. An extract from *Luke* 17:20–21. "And when he was demanded of the Pharisees, when the kingdom of God should come, he answered them and said, The kingdom of God cometh not with observation: Neither shall they say, Lo here! or, lo there! for, behold, the kingdom of God is within you." 《聖經‧路加福音》第 17 章第 20–21 節：「法利賽人問耶穌：神的國幾時來到？祂回答說：神的國來到不是眼所能見的。人也不得說：看哪，在這裡！看哪，在那裡！因為神的國就在你們心裡。」

Non-Violence: The Doctrine of the Sword

印度聖雄甘地：
非暴力，武力的法則

甘地一生為印度的獨立而奮鬥，帶領國家脫離英國的殖民統治。聖雄（Mahatma），是印度詩人泰戈爾（Rabindranath Tagore, 1861–1941）給予他的稱號，意思是「偉大的靈魂」。

甘地於 1888 年留學英國倫敦大學，修習法律。1893 年，甘地被一家印度公司派至南非，後來參與了南非的公民權利運動，並曾於 1913 年被捕。在南非的這段期間，甘地成了社會政治活動家，其不服從的非暴力抵抗也逐漸成形。

第一次世界大戰時，甘地返回印度。戰後，他參與國大黨的獨立運動，以不合作運動和絕食抗議等活動，受到國際關注。第二次世界大戰之後，甘地希望印度能夠獨立，成為一個完整的國家，但最後為了獨立，甘地接受讓印度與巴基斯坦分別獨立的方案，巴基斯坦於是成為一個獨立的穆斯林國家。

甘地的「非暴力」思想，影響後世極深，並成為許多民權鬥士的指導方針。像金恩博士和曼德拉，都受到甘地很大的啟發。

在 1937 年到 1948 年之間，甘地曾獲得過五次諾貝爾和平獎的提名，但始終沒有得名。多年以後，諾貝爾委員會曾對此公開表示過遺憾。在 20 世紀末時，《時代》雜誌曾評選 20 世紀的風雲人物，甘地名列前三名，其他兩名則分別是愛因斯坦和小羅斯福總統。

Speaker	印度聖雄甘地 （Mohandas Karamchand Gandhi, 1869–1948）
Time	1920 年 8 月 11 日
Place	印度西部阿默特巴德市（Ahmedabad, India）

◉ 錄音　◉ 擷錄

22

In this age of the rule of brute force, it is almost impossible for anyone to believe that anyone else could possibly reject the law of final supremacy of brute force. And so I receive anonymous letters advising me that I must not interfere with the progress of non-cooperation even though popular violence may break out.

Others come to me and assuming that secretly I must be plotting violence, inquire when the happy moment for declaring open violence to arrive. They assure me that English never yield to anything but violence secret or open. Yet others I am informed, believe that I am the most rascally person living in India because I never give out my real intention and that they have not a shadow of a doubt that I believe in violence just as much as most people do.

Such being the hold that the doctrine of the sword has on the majority of mankind, and as success of non-cooperation depends principally on absence of violence during its pendency[1] and as my views in this matter affect the conduct of large number of people. I am anxious to state them as clearly as possible.

I do believe that, where there is only a choice between cowardice and violence, I would advise violence. Thus when my eldest son asked me what he should have done had he been present when I was almost fatally assaulted in 1908, whether he should have used his physical force which he could and wanted to use, and defended me, I told him that it was his duty to defend me even by using violence.

Hence it was that I took part in the Boer War[2], the so-called Zulu Rebellion[3] and the late war. Hence also do I advocate training in arms for those who believe in the method of violence. I would rather have India resort to arms in order to defend her honor than that she should, in a cowardly manner, become or remain a helpless witness to her own dishonor. →

在這個武力當道的時代，幾乎沒有人會相信有人可以放棄訴諸武力這種終極手段。也因此，我收到不具名的信，勸我不要去干預不合作運動的進行，就算有可能爆發大規模的武力衝突。

還有一些人來找我，以為我一定暗中在策畫暴力活動，他們問我，何時要宣告展開令人亢奮的武力抗爭活動？他們跟我打包票說，英國人只會妥協於武力，不管是祕密還是公然進行的武力活動。我甚至聽說，還有人認為我是當今印度最無賴的分子，因為我從不說真心話，他們毫不懷疑地認定我崇尚武力，就像大部分的人一樣。

一般人都是這樣認為武力法則主宰了多數人類，而不合作運動的成功與否，主要就在於運動期間不能有暴力衝突，我對這一點的看法，影響了不少人的行為。我很想就這一點盡可能地加以闡釋清楚。

我也認為，迫不得已要在怯懦和暴力之間做出選擇的話，我會建議選擇暴力。1908 年，我遭到襲擊，幾乎喪生，我的大兒子問我，要是他在現場的話，他應該怎麼做？他很想動手回擊以保護我，他可以這樣做嗎？我告訴他，就算是動手動腳來保護我，也是他的一種責任。

自從那個事件之後，我參加了波爾戰爭，也就是祖魯人叛亂事件以及後續的戰爭。從那時候起，我也和那些崇尚武力手段的人士站在同一陣線，擁護軍事訓練。倘若因為懦弱而眼睜睜看著印度遭受屈辱，那我寧可訴諸武力，以守護印度。

the statue of Mahatma Gandhi in San Francisco

Mahatma Gandhi (1869–1948)

1. pendency [ˈpɛndənsi] (n.) the quality or state of being pendent or suspended 懸而未決
2. Boer War: a war fought from 1899 to 1902 between an alliance of the Boer governments of the Transvaal and the Orange Free State on the one hand and Great Britain on the other hand 波爾戰爭（1899–1902 年，英國人與波爾人的戰爭）
3. Zulu Rebellion: a war in 1879 between the British Empire and the Zulu Empire 祖魯戰爭

23

But I believe that non-violence is infinitely superior to violence, forgiveness is more manly than punishment, forgiveness adorns a soldier. But abstinence[4] is forgiveness only when there is the power to punish; it is meaningless when it pretends to proceed from a helpless treasure. A mouse hardly forgives a cat when it allows itself to be torn to pieces by her.

I therefore appreciate the sentiment of those who cry out for the punishment of General Dyer[5] and his ilk[6]. They would tear him to pieces if thy could. But I do not believe Indian to be helpless. I do not believe myself to be a helpless creature. Only I want to use India's and my strength for a better purpose.

Let me no be misunderstood. Strength does no come from physical capacity. It comes from an indomitable[7] will. An average Zulu is any way more than a match for an average Englishman in bodily capacity. But he flees from an English boy, because he fears death and is nerveless in spite of his burly figure.

We in India may in a moment realize that one hundred thousand Englishmen need not frighten three hundred million human beings. A definite forgiveness would therefore, mean a definite recognition of our strength. →

4. abstinence ['æbstɪnəns] (n.) restraint from indulging a desire for something 節制
5. Reginald Dyer (1864–1927): a British Indian Army officer responsible for the Jallianwala Bagh massacre 一位曾執行大屠殺的英國將領
6. ilk [ɪlk] (n.) a kind of person 同類
7. indomitable [ɪn'dɑːmɪtəbəl] (a.) not to be conquered; unyielding 不屈不撓的

　　但是，我相信非暴力遠遠地勝過於武力。寬恕，要比動粗還更有男子氣概，更能顯示出戰士的威風。然而，在可以為之而不為的情況下，這樣的武力克制才算得上是一種寬恕。如果是因為勢不可為，而拿來當作逃遁的藉口，那就不是這麼一回事了。屈服於貓爪下的老鼠，是不能說牠寬恕了貓的。

　　因此，對於那些主張懲罰戴爾將軍和其爪牙的人，我很能體會他們的心情，他們恨不得將他碎屍萬段。然而，我並不認為印度人是無能為力的，我也不認為自己是一個無能為力的人。我想做的，只是想讓印度同胞和我自己的能力，能夠發揮於一個更好的目標上。

　　大家不要誤會了我的意思。力量，不是來自於身體的蠻力，而是來自於不屈不撓的意志。在身體的氣力上，一個中等體型的祖魯人，是足以和另一個中等體型的英國人互相對抗的，然而，當他看到一個英國小男孩時，儘管他塊頭要大得多，他卻會拔腿就跑，因為他怕自己小命不保。

　　在印度，我們可能意識過，即使只有十萬個英國人，但就算來個三億的人馬，也毋須害怕。因此，要有一個真正的寬恕，就必須對我們自己的力量有一個明確的認識。

24

With enlightened forgiveness must come a mighty wave of strength in us which would make it impossible for a Dyer and a Frank Johnson to heap affront[8] on India's devoted head. We feel too downtrodden not to be angry and revengeful. But I must not refrain from saying that India can gain more by waiving the right of punishment. We have better work to do, a better mission to deliver to the world.

I am not a visionary. I claim to be a practical idealist. The religion of non-violence is not meant merely for the rishis holy people and saints. It is meant for the common people as well. Non-violence is the law of our species as violence is the law of the brute, and he knows no law but that of physical might. The dignity of man requires obedience to a higher law—to the strength of the spirit.

I have therefore ventured to place before Indian the ancient law of self-sacrifice. For satyagraha and its off shoots, non-cooperation and civil resistance are nothing but new names for the law of suffering. The rishis who discovered the law of non-violence in the midst of violence, were greater geniuses than Newton. They were themselves greater warriors than Wellington[9]. Having themselves known the use of arms, they realized their uselessness, and taught a weary world that its salvation lay not through violence but through non-violence.

Non-violence in its dynamic condition means conscious suffering. It does not mean meek submission to the will of the evil-doer, but it means the pitting of one's whole soul against the will of the tyrant. Working under this law of our being, it is possible for a single individual to defy[10] the whole might of an unjust empire to save his honor, his religion, his soul, and lay the foundation for that empire's fall or its regeneration.

11 非暴力‧武力的法則

8. affront [əˈfrʌnt] (n.) an open insult or giving of offense to somebody 公然侮辱
9. The Duke of Wellington, Arthur Wellesley (1769–1852) 第一代威靈頓公爵
10. defy [dɪˈfaɪ] (v.) to refuse to obey a person, decision, law, situation, etc. 公然反抗

　　覺悟性的寬恕，必然來自於內心裡強大的力量，這種力量會使得那一幫英國人根本不敢爬到印度人的頭上撒野。我們感到被蹂躪得很徹底，所以不敢言怒，也不敢回擊。我不得不這麼說，印度只要揮旗起義，就能有所改善，但是，我們還有更好的事業可以奮鬥，可以為全世界執行更好的任務。

　　我不是一個空想家，我主張要做一個實際的理想家。真理堅固的信仰，不是神仙聖人才需要修持的，對一般凡夫俗子而言也是有必要的。非暴力是我們人類的法則，暴力是野蠻世界的法則，它只有蠻力而無法律可言。人類尊嚴需要依循於一個更高的法則——依循於內在的力量。

　　因此，我才向印度人提出了「犧牲奉獻」這條古老的法則。Satyagraha（真理堅固）和其衍生出的概念——不合作運動與非暴力抵抗——都只是苦行法則的新名稱罷了。在暴力之中發現非暴力法則的神仙聖人，他們的發明比牛頓更具天才，他們也比威靈頓公爵更驍勇善戰。他們領悟到武力不能解決問題，所以教導疲乏的世人，解決之道不在於武力，而在於非暴力。

　　非暴力的進行，是一種醒覺性的苦行。它決非是指卑微地臣服於淫威之下，而是指威武不能屈。只要能依循這條生存的法則，單槍匹馬的一個人就可能成為足以與整個邪惡帝國抗衡的力量，能夠挽救其榮譽、宗教和精神，並成為帝國失敗或改革的基礎。

Our March to Freedom Is Irreversible

Release From Prison

曼德拉出獄演講：
邁向民主的腳步不
會倒退

南非的民族鬥士曼德拉出生於一個部落酋長家庭，他身為長子，是酋長繼承人，但他選擇為人權而戰，終生奉獻於人類的自由與和平。他因為致力於反對種族隔離制度，1962 年 8 月被捕入獄，囚禁在大西洋羅本島（Robben Island）約 20 年，接著數次移監，身陷囹圄長達 27 年。

1964 年，南非白人政府對他提出叛國罪，指控他密謀推翻政權。本篇演說結尾所提及的引言，即是他當年在審判法庭上所做的陳述詞。1990 年，南非當局在國內外的強大輿論壓力下，不得已才釋放了已經 72 歲的曼德拉。1990 年 2 月 11 日，曼德拉發表了這篇出獄後的首次演講。

南非自 1940 年代開始實施的種族隔離政策，終於在 1990 年廢除。1994 年 5 月，曼德拉成為南非第一位黑人總統。曼德拉四十年來獲得的榮譽獎項不計其數，並於 1993 年獲得諾貝爾和平獎。

2009 年 7 月 18 日，在曼德拉 91 歲生日這一天，南非將 7 月 18 日訂定為「曼德拉日」（Mandela Day），呼籲人們在這一天至少花 67 分鐘參與社會公益活動，以紀念曼德拉為人權運動奮鬥的 67 年。

Nelson Mandela's Prison Cell, Robben Island, South Africa
(Author: Paul Mannix)

Speaker	南非的民族鬥士曼德拉 （Nelson Mandela, 1918–2013）
Time	1990 年 2 月 11 日
Place	南非開普敦（Cape Town, South Africa）

☉ 錄音　☉ 擷錄

Entrance to Robben Island Prison, South Africa

Nelson Mandela Museum in Mthatha, Eastern Cape, South Africa

Nelson Mandela Bridge in Johannesburg, South Africa

Friends, comrades and fellow South Africans.

I greet you all in the name of peace, democracy and freedom for all. I stand here before you not as a prophet but as a humble servant of you, the people. Your tireless and heroic sacrifices have made it possible for me to be here today. I therefore place the remaining years of my life in your hands.

On this day of my release, I extend my sincere and warmest gratitude to the millions of my compatriots[1] and those in every corner of the globe who have campaigned tirelessly for my release.

Today the majority of South Africans, black and white, recognize that apartheid[2] has no future. It has to be ended by our own decisive mass action in order to build peace and security. The mass campaign of defiance and other actions of our organization and people can only culminate in the establishment of democracy. →

各位朋友，各位同仁，各位南非的同胞們：

我以全人類的和平、民主和自由之名，來向你們大家致意。我站在這裡，站在你們大家的面前，並不是因為我是什麼使者，而是因為我是你們一個身分卑微的僕人。要不是有你們不懈的英勇犧牲和奉獻，我今天是不可能站在這裡的，因此，我要把我往後的餘生獻給你們。

今天，是我獲釋的日子，我要向千百萬名同胞，向全球各地為我不斷奔走、爭取釋放的人們，致上最真誠由衷的感謝。

今天，大多數的南非人，不管是黑人還是白人，都了解到種族隔離的政策是毫無前途的。這需要透過我們自己堅定的群眾運動，來結束這種制度，以建立和平安全的社會。除非我們建立起民主制度，否則大規模的抗爭活動，或是我們這個組織或人民的其他活動，就沒有終止的一天。

1. compatriot [kəmˈpeɪtriət] (n.) person from your own country 同胞
2. apartheid [əˈpɑːrtaɪt] (n.) a former policy of segregation and political and economic discrimination against non-European groups in the South Africa 南非的種族隔離政策

Mandela Day

make an imprint
a 46664 celebration.

The destruction caused by apartheid on our subcontinent is incalculable. The fabric of family life of millions of my people has been shattered. Millions are homeless and unemployed. Our economy lies in ruins and our people are embroiled in political strife.

The factors which necessitated the armed struggle still exist today. We have no option but to continue. We express the hope that a climate conducive to a negotiated settlement will be created soon so that there may no longer be the need for the armed struggle.

I am a loyal and disciplined member of the African National Congress[3]. I am therefore in full agreement with all of its objectives, strategies and tactics. The need to unite the people of our country is as important a task now as it always has been. No individual leader is able to take on this enormous task on his own.

Our struggle has reached a decisive moment. We call on our people to seize this moment so that the process towards democracy is rapid and uninterrupted. We have waited too long for our freedom. We can no longer wait. Now is the time to intensify the struggle on all fronts. To relax our efforts now would be a mistake which generations to come will not be able to forgive. The sight of freedom looming[4] on the horizon should encourage us to redouble our efforts.

It is only through disciplined mass action that our victory can be assured. We call on our white compatriots to join us in the shaping of a new South Africa. The freedom movement is a political home for you too. We call on the international community to continue the campaign to isolate the apartheid regime. To lift sanctions[5] now would be to run the risk of aborting the process towards the complete eradication[6] of apartheid. →

種族隔離為這塊土地所帶來的傷害，難以估計。我們數百萬的黑人家庭被拆散，數百萬的人民流離失所，無法工作。我們的經濟崩盤，人民飽受政治鬥爭的煎熬。

今天，不得不以武力抗爭的原因仍然存在著。我們只能繼續下去，沒有其他的選擇。我們期待，能盡快形成有利於談判解決的情勢，以便終止武力抗爭。

我是非洲國民大會遵守紀律的忠誠分子，我完全贊同其所提出來的目標、戰略和策略。現在需要全國人民團結一致起來，這始終都是最關鍵的一個點。任何領導者，都無法獨自承擔這些重責大任的。

我們的奮鬥已經到了一個決定性的時刻，我呼籲人們抓住這個時機，以便加快民主化的過程，讓這個過程不會受到阻撓。我們等待自由，已經等待太久了，我們無法再等下去了。現在，就是全面加緊奮鬥的時刻了！如果我們現在鬆懈了，那將會是我們後代子孫所無法原諒的一個錯誤！地平線上浮現的自由蜃景，就足以激勵我們加倍地努力奮鬥。

只有透過有紀律的群眾活動，才能保證我們可以贏得勝利。我們呼籲我們的白人同胞們也一起加入我們的行列，一起打造一個嶄新的南非共和國。對於自由的爭取，也是你們政治上追求的終點。我們也呼籲國際社會繼續採取行動，繼續孤立這個實行種族隔離制度的政權。如果現在停止國際制裁，那徹底消除種族隔離的進展就會有夭折的危險。

---

3. African National Congress: a South African political party founded in 1912 that fought against apartheid 非洲國民大會

4. loom [luːm] (v.) to appear as a large or indistinct, and sometimes menacing, shape 隱約地出現

5. sanctions [ˈsæŋkʃəns] (n.) (pl.) a measure taken by one or more nations to apply pressure on another nation to conform to international law or opinion 國際制裁

6. eradication [ɪˌrædɪˈkeɪʃən] (n.) the complete destruction of every trace of something 消滅；根除

Photographer: Alet van Huyssteen

27

Our march to freedom is irreversible. We must not allow fear to stand in our way. Universal suffrage[7] on a common voters' role in a united democratic and non-racial South Africa is the only way to peace and racial harmony.

In conclusion I wish to quote my own words during my trial in 1964. They are true today as they were then:

"I have fought against white domination and I have fought against black domination. I have cherished the ideal of a democratic and free society in which all persons live together in harmony and with equal opportunities. It is an ideal which I hope to live for and to achieve. But if needs be, it is an ideal for which I am prepared to die."

我們邁向自由的腳步是不會倒退的，我們決不會讓恐懼阻擋在我們前方的路上。在一個聯合民主、不分膚色的南非實現全民普選，是我們邁向和平與種族和諧的唯一道路。

最後，我想引用我自己在 1964 年受審時所說過的話。這些話不論是在當時，還是在今日，我都還是真心這樣想的：

「我為反對白人統治而抗爭，也為反對黑人統治而抗爭。我珍視民主和自由社會的理想，在那樣的社會裡，所有人都能夠和平共處，而且每個人都擁有平等的機會。我想要為這個理想而活，我想要實現它。然而，如果有需要，我也準備為這個理想而死。」

7. suffrage ['sʌfrɪdʒ] (n.) the right to vote in an election 投票；選擇權

Old Soldiers Never Die

麥克阿瑟國會告別演說：
老兵不死，只是凋零

麥克阿瑟將軍出生於阿肯色州的軍人世家，1898 年，他考取西點軍校，並以百年來最佳的優異成績畢業。麥克阿瑟縱橫沙場有半世紀之久，戰功彪炳，獲頒美國最高的軍事榮銜「榮譽勳章」（Medal of Honor）。

1919 年，在他 39 歲那一年被任命為西點軍校校長，成為西點軍校史上最年輕的校長，後於 1937 年退役。1941 年，第二次世界大戰爆發，他被徵召擔任遠東軍總司令。1944 年，升為五星上將。戰後 1945–1951 年間，擔任盟軍總司令，負責日本的重建工作。

1950 年 6 月 25 日，北韓領導人金日成進攻南韓，6 月 27 日杜魯門總統下令美軍參戰，聯合國安理會隨後也組織軍隊參戰，由麥克阿瑟擔任總司令。後來杜魯門總統指示他只能打一場有限的戰爭，麥克阿瑟公開反對。1951 年 4 月 11 日，杜魯門以「未能全力支持美國和聯合國的政策」為由，將之撤職。

麥克阿瑟回到美國後，在華盛頓受到了萬人空巷的英雄式歡迎。1951 年 4 月 19 日，麥克阿瑟在國會大廈發表了這篇著名的《老兵不死》的告別演說。其中最膾炙人口的一句話就是：

Old soldiers never die; they just fade away.
老兵不死，只是凋零。

Speaker	美國名將麥克阿瑟將軍（Douglas MacArthur, 1880–1964）
Time	1951 年 4 月 19 日
Place	美國國會大廈（US Capitol）

▣ 原音重現 ▣ 擷錄

The Memorial to Gen. MacArthur's Leyte Landing in the Philippines

28

MacArthur's Leyte Landing: "I have returned."

I stand on this rostrum[1] with a sense of deep humility and great pride—humility in the wake of those great architects of our history who have stood here before me, pride in the reflection that this home of legislative debate represents human liberty in the purest form yet devised.

Here are centered the hopes and aspirations and faith of the entire human race. I do not stand here as advocate for any partisan[2] cause, for the issues are fundamental and reach quite beyond the realm of partisan considerations. They must be resolved on the highest plane of national interest if our course is to prove sound and our future protected.

I trust, therefore, that you will do me the justice of receiving that which I have to say as solely expressing the considered viewpoint of a fellow American. I address you with neither rancor[3] nor bitterness in the fading twilight of life, with but one purpose in mind: to serve my country. →

　　站在這個演講臺上，我懷著十分謙卑，卻也十分驕傲的心情。我謙卑，是因為在我之前，有許多我們歷史上的偉大創造者也曾經在這裡發言過；我驕傲，是因為我想到，這個最早容許立法辯論的地方，正代表著人類有史以來最純粹的一種自由。

　　這個地方，是全人類之希望、抱負和信仰的中心。我站在這裡，不是為了任何黨派而發言，我要談的是最根本的問題，是超越黨派的。如果要證明我們的路線是正確的，要保障我們的未來，那麼在制定有關國家利益的最高綱領時，就必須解決這些問題。

　　因此，我相信，當我只是陳述出一個身為美國公民的熱切觀點後，你們就能接受我所說的話了。我已經進入日薄西山的晚年，在這裡對你們談話的我，心中沒有仇恨、沒有痛苦，只有一個目標：為我的國家服務。

1. rostrum [ˈrɑːstrəm] (n.) small platform on which a person making a speech 講臺
2. partisan [ˌpɑːrtɪzən] (a.) devoted to a party 黨派的
3. rancor [ˈræŋkɔr] (n.) a feeling of deep and bitter anger and ill-will 激烈的憎惡

29

I am closing my fifty-two years of military service. When I joined the army, even before the turn of the century, it was the fulfillment of all my boyish hopes and dreams.

The world has turned over many times since I took the oath on the plain at West Point[4], and the hopes and dreams have long since vanished, but I still remember the refrain of one of the most popular barracks[5] ballads of that day which proclaimed most proudly that old soldiers never die; they just fade away.

And like the old soldier of that ballad, I now close my military career and just fade away, an old soldier who tried to do his duty as God gave him the light to see that duty.

Good-bye.

我即將結束我五十二年的軍旅生涯。我在上個世紀末就加入軍隊,這讓我實現了我小時候的所有願望與夢想。

從我在西點軍校的草坪上做過宣誓以來,世界已經經歷了許多次的轉變,而我那些兒時的願望與夢想,也早已不復存在。然而,我依然記得當年曾經最流行的一首軍歌,我記得它的副歌部分,它神氣地唱道:老兵不死,只是凋零。

就像這首歌中的老兵一樣,如今我將結束我的軍旅生涯,淡出舞臺。這是一個盡力依照上帝所指引的那樣,努力去完成職責的老兵。

再見!

---

4. West Point: a U.S. military installation in southeast New York 美國西點軍校
5. barracks ['bærəks] (n.) (pl.) a large building or group of buildings for housing soldiers 軍營

14

Arms Can Bring No Security

愛因斯坦：
武器捍衛不了國土

愛因斯坦生於德國多瑙河畔的烏爾姆（Ulm），父母都是猶太人；六個星期大時，全家搬到慕尼黑，之後又舉家遷居至義大利米蘭。1896 年，他進入瑞士一所學院就讀；1901 年，他取得瑞士國籍。1905 年，他發表了六篇劃時代的論文，提出了狹義相對論和光量子論的觀點，這一年因此被稱為愛因斯坦的奇蹟年（Miracle Year）。1915 年，發表了廣義相對論。

第一次世界大戰爆發後，他投入公開和地下的反戰活動。1921 年，獲得諾貝爾物理學獎。1933 年，納粹黨取得德國政權，他成了納粹在科學界首要的迫害對象；同年 10 月，他前往美國擔任普林斯頓高級研究院的教授，並於 1940 年取得美國國籍。

1937 年，他探訪當時住在美國加州的英國演員及導演查理・卓別林（Charles Chaplin, 1889–1977）。三年後，卓別林在自導自演的電影《大獨裁者》（The Great Dictator）中，演出了一段對納粹的精彩指控。

1939 年，他上書小羅斯福總統，建議研發原子彈，以防被德國搶先製造。美國後來在廣島和長崎投下原子彈，他對此表達了強烈的不滿。他是個和平主義者和人道主義者，1955 年，在他去世的前幾天，他簽署了反核武的《羅素—愛因斯坦宣言》（Russell-Einstein Manifesto）。

為了紀念愛因斯坦的成就，1952 年合成的原子序數 99 之放射性化學元素，就以他的姓取名為「鑀」。2009 年，在諾貝爾獎各獎項即將揭曉之際，諾貝爾基金會評出了諾貝爾獎百餘年以來最受尊崇的三位獲獎者，愛因斯坦是其中的一位，其他兩位分是是 1964 年和平獎得主馬丁路德金，以及 1979 年和平獎得主德蕾莎修女。

Speaker　物理學家愛因斯坦（Albert Einstein, 1879–1955）

Time　1950 年 2 月 19 日

Place　美國電視演説

☑ 錄音　☑ 擷錄

30

I am grateful to you for the opportunity to express my conviction in this most important political question.

The idea of achieving security through national armament is, at the present state of military technique, a disastrous illusion. On the part of the United States, this illusion has been particularly fostered by the fact that this country succeeded first in producing an atomic bomb. The belief seemed to prevail that in the end it were possible to achieve decisive military superiority.

In this way, any potential opponent would be intimidated, and security, so ardently desired by all of us, brought to us and all of humanity. The maxim which we have been following during these last five years has been, in short: security through superior military power, whatever the cost.

The armament race between the USA and the USSR, originally supposed to be a preventive measure, assumes a hysterical character. On both sides, the means to mass destruction are perfected with feverish[1] haste, behind the respective walls of secrecy. The H-bomb[2] appears on the public horizon as a probably attainable goal. Its accelerated development has been solemnly proclaimed by the president.

If successful, radioactive poisoning of the atmosphere and hence annihilation of any life on earth has been brought within the range of technical possibilities. The ghost-like character of this development lies in its apparently compulsory trend. Every step appears as the unavoidable consequence of the preceding one. In the end, there beckons more and more clearly general annihilation.

Is there any way out of this impasse created by man himself? All of us, and particularly those who are responsible for the attitude of the US and the USSR, should realize that we may have vanquished an external enemy[3], but have been incapable of getting rid of the mentality created by the war. →

很高興能有機會就這個極為重要的政治議題談談自己的見解。

就目前的軍事發展情況來看，幻想藉由加強軍備來捍衛國土，只會招致災難性的後果。美國率先研發出了原子彈，因此特別會懷抱這種幻想。一般人認為，美國最終還是會取得決定性的軍事優勢。

如此一來，任何潛在的對手都會畏懼三分，而大家所熱切期盼的安全保障，便會降臨在我們以及全人類身上。簡單來說，我們這五年來一直恪守的準則就是：就算不惜任何代價，也要取得軍事優勢，以確保國家安全。

美國和蘇聯之間的軍備競賽的初衷是為了防止戰爭的發生，而現在卻演變到一發不可收拾的地步。在被列為國家機密的情況下，雙方都以狂熱的速度完善其大規模殺傷武器。氫彈的研發完成，指日可待。總統也正式發表了這項加速發展的聲明。

一旦氫彈研發完成，大氣層可能會遭到放射性物質污染，因而導致地球生物的滅絕。這項發展顯然已經成為一種無法遏止的勢態，而這正是它的可怕之處。一旦踏上了這條不歸路，全人類滅亡的日子最終也會步步逼近。

在這個人類所構建的死巷中，我們還有別的出路嗎？我們每個人，尤其是美國和蘇聯的領導者，都應該清楚這一點：我們也許可以戰勝外面的敵人，但卻還不能消除戰爭所引起的內心恐懼。

a waxwork of Albert Einstein

Albert Einstein (1879–1955)

1. feverish [ˈfiːvərɪʃ] (a.) showing intense agitation, excitement, or emotion 發燒的；發熱的

2. H-bomb (hydrogen bomb): an explosive weapon of mass destruction in which huge amounts of energy are released by the fusion of hydrogen nuclei 氫彈

3. Einstein refers to the Axis powers of World War II (Germany, Italy, and Japan). 在此指軸心國（第二次世界大戰德、義、日等國）

Albert Einstein (1879–1955)

31

It is impossible to achieve peace as long as every single action is taken with a possible future conflict in view. The leading point of view of all political action should therefore be: What can we do to bring about a peaceful co-existence and even loyal co-operation of the nations?

The first problem is to do away with mutual fear and distrust. Solemn renunciation[4] of violence (not only with respect to means of mass destruction) is undoubtedly necessary.

Such renunciation, however, can only be effective if at the same time a supra-national judicial and executive body is set up, empowered to decide questions of immediate concern to the security of the nations. Even a declaration of the nations to collaborate loyally in the realization of such a "restricted world government" would considerably reduce the imminent danger of war.

In the last analysis, every kind of peaceful co-operation among men is primarily based on mutual[5] trust and only secondly on institutions such as courts of justice and police. This holds for nations as well as for individuals. And the basis of trust is loyal give and take[6]. ◀

只要我們採取的行動具有未來衝突的可能性，和平就不會實現。因此，主導一切政治活動的原則應該是：如何才能實現國與國之間的和平共存，甚至是真誠合作呢？

首先，我們必須消除彼此的恐懼和猜疑。鄭重聲明放棄使用武力（不僅是放棄大規模殺傷武器），無疑是十分重要的。

然而，要有效地做到放棄武力，必須同時成立一個超越國界的司法和執行機構，授權解決與各國安全密切相關的問題。儘管只是幾個國家聯合聲明，表達真誠合作的意願，實現這種「權力有限的世界政府」，也能夠大大緩和迫在眉睫的戰爭危機。

總而言之，互相信任是人類和平合作的首要基礎，其次才是諸如法庭和警官之類的機構。這不僅適用於國家與國家之間，人與人之間亦是如此。而信任的基礎建立於誠心誠意的互讓。

4. renunciation [rɪˌnʌnsɪˈeɪʃən] (n.) an official declaration giving up a title, office, claim, or privilege （權利等的）宣告放棄

5. mutual [ˈmjuːtʃʊəl] (a.) shared by or common to two or more people or groups 相互的；共有的

6. give and take: mutual cooperation and understanding between people or groups, often involving concessions on all sides 互相遷就；互讓

15

Shall We Choose Death?

英國哲學家羅素：
我們該選擇死亡嗎？

英國哲學家伯特蘭・羅素出生於貴族家庭，祖父曾兩次出任英國首相。他在年幼時，父母就雙雙過世，由祖父母撫養長大。1890 年，他進入劍橋大學三一學院，後來成為學院的研究員及英國皇家學會成員。

1920 年，羅素訪問俄國和中國，在北京講學一年，與美國的杜威同時間在中國講學。他後來著有《中國問題》一書，孫中山稱他是「唯一真正瞭解中國的西方人」。當年徐志摩遠赴英國想拜羅素為師，羅素卻已離開劍橋大學，徐志摩失望之餘，於1928 年寫下了《再別康橋》一詩。

羅素是二十世紀最具影響力的哲學家之一。他力倡和平，曾因為反對英國參加第一次世界大戰而被罰款，並失去三一學院的教職。

他也曾參與美國總統甘迺迪遇刺事件的調查，是最早幾個對官方說詞提出質疑的人。1950 年，他獲得諾貝爾文學獎，表揚其著作的重要性，以及他的人道主義理想和對思想自由的追求。

1954 年，氫彈爆破成功，羅素意識到核武可能給人類帶來的災難，這也是本篇演講的主題。1955 年 7 月，羅素發表了著名的《羅素—愛因斯坦宣言》（Russell-Einstein Manifesto），宣言中對核武的危險深表憂慮，呼籲各國領導人以和平的方式解決國際衝突。

1961 年，89 歲高齡的羅素參與核武裁軍的遊行後被拘禁了 7天。他也是位反越戰的人士，1967 年，他還和法國哲學家沙特（Jean-Paul Sartre）成立了一個民間法庭（後來稱為「羅素法庭」），揭露美國的戰爭罪行。

Speaker 英國哲學家羅素
（Bertrand Russell, 1872–1970）

Time 1954 年 12 月 30 日

▣ 錄音 ▣ 全文收錄

32

I am speaking not as a Briton, not as a European, not as a member of a western democracy, but as a human being, a member of the species Man, whose continued existence is in doubt. The world is full of conflicts: Jews and Arabs; Indians and Pakistanis; white men and Negroes in Africa; and, overshadowing all minor conflicts, the titanic struggle between communism and anticommunism.

Almost everybody who is politically conscious has strong feelings about one or more of these issues; but I want you, if you can, to set aside such feelings for the moment and consider yourself only as a member of a biological species which has had a remarkable history and whose disappearance none of us can desire.

I shall try to say no single word which should appeal to one group rather than to another. All, equally, are in peril, and, if the peril is understood, there is hope that they may collectively avert it. We have to learn to think in a new way. We have to learn to ask ourselves not what steps can be taken to give military victory to whatever group we prefer, for there no longer are such steps.

The question we have to ask ourselves is: What steps can be taken to prevent a military contest of which the issue must be disastrous to all sides?

The general public, and even many men in positions of authority, have not realized what would be involved in a war with hydrogen[1] bombs. The general public still thinks in terms of the obliteration[2] of cities. It is understood that the new bombs are more powerful than the old and that, while one atomic bomb could obliterate Hiroshima, one hydrogen bomb could obliterate the largest cities such as London, New York, and Moscow.

Here, then, is the problem which I present to you, stark[3] and dreadful and inescapable: Shall we put an end to the human race; or shall mankind renounce war? →

我現在發言，不是以一個英國人的身分，不是以一個歐洲人的身分，也不是以一個西方民主國家人士的身分來發言，而是以一個人類的身分，以一個不知能否繼續生存下去的人類的身分來發言。這個世界充滿了衝突：猶太人和阿拉伯人的衝突，印度人和巴基斯坦人的衝突，非洲白人和黑人的衝突，還有共產國家和非共產國家之間的巨大衝突，這個衝突使得所有的小型衝突都相形見絀。

幾乎每一個具有政治意識的人，對這些議題或多或少都有強烈的感觸。然而，如果可以，我請你暫時把這些感觸拋開，僅僅把自己當成是人類這種物種的一員。這個物種擁有非凡的歷史，而我們都不希望看到這個物種滅絕。

可能會迎合某一群人而冷落另一群人的話，我都將盡量不提。我們大家都站在同一條船上，而如果我們能夠認識這場災難，那我們就有希望可以合力來避開災難。我們必須要學習用一種新的方式來思惟，我必須學著問問自己的，不是採取什麼措施可以使同盟國獲得軍事上的勝利，因為此時此刻根本談不上這種措施。

我們必須自問的問題是：我們能採取什麼樣的措施，來避免可能導致毀滅性災難的軍事競賽？

一般人，甚至是許多政府官員，都還不清楚一場氫彈戰爭到底意謂著什麼。一般大眾仍舊從城市被毀的概念上來思考。一般都知道，新型炸彈比舊式的炸彈更具威力，而且一個原子彈就可以炸毀一個廣島市，而一顆氫彈能夠炸毀像倫敦、紐約或莫斯科這樣的大型都市。

因此在這裡，我要向各位所提出的，就是這樣一個赤裸裸、可怕、無法回避的問題：我們應該毀滅、終結人類，還是人類應該拋棄戰爭？

a statue of Bertrand Russell

Bertrand Russell (1872–1970)

1. hydrogen [ˈhaɪdrədʒən] (n.) the lightest gas, with no color, taste or smell, that combines with oxygen to form water 氫

2. obliteration [ə,blɪtəˈreɪʃən] (n.) destruction by annihilating something 整體毀滅

3. stark [stɑːrk] (a.) complete or extreme 赤裸裸的；明顯的

People will not face this alternative because it is so difficult to abolish war. The abolition of war will demand distasteful limitations of national sovereignty. But what perhaps impedes[4] understanding of the situation more than anything else is that the term "mankind" feels vague and abstract.

People scarcely realize in imagination that the danger is to themselves and their children and their grandchildren, and not only to a dimly apprehended humanity. And so they hope that perhaps war may be allowed to continue provided modern weapons are prohibited.

I am afraid this hope is illusory. Whatever agreements not to use hydrogen bombs had been reached in time of peace, they would no longer be considered binding in time of war, and both sides would set to work to manufacture hydrogen bombs as soon as war broke out, for if one side manufactured the bombs and the other did not, the side that manufactured them would inevitably be victorious.

As geological time is reckoned, Man has so far existed only for a very short period—one million years at the most. What he has achieved, especially during the last 6,000 years, is something utterly new in the history of the Cosmos, so far at least as we are acquainted with it. For countless ages the sun rose and set, the moon waxed and waned, the stars shone in the night, but it was only with the coming of Man that these things were understood.

In the great world of astronomy and in the little world of the atom, Man has unveiled secrets which might have been thought undiscoverable. In art and literature and religion, some men have shown a sublimity of feeling which makes the species worth preserving. →

我們該選擇死亡嗎？

4. impede [ɪmˈpiːd] (v.) to slow down or cause problems for the achievement or finishing of something 妨礙

Bertrand Russell prepares to speak in Trafalgar Square at the end of the Aldermaston march in London, April 3, 1961 (Author: Austin Underwood)

人們不願面對這個抉擇，因為要消滅戰爭太難了。要消滅戰爭，就會要求限制國家主權，而這讓人難以接受。或許，阻礙人們去認清情勢的最大原因，是因為「人類」這個字眼顯得太過籠統而抽象。

人們並沒有去想像這種危險性會如何地殃及自己，殃及我們的後代子孫，實則這並不是只是籠籠統統地說會危及人類而已。人們相信，只要禁止使用現代武器，戰爭還是可以繼續下去的。

恐怕這種願望只是一種痴心妄想。人們只有在和平時期才會簽署禁用氫彈的協議，要是碰到了戰爭，就會毫無約束力。一旦戰爭爆發，雙方就會著手製造氫彈，因為誰有氫彈，誰就會贏。

按照地質年代來計算，人類存在的時間其實很短，頂多是一百萬年而已。而人類所達到的成就，特別是最近這六千年以來的發展，在宇宙史上是全新的一頁，起碼就我們所知的宇宙而言是如此。恆久遠以來，日出日落，月盈月缺，天上的星斗，一直到人類出現了之後，這些現象才被認識。

在天文學的宏觀世界和原子的微觀世界裡，人類揭露了這些曾經被認為是無法得知的祕密。在藝術、文學和宗教裡，人們顯現了崇高的情感，讓人類成為值得延續下去的物種。

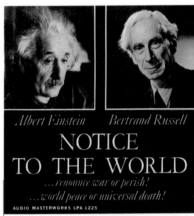

Albert Einstein   *Bertrand Russell*

NOTICE
TO THE WORLD
...renounce war or perish!
...world peace or universal death!
AUDIO MASTERWORKS LPA 1225

Is all this to end in trivial horror because so few are able to think of Man rather than of this or that group of men? Is our race so destitute[5] of wisdom, so incapable of impartial love, so blind even to the simplest dictates of self-preservation, that the last proof of its silly cleverness is to be the extermination of all life on our planet?—for it will be not only men who will perish, but also the animals, whom no one can accuse of communism or anticommunism.

I cannot believe that this is to be the end. I would have men forget their quarrels for a moment and reflect that, if they will allow themselves to survive, there is every reason to expect the triumphs of the future to exceed immeasurably the triumphs of the past.

There lies before us, if we choose, continual progress in happiness, knowledge, and wisdom. Shall we, instead, choose death, because we cannot forget our quarrels?

I appeal, as a human being to human beings: remember your humanity, and forget the rest. If you can do so, the way lies open to a new Paradise; if you cannot, nothing lies before you but universal death. ◀

　　這一切都將在毫無價值的災難中告終嗎？只因為大多數人只考慮到這一群人或那一群人，而無法考慮到全人類嗎？我們人類是這麼缺乏智慧的嗎？我們的愛是這麼狹隘的嗎？我們是這麼盲目的嗎，連自我保存這種最簡單的聲音都聽不到？我們非得把整個地球的生命都毀滅，才能知道自己的聰明才智原來是多麼愚蠢嗎？——被毀滅的不只是人類，還包括其他的動物，這些動物不會指控是共產主義還是反共產主義。

　　我無法相信人類會走上這樣的結局。人類如果想繼續生存下去，就應該要把爭執拋到一邊，想一想，人類有千百個理由，足以期待未來的成就能大大超越過往的成就。

　　如果讓我們選擇，擺在我們眼前的，將是不斷前進的幸福、知識和智慧。又或者，只因為我們不願意放下爭執，所以我們寧可選擇死亡？

　　身為人類，我要向所有的人類呼籲：記住你的人性，其餘的都拋到腦後吧。如果可以做到這一點，前方的路就會通向一個新的天堂；如果做不到，眼前除了世界性的毀滅，將一無所有。

5. destitute ['dɛstɪtuːt]
(a.) lacking a
particular quality
缺乏的

16

Strike Against War

海倫・凱勒：
不要順從於毀滅者

海倫・凱勒在一歲半左右因為染上猩紅熱，喪失視力與聽力。後來在老師蘇利文（Anne Sullivan）不懈的教導下，開始學習手語、點字和說話。海倫・凱勒畢業於雷德克利夫學院（Radcliffe College），她終其一生都在為失能人士奔走，爭取資源。1955 年，哈佛大學頒發給她榮譽學位，成為歷史上第一個受此殊榮的女性。

海倫・凱勒從童年時期起，就會被每一任美國總統邀請至白宮做客。1964 年，詹森總統還頒發給她「總統自由勳章」（Presidential Medal of Freedom），這是美國最高的平民榮譽之一。

她一生出版過 14 本著作，還有其他一些文章。1903 年，她出版自傳《我的生活》（The Story of My Life）。1954年發行的電影《海倫凱勒傳》（The Unconquered），由她自己擔任主演，本片還獲得了奧斯卡最佳紀錄片獎。

1946 年，她擔任美國全球盲人基金會國際關係顧問，開始奔走世界。她爭取興建盲人學校，訪問醫院病人，此外，她也為貧民及黑人爭取權益，提倡世界和平。

1971 年，國際獅子會宣佈將海倫・凱勒逝世的日子 6 月1 日，訂為全球的「海倫凱勒紀念日」，在這一天，全球的獅子會都會舉辦視力相關的服務活動。

Speaker 美國知名盲聾人士海倫・凱勒
（Helen Adams Keller, 1880–1968）

Time 1916 年 1 月 5 日

Place 美國紐約市（New York City, USA）

◉ 錄音 ◉ 擷錄

35

To begin with, I have a word to say to my good friends, the editors, and others who are moved to pity me. Some people are grieved because they imagine I am in the hands of unscrupulous[1] persons who lead me astray and persuade me to espouse[2] unpopular causes and make me the mouthpiece of their propaganda. Now, let it be understood once and for all that I do not want their pity; I would not change places with one of them. I know what I am talking about.

My sources of information are as good and reliable as anybody else's. I have papers and magazines from England, France, Germany and Austria that I can read myself. Not all the editors I have met can do that. Quite a number of them have to take their French and German second hand. No, I will not disparage[3] the editors. They are an overworked, misunderstood class. Let them remember, though, that if I cannot see the fire at the end of their cigarettes, neither can they thread a needle in the dark. All I ask, gentlemen, is a fair field and no favor. I have entered the fight against preparedness[4] and against the economic system under which we live. It is to be a fight to the finish, and I ask no quarter[5].

Congress is not preparing to defend the people of the United States. It is planning to protect the capital of American speculators and investors in Mexico, South America, China, and the Philippine Islands. Incidentally, this preparation will benefit the manufacturers of munitions[6] and war machines. →

1. unscrupulous [ʌnˈskruːpjʊləs] (a.) lacking honesty and oblivious to what is honorable 肆無忌憚的；無恥的
2. espouse [ɪˈspaʊz] (v.) to become involved with or support an activity or opinion 擁護；信奉
3. disparage [dɪˈspærɪdʒ] (v.) to express a negative opinion of 貶低
4. preparedness [prɪˈpɛrədnɪs] (n.) a state of readiness, especially for war 戰備
5. quarter [ˈkwɔːrtər] (n.) mercy offered to a defeated enemy 對敵人的寬恕
6. munitions [mjuːˈnɪʃəns] (n.) (pl.) military supplies 軍需品；軍火

　　首先，我要跟我的好朋友、編輯以及其他受我感動而同情我的人説一些話。有些人覺得很傷心，因為他們覺得我被一些無恥的人掌控並誤導，使我去擁護一些不得人心的想法，進而成為他們宣傳的利器。現在我要再一次地説清楚，我並不需要其他人的同情，我的立場更不會因為他人而改變，而且我很清楚自己在説些什麼。

　　我的消息來源和其他人一樣可靠。我有來自英國、法國、德國和奧地利的報紙雜誌，而且我可以靠自己來閱讀，在我認識的編輯裡，並不是人人都可以做這麼多閱讀，他們當中有些人甚至只能閱讀法國和德國的二手消息。當然，我並不是要貶低這些編輯，他們常常工作過度，也常被誤解。我只是想讓他們知道，他們所得到的消息，並不會比我多。諸位，我要求的僅是一個公平、沒有任何偏袒的空間。我一直堅決反戰，也反對我們現在的經濟體系。這是一場不達目標、決不放棄的奮鬥，我決不會妥協。

　　國會並不準備保護美國人民，而是只打算保護美國金主在墨西哥、南美洲、中國和菲律賓所投資的資金。附帶一提的是，這會造福彈藥及軍火製造商。

36

Until recently there were uses in the United States for the money taken from the workers. But American labor is exploited[7] almost to the limit now, and our national resources[8] have all been appropriated[9]. Still the profits keep piling up new capital. Our flourishing industry in implements of murder is filling the vaults[10] of New York's banks with gold. And a dollar that is not being used to make a slave of some human being is not fulfilling its purpose in the capitalistic scheme. That dollar must be invested in South America, Mexico, China, or the Philippines.

Every modern war has had its root in exploitation. The Civil War was fought to decide whether to slaveholders of the South or the capitalists of the North should exploit the West. The Spanish-American War decided that the United States should exploit Cuba and the Philippines. The South African War decided that the British should exploit the diamond mines. The Russo-Japanese War decided that Japan should exploit Korea. The present war is to decide who shall exploit the Balkans, Turkey, Persia, Egypt, India, China, Africa.

And we are whetting[11] our sword to scare the victors into sharing the spoils with us. Now, the workers are not interested in the spoils; they will not get any of them anyway.

Strike against all ordinances[12] and laws and institutions that continue the slaughter of peace and the butcheries of war. Strike against war, for without you no battles can be fought. Strike against manufacturing shrapnel[13] and gas bombs and all other tools of murder. Strike against preparedness that means death and misery to millions of human being. Be not dumb, obedient slaves in an army of destruction. Be heroes in an army of construction.

時至今日，美國仍從勞工手中奪走大把鈔票，並且別有用途。美國的勞工已經被剝削殆盡，國家財力被掏空，而利潤所得仍不斷轉作新資本之用。對剝削者而言，我們欣欣向榮的工業，是他們中飽紐約銀行金庫的工具。他們的每一毛錢，若非用於奴役一些人們，來成就他們的資本主義大業，那麼這些錢就一定是用來投資南美洲、墨西哥、中國或菲律賓。

現代的每一場戰爭，都根源於有利可圖的剝削。美國南北戰爭決定了是由南方的奴隸主、還是北方的資本家可以來剝削西部。美西戰爭讓美國得到了古巴和菲律賓。南非戰爭讓英國拿到了鑽石礦脈。日俄戰爭讓日本奪取了韓國。而現在這場戰爭決定了將來誰可以剝削巴爾幹地區、土耳其、波斯、埃及、印度、中國和非洲等國。

我們正磨利我們的刀，威嚇那些勝利者分我們一杯羹。工人對於這些事情則一點都不感興趣，因為他們不會得到任何的好處。

反對那些會繼續殲滅和平、屠殺人類的所有條例、法律和機構！反對戰爭吧！你要是不參與，就不會有戰爭。反對砲彈製造商、毒氣彈等等的殺人工具吧！反對備戰吧！那代表著數百萬人的死亡或苦難。不要沉默地乖乖順從於毀滅者！要當一個創造的英雄！

a statue of Helen Keller

Helen Keller (1880–1968)

7. exploit [ɪkˈsplɔɪt] (v.) to use someone or something unfairly for your own advantage 剝削

8. resources [rɪˈsɔːrsɪs] (n.) (pl.) the collective wealth of a country 國家財力

9. appropriate [əˈproʊprɪət] (v.) to take something that belongs to or is associated with somebody else for yourself 盜用；佔用

10. vault [vɑːlt] (n.) a room, especially in a bank which is used to store money or valuable things 金庫房

11. whet [wɛt] (v.) to make keen or more acute 磨利

12. ordinance [ˈɔːrdənəns] (n.) a law or rule made by a government or authority 法令

13. shrapnel [ˈʃræpnəl] (n.) metal balls or fragments that are scattered when a shell, bomb, or bullet explodes 榴霰彈

17

The Perils of Indifference

集中營倖存者維瑟爾：
冷漠的危險

伊利‧維瑟爾出生於今日的羅馬尼亞境內，是猶太人大屠殺中的倖存者。

1944 年，15 歲的維瑟爾被關進位於波蘭的奧斯威辛集中營（Auschwitz concentration camp），他把這段悲慘的經歷寫成自傳《夜》（Night），於 1958 年出版，本書與《安妮的日記》和義大利作家普里莫‧萊維（Primo Levi）的集中營回憶錄《如果這是一個人》（If This Is a Man）齊名。

《夜》最初以猶太人的意第緒語寫成，最先被翻譯成法文版。本書一開始被多家出版社退稿，後來經過 1952 年諾貝爾文學獎得主的法國作家弗朗索瓦‧莫里克亞（Francois Mauriac）的奔走，才付梓出版。維瑟爾的著作達 57 本，在文學、宗教學和靈性上多有發揮。

1963 年，維瑟爾成為美國公民。1986 年，他獲得諾貝爾和平獎，挪威諾貝爾委員會稱他為「人類的使者」，為和平與人性尊嚴而奮鬥。

Speaker	猶太作家和政治家維瑟爾 （Elie Wiesel, 1928–）
Time	1999 年 4 月 12 日
Place	美國白宮東廂（華盛頓哥倫比亞特區） （East Room of the White House, USA）

◉ 原音重現　◉ 擷錄

37

We are on the threshold of a new century, a new millennium. What will the legacy of this vanishing century be? How will it be remembered in the new millennium? Surely it will be judged, and judged severely, in both moral and metaphysical terms.

These failures have cast a dark shadow over humanity: two World Wars, countless civil wars, the senseless chain of assassinations—Gandhi, the Kennedys, Martin Luther King, Sadat[1], Rabin[2]—bloodbaths in Cambodia and Nigeria, India and Pakistan, Ireland and Rwanda, Eritrea and Ethiopia, Sarajevo and Kosovo; the inhumanity in the gulag[3] and the tragedy of Hiroshima. And, on a different level, of course, Auschwitz and Treblinka[4]. So much violence, so much indifference.

What is indifference? Etymologically, the word means "no difference." A strange and unnatural state in which the lines blur between light and darkness, dusk and dawn, crime and punishment, cruelty and compassion, good and evil.

What are its courses and inescapable consequences? Is it a philosophy? Is there a philosophy of indifference conceivable? Can one possibly view indifference as a virtue? Is it necessary at times to practice it simply to keep one's sanity, live normally, enjoy a fine meal and a glass of wine, as the world around us experiences harrowing upheavals?

Of course, indifference can be tempting—more than that, seductive. It is so much easier to look away from victims. It is so much easier to avoid such rude interruptions to our work, our dreams, our hopes. It is, after all, awkward, troublesome, to be involved in another person's pain and despair.

Yet, for the person who is indifferent, his or her neighbor are of no consequence. And, therefore, their lives are meaningless. Their hidden or even visible anguish is of no interest. Indifference reduces the other to an abstraction.

In a way, to be indifferent to that suffering is what makes the human being inhuman. Indifference, after all, is more dangerous than anger and hatred. →

我們來到了一個新世紀的開始，一個新的千禧年。過去的這一個世紀，留給了人們什麼？在新的千禧年裡，人們回顧過去，又將記著什麼？毫無疑問地，過去這一個世紀，在道德和哲學上都將受到嚴厲的批判。

這些失敗讓人性蒙上了一層陰影：兩次的世界大戰，數不清的內亂，還有一樁樁愚蠢的刺殺事件——甘地、甘迺迪兄弟、馬丁·路德·金恩、薩達特、拉賓——還有各地的血腥屠殺，像是柬埔寨、奈及利亞、印度、巴基斯坦、愛爾蘭、盧安達、厄利垂亞、衣索匹亞、塞拉耶佛、科索夫；還有，慘無人道的前蘇聯古拉格勞改營，以及廣島的（原子彈）悲劇。當然了，另外還有不同性質的奧斯威辛和特雷布林卡集中營。這麼多的暴力，這麼多的冷漠！

什麼是「冷漠」？就語源學上來說，這個字是指「沒有差別」。這是一種奇怪、不自然的狀態，在明與暗、晨與昏、罪與罰、殘酷與同情、善與惡之間的界線，模糊不清。

是什麼造就了「冷漠」？這會導致什麼樣無可避免的結果？「冷漠」能算是一門哲學嗎？我們能信奉這門哲學嗎？有沒有可能將「冷漠」視為一種美德？當周遭的世界歷經慘痛的巨變時，為了保持心理的健康，以便過正常的生活、享受美食醇酒，有時冷漠一下，是否是必需的？

當然，冷漠是頗具吸引力的，甚至是極具誘惑性的。對受難者視而不見，事情會變得容易多了。避免去妄加打斷我們的工作、夢想和願望，事情也會簡單多了。畢竟，陷入別人的痛苦和絕望之中，棘手又麻煩。

然而，對冷漠的人來說，鄰居不占任何分量，旁人的生命不具任何意義，就算別人在受苦，他也都無關緊要。在冷漠人的心裡，別人的存在只是一種概念上的存在。

在某方面來說，對受苦受難的冷漠，會讓人類失去人性。畢竟，冷漠比憤怒和仇恨更危險。

1. Anwar Sadat (1918–1981): an Egyptian statesman and president of Egypt
   埃及總統薩達特

2. Yitzhak Rabin (1922–1995): an Israeli politician and general
   以色列總理拉賓

3. gulag [ˈguːlɑːɡ] (n.) a Russian prison camp for political prisoners
   古拉格（前蘇聯的勞改營）

4. Treblinka: a Nazi concentration camp in Poland, near Warsaw
   波蘭的納粹集中營

38

Anger can at times be creative. One writes a great poem, a great symphony, one does something special for the sake of humanity because one is angry at the injustice that one witnesses. But indifference is never creative. Even hatred at times may elicit[5] a response. You fight it. You denounce[6] it. You disarm it. Indifference elicits no response. Indifference is not a response.

Indifference is not a beginning, it is an end. And, therefore, indifference is always the friend of the enemy, for it benefits the aggressor—never his victim, whose pain is magnified when he or she feels forgotten. The political prisoner in his cell, the hungry children, the homeless refugees—not to respond to their plight, not to relieve their solitude by offering them a spark of hope is to exile them from human memory. And in denying their humanity we betray our own. Indifference, then, is not only a sin, it is a punishment. And this is one of the most important lessons of this outgoing century's wide-ranging experiments in good and evil.

Does it mean that we have learned from the past? Does it mean that society has changed? Has the human being become less indifferent and more human? Have we really learned from our experiences? Are we less insensitive to the plight of victims of ethnic cleansing and other forms of injustices in places near and far?

Is today's justified intervention in Kosovo, led by you, Mr. President, a lasting warning that never again will the deportation[7], the terrorization of children and their parents be allowed anywhere in the world? Will it discourage other dictators in other lands to do the same?

What about the children? Oh, we see them on television, we read about them in the papers, and we do so with a broken heart. Their fate is always the most tragic, inevitably. When adults wage war, children perish. We see their faces, their eyes. Do we hear their pleas? Do we feel their pain, their agony? Every minute one of them dies of disease, violence, famine. Some of them—so many of them—could be saved.

有時，憤怒可以激發創造力。一個人可能因為看到不公不義的事情而義憤填膺，因而出於人道，創作出偉大的詩、交響樂，或是做出一些特別的事情。但是冷漠呢，它永遠都不會有任何的創造性。連仇恨有時都能激起反應，人們會起來抗爭、譴責，然後歸於緩和，而冷漠永遠都不會有任何的反應。冷漠本身並不是一種反應。

冷漠不是事情的開始，而是結束。也因此，冷漠是敵人的好朋友，因為它只會庇蔭侵略者——不會造福受難者，它加深了受難者的痛苦，因為他們感到自己被遺忘。蹲在牢裡的政治犯，饑餓的兒童，無家可歸的難民——我們對他們的困境視若無睹，他們孤立無援，我們連一絲希望都沒有提供給他們，這就意味著將他們驅逐出人類的記憶之中。否定他們的人性，就意味著出賣我們自己的人性。也因此，冷漠不只是一種罪惡，也是一種懲罰。在過去這個世紀的大規模「善與惡」的實驗中，這是最重要的一課。

這是否就意謂著我們已經學到了教訓？這是否表示社會已經有所改變了？人類是否就變得不再冷漠、找回了更多的人性？我們真的從過去的經驗中學到了一課嗎？對種族屠殺和其他遭受迫害的受害者所處的困境，無論距離遠近，我們是否不再那麼麻木不仁了？

總統先生，現在由您領導的對科索夫的人道介入，是否是發出一個持續的警告：我們不允許世界任何一個角落，再有兒童和父母遭到驅逐及恐嚇？這是否能遏阻其他國家的獨裁者不會做同樣的事情？

那孩子們呢？哦，我們在電視上看到他們時，在報紙上讀到他們時，心中十分沉痛。不可避免的，他們的命運總是最悽慘的。大人們發動戰爭，孩子們就遭受毀滅。我們看看他們的臉孔，看看他們的眼睛，我們是否聽到了他們懇求的聲音？我們是否感受到他們的痛苦和悲傷？每一分鐘，就有一名兒童死於疾病、暴力或饑荒。其中有一些人——實際上是很多人——他們原本都是可以被拯救出來的。

5. elicit [ɪˈlɪsɪt] (v.)
   to get or produce
   something, especially
   information or a
   reaction 誘出；引出

6. denounce [dɪˈnaʊns]
   (v.) to speak out
   against 譴責

7. deportation [ˌdiːpɔːrˈteɪʃən] (n.) the
   removal from a
   country of an alien
   whose presence
   is unlawful or
   prejudicial 驅逐出境

On Charity and Humor

英國文學家薩克雷：
論慈善與幽默

薩克雷是維多利亞時代極具代表性的小說家，與狄更斯齊名，他們兩人都是現實主義小說家，被喻為「小說雙傑」，兩人的代表作分別為《浮華世界》（Vanity Fair）和《塊肉餘生錄》（David Copperfield），這兩部作品也被喻為 19 世紀英國文學的兩塊瑰寶。

薩克雷出生於印度的加爾各答，父親是東印度公司的員工，五歲時父親過世，母親便帶他返回英國，由外婆撫養長大。1829 年，進入劍橋大學就學，讀了一年後被退學，之後四處遊走，一事無成。

1833 年，薩克雷存款的銀行倒閉，他因此破產，但卻也讓他從此振作起來面對現實生活，並以寫稿謀生。他在報章雜誌投過不少稿，也出過幾部書，風評都還不錯，但一直到 1847 年發表《浮華世界》後，才被公認為是一個偉大的小說天才。薩克雷擅長描繪英國上流中產階層社會的生活，他的人物角色生動，深刻表現出現實生活中交錯的道德、罪惡、虛華和腐敗。

薩克雷一生的創作很多，全集多達 35 卷。他的筆鋒犀利，語調幽默，在英國文學史上佔有重要的地位。他除了勤於筆耕，後來還到英國各地和美國去做演講，這篇演說就是他在紐約時，代表某慈善機構所做的演講。

Speaker	英國小説家薩克雷 （William Makepeace Thackeray, 1811–1863）
Time	1852 年
Place	美國紐約市（代表某慈善機構發表演説） （New York City, USA）

▣ 錄音　▣ 擷錄

39

Besides contributing to our stock of happiness, to our harmless laughter and amusement, to our scorn for falsehood and pretension, to our righteous hatred of hypocrisy, to our education in the perception of truth, our love of honesty, our knowledge of life, and shrewd guidance through the world, have not our humorous writers, our gay and kind weekday preachers, done much in support of that holy cause which has assembled you in this place, and which you are all abetting[1],—the cause of love and charity, the cause of the poor, the weak, and the unhappy; the sweet mission of love and tenderness, and peace and goodwill toward men?

That same theme which is urged upon you by the eloquence and example of good men to whom you are delighted listeners on Sabbath days is taught in his way and according to his power by the humorous writer, the commentator on everyday life and manners.

And as you are here assembled for a charitable purpose, giving your contributions at the door to benefit deserving people who need them, I like to hope and think that the men of our calling[2] have done something in aid of the cause of charity, and have helped, with kind words and kind thoughts at least, to confer happiness and to do good.

If the humorous writers claim to be weekday preachers, have they conferred any benefit by their sermons? Are people happier, better, better disposed to their neighbors, more inclined to do works of kindness, to love, forbear, forgive, pity, after reading in Addison, in Steele, in Fielding, in Goldsmith, in Hood, in Dickens? →

1. abet [əˈbɛt] (v.) to assist or encourage 幫助；支持
2. calling [ˈkɑːlɪŋ] (n.) the particular occupation for which you are trained 職業

William Makepeace Thackeray
and His Mother (c. 1813)

　　我們幽默的作家們，這些在非安息日也照樣天天傳教的好心作家們，他們除了為我們增添生活情趣，講一些無傷大雅的逗趣言論，摒斥虛情假意，義正嚴詞的痛斥虛偽造作，啟發世人認識真理，說明誠實的可貴，教導生活知識，引導人們的處世之道外，他們不是也對神聖事業的支持不遺餘力？這是你們聚集在這裡、努力促成的神聖事業——這是愛與慈善的事業，貧困者、弱勢者和不幸者的事業，這是一項出於愛護與溫情、致力於人類和平與友好的甜蜜使命。

　　牧師在安息日以流利口才和生動事跡向你們宣講的主題，幽默作家則以他特有的方式和魅力向你們講述，他們是日常生活規範的評論家。

　　你們抱著行善的目的聚集在這裡，在門口幫忙為那些需要幫助的人，我希望，而且我相信，做我們這一行的也能有益於公益事業，最起碼，能用好言善語來給予快樂、造福人群。

　　如果說幽默作家是天天傳教的傳教士，那麼他們的佈道是否有益於人心？在讀過艾迪生、史第爾、菲爾丁、哥德史密斯、胡德和狄更斯的作品之後，和以前比起來，是否變得更快樂些？為人是否更好些？和鄰居相處是否更和睦些？是否更願意做好事？更願意去關愛別人、克制自己、寬恕別人、同情別人？

40

I hope and believe so, and fancy that in writing they are also acting charitably, contributing with the means which Heaven supplies them to forward the end which brings you, too, together.

I have said myself somewhere, that humor is wit and love; I am sure, at any rate, that the best humor is that which contains most humanity, that which is flavored throughout with tenderness and kindness.

This love does not demand constant utterance or actual expression, as a good father, in conversation with his children or wife, is not perpetually embracing them or making protestations of his love. He shows his love by his conduct, by his fidelity, by his watchful desire to make the beloved person happy; it influences all his words and actions; suffuses his whole being; it sets the father cheerily to work through the long day, supports him through the tedious labor of the weary absence or journey, and sends him happy home again, yearning toward the wife and children.

And so with a loving humor: I think, it is a genial writer's habit of being; it is the kind, gentle spirit's way of looking out on the world—that sweet friendliness which fills his heart and his style. ◀

　　但願如此，我也相信確實如此。我想，作家們在寫作時也是出於慈善的，上帝賜予他們寫作的本領來推動慈善，這也是我們大家齊聚一堂的原因。

　　我曾在某處說過，幽默就是風趣和愛。我確信，最佳的幽默蘊含著最多的人性，溫情和仁慈貫穿其中，使之生色。

　　這種愛不需要在口頭或行為上一直不斷地做表達，就好比一個好父親，他在和妻兒說話時，不會一直抱著對方或是聲明自己的愛。他是透過行為、忠誠和希望對方快樂的真摯願望，來表現他的愛。這份愛會影響他的語言和行為，讓他整個人都洋溢著愛。這份愛會讓父親整天的工作都充滿活力，會在他出門或出差的疲累旅程中支撐著他，讓他在思念妻兒的心情中歡歡喜喜地回到家。

　　出於愛心的幽默也是如此。我想，這正是一個真誠作家的習性，這是一個仁慈和善的人看待世界的方式──甜蜜的情誼會洋溢在他的心裡頭，並且呈現在他的風格之中。

Truths of the Heart

Speech Accepting the Nobel Prize in Literature

福克納諾貝爾得獎感言：
心靈的真諦

威廉‧福克納生於密西西比州，在氣息濃厚的美國南方長大。他的作品大都以密西西比河畔為背景，故事內容描繪生動而深刻。他是美國南方文學派的創始人，也是最具影響力的現代派小說家之一，代表作有《喧嘩與騷動》（*The Sound and the Fury*）、《八月之光》（*Light in August*）等。

福克納也寫推理小說，出版過一系列的犯罪小說《馬棄兵》（*Knight's Gambit*）。他後來搬到好萊塢，成了電影編劇，作品有《夜長夢多》（*The Big Sleep*）和《猶有似無》（*To Have and Have Not*）等。

1949 年，福克納獲得了諾貝爾文學獎。在這篇膾炙人口的簡短謝辭中，福克納把寫作的志業和人類的本質及命運連結了起來。

獲獎後，他捐出獎金，成立了「國際筆會／福克納基金會」（PEN/Faulkner Foundation），每年頒發「國際筆會／福克納小說獎」（PEN/Faulkner Award for Fiction），以鼓勵文學新人。

此篇得獎感言為經過修潤後收錄在《福克納文集》（*The Faulkner Reader*）一書中的版本，本書所收錄的錄音則為未經修潤的版本，特此註明。

Speaker	美國文學家威廉‧福克納 （William Faulkner, 1897–1962）
Time	1950 年 12 月 10 日
Place	瑞典首都斯德哥爾摩市政廳 （Stockholm City Hall, Sweden）

◙ 原音重現　◙ 全篇收錄

Copyright © The Nobel Foundation 2012
Audio copyright to © Nobel Media AB

William Faulkner (1897–1962)

41

Ladies and gentlemen,

I feel that this award was not made to me as a man, but to my work—life's work in the agony and sweat of the human spirit, not for glory and least of all for profit, but to create out of the materials of the human spirit something which did not exist before. So this award is only mine in trust.

It will not be difficult to find a dedication for the money part of it commensurate with the purpose and significance of its origin. But I would like to do the same with the acclaim too, by using this moment as a pinnacle from which I might be listened to by the young men and women already dedicated to the same anguish and travail[1], among whom is already that one who will someday stand where I am standing.

Our tragedy today is a general and universal physical fear so long sustained by now that we can even bear it. There are no longer problems of the spirit. There is only the question: When will I be blown up? Because of this, the young man or woman writing today has forgotten the problems of the human heart in conflict with itself which alone can make good writing because only that is worth writing about, worth the agony and the sweat.

He must learn them again. He must teach himself that the basest[2] of all things is to be afraid; and, teaching himself that, forget it forever, leaving no room in his workshop for anything but the old verities[3] and truths of the heart, the universal truths lacking which any story is ephemeral[4] and doomed—love and honor and pity and pride and compassion and sacrifice.

Until he does so, he labors under a curse. He writes not of love but of lust, of defeats in which nobody loses anything of value, of victories without hope and, worst of all, without pity or compassion. His griefs grieve on no universal bones, leaving no scars. He writes not of the heart but of the glands[5]. →

各位先生女士：

　　我感到這個獎項並不是授予我個人，而是授予我的這份工作的——我這份職志的工作，是在人類內心極大痛苦與焦慮中進行的，不是為了名，不是為了利，而是為了從人類的靈魂中汲取素材，創造出一些東西來。因此，這個獎項我只是代為託管罷了。

　　要講出與獎金同等重量，並符合獎項精神的獻詞，並非難事。但我想利用這個時刻，利用這個舉世矚目的講壇，對那些與我有著同樣痛苦與艱難的青年男女致意，在他們之中，有人日後也必將站在我現在所站的地方。

　　我們今天的悲劇是，外面的世界長期普遍瀰漫著恐懼，我們也都習慣了這種恐懼。現在浮現的不再是心靈上的問題，人們唯一擔心的問題是：我什麼時候會遭受到攻擊？也因為如此，現在年輕人在寫作時都忘記了人類心靈本身的內在衝突，而只有這種內在衝突的題材才能寫出好的作品，才是值得著墨，值得嘔心瀝血去創作的。

　　他必須重新學習去讓自己明白：恐懼其實是最不足為道的。他必須學習將恐懼永遠驅逐出去，讓作品中只存在心靈中亙古不變的真理。缺少了這些普世的真理——愛、榮譽、憐憫、自尊、仁慈和奉獻——任何小說都只是浮光掠影，不會成功。

　　如果沒有做到這些，他是在詛咒之下工作。他描寫的愛，會變成情欲；他描寫的失敗，實則毫無所失；他描寫的成功，透不出絲毫的希望；最慘的是，作品之中毫無憐憫或慈悲。他描寫的悲傷不是為了世上的生靈，無法留下深刻的痕跡。這樣的作品不是來自心靈，而是來自腺體的分泌。

1. travail [ˈtræveɪl] (n.) a very difficult situation, or a situation in which you must work very hard 艱難；痛苦
2. base [beɪs] (a.) having no value 沒有價值的
3. verities [ˈverɪtɪz] (n.) (pl.) something that is true, as a principle, belief, etc. 真理
4. ephemeral [ɪˈfemərəl] (a.) enduring a very short time 短暫的
5. gland [glænd] (n.) an organ of the body which secretes particular chemical substances 腺

42

Until he learns these things, he will write as though he stood among and watched the end of man. I decline to accept the end of man. It is easy enough to say that man is immortal simply because he will endure: that when the last ding-dong of doom has clanged and faded from the last worthless rock hanging tideless in the last red and dying evening, that even then there will still be one more sound: that of his puny inexhaustible voice, still talking.

* I refuse to accept this. I believe that man will not merely endure: he will prevail. He is immortal, not because he alone among creatures has an inexhaustible voice, but because he has a soul, a spirit capable of compassion and sacrifice and endurance.

The poet's, the writer's, duty is to write about these things. It is his privilege to help man endure by lifting his heart, by reminding him of the courage and honor and hope and pride and compassion and pity and sacrifice which have been the glory of his past. The poet's voice need not merely be the record of man, it can be one of the props, the pillars to help him endure and prevail. ◀

19
心
靈
的
真
諦

* 此頁最後兩段，原音音檔闕如。

　　寫作者在尚未重新認識這些之前，他在寫作時會好比是站在人群之中，目睹著世界末日。我並不認同世界末日的說法，我倒寧可說人類會世世代代地延續下去。即使最後一位人類的喪鐘已經敲響，鐘響在落日的餘暉中，消失在海潮最後退去的崖邊──即使是在這樣的時刻裡，仍然還可以聽到人類綿延不斷的微弱說話聲。

　　我不認同世界末日的說法，我認為人類不僅會繼續延續下去，而且會愈來愈好。人類會永恆的延續下去，不只是因為萬物之中人類綿延不斷的說話聲，更是因為人類擁有靈魂，具有慈悲、奉獻和堅忍的精神。

　　詩人和作家的責任，就是把這些東西寫出來。提昇人們的心靈，喚醒人類向來所擁有的光榮──勇氣、榮譽、希望、自尊、慈悲、憐憫和奉獻──以幫助人類繼續延續下去，這就是寫作者的殊榮。詩人不應該只是寫寫人類的生活記錄，詩人應該成為人類的中流砥柱，幫助人類延續、繁榮下去。

Our Family Creed
The Things That Make Life Most Worth Living

洛克斐勒家訓：
讓生命有意義的方法

美國石油大王洛克菲勒（John Davison Rockefeller, 1839–1937），是人類近代史上的首富，他在 1870 年創立了標準石油公司（Standard Oil），曾經壟斷全美 90% 的石油市場。1911 年，才因反壟斷法（Anti-Trust Law）而被下令分成 34 家公司。

洛克菲勒出身貧窮，個人的生活節制而規律。他沉默寡言，行事低調，一生勤儉持家。他在年輕時拿到第一份薪水之後，就固定將十分之一的薪水捐獻給教會。1897 年之後，他致力於慈善事業，捐出了大部分的財產，並創辦了芝加哥大學和洛克斐勒大學。

小約翰‧洛克斐勒（John Davison Rockefeller, Jr., 1874–1960）是洛克斐勒的獨生子，他繼承了父親大部分的事業。這篇洛氏家訓是他在電臺上所發表的，當時正值第二次世界大戰，電臺在進行一系列節目，主題是「可以讓生命活得有意義的方法」（The Things That Make Life Most Worth Living），小約翰‧洛克斐勒就是在這時候發表了洛氏家訓。

Speaker 小約翰‧洛克斐勒
（John Davison Rockefeller, Jr., 1874–1960）

Time 1941 年 7 月 8 日

Place 美國廣播電臺

▣ 錄音 ▣ 擷錄

John D. Rockefeller (left) and his son John D. Rockefeller Jr.

43

They are the principles on which my wife and I have tried to bring up our family. They are the principles in which my father believed—and by which he governed his life. They are the principles, many of them, which I learned at my mother's knee.

They point the way to usefulness and happiness in life, to courage and peace in death. If they mean to you what they mean to me, they may perhaps be helpful also to our sons for their guidance and inspiration. Let me state them:

I believe in the supreme worth of the individual and in his right to life, liberty and the pursuit of happiness.

I believe that every right implies a responsibility; every opportunity, an obligation; every possession, a duty.

I believe that the law was made for man and not man for the law; that government is the servant of the people and not their master.

I believe in the dignity of labor, whether with head or hand; that the world owes no man a living but that it owes every man an opportunity to make a living.

I believe that thrift[1] is essential to well ordered living and that economy is a prime requisite[2] of a sound financial structure, whether in government, business or personal affairs.

I believe that truth and justice are fundamental to an enduring social order.

I believe in the sacredness of a promise, that a man's word should be as good as his bond, that character—not wealth or power or position—is of supreme worth. →

這是一些我和妻子努力用來持家教子的訓言，它們是我父親的守訓，是他安身立命的原則。在這些訓言當中，有不少是我在我母親膝下學到的。

這些訓言，能夠讓人在活著的時候，能夠活得快樂、有意義，在面臨死亡的時候，能夠勇敢平靜地離去。如果你跟我一樣，也認為這些訓言深具意義，那或許它們對我們子女的教導和啟發也會很有幫助。且讓我加以陳述如下：

我深信，每個個體都具有無上的價值，而且都有生存、自由和追求幸福的權利。

我深信，每一項權利都含有一份職責，每一個機會都含有一份義務，每一個擁有都伴隨一份責任。

我深信，法律是為人而設立的，人不應該犧牲在法律之下。政府是人民的公僕，而不是人民的主人。

我深信，工作是一種尊嚴的活動，不論是用腦力還是用體力。世界並不負責去養活人們，但它應該給每一個人都擁有謀生的機會。

我深信，節儉是井然有序的生活之所必需。不管對於政府、企業或是個人來說，要擁有良好的經濟狀況，節約都是不可或缺的。

我深信，真理和正義是社會長治久安的基礎。

我深信，承諾是具有神聖性的，一句承諾應該如同契約一樣有效。具有崇高價值的是一諾千金的人格，而非財力或權勢。

John D. Rockefeller's
(by John Singer Sargent in 1917)

1. thrift [θrɪft] (n.) the careful use of money, especially by avoiding waste 節儉
2. requisite ['rɛkwɪzɪt] (n.) something that is necessary or indispensable 必要條件

Saint John (painting by Odilon Redon, 1892)

44

I believe that the rendering of useful service is the common duty of mankind and that only in the purifying fire of sacrifice is the dross of selfishness consumed and the greatness of the human soul set free.

I believe in an all-wise and all-loving God, named by whatever name, and that the individual's highest fulfillment, greatest happiness and widest usefulness are to be found in living in harmony with His will.

I believe that love is the greatest thing in the world; that it alone can overcome hate; that right can and will triumph over might.

These are the principles, however formulated, for which all good men and women throughout the world, irrespective of race or creed, education, social position or occupation, are standing, and for which many of them are suffering and dying. These are the principles upon which alone a new world recognizing the brotherhood of man and the fatherhood of God can be established. ◀

　　我深信，能確實地對社會做出貢獻，是全人類的共同責任。唯有犧牲奉獻的火焰，才能燒毀自私自利的渣滓，崇高的人類靈魂也才得以被釋放出來。

　　我深信，有一個全知全能、博愛世人的上帝存在，不管你用什麼名字來稱呼祂。個人最高的實現、最大的幸福和最大的意義，都能夠在符合上帝旨意的生活中找到。

　　我深信，愛是世界上最偉大的東西，只有愛才能戰勝仇恨，公理也將會戰勝強權。

　　不管如何陳述，這些就是守訓了。世界上所有良善的男女，不分種族、信仰、教育、身分或職業，都共同謹守這些訓言，他們當中有些人還為此正在受著苦難或瀕臨死亡。唯有依循這些守訓，才能建立一個人類友愛、上帝慈愛的新世界。

Lou Gehrig's Farewell Speech

The Luckiest Man on Earth

洋基鐵馬賈里格告別演說：
我是世界上最幸運的人

賈里格出生於紐約市，雙親是來自德國的移民。他終生效力於紐約的洋基職棒隊伍，因為鮮少受傷，素有「鐵馬」（Iron Horse）之稱。但事實上，在他後期接受 X 光檢查之後，才發現雙手共有 17 處骨折。

在 1925–1939 年這 14 年之間，他連續出賽了 2,130 場比賽，一直到罹患了漸凍人症（肌肉萎縮性側索硬化症）才停止出賽，而這種疾病後來也被稱為「賈里格症」（Lou Gehrig's Disease）。

賈里格的打擊表現出色，生涯共有 7 個球季的打點超過 150，而且連續 13 季打點都破百。自 1933 年開始舉辦明星賽後，他每個球季都入選明星隊。

1939 年，在他宣佈引退後尚未滿一年時，美國棒球作家協會就全數通過票數，破例讓他提早進入棒球名人堂，而他也是歷史上第一個球衣背號（4 號）跟著球員一起退休的職棒球員。

1938 年的球季中，賈里格的表現大不如前。他的行動越來越不靈活，甚至會無預警地摔倒。1939 年春訓時，賈里格的身體仍然無法恢復氣力，甚至連一個番茄醬罐頭都打不開。➜

Bottom row, third and fourth from the left:
Lou Gehrig and Babe Ruth (1931)

Speaker	洋基棒球隊傳奇球星賈里格 （Lou Gehrig, 1903–1941）
Time	1939 年 7 月 4 日
Place	紐約洋基舊球場（Yankee Stadium, USA）

◉ 錄音　◉ 全篇收錄

1939 年 5 月 2 日，在底特律老虎隊的主場上，賈里格主動要求
坐板凳。比賽開始前，球場播報員廣播說：「這場比賽將是過去
2,130 場比賽以來，盧・賈里格首度未被列在洋基的先發打序
上。」全場的底特律球迷聽了之後全部起立鼓掌致敬。之後，賈
里格仍繼續跟著球隊移動，但是身體狀況迅速惡化。

1939 年 6 月 13 日，賈里格去了一家診所，6 月 19 日，他在
生日的這一天，被確診為罹患漸凍人症，而且診斷壽命最多只
剩三年。6 月 21 日，洋基隊宣佈賈里格因病退休，但仍會以隊
長的身分隨隊出征。

兩個星期後，1939 年 7 月 4 日，在賈里格引退的這一天，洋基
將這一日命名為「盧・賈里格日」，並且特別做了許多的慶祝活
動。在賈里格發表了這篇著名的引退演說之後，全場爆滿的觀
眾起立鼓掌長達兩分鐘。

1939 年 12 月 7 日，他破例被提早選入名人堂，但卻因為身體
過於虛弱，而無法參加特別為他舉行的紀念儀式。→

1939 年 10 月，紐約市長聘請賈里格出任紐約市的假釋官。賈里格在這個工作上盡忠職守，每天規律地上下班，直到過世前的一個月為止。1941 年 6 月 2 日，賈里格在家中溘然長逝，享年 37 歲，紐約市為此降半旗致哀。

1942 年，賈里格的傳記電影《洋基之光》(*The Pride of the Yankees*) 開拍。電影推出後異常轟動，為年度十大賣座影片。此外，賈里格也是少數獲得美國郵政總局發行紀念郵票殊榮的運動員。

賈里格這篇引退演說，被譽為棒球史上的《蓋茨堡宣言》，是運動場上最動人、最令人難忘的演說，也是美國 20 世紀最偉大演說之一，足以與林肯的《蓋茨堡宣言》和金恩博士的《我有一個夢想》媲美。

45

Fans, for the past two weeks you have been reading about a bad break I got. Yet today I consider myself the luckiest man on the face of the earth.

I have been in ballparks for seventeen years and have never received anything but kindness and encouragement from you fans. Look at these grand men. Which of you wouldn't consider it the highlight of his career just to associate with them for even one day?

Sure I'm lucky.

Who wouldn't consider it an honor to have known Jacob Ruppert? Also, the builder of baseball's greatest empire, Ed Barrow? To have spent six years with that wonderful little fellow, Miller Huggins? Then to have spent the next nine years with that outstanding leader, that smart student of psychology, the best manager in baseball today, Joe McCarthy?

Sure I'm lucky.

When the New York Giants[1], a team you would give your right arm to beat, and vice versa, sends you a gift—that's something. When everybody down to the groundskeepers and those boys in white coats remember you with trophies—that's something.

When you have a wonderful mother-in-law who takes sides with you in squabbles with her own daughter—that's something.

When you have a father and a mother who work all their lives so you can have an education and build your body—it's a blessing.

When you have a wife who has been a tower of strength and shown more courage than you dreamed existed—that's the finest I know.

So, I close in saying that I might have been given a bad break, but I've got an awful lot to live for.

Thank you.

球迷們，過去這兩個星期，你們都聽說了我的壞消息。但是，今天，我卻認為自己是世界上最幸運的人。

我在球場待了 17 年，我所收到的，全是你們球迷滿滿的愛護與鼓勵。看看這些高尚的人們，即使只有一天的時間能和他們相聚一堂，就是生命中最精彩的一刻，你們有誰不會這樣認為呢？

無疑地，我是很幸運的。

能與 Jacob Ruppert（球團老闆）相識，誰不會認為這是很榮幸的事？還有，能認識偉大棒球帝國的 Ed Barrow，不也是與有榮焉嗎？能和厲害的小個兒 Miller Huggins 一起度過六年的時間，不也是很榮幸的嗎？接著，我和 Joe McCarthy 相處了九年的時間，他是一個傑出的領導者，一個聰明的心理學學生，也是今日球壇最好的教練，這能不感到榮幸嗎？

無疑地，我是很幸運的。

紐約巨人隊是一支你非常想打倒的隊伍，反之，他們也想打到你。當他們送給你一份禮物時，這是意義非凡的。當每個的球場工作人員和穿著白色外套的球僮，記得你這個人以及你所獲得過的獎項，這是意義非凡的。

當你有一個很棒的岳母，她站在你這邊和她的女兒拌嘴時，這是意義非凡的。

當你有一個爸爸和一個媽媽，他們辛勤工作以賺取你的教育費和伙食費時，這是蒙受天佑的。

當你有一個妻子，當她充滿無比的力量，展現出超乎想像的勇氣時，這是我所知道最美好的事情。

最後，我要講的是，我雖然聽到了壞消息，但我擁有這麼多我要好好為之活下去的東西。

謝謝！

Lou Gehrig bade farewell to fans at Yankee Stadium. (July 4, 1939)

1. New York Giants 紐約巨人隊，後來搬到舊金山，改為舊金山巨人隊

Courage

馬克‧吐溫：
勇氣

馬克‧吐溫被譽為美國文學之父、美國文學界的林肯，是美國文學中最具代表性的作家。他來自密蘇里州一個貧窮的家庭，所以他的學識與文筆，都是靠自學而來的。他年輕時，特別喜歡閱讀莎士比亞、狄更斯和西班牙文學家塞凡提斯等人的作品。

當時密蘇里州是奴隸州，而黑奴的故事也成為他小說中常見的主題，像是《湯姆歷險記》（*The Adventures of Tom Sawyer*）和《頑童流浪記》（*Adventures of Huckleberry Finn*）。《湯姆歷險記》是全世界最家喻戶曉的一本名著。而《頑童流浪記》則是公認最偉大的美國小說之一，它是美國文學史上具劃時代意義的寫實主義作品，被喻為「美國版的魯賓遜漂流記」，也是馬克‧吐溫登峰造極之作，作家海明威甚至說：

All modern American literature comes from one book by Mark Twain called *Huckleberry Finn*.
美國所有的現代文學，都濫觴於馬克‧吐溫的一本書《頑童流浪記》。

馬克‧吐溫的作品以幽默諷刺著稱，這篇演說是在一場牛排的餐會上所發表的，當然是不改其詼諧逗趣的風格。

Speaker	美國大文豪馬克・吐溫（Mark Twain, 1835-1910）
Time	1908 年 4 月 18 日
Place	美國紐約市某一餐會（New York City, USA）

◉ 錄音　◉ 全篇收錄

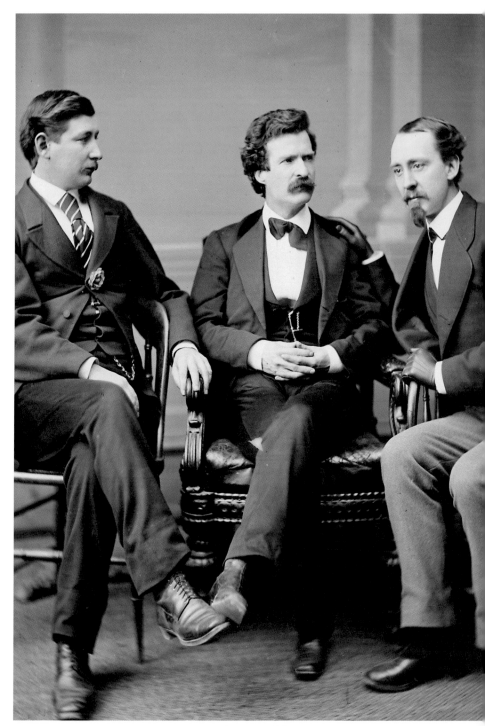

Mark Twain (middle)

46

In the matter of courage we all have our limits.

There never was a hero who did not have his bounds. I suppose it may be said of Nelson[1] and all the others whose courage has been advertised that there came times in their lives when their bravery knew it had come to its limit.

I have found mine a good many times. Sometimes this was expected— often it was unexpected. I know a man who is not afraid to sleep with a rattlesnake, but you could not get him to sleep with a safety-razor.

I never had the courage to talk across a long, narrow room I should be at the end of the room facing all the audience. If I attempt to talk across a room I find myself turning this way and that, and thus at alternate periods I have part of the audience behind me. You ought never to have any part of the audience behind you; you never can tell what they are going to do.

I'll sit down.

説到勇氣這種東西，我們每個人都會碰到極限。

沒有哪位英雄人物是可以什麼都不怕的。一般人可能會想到名將尼爾森，還有那些英勇事跡被廣為傳頌的人，我想在他們的一生中，也有拿不出勇氣的時候。

我就曾多次遇到這種狀況，有時候是怕得很合理，但大部分的時候都是怕得莫名其妙。我認識一位老兄，他敢跟一條響尾蛇同眠，可你無法讓他與安全刮鬍刀共眠。

我呢，就怕在狹長型的房間中央做演講，那我一定得站在房間的一頭，來面對所有的觀眾。我要是站在房間中央演講，我的人就會不停地轉過來轉過去，在我的身後總是會有觀眾，但你是不能背對任何觀眾的，誰知道他們會突如其來地對你做出什麼事！

我要坐下了。

---

1. Nelson Appleton Miles (1839–1925): a U.S. army officer 美國名將尼爾森

Tribute to a Dog

為老鼓忠犬辯護：
忠犬禮讚

維斯特是美國密蘇里州人，1879–1903 年間擔任美國參議員，是當時有名的演說家和辯論家。當年，他在密蘇里州一個小鎮上擔任律師時，他的當事人控訴自己的狗被殺害，這篇《忠犬禮讚》就是維斯特在法庭上所作的結案陳詞。最後，他贏得了這場訴訟。

這樁訴訟案的原委是：在華堡（Warrensburg）這個鎮上，波頓先生（Charles Burden）養了一隻叫作「老鼓」（Old Drum）的愛狗，一天晚上，老鼓跑到隔壁洪思比（Leonidas Hornsby）的後院，洪思比是波頓姐妹的丈夫，還會帶老鼓去打獵，但他卻仍懷疑老鼓就是殺害他家羊隻的兇手，於是開槍將老鼓擊斃。

波頓先生旋即告上法庭，這場奇特的官司，一直打到了密蘇里州的最高法院。在終審時，維斯特這篇《忠犬禮讚》的辯詞，感動了法官和陪審團。

隨後，這篇演說就成為了愛狗人士的最愛，當地人還在華堡法院前立了忠犬老鼓的雕像，並將這篇辯詞刻在底座上。

常言道：「狗是人類最好的朋友。」就是源自於這篇辯文。

Speaker	美國參議員維斯特 （George Graham Vest, 1830–1904）
Time	1870 年 9 月 23 日
Place	美國密蘇里州最高法院 （Missouri Supreme Court, USA）

◉ 錄音　◉ 全篇收錄

Gentlemen of the Jury:

The best friend a man has in the world may turn against him and become his enemy. His son or daughter that he has reared with loving care may prove ungrateful. Those who are nearest and dearest to us, those whom we trust with our happiness and our good name may become traitors to their faith.

The money that a man has, he may lose. It flies away from him, perhaps when he needs it most. A man's reputation may be sacrificed in a moment of ill-considered action. The people who are prone to fall on their knees to do us honor when success is with us, may be the first to throw the stone of malice when failure settles its cloud upon our heads.

The one absolutely unselfish friend that man can have in this selfish world, the one that never deserts him, the one that never proves ungrateful or treacherous is his dog. A man's dog stands by him in prosperity and in poverty, in health and in sickness.

He will sleep on the cold ground, where the wintry winds blow and the snow drives fiercely, if only he may be near his master's side. He will kiss the hand that has no food to offer. He will lick the wounds and sores that come in encounters with the roughness of the world. He guards the sleep of his pauper master as if he were a prince.

When all other friends desert, he remains. When riches take wings, and reputation falls to pieces, he is as constant in his love as the sun in its journey through the heavens.

If fortune drives the master forth, an outcast in the world, friendless and homeless, the faithful dog asks no higher privilege than that of accompanying him, to guard him against danger, to fight against his enemies.

And when the last scene of all comes, and death takes his master in its embrace and his body is laid away in the cold ground, no matter if all other friends pursue their way, there by the graveside will the noble dog be found, his head between his paws, his eyes sad, but open in alert watchfulness, faithful and true even in death. ◀

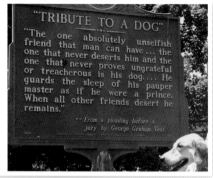

各位陪審團：

　　人生在世，最好的朋友也可能反目成仇。就算是自己細心呵護、養育長大的兒女，也可能忘恩負義。那些我們最親密、最親愛的人，那些我們寄託幸福和名譽的人，也可能違背他們當初的誓言。

　　人們擁有的財富，有可能會失去，甚至可能是在最需要的時候，財富不翼而飛。人的聲譽，有可能因為一時的疏失而毀於一旦。曾在我們飛黃騰達之時對我們畢恭畢敬的人，有可能在我們落難的時候，率先對我們落井下石。

　　在這個冷暖世間裡，唯一真正不會自私、不會遺棄你、不會忘恩負義、不會背叛你的朋友，就是你的狗。不論你是富貴還是貧賤，是健康還是生病，你的狗都會守在你身邊。

　　只要能夠待在主人的身邊，即使北風嘯嘯、大雪紛飛，牠都甘願睡在冰冷的地上。當主人的手上並沒有東西要給牠吃時，牠還是會去舔拭主人的雙手。當主人遭遇人世的險惡時，牠也會去舔撫主人的傷痕。當窮困潦倒的主人入睡時，牠也會守護在一旁，就好像在守護王子一樣。

　　當所有的人都離棄主人而去時，只有牠仍然忠心守護。當財富與名聲都煙消雲散時，牠的忠心就如同每天的日升日落一樣，永恆不變。

　　如果主人遭受無情命運的擺弄，被世界遺棄，孤苦無依、無家可歸時，忠犬的唯一要求，就是與主人相伴，保護主人的安全，讓他不會遭遇危險，一起對抗主人的敵人。

　　當到了人生的最後一刻，死神帶走了主人，牠仍會圍繞在主人的身邊，躺在一旁冰冷的地面上。不論主人的其他朋友是否都各奔東西了，這隻忠狗還是會守護在主人的墓旁。牠的頭會趴在兩掌之間，流露出傷心的眼神，但仍然保持高度的機警，忠心耿耿，至死不渝。

To Temper Justice With Mercy

Mercy for Leopold and Loeb | 丹諾律師為少年請纓：用仁慈之心行正義之事

丹諾律師是美國的傳奇性辯護律師，而且也是一位成功的演説家和作家。他在將近 60 年的律師生涯中，為勞工領袖、黑人、窮人等等各種弱勢的被告做過無數次成功的辯護，展現出他無比的正義感和道德勇氣，也使他在律師界得到了「老獅」（Old Lion）的封號。

丹諾律師也著有《丹諾自傳》，這本書曾入選美國律師協會評選出的「20 世紀律師必讀的十大好書」。在自傳裡，丹諾律師回憶了他數十年來所處理過的案件，他的專業能力和人道關懷，令許多人深受啟迪。

這篇是針對「李歐帕德與勒伯案」（Leopold and Loeb）所做的辯護詞，他在法庭上為他們辯護了三天，以下是結論的高潮。李歐帕德和勒伯是兩個公子哥兒，兩人結夥進行了一件冷血的綁票謀殺案，成為最早在美國被稱為「世紀犯罪」的重大刑事案件。

一方面，這是一椿罪不可赦的惡行，另一方被告是兩位富家子弟，這對丹諾本人來説是特別棘手的案件。後來，反對死刑的丹諾還是成功地讓兩名被告免於極刑。

這椿世紀轟動的案件，多次被編成戲劇上演，其中最經典的就屬希區考克（Alfred Hitchcock, 1899–1980）於 1948 年發行的電影《奪魂索》（Rope）。

Speaker	美國知名律師丹諾 （Clarence Darrow, 1857–1938）
Time	1924 年 9 月
Place	美國芝加哥地方法院 （Municipal Court of Chicago, USA）

☑ 錄音　☑ 擷錄

There are causes for this terrible crime. There are causes as I have said for everything that happens in the world. War is a part of it; education is a part of it; birth is a part of it; money is a part of it—all these conspired to compass the destruction of these two poor boys.

Has the court any right to consider anything but these two boys? The State says that your Honor has a right to consider the welfare of the community, as you have. If the welfare of the community would be benefited by taking these lives, well and good[1]. I think it would work evil that no one could measure.

I do not know how much salvage[2] there is in these two boys. I hate to say it in their presence, but what is there to look forward to? I do not know but what your Honor would be merciful to them, but not merciful to civilization, and not merciful to those who would be left behind if you tied a rope around their necks and let them die.

I would not tell this court that I do not hope that some time, when life and age have changed their bodies, as they do, and have changed their emotions, as they do—that they may once more return to life. I would be the last person on earth to close the door of hope to any human being that lives, and least of all to my clients. But what have they to look forward to? Nothing. And I think here of the stanza of Housman[3]:

Now hollow fires burn out to black,
And lights are fluttering low:
Square your shoulders, lift your pack
And leave your friends and go.
O never fear, lads, naught's to dread,
Look not left nor right:
In all the endless road you tread
There's nothing but the night. →

24

用仁慈之心行正義之事

這樁可怕的罪行是事出有因的。正如我所説過的，世界上所發生的一切，都必然事出有因。戰爭是原因之一，教育是原因之一，出身是原因之一，金錢也是原因之一——所有的這些原因湊在一起，就促成了這兩個可憐孩子的毀滅。

法庭有權不去考慮這兩個孩子嗎？州法律給予法官閣下有權考量社會安康的權利，這也正是你們在執行的權力。如果取走這兩個孩子的性命，就能換得社會的安康，那也就罷了。但我想這樣做的負面效果是難以估計的。

我不知道這兩個孩子還有多少希望可言，我不想在他們面前談論這一點，但我們還能企盼什麼？我只知道，如果對他們判以絞刑處死，那法庭是寬待了被告，對文明卻是殘酷的，對那些後來的人也是殘忍的。

我並不想在法庭上説，我並不期待許久之後，當時間歲月流逝，他們的身心不復以往之後，他們是否還會重新回到生活之中。對於任何一個在世的人，我會是最後一個去關閉其希望之門的人，最起碼，對我的當事人來說是如此。然而，這兩個孩子還能期待什麼未來？無可期待啊！這讓我想到了英國詩人豪斯曼的一首詩：

Clarence Darrow (1857–1938)

1. well and good: used to indicate calm acceptance, as of a decision 決定冷靜接受
2. salvage [ˈsælvɪdʒ] (n.) save something from destruction 挽救
3. Alfred Edward Housman (1859–1936): an English poet 英國詩人豪斯曼

　　　無力的火焰即將在黑夜中燃盡，
　　　火光在搖曳中逐漸隱去，
　　　挺起你的肩膀，背起你的背包
　　　告別你的友人離去吧。
　　　別怕，少年郎，什麼都不要怕，
　　　切莫左顧右盼：
　　　你眼前踏上的這條永無止境的路
　　　只有無盡的夜晚。

Your Honor stands between the past and the future. You may hang these boys. But in doing it you will turn your face toward the past. In doing it you are making it harder for every other boy who in ignorance and darkness must grope his way through the mazes which only childhood knows. In doing it you will make it harder for unborn children.

You may save them and make it easier for every child that sometime may stand where these boys stand. You will make it easier for every human being with an aspiration and a vision and a hope and a fate.

I am pleading for the future; I am pleading for a time when hatred and cruelty will not control the hearts of men. When we can learn by reason and judgment and understanding and faith that all life is worth saving, and that mercy is the highest attribute of man.

I feel that I should apologize for the length of time I have taken. This case may not be as important as I think it is, and I am sure I do not need to tell this court, or to tell my friends that I would fight just as hard for the poor as for the rich.

If I should succeed, my greatest reward and my greatest hope will be that for the countless unfortunates who must tread the same road in blind childhood that these poor boys have trod—that I have done something to help human understanding, to temper justice with mercy, to overcome hate with love.

I was reading last night of the aspiration of the old Persian poet, Omar Khayyam. It appealed to me as the highest that I can vision. I wish it was in my heart, and I wish it was in the hearts of all.

So I be written in the Book of Love,
I do not care about that Book above.
Erase my name or write it as you will,
So I be written in the Book of Love. ◀

(L–R) Loeb and Leopold (L–R) Leopold, Clarence Darrow and Loeb

　　法官閣下站在過去與未來之間，您可以絞死這兩個孩子，只是當您這樣做的同時，您的臉是望向過去的。這樣做的結果，對無知愚昧、只能在迷惘中摸索著前進的孩子來說，是難以接受的，這是孩子們才有的迷惘。這樣做的結果，無異於是讓每一個尚未出世的孩子，都擁有了一個更艱難的未來。

　　您可能可以拯救這兩個孩子一命，並且對未來和這些孩子身處相同處境的每個孩子寬容一些，對每一個具有抱負、憧憬、希望和命運的人來說，也是如此。

　　我是在為未來做辯護，在為仇恨與冷酷不再支配人心的那一刻做辯護。當我們能透過理性、判斷、理解和信任，明白到一切生靈都是值得被拯救時，仁慈就會成為人類最高貴的美德。

　　我想，我要為自己占用了這麼久的時間而道歉，這件案子或許不如我所想的那麼重要，我也毋需向法庭或我的友人說明，不論我的當事人是貧是富，我都會同樣為之奮鬥。

　　如果我成功了，那我最大的酬償和願望，就是希望那些無數的不幸孩子，當他們在無知的年少時代，無可避免地也踏上了這兩個可憐孩子所走的路時──我起碼做出了一點事，讓人們能多理解他們，讓正義與仁慈能並行不悖，並且能用愛來征服仇恨。

　　昨天晚上，我讀到了古代波斯詩人歐瑪‧開揚的抱負。它吸引了我，因為它提出了我所能想像的最高理想，我希望這也是我心裡所願的，也是大家心裡所盼的：

> 我如是地被寫入《愛之書》，
> 我並不在乎這本書將會如何。
> 任你擦去或是寫上我的名字，
> 我如是地被寫入《愛之書》。

Nothing Is Impossible

Christopher Reeve's DNC speech

「超人」李維演說：
沒有不可能的事情

李維出生於紐約市，是美國《超人》電視、電影系列的第三代超人，在 1978–1987 年間，主演過四部《超人》電影。1995 年 5 月，他在參加馬術比賽時發生意外，脊椎嚴重受傷，造成全身癱瘓。此後，他投身於社會公益事業，成立基金會，為癱瘓症研究籌集資金，致力於推動醫學研究，經常舉辦巡迴演講，鼓勵癱瘓病人。他也遊說國會立法，讓意外傷患獲得更好的保險保障。

他曾誓言 50 歲時要重新站起來，這個願望後來雖未能實現，但他重新恢復全身 70% 以上的感覺，並且能夠移動全身大多數的關節，讓醫界大感驚訝，也為脊髓醫療帶來了光明的前景。2004 年 10 月，在走過九年多癱瘓的人生歲月之後，他因心肌梗塞逝世，享年 52 歲。

李維成功扮演了電影上的超人形象，在現實生活裡，他更是一個不折不扣的英雄，激勵著人們，並且在許多層面上造福了很多的人。他曾説：

A hero is an ordinary individual who finds the strength to persevere and endure in spite of overwhelming obstacles.

英雄，乃是一個凡人在遇到無法抵抗的逆境時，
能夠找到勇氣，繼續奮鬥、堅持下去的人。

Speaker 美國知名男演員克里斯多福・李維
（Christopher D'Olier Reeve, 1952–2004）

Time 1996 年 8 月 26 日

Place 1996 年美國民主黨全國大會（美國芝加哥）
（1996 Democratic National Convention, Chicago, USA）

▣ 原音重現　▣ 全篇收錄

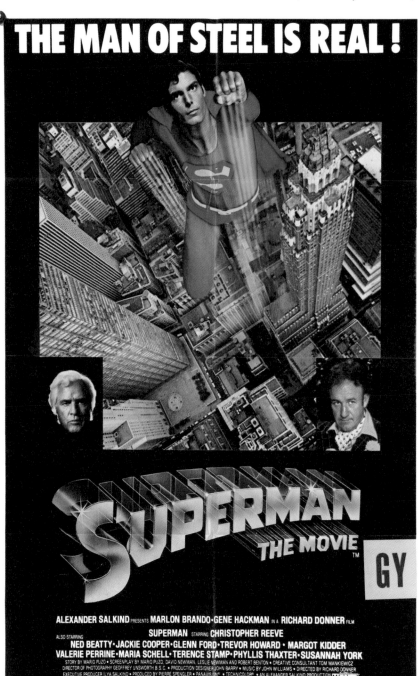

50

The last few years we've heard a lot about something called family values. And like many of you I've struggled to figure out what that means. And since my accident I found a definition that seems to make sense. I think it means that we're all family. And that we all have value.

Now, if that's true, if America really is a family, then we have to recognize that many members of our family are hurting. And just to take one aspect of it, one in five of us have some kind of disability. You may have Parkinson's Disease[1] or a neighbor with a spinal cord[2] injury or a brother with AIDS. And if we're really committed to this idea of family, we've got to do something about it.

Now, first of all, our nation cannot tolerate discrimination of any kind. And that's why the Americans With Disabilities Act is so important. It must be honored everywhere. It is a civil rights law that is tearing down barriers both in architecture and in attitude. Its purpose is to give the disabled access not only to buildings but to every opportunity in society.

Now I strongly believe our nation must give its full support to the care givers who are helping people with disabilities lead independent lives.

Now, of course, we have to balance the budget. And we will. We have to be extremely careful with every dollar we spend. But we've also got to take care of our family. And not slash[3] programs that people need. Now, one of the smartest things we could do about disability is to invest in research that will protect us from diseases, and will lead to cures.

This country already has a long history of doing it. When we put our minds to a problem, we find solutions. But our scientists can do more. We've got to give them the chance. And that means more funding for research. →

在過去的幾年裡，我們常常聽到人們在談「家庭價值」，我也和很多人一樣，一直在思索那究竟是什麼意思。然而在我發生了意外之後，我找到了一個頗有意義的解釋。我認為，它意謂著我們同屬於一個大家庭，意謂著我們每一個人都有自己的價值。

現在，如果這是真的，如果美國的確是一個大家庭，那麼我們就必須意識到，我們有很多的家人正在遭受著痛苦。我們單從某一方面舉例來説，我們每五個人當中，就有一個人具有某方面的失能。可能是你自己罹患了帕金森氏症，或是鄰居是個脊椎損傷者，或是你的兄弟得了愛滋病。如果我們真的都把他們當成家人一般，那我們就該有所行動。

現在，首先是我們的國家不能容許任何的歧視存在，而這也就是《美國失能保障法案》如此重要的原因，它應該普遍地被遵行，這是民權法的一部份，用來消弭結構上和態度上的各種障礙。它的用意不只是為失能人士提供通行便利，更要為他們爭取社會上每一個平等的機會。

現在，我深深地認為，我們的國家應該要不遺餘力地協助看護者，因為他們幫助那些失能人士活出獨立自主的人生。

現在，我們當然要讓預算取得平衡，我們一定得這樣做，任何的開銷都要深思熟慮，但我們也要照顧好我們的家人，不能隨意削減必要的預算。現在，對於失能的問題，最明智的作法是把預算投注在醫學研究上，這樣才能幫助我們免於疾病之苦，或是找到痊癒的方法。

我們國家在這方面的推動已經行之有年，當我們把心力貢獻在某個問題上，我們一定可以找到解決之道，然而我們的科學家在這方面可以做得更多。我們必須提供他們這個機會，也就是説，我們需要更多的研究資金。

Christopher Reeve
(1952–2004)

1. Parkinson's Disease: a progressive nervous disorder marked by symptoms of trembling hands, lifeless face, etc. 帕金森氏症

2. spinal cord: thick cord of nerve tissue 脊髓

3. slash [slæʃ] (v.) to cut drastically 大幅削減

51

Right now, for example, about a quarter million Americans have a spinal cord injury, and our government spends about $8.7 billion a year just maintaining these members of our family. But we only spend $40 million a year on research that would actually improve the quality of their lives and get them off public assistance or even cure them. We've got to be smarter and do better.

The money we invest in research today is going to determine the quality of life for members of our family tomorrow. Now, during my rehabilitation[4] I met a young man named Gregory Patterson. He was innocently driving through Newark, New Jersey, and a stray bullet from a gang shooting went through a car window right into his neck and severed[5] his spinal cord. Five years ago he might have died. Today because of research, he's alive.

But merely being alive, merely being alive is not enough. We have a moral and an economic responsibility to ease his suffering. And to prevent others from experiencing such pain. And to do that we don't need to raise taxes. We just need to raise our expectations.

Now, America has a tradition that many nations probably envy. We frequently achieve the impossible. But that's part of our national character. That's what got us from one coast to another. That's what got us the largest economy in the world. That's what got us to the moon. Now, in my room while I was in rehab, there was a picture of the space shuttle blasting off. It was autographed by every astronaut down at NASA[6]. On the top of that picture it says, "We found nothing is impossible."

Now, that should be our motto. It's not a Democratic motto, not a Republican motto. It's an American motto. It's not something one party can do alone. It's something we as a nation have to do together. →

舉例來說，現今美國大約有二十五萬人受脊椎損傷之苦，我們政府每年花八十七億元照顧這些人，卻只撥四千萬元在研究經費上，但這些研究才能真正改善他們的生活品質，讓他們不用再依賴公共援助，甚至可以使他們痊癒。所以我們必須睿智一點，把它做得更完善。

　　我們投注在研究上的經費，將會決定我們這個大家庭每一成員未來的生活品質。在我復健的過程中，我認識了一位名叫格雷戈里‧帕特森的年輕人，他安份地開著車行經新澤西州的紐瓦克時，一顆突如其來的子彈射穿了他的車窗，打到了他的頸部，傷到了他的脊髓。這種情況在五年前可能是不治的，但今日因為有醫學研究，所以他仍然活著。

　　然而僅僅只是活著，僅僅只是活著是不夠的！我們有道德和經濟上的責任去減輕他的痛苦，並且要避免其他人再去承受這種痛苦。要做到這一點，我們不需要加稅，我們只要把期望提高就可以。

　　現在，美國有一個讓許多國家艷羨的傳統：我們總是把不可能化為可能，這是我們民族特質的一部分。正是這個特質讓我們開墾了大陸，讓我們造就了世界最大的經濟體，讓我們登上了月球。現在在我復健的房間裡，有一張太空梭升空的照片，上頭還有美國國家太空總署每一位太空人的親筆簽名。在照片的上端寫著：「我們發現，沒有什麼事情是不可能的。」

　　這一句話也應該成為我們的座右銘。這不是民主黨的座右銘，不是共和黨的座右銘，它應該是我們每一位美國人的座右銘。這不是某一個政黨可以獨力做到的事情，這是我們全國人民要上下齊心去做的事情。

4. rehabilitation [ˌriːhəbɪlɪ'teɪʃən] (n.) the treatment of physical disabilities by massage and electrotherapy and exercises 復健

5. sever ['sɛvər] (v.) to cut off from a whole 裂開

6. National Aeronautics and Space Administration 美國國家太空總署

52

So many of our dreams, so many dreams at first seem impossible, and then they seem improbable. And then when we summon the will, they soon become inevitable.

So if we can conquer outer space, we should be able to conquer inner space, too. And that's the frontier of the brain, the central nervous system and all the afflictions[7] of the body that destroys so many lives and rob our country of so many potential.

Research can provide hope for people who suffer from Alzheimer's[8]. We've already discovered the gene that causes it. Research can provide hope for people like Muhammad Ali and the Reverend Billy Graham who suffer from Parkinson's. Research can provide hope for the millions of Americans like Kirk Douglas who suffer from stroke. We can ease the pain of people like Barbara Jordan who battle Multiple Sclerosis[9]. We can help people like Barbara Glazer.

Now we know the nerves of the spinal cord can regenerate. We are on our way to helping millions of people around the world, millions of people around the world like me, up and out of these wheelchairs.

Now, 56 years ago, FDR[10] dedicated[11] new buildings for the National Institutes of Health. He said that, "The defense this nation seeks involves a great deal more than building airplanes, ships, guns and bombs. We cannot be a strong nation unless we are a healthy nation."

He could have said that today. President Roosevelt showed us that a man who could barely lift himself out of a wheelchair could still lift this nation out of despair. And I believe—and so does this administration— in the most important principle, the most important principle that FDR taught us.

America does not let its needy citizens fend[12] for themselves. America is stronger when all of us take care of all of us. Giving new life to that ideal is the challenge before us tonight. Thank you very much. ◀

曾經我們有很多的夢想，它們一剛開始時看起來都是不可能的，之後我們還是覺得不大可能實現，但一旦我們拿出決心，就變得必然會實現了。

所以，如果我們都能征服外太空了，那我們就應該也能征服人體。這是關於大腦的未知領域、中樞神經系統，以及所有的身體疾病，這些疾病奪走了很多人的性命，讓我們國家喪失了很多的潛力。

醫學研究能帶給阿茲海默患者一線曙光，我們已經找出了致病的基因；研究也能為像拳王阿里和葛理翰牧師這些罹患帕金森氏症的人帶來希望；研究也能為像寇克・道格拉斯（美國演員）等數百萬的美國中風患者帶來一線生機。我們也可以幫助像芭芭拉・喬丹（美國前女性黑人議員）這種多發性硬化症患者減輕病痛，或是幫助像芭芭拉・葛萊瑟（美國女演員）這些人。

現在我們發現脊髓損傷患者的神經可以再生。我們正在邁向一個前景，可以幫助這世界上數百萬的人們，他們和我一樣都得靠輪椅來活動。

56 年前，小羅斯福總統出席國家衛生研究院新大樓的落成典禮時說道：「我們的國防並不只是建立在飛機、軍艦、槍砲和炸彈的數量上，如果沒有健康的國民，就不可能有富強的國家。」

我想就算是在今天，他也會說同樣的話。小羅斯福總統自己就是一個例子，他讓我們知道一個坐在輪椅上的人，也可以帶領這個國家走出絕望。我，和我們的政府都相信羅斯福總統所教導的這句話，這是我們最重要的原則。

美國不可能對需要幫助的人民棄之不顧。當我們大家都能夠彼此照顧，美國就會變得更強大。今晚，賦予這個理想新的生命，是我們眼前所要奮鬥的目標。謝謝大家。

7. affliction [əˈflɪkʃən] (n.) something that makes you suffer 肉體或精神上的痛苦
8. Alzheimer's disease: a medical disorder causing dementia 阿茲海默症
9. sclerosis [sklɪˈroʊsɪs] (n.) any pathological hardening or thickening of tissue 硬化症
10. Franklin Delano Roosevelt (1882-1945): 32nd President of the United States 小羅斯福總統
11. dedicate [ˈdedɪkeɪt] (v.) to open to public use, as of a highway, park, or building 為……舉行落成典禮
12. fend [fend] (v.) to look after somebody 照料

The Audacity of Hope

歐巴馬基調演說：
無畏的希望

2004 年 7 月，在美國民主黨舉行的全國代表大會上，當時還是一位州議員的歐巴馬，被派任發表黨綱和政策的「基調演講」（Keynote Address），他親自擬稿，演說慷慨激昂，也因為這次震驚四座的成功演講，歐巴馬成為政壇一顆耀眼的新星。

這次演講的題目是〈無畏的希望〉（The Audacity of Hope），這也成為歐巴馬日後著作的書名。在英國《每日電訊報》2008 年所評選出 20–21 世紀最重要的 25 場政治演説中，這場演講名列其中。

歐巴馬口齒便給，非常擅於演講，而且比明星更有光環。他在政壇急速崛起，深受美國民眾所喜愛，成為全國知名的政治明星。

四年後，他傳奇性地當選美國總統，成為美國史上第一位黑人總統，實現了金恩博士的一個夢想。

Speaker　美國州議員歐巴馬（Barack Hussein Obama II, 1961–）

Time　2004 年 7 月 27 日

Place　美國波士頓艦隊中心體育館（Fleet Center, Boston）
　　　1976 年民主黨全國大會基調演說
　　　（Democratic National Convention Keynote Address, USA）

☒ 原音重現　☒ 擷錄

53

On behalf of the great state of Illinois, crossroads of a nation, Land of Lincoln, let me express my deepest gratitude for the privilege of addressing this convention. Tonight is a particular honor for me because, let's face it, my presence on this stage is pretty unlikely.

My father was a foreign student, born and raised in a small village in Kenya. He grew up herding goats, went to school in a tin-roof shack. His father—my grandfather—was a cook, a domestic servant to the British. But my grandfather had larger dreams for his son. Through hard work and perseverance my father got a scholarship to study in a magical place, America, that shone as a beacon of freedom and opportunity to so many who had come before.

While studying here, my father met my mother. She was born in a town on the other side of the world, in Kansas. Her father worked on oil rigs[1] and farms through most of the Depression[2]. The day after Pearl Harbor my grandfather signed up for duty; joined Patton's[3] army, marched across Europe.

Back home, my grandmother raised a baby and went to work on a bomber assembly line. After the war, they studied on the G.I. Bill[4], bought a house through F.H.A.[5], and later moved west all the way to Hawaii in search of opportunity. And they, too, had big dreams for their daughter. A common dream, born of two continents.

My parents shared not only an improbable love, they shared an abiding faith in the possibilities of this nation. They would give me an African name, Barack, or "blessed," believing that in a tolerant America your name is no barrier to success. They imagined—They imagined me going to the best schools in the land, even though they weren't rich, because in a generous America you don't have to be rich to achieve your potential. →

偉大的伊利諾州，是全國的交通樞紐，是「林肯之州」，我身為州代表，能有這個殊榮在大會上致詞，我在此致上深深的感恩之情。今晚對我來說，是特別的光榮，因為，就這麼說吧，我能站在這個講臺上，簡直是不可能的事。

我父親是一個外國留學生，他在肯亞的一個小村莊裡出生長大。他小時候要牧羊，上的是鐵皮屋頂搭成的學校，簡陋不堪。他的父親，也就是我的祖父，在為英國人幫傭煮飯，但他對兒子有很深的期許。父親憑藉著不懈的努力和毅力，獲得了一份獎學金，可以到一個神奇的國家留學——美國，對前來這個國家的許許多多人而言，這裡閃耀著自由和機會的火光。

在美國留學期間，我的父親遇見了我的母親。我的母親出生於地球的另一端——美國的堪薩斯州。我的外祖父在石油井和田地上工作，以此熬過了經濟大蕭條時期。珍珠港事變之後的隔天，外祖父報名從軍，加入了巴頓將軍的軍隊，踏遍了歐洲。

在家鄉的那一端，外祖母要養育一個孩子，她找了一份轟炸機生產線的工作。戰爭結束後，他們根據《士兵福利法案》，透過「美國住房管理局」買了一間房子，後來，他們舉家西遷搬到了夏威夷，想找找看有沒有比較好的發展機會。他們同樣也對自己的女兒望女成鳳，雖然來自於不同的世界，但他們都有著同樣的夢想。

我的父母親締結了少見的異國婚姻，而且他們都相信這個國家遍地都是機會。他們為我取了一個非洲的名字「Barack」，這是「天佑」的意思，他們相信，在這個包容的國度裡，名字並不會成為成功的羈絆。雖然他們的生活並不寬裕，但他們還是設法讓我去上當地最好的學校，因為在富庶的美國，無論貧富貴賤，人人都有發展的潛能。

Barack Obama (1961–)

1. oil rig: the equipment used for drilling for 油井設備

2. Great Depression: the economic crisis beginning with the stock market crash in 1929 and continuing through the 1930s 1929 年至 1933 年之間的全球性經濟大蕭條

3. George Smith Patton (1885–1945): a U.S. general 美國巴頓將軍

4. G.I. Bill: Servicemen's Readjustment Act 士兵福利法案

5. Federal Housing Administration: a federal agency that insures residential mortgages and assists certain groups of home buyers 美國住房管理局

54

They're both passed away now. And yet, I know that on this night they look down on me with great pride.

They stand here—And I stand here today, grateful for the diversity of my heritage, aware that my parents' dreams live on in my two precious daughters. I stand here knowing that my story is part of the larger American story, that I owe a debt to all of those who came before me, and that, in no other country on earth, is my story even possible.

Tonight, we gather to affirm the greatness of our Nation—not because of the height of our skyscrapers, or the power of our military, or the size of our economy. Our pride is based on a very simple premise, summed up in a declaration made over two hundred years ago:

We hold these truths to be self-evident, that all men are created equal, that they are endowed by their Creator with certain inalienable rights, that among these are Life, Liberty and the pursuit of Happiness.[6]

That is the true genius of America, a faith—a faith in simple dreams, an insistence on small miracles; that we can tuck in our children at night and know that they are fed and clothed and safe from harm; that we can say what we think, write what we think, without hearing a sudden knock on the door; that we can have an idea and start our own business without paying a bribe; that we can participate in the political process without fear of retribution, and that our votes will be counted—at least most of the time.

This year, in this election we are called to reaffirm our values and our commitments, to hold them against a hard reality and see how we're measuring up to the legacy of our forbearers and the promise of future generations. →

如今，我的雙親都已經過世了，但是我知道，今晚，他們會在天上看著我，為我感到驕傲不已。

他們站在這裡——今天，我站在這裡，我感激我身上流著兩種血脈，我知道，我雙親的夢想，將會在我兩個寶貝女兒的身上延續下去。我站在這裡，我知道我個人的故事，就是整個美國故事的一個部分。拜所有踏上這塊土地的先人們所賜，若不是因為在美國，我的故事無論如何是不可能發生的。

今晚，我們齊聚一堂，再度證明了這個國家的偉大——其偉大並非在於高聳入天的摩天大樓，並非在於強大的軍事力量，並非在於我們雄厚的經濟實力。我們之所以引以為豪，是因為一個非常簡單的前提，這是在兩百年前所做的一個精華宣言：

> 這個真理是不言而喻的，那就是，人人生而平等。造物主賜予人不可剝奪的權利，那就是生存、自由和追求幸福的權利。

6. An extract from the *United States Declaration of Independence*
出自《美國獨立宣言》

這是美國真正的原創精神，這是對簡單夢想的一種信仰，始終相信著一直會有點點滴滴的奇蹟發生。夜晚，當我們為孩子們蓋上棉被時，我們知道他們得到了溫飽，安全無虞；我們可以說我們想說的話，寫我們想寫的東西，不用害怕會有人突然敲門來調查；我們可以發揮點子，自由創業，不用去賄賂收買；我們可以參與政治，不用擔心會被清算；我們的每一張選票都是有效的，起碼絕大部分都是這樣子的。

在今年的選舉中，我們要重申我們的核心價值和所肩負的責任，以此渡過難關，並看看我們可以如何地繼往開來。

55

People don't expect—People don't expect government to solve all their problems. But they sense, deep in their bones, that with just a slight change in priorities, we can make sure that every child in America has a decent shot at life, and that the doors of opportunity remain open to all.

You know, a while back—a while back I met a young man named Shamus in a V.F.W.[7] Hall in East Moline, Illinois. He was a good-looking kid—six two, six three, clear eyed, with an easy smile. He told me he'd joined the Marines and was heading to Iraq the following week. And as I listened to him explain why he'd enlisted, the absolute faith he had in our country and its leaders, his devotion to duty and service, I thought this young man was all that any of us might ever hope for in a child.

But then I asked myself, "Are we serving Shamus as well as he is serving us?" I thought of the 900 men and women—sons and daughters, husbands and wives, friends and neighbors, who won't be returning to their own hometowns. I thought of the families I've met who were struggling to get by without a loved one's full income, or whose loved ones had returned with a limb missing or nerves shattered, but still lacked long-term health benefits because they were Reservists[8].

When we send our young men and women into harm's way, we have a solemn obligation not to fudge[9] the numbers or shade the truth about why they're going, to care for their families while they're gone, to tend to the soldiers upon their return, and to never ever go to war without enough troops to win the war, secure the peace, and earn the respect of the world.

It is that fundamental belief—It is that fundamental belief: I am my brother's keeper. I am my sister's keeper that makes this country work. It's what allows us to pursue our individual dreams and yet still come together as one American family. E pluribus unum[10]: "Out of many, one." →

人民並不期待政府要解決所有的問題，但他們深深地感受到，只要政府的工作重點能做一些些調整，我們就能確保美國的每一個孩子都能夠茁壯長大，確保機會之門會同時為所有人都敞開。

前不久，在伊利諾州東莫林市的「美國海外退伍軍人大會堂」裡，我遇見了一個叫做謝莫斯的年輕人，他長相英俊，身高約一米九，他眼睛清澈，笑容可掬。他説他加入了美國海軍陸戰隊，下個星期就要前往伊拉克。當我聽他講到入伍的原因時，他對國家和領袖有著絕對的信賴，完全忠於自己的職責，我想這位年輕人的特質，大概就是為人父母最想在自己孩子身上所看到的。

於是我自問：「我們對謝莫斯所做的，是否與他所付出的相當？」我想到，在這次的戰爭中，已有九百多位軍人捐軀，他們是別人的兒女、丈夫、妻子、朋友、鄰居，他們將再也不會回來了。我想到我遇到的那些家庭，他們有的頓失經濟支柱、陷入困境，或是要面對身體傷殘或精神崩潰的歸鄉軍人，他們沒有長期的醫療津貼，因為他們是後備役軍人。

當我們把這些年輕人送入險境時，對於他們出征的原因，我們絕對不可以隱瞞情資和真相，而且務必在期間好好關照他們的家人。等他們榮歸故里後，也務必好好照顧他們的生活。此外，如果沒有足夠的軍隊，沒有足夠的勝算可以打贏戰爭、保衛和平、贏得威望，那就不應該參戰。

就因為這個根本的信仰，而這根本的信仰是——我們是一家人——才讓這個國家發展到今天。我們因而一方面得以追求我們個人的夢想，另一方面得以凝聚成一個美國大家庭。E pluribus unum：「合眾為一。」

Honor Guard marching at Veterans of Foreign Wars (VFW) annual parade

7. Veterans of Foreign Wars: an organization of United States war veterans
   美國海外退伍軍人

8. reservist [rɪˈzɜːrvɪst] (n.) a member of the reserved military force
   後備軍人

9. fudge [fʌdʒ] (v.) to avoid giving a clear answer about something 捏造

10. one out of many (the motto of the US)
    〔拉〕合眾為一（美國標語）

56

Now even as we speak, there are those who are preparing to divide us—the spin masters, the negative ad peddlers who embrace the politics of "anything goes." Well, I say to them tonight, there is not a liberal America and a conservative America—there is the United States of America. There is not a Black America and a White America and Latino America and Asian America—there's the United States of America.

In the end—In the end—In the end, that's what this election is about. Do we participate in a politics of cynicism[11] or do we participate in a politics of hope?

John Kerry calls on us to hope. John Edwards calls on us to hope. I'm not talking about blind optimism here—the almost willful ignorance that thinks unemployment will go away if we just don't think about it, or the health care crisis will solve itself if we just ignore it.

That's not what I'm talking about. I'm talking about something more substantial. It's the hope of slaves sitting around a fire singing freedom songs; the hope of immigrants setting out for distant shores; the hope of a young naval lieutenant[12] bravely patrolling the Mekong Delta[13]; the hope of a millworker's son who dares to defy the odds; the hope of a skinny kid with a funny name who believes that America has a place for him, too.

Hope—Hope in the face of difficulty. Hope in the face of uncertainty. The audacity[14] of hope! ◖

---

11. cynicism ['sɪnɪsɪzəm] (n.) believing that people are only interested in themselves and are not sincere 譏笑；犬儒主義
12. lieutenant [luː'tenənt] (n.) an officer in the U.S. navy 海軍上尉
13. Mekong Delta: the delta of the Mekong River in Vietnam 湄公河三角洲
14. audacity [ɔː'dæsɪti] (n.) fearless daring 無畏

　　現在，在我們說話的這個當下，就有那麼些人企圖分化我們，他們透過輿論操縱和負面宣傳，採取無所不用其極的手段。今晚，我要向這些人說，並沒有一個自由美國和一個保守美國的分別存在──只有一個美利堅合眾國的存在。也沒有所謂黑人美國、白人美國、拉丁美國或是亞裔美國的存在──只有一個美利堅合眾國的存在。

　　說到底，這個才是這一次選舉的意義所在。我們想要參與的政治，是一個唱衰的政治，還是一個充滿希望的政治？

　　約翰‧克里號召我們要懷抱希望，約翰‧愛德華茲號召我們要懷抱希望。我在這裡所講的不是說要盲目的樂觀──以為只要不去談論失業的問題，問題就會消失，或是對醫療危機視而不見，危機就不會存在。

　　這不是我要談的樂觀，我所要談的是更根本的問題。奴隸圍在火堆旁唱著歌頌自由的歌曲，是因為心存希望；移民者千里迢迢、遠涉重洋，是因為心存希望；年輕的海軍上尉在湄公河三角洲勇敢的巡邏放哨，是因為心存希望；出身寒門的孩子敢於挑戰命運，是因為心存希望；我這個名字怪怪的瘦小子相信美國這塊土地上必有容身之處，也是因為心存希望。

　　這個希望──正面迎向困境，正面迎向未知的未來，這個就是無畏的希望！

United States Declaration of Independence

美國獨立宣言

1775 年 4 月 19 日，美國獨立戰爭（1775–1783）正式開打。隔年 6 月，亞當斯（John Adams）*、富蘭克林（Benjamin Franklin）、傑佛遜（Thomas Jefferson）**、李文斯頓（Robert R. Livingston）和謝爾曼（Roger Sherman），五人共議撰寫獨立宣言，宣言由傑佛遜起草，後由富蘭克林和亞當斯加以修訂。

同年 7 月 4 日，來自北美洲十三個英屬殖民地的議會代表，在費城所舉行的第二次大陸會議上，批准通過《美國獨立宣言》，宣告獨立，這一天後來也成為美國的國慶日。

同年 8 月 2 日，完成《獨立宣言》的簽署，共有來自十三州的 56 位代表者簽署。獨立戰爭結束後，英美於 1783 年簽署《巴黎條約》（Treaty of Paris），英國遂承認美國獨立。《獨立宣言》指出了民主、自由和人權的基本哲學，全文最精髓的地方就是：

We hold these truths to be sacred and undeniable; that all men are created equal and independent; that from that equal creation they derive right inherent and inalienable, among which are the preservation of life, and liberty, and the pursuit of happiness.

我們認為，以下這個真理是神聖而不可否認的，那就是：人人生而平等獨立。造物主賜予每個人與生俱來不可剝奪的權利，那就是：生存、自由和追求幸福的權利。

* 之後成為美國第一任副總統，繼之成為美國第二任總統，也是第一位入住白宮的總統。
** 之後成為美國第二任副總統，繼之成為美國第三任總統。

Speaker 北美洲十三個英屬殖民地的議會代表
（the unanimous Declaration of the thirteen
United States of America）

Time 1776 年 7 月 4 日

Place 費城，第二次大陸會議
（Second Continental Congress in Philadelphia）

▣ 約翰・甘迺迪誦讀　▣ 擷錄

57

When in the Course of human events, it becomes necessary for one people to dissolve the political bands which have connected them with another, and to assume among the powers of the earth, the separate and equal station to which the Laws of Nature and of Nature's God entitle them, a decent respect to the opinions of mankind requires that they should declare the causes which impel them to the separation.

We hold these truths to be self-evident, that all men are created equal, that they are endowed by their Creator with certain unalienable Rights, that among these are Life, Liberty and the pursuit of Happiness.

—That to secure these rights, Governments are instituted among Men, deriving their just powers from the consent of the governed,

—That whenever any Form of Government becomes destructive of these ends, it is the Right of the People to alter or to abolish it, and to institute new Government, laying its foundation on such principles and organizing its powers in such form, as to them shall seem most likely to effect their Safety and Happiness.

Prudence, indeed, will dictate that Governments long established should not be changed for light and transient causes; and accordingly all experience hath shewn, that mankind are more disposed to suffer, while evils are sufferable, than to right themselves by abolishing the forms to which they are accustomed.

But when a long train of abuses and usurpations[1], pursuing invariably the same Object evinces[2] a design to reduce them under absolute Despotism[3], it is their right, it is their duty, to throw off such Government, and to provide new Guards for their future security.—Such has been the patient sufferance of these Colonies; and such is now the necessity which constrains them to alter their former Systems of Government. →

27
美國獨立宣言

1. usurpation [ˌjuːsɜːrˈpeɪʃən] (n.) wrongfully seizing and holding by force 奪取
2. evince [ɪˈvɪns] (v.) to make obvious or show clearly 顯示出
3. despotism [ˈdespətɪzəm] (n.) a form of government in which the ruler is an absolute dictator 專制統治

L–R: John Adams, Benjamin Franklin, Thomas Jefferson, Robert R. Livingston, and Roger Sherman

在人類發展的過程中，當一個民族要脫離和另一個民族的政治從屬關係，並遵循自然法則與上帝旨意所授予，而成為一個獨立且平等的國家，躋身世界列國之林時，出於對人類輿論的尊重，應該將其不得不獨立出來的原因，公告於世。

我們認為，以下這個真理是不言而喻的，那就是：人人生而平等。造物主賜予人不可剝奪的權利，那就是：生存、自由和追求幸福的權利。

——正是為了確保這些權利，人們才建立了政府，而政府的合法權利，是經由人民所同意授予的，

——任何一種型態的政府，一旦違悖了這些目標，人民就有權利去改變或廢除它，並建立新的政府。新政府賴以奠基的原則，以及其組織權力的型態，都應該要最有利於人民的安全與幸福。

確實，出於慎重，對於建立已久的政府，不宜因為輕微或一時的原因，就妄加變更。況且根據所有的經驗法則來看，人類更傾向於忍受，只要尚能忍受，人們就寧可忍受，也不願去廢除已經習慣了的政府。

然而，當濫用職權、巧取豪奪的情況層出不窮，顯示出政府所追求的目標是要對人民行高壓的專制統治，那麼去推翻這樣的一個政府，並為日後的安危建立一個新的保障，就是人民的權利與責任——而這就也是殖民地人民以前逆來順受，現在卻不得不改變原有的政府制度的原因了。

58

In every stage of these Oppressions We have Petitioned for Redress[4] in the most humble terms: Our repeated Petitions have been answered only by repeated injury. A Prince whose character is thus marked by every act which may define a Tyrant, is unfit to be the ruler of a free people.

Nor have We been wanting in attentions to our British brethren[5]. We have warned them from time to time of attempts by their legislature to extend an unwarrantable jurisdiction[6] over us. We have reminded them of the circumstances of our emigration and settlement here. We have appealed to their native justice and magnanimity, and we have conjured[7] them by the ties of our common kindred to disavow[8] these usurpations, which, would inevitably interrupt our connections and correspondence.

They too have been deaf to the voice of justice and of consanguinity[9]. We must, therefore, acquiesce[10] in the necessity, which denounces our Separation, and hold them, as we hold the rest of mankind, Enemies in War, in Peace Friends.

We, therefore, the Representatives of the United States of America, in General Congress, Assembled, appealing to the Supreme Judge of the world for the rectitude[11] of our intentions, do, in the Name, and by Authority of the good People of these Colonies, solemnly publish and declare, That these United Colonies are, and of Right ought to be Free and Independent States; that they are Absolved from all Allegiance to the British Crown, and that all political connection between them and the State of Great Britain, is and ought to be totally dissolved; and that as Free and Independent States, they have full Power to levy[12] War, conclude Peace, contract Alliances, establish Commerce, and to do all other Acts and Things which Independent States may of right do.

And for the support of this Declaration, with a firm reliance on the protection of divine Providence, we mutually pledge to each other our Lives, our Fortunes and our sacred Honor. ◖

我們每一次在遭受壓迫時，都用了最謙卑的言語請求改善，然而每一次請求所得到的回應，都是一次又一次的傷害。一個君主，當他的每一個行為都屬於暴君的行為時，那他就不再適合擔任自由人民的統治者。

我們不是沒有顧及我們英國的弟兄。我們一再提醒他們，他們的立法機關企圖對我們進行不合理的管制。我們也向他們說明過人民在這裡移民與定居的情況。我們曾經請求他們大發慈悲，看在我們是同文同種的份上，不要再掠奪我們，以免影響到彼此的關係和往來。

然而，他們對於這些正義和血緣的呼喊，仍舊充耳不聞。因此，我們不得不宣布和他們脫離關係，將他們視為一般國家，也就是說：與我們為敵的，就是敵人，與我們友好的，就是朋友。

所以我們這些美利堅合眾國的代表們，我們前來參加這次的大陸會議，以各殖民地善良人民的名義，經過他們的授權，向世界最崇高的正義呼籲，說明我們嚴正的意向，並且鄭重地發表和宣布：我們這些聯合起來的殖民地，現在是，也理當是自由獨立的國家；我們取消一切對英國王室效忠的義務，從此之後，我們和大不列顛國家之間的一切政治聯繫全面斷絕，而且理當斷絕；身為一個自由獨立的國家，我們有完全的權力可以自行宣戰、締和、結盟、通商，我們可以行使一個獨立國家有權行使的一切行動和事務。

為了擁護此一宣言，我們懷著蒙受上帝庇佑的堅定信心，以我們的性命、財產和神聖的名譽，互相宣誓。

4. redress [rɪˈdrɛs] (n.) act of correcting an error or a fault or an evil 矯正
5. brethren [ˈbrɛðrən] (n.) (plural form of brother) the lay members of a male religious order（brother 的複數形）弟兄；道友
6. jurisdiction [ˌdʒʊərɪsˈdɪkʃən] (n.) the territory within which power can be exercised 管轄範圍
7. conjure [ˈkʌndʒər] (v.) to ask for or request earnestly 召喚
8. disavow [ˌdɪsəˈvaʊ] (n.) refuse to acknowledge 拒絕；推翻
9. consanguinity [ˌkɑːnsæŋˈgwɪnɪti] (n.) when people are members of the same family 血親關係；同族
10. acquiesce [ˌækwiˈɛs] (v.) to accept or agree to something, often unwillingly 默認
11. rectitude [ˈrɛkɪtuːd] (n.) behavior that is honest and morally correct 正直
12. levy [ˈlɛvi] (v.) to declare war on somebody 發動（戰爭）

Give Me Liberty or Give Me Death

不自由，毋寧死

派屈克·亨利（Patrick Henry，1736–1799）是美國獨立革命時代的政治人物，為美國的開國元老之一，曾兩次出任維吉尼亞州州長。1775 年 3 月 23 日，他在維吉尼亞州里奇蒙的聖約翰教堂發表了這篇著名的《不自由，毋寧死》演說。

這篇演講在美國革命的文獻史上佔有重要的一頁，當時，北美殖民地正處於主戰派和主和派的抉擇之際，而派屈克·亨利代表了主戰派的觀點。他在這場演講中，以客觀的事實駁斥主和派，說明獨立戰爭的無可避免，並呼籲人們為自由而戰。

在這篇演說發表不到一個月之後，同年的 4 月 19 日，美國獨立戰爭（1775–1783）的第一槍終於打響，派屈克·亨利這句「Give me liberty or give me death」讓美國殖民地人民熱血澎湃，象徵了獨立戰爭的精神與勇氣。

獨立戰爭整整持續了八年又四個多月，美國以寡敵眾，贏得勝利，因而帶動了拉丁美洲殖民地的獨立風潮，影響力持續到拉丁美洲獨立戰爭（1808–1826）。

另外，美國獨立戰爭也間接引發了法國大革命（1789–1799），「不自由，毋寧死」這句激動人心的口號，也是法國大革命當時的流行口號。

Speaker 美國革命時期的演説家和政治家派屈克·亨利
（Patrick Henry, 1736–1799）

Time 1775 年 3 月 23 日

Place 維吉尼亞州里奇蒙聖約翰教堂
（St. John's Church in Richmond, Virginia）

☑ 錄音　☑ 全篇收錄

No man thinks more highly than I do of the patriotism, as well as abilities, of the very worthy gentlemen who have just addressed the House. But different men often see the same subject in different lights; and, therefore, I hope it will not be thought disrespectful to those gentlemen if, entertaining as I do opinions of a character very opposite to theirs, I shall speak forth my sentiments freely and without reserve. This is no time for ceremony.

The questing before the House is one of awful moment to this country. For my own part, I consider it as nothing less than a question of freedom or slavery; and in proportion to the magnitude of the subject ought to be the freedom of the debate. It is only in this way that we can hope to arrive at truth, and fulfill the great responsibility which we hold to God and our country. Should I keep back my opinions at such a time, through fear of giving offense, I should consider myself as guilty of treason towards my country, and of an act of disloyalty toward the Majesty of Heaven, which I revere above all earthly kings.

Mr. President, it is natural to man to indulge in the illusions of hope. We are apt to shut our eyes against a painful truth, and listen to the song of that siren[1] till she transforms us into beasts. Is this the part of wise men, engaged in a great and arduous struggle for liberty? Are we disposed to be of the number of those who, having eyes, see not, and, having ears, hear not, the things which so nearly concern their temporal salvation? For my part, whatever anguish of spirit it may cost, I am willing to know the whole truth; to know the worst, and to provide for it.

I have but one lamp by which my feet are guided, and that is the lamp of experience. I know of no way of judging of the future but by the past. And judging by the past, I wish to know what there has been in the conduct of the British ministry for the last ten years to justify those hopes with which gentlemen have been pleased to solace[2] themselves and the House. Is it that insidious smile with which our petition has been lately received? Trust it not, sir; it will prove a snare to your feet.

Suffer not yourselves to be betrayed with a kiss. Ask yourselves how this gracious reception of our petition comports[3] with those warlike preparations which cover our waters and darken our land. Are fleets and armies necessary to a work of love and reconciliation? Have we shown ourselves so unwilling to be reconciled that force must be called in to win back our love? Let us not deceive ourselves, sir. These are the implements of war and subjugation; the last arguments to which kings resort. →

對於剛剛在議會上發言的傑出人士們，我比誰都更欽佩他們的愛國情操和能力。但每個人的見解各有不同，我也會坦誠直言，如果我的意見和他們相左，請見諒，我並無冒犯之意，而且現在也不是講求客套的時候。

我們在這議會上所提出的問題，攸關國家的存亡時刻。就我個人來看，我認為這是一個不折不扣的自由與奴役的問題。這個問題事關重大，大家應該盡量各抒己見，這樣我們才能夠釐清真相，也才不會辜負上帝與祖國所賦予我們的重責大任。在這種時刻，如果因為害怕冒犯別人而噤口，我認為這無異於是背叛了自己的國家，也是違背了上帝，違背了這位塵世之上的王。

議長先生，人類天性就傾向於被美好的假象所迷惑。我們傾向於蒙住眼睛，不願正視痛苦的現實，甘願被海妖的歌聲所迷惑、落入圈套。在為自由艱苦奮鬥之際，這是明智之舉嗎？對於如此攸關世間自由的事情，我們甘願成為視而不見，充耳不聞的人嗎？就我來說，無論內心會承受多少痛苦，我都想了解事實的真相，明白最壞的情況，然後為之做好準備。

我只有一盞明燈可以指示前路，這盞明燈就是經驗，我只能依過去的經驗來判斷未來。按照過去的經驗來看，我想知道的是，這十年來，英國政府的所作所為到底帶來了什麼希望，足以讓各位和議會感到欣慰？難道是他們最近接受我們請願書時，所露出的那種狡詐的微笑？各位，別上當了，那不過是笑裡藏刀。

我們不要被人偷偷賣掉了都還不知道！且讓我們自問：他們接受我們的請願書時，一副態度親切的樣子，但一方面卻又在我們的土地和海域上部署大規模的軍備，這兩者如何能相稱？難道是因為出於對我們的愛護與善意，所以要動用到戰艦和軍隊？難道因為我們做了不願和解的表態，所以他們要用武力來挽回我們的心？諸位，我們不要再自欺欺人了，那些是戰爭和征服的工具，是英王最後要拿出來的手段。

---

1. siren [ˈsaɪrən] (n.) a group of women in ancient Greek stories, whose beautiful singing made sailors sail towards them into dangerous water
   〔希臘神話〕以歌聲吸引水手並使船隻遇難的海妖

2. solace [ˈsɑːlɪs] (v.) to give moral or emotional strength to 安慰

3. comport [kəmˈpɔːrt] (v.) to behave in a certain manner 相符合

I ask gentlemen, sir, what means this martial array, if its purpose be not to force us to submission? Can gentlemen assign any other possible motive for it? Has Great Britain any enemy, in this quarter of the world, to call for all this accumulation of navies and armies? No, sir, she has none. They are meant for us: they can be meant for no other. They are sent over to bind and rivet upon us those chains which the British ministry have been so long forging.

And what have we to oppose to them? Shall we try argument? Sir, we have been trying that for the last ten years. Have we anything new to offer upon the subject? Nothing. We have held the subject up in every light of which it is capable; but it has been all in vain. Shall we resort to entreaty and humble supplication? What terms shall we find which have not been already exhausted?

Let us not, I beseech you, sir, deceive ourselves. Sir, we have done everything that could be done to avert the storm which is now coming on. We have petitioned; we have remonstrated; we have supplicated; we have prostrated[4] ourselves before the throne, and have implored its interposition to arrest the tyrannical hands of the ministry and Parliament. Our petitions have been slighted; our remonstrances have produced additional violence and insult; our supplications have been disregarded; and we have been spurned, with contempt, from the foot of the throne! In vain, after these things, may we indulge the fond hope of peace and reconciliation. →

28
不自由，毋寧死

　　各位，我請問你們，如果他們的目的不是要逼我們歸順，那為什麼要部署軍隊？各位能指出他們還有什麼其他可能的動機嗎？在北美這一帶，大英帝國還有什麼敵人需要勞動他們這樣動員海陸軍力的？各位，他們沒有其他的敵人了，他們完全是針對我們而來的，這裡不可能有其他的敵人。他們是派來把我們套緊鐵鏈的，英國政府長久以來就一直想把我們套牢。

　　我們要如何來對抗他們？我們還要靠辯論嗎？各位，我們為此已經爭吵了十年了，我們還能為這個議題提出什麼新的觀點？沒有什麼新的觀點了，我們能談的都談了，什麼結果都沒有。難道我們還要苦苦地哀求下去嗎？我們還有什麼方法沒用過的？

　　各位，我請求你們，不要再自欺欺人了。為了阻止這場即將來臨的大風暴，我們能做的都做了。我們請願過，我們抗議過，我們乞求過。我們跪在英王的御座面前，懇請他出面制止國會和內閣的暴行，但他對我們的請願不屑一顧，我們的抗議反而換來了更多的鎮壓和侮辱。他們對我們的懇求置之不理，把我們從御座旁邊一腳踢開！我們做的這些努力全都是白費的，我們難道還會沉迷於虛無飄渺的和平願望之中。

| 4. prostrate ['prɑːˈstreɪt] (v.) to lie prone or stretched out with the face downward 俯臥；拜倒

There is no longer any room for hope. If we wish to be free—if we mean to preserve inviolate those inestimable privileges for which we have been so long contending—if we mean not basely to abandon the noble struggle in which we have been so long engaged, and which we have pledged ourselves never to abandon until the glorious object of our contest shall be obtained—we must fight! I repeat it, sir, we must fight! An appeal to arms and to the God of hosts is all that is left us!

They tell us, sir, that we are weak; unable to cope with so formidable an adversary. But when shall we be stronger? Will it be the next week, or the next year? Will it be when we are totally disarmed, and when a British guard shall be stationed in every house? Shall we gather strength by irresolution and inaction? Shall we acquire the means of effectual resistance by lying supinely[5] on our backs and hugging the delusive phantom of hope, until our enemies shall have bound us hand and foot?

Sir, we are not weak if we make a proper use of those means which the God of nature hath placed in our power. The millions of people, armed in the holy cause of liberty, and in such a country as that which we possess, are invincible by any force which our enemy can send against us.

Besides, sir, we shall not fight our battles alone. There is a just God who presides over the destinies of nations, and who will raise up friends to fight our battles for us. The battle, sir, is not to the strong alone; it is to the vigilant[6], the active, the brave. Besides, sir, we have no election. If we were base enough to desire it, it is now too late to retire from the contest.

There is no retreat but in submission and slavery! Our chains are forged! Their clanking may be heard on the plains of Boston! The war is inevitable—and let it come! I repeat it, sir, let it come.

It is in vain, sir, to extenuate[7] the matter. Gentlemen may cry, Peace, Peace—but there is no peace. The war is actually begun! The next gale that sweeps from the north will bring to our ears the clash of resounding arms! Our brethren are already in the field! Why stand we here idle? What is it that gentlemen wish? What would they have? Is life so dear, or peace so sweet, as to be purchased at the price of chains and slavery? Forbid it, Almighty God! I know not what course others may take; but as for me, give me liberty or give me death!

28

不
自
由
，
毋
寧
死

這是毫無和平的希望的，如果我們想獲得自由——如果我們想維護那些我們為之奮鬥已久的珍貴權利——如果我們不願意就這樣放棄我們長久以來所獻身的崇高奮鬥，我們曾誓言不達這光榮的目標、誓不罷手——那我們就必須為之而戰！諸位，讓我再說一次，我們必須為之而戰！我們唯一能做的，就是訴諸武力，並求助於萬邦之主的上帝。

各位，他們說我們很弱小，不可能打贏這麼一個強大的敵人。那我們何時才要強大起來？下個星期，還是明年？是不是要等到我們都繳械了，英國士兵可以隨意駐紮我們的民房時，我們才要強大起來？我們這樣子猶猶豫豫、毫無作為，是否就會強大起來？難道我們高枕而臥，抱著虛妄不實的願望，等到敵人捆住了我們的手腳，我們就能找到有效的禦敵之策？

各位，只要我們善加運用上帝所賦予的天賜力量，我們就不是弱者。一旦數百萬的人民站在自己的土地上，為神聖的自由而戰，那麼任何敵人都無法征服我們。

此外，各位，我們也將不是孤軍奮戰的，公正的上帝主宰著各國的命運，祂將找來盟友一齊為我們而戰。各位，戰爭的勝利並非只屬於強者，它也屬於那些機警、主動和勇敢的人們。更何況，各位，我們已經別無選擇了，就算我們軟弱想退縮，我們現在也騎虎難下了。

我們已經沒有退路了，除非我們甘願投降、甘願被奴役！用來囚禁我們的鍊鎖已經打造好了！波士頓的草原上已經聽得到鋃鐺的鐐銬聲了！這場戰爭已經無可避免了——就讓我們迎戰吧！各位，我再說一次，就讓我們來迎戰吧！

各位，粉飾太平是沒有用的。各位先生可以高喊「和平，和平」——但事實上根本是毫無和平可言的，因為戰爭已經開打了！很快地，北風就會捎來作戰的鏗鏘聲響！我們的弟兄們已經奔赴戰場了！我們還站在這裡做什麼？各位心裡頭所期待的到底是什麼？會得到的又是什麼？生命就如此可貴、和平就如此珍貴，所以甘願被套上枷鎖、甘願被奴役？全能的上帝，請不要讓這種事發生！我不知道別人還有什麼做法，但對我來說，不自由，毋寧死！

---

5. supinely [suˈpaɪnli] (adv.) (lying) flat on your back, looking up 仰臥地；懶散地

6. vigilant [ˈvɪdʒɪlənt] (a.) carefully observant or attentive 警戒的

7. extenuate [ɪksˈtɛnjueɪt] (v.) to lessen or to try to lessen the seriousness or extent of 減輕過失

29

Thomas Jefferson: The Creed of Our Political Faith

傑佛遜第一次就職演說：我們的政治信念

在美國總統就職演說的歷史上，有四場是史學家公認最偉大的演說，分別是：傑佛遜第一次就職演說（1801）、林肯第二次就職演說（1865）、小羅斯福第一次就職演說（1933），以及甘迺迪的就職演說（1961）。本書將會陸續介紹這四篇就職演說。

美國獨立戰爭（1775–1783）結束後，1783 年 9 月 3 日，英國簽下《巴黎條約》，正式承認美國的獨立。1789 年，美國憲法正式生效後，同年誕生了美國歷史上的第一位總統喬治·華盛頓（George Washington）。華盛頓連任兩屆之後（任期 1789–1797 年），繼之的總統是約翰·亞當斯（John Adams，任期 1797–1801 年），之後傑佛遜繼任第三任總統，並連任兩屆（任期 1801–1809 年）。

傑佛遜也是美國《獨立宣言》（1776 年）的起草人，他多才多藝，同時是一位建築師、發明家、科學家。他能夠閱讀五種以上的語言。此外，他也是《宗教自由法》、《西部土地法》等等官方文獻的起草人，並創辦了維吉尼亞大學。

傑佛遜鼓吹民主，而且能夠結合崇高的理想與實際情況。他在這一篇第一次就職演講中，闡述了民主哲學，是民主思想的經典之作。

Speaker 美國第三任總統傑佛遜
（Thomas Jefferson, 1743–1826）

Time 1801 年 3 月 4 日

Place 美國華盛頓特區（Washington, D.C.）

☑ 錄音 ☑ 擷錄

Thomas Jefferson (1743–1826)

62

During the contest of opinion through which we have past, the animation of discussions and of exertions[1] has sometimes worn an aspect which might impose on strangers unused to think freely, and to speak and to write what they think; but this being now decided by the voice of the nation, announced according to the rules of the constitution all will of course arrange themselves under the will of the law, and unite in common efforts for the common good.

All too will bear in mind this sacred principle, that though the will of the majority is in all cases to prevail, that will, to be rightful, must be reasonable; that the minority possess their equal rights, which equal laws must protect, and to violate would be oppression.

Let us then, fellow citizens, unite with one heart and one mind, let us restore to social intercourse that harmony and affection without which liberty, and even life itself, are but dreary things.

And let us reflect that having banished from our land that religious intolerance under which mankind so long bled and suffered, we have yet gained little if we countenance[2] a political intolerance, as despotic[3], as wicked, and capable of as bitter and bloody persecutions[4].

Let us then, with courage and confidence, pursue our own federal and republican principles; our attachment to union and representative government.

Still one thing more, fellow citizens, a wise and frugal government, which shall restrain men from injuring one another, shall leave them otherwise free to regulate their own pursuits of industry and improvement, and shall not take from the mouth of labor the bread it has earned. This is the sum of good government; and this is necessary to close the circle of our felicities[5].

About to enter, fellow citizens, on the exercise of duties which comprehend everything dear and valuable to you, it is proper you should understand what I deem *the essential principles of our government*, and consequently those which ought to shape its administration. I will compress them within the narrowest compass they will bear, stating the general principle, but not all its limitations.

—Equal and exact justice to all men, of whatever state or persuasion, religious or political;

—peace, commerce, and honest friendship with all nations, entangling alliances with none; →

我們經歷了一段時期的爭論，大家討論得沸沸揚揚，各自競相奔走。那些還不習慣自由思考和自由寫作的人士見到這種情形，可能會相顧失色。但如今國家已經由人民做出決定，並根據憲法規定來加以宣讀，大家都要遵守法紀，並且團結一致，為共同的利益而奮鬥。

大家也會牢牢記住一項神聖的原則，那就是：雖然凡事都要以多數人的意見為主，但意見還是要合情合理；而主張少數意見的人也擁有同等的權利，應受平等的法律來保護，如有違犯，即是迫害。

所以各位同胞，我們應當上下一心團結起來，恢復和諧溫馨的社會交流，否則自由——甚至連生活本身——都會變成是一種惡夢。

我們還應該反思：我們已經將那種長久以來造成人類衝突與苦難的排他性宗教，謝絕在我們的大門之外，而如果我們又鼓勵一言堂的政治，專制、邪惡、進行殘酷血腥的迫害，那我們其實並沒有什麼太大的進步。

因此各位，我們應當秉著勇氣和信心，追求我們自己的聯邦、共和原則，擁護聯邦和代議政體。

各位同胞，我們另外還需要的是一個明智和節儉的政府。這樣的政府能夠防止人們互相迫害，並且讓人民得以自由地追求事業與進步，不會剝奪人民的所得。這是一個良好政府的要旨，也是人民安樂的必要條件。

各位同胞，我即將開始執行我的職責，其中涵蓋了人民們所珍視的一切東西，所以人民有必要了解我所謂的「政府基本原則」，這些原則將會導出我們的施政方針。以下我將簡單陳述大方向，我只講一般的原則，不會談及全部範疇。

　　——不論出身於什麼地位、信念、宗教或黨派，人人都享有平等和公正的待遇；

　　——與所有國家和平相處，互通有無，敦睦邦交，但不與他國結盟，以免糾纏不清；

1. exertion [ɪgˈzɜːrʃən] (n.) use of physical or mental energy 努力
2. countenance [ˈkaʊntɪnəns] (v.) to give support to 支持
3. despotic [deˈspɑːtɪk] (a.) absolute in power 專橫的
4. persecution [ˌpɜːrsɪˈkjuːʃən] (n.) unfair treatment over a long period of time because of race, religion, or political beliefs 迫害
5. felicity [fɪˈlɪsɪti] (n.) happiness or contentment 幸福

—the support of the state governments in all their rights, as the most competent administrations for our domestic concerns, and the surest bulwarks[6] against anti-republican tendencies;

—the preservation of the General government in its whole constitutional vigor[7], as the sheet anchor[8] of our peace at home, and safety abroad;

—a jealous[9] care of the right of election by the people, a mild and safe corrective of abuses which are lopped by the sword of revolution where peaceable remedies are unprovided;

—absolute acquiescence[10] in the decisions of the majority, the vital principle of republics, from which is no appeal but to force, the vital principle and immediate parent of the despotism[11];

—a well disciplined militia[12], our best reliance in peace, and for the first moments of war, till regulars may relieve them;

—the supremacy of the civil over the military authority;

—economy in the public expense, that labor may be lightly burthened;

—the honest payment of our debts and sacred preservation of the public faith;

—encouragement of agriculture, and of commerce as its handmaid;

—the diffusion of information, and arraignment[13] of all abuses at the bar of the public reason[14];

—freedom of religion; freedom of the press; and freedom of person, under the protection of the Habeas Corpus[15]; and trial by juries impartially selected.

These principles form the bright constellation, which has gone before us and guided our steps through an age of revolution and reformation. The wisdom of our sages, and blood of our heroes have been devoted to their attainment; they should be the creed of our political faith; the text of civic instruction, the touchstone by which to try the services of those we trust; and should we wander from them in moments of error or of alarm, let us hasten to retrace our steps, and to regain the road which alone leads to peace, liberty, and safety.

——支持州政府的所有權利，讓各州足堪治理內政事務，並使各州成為抵擋「反共和潮流」的最佳堡壘；

——維護中央政府具有憲法上的完整效力，並使中央政府成為國內和平和對外安全的後盾；

——小心維護人民的選舉權，獨立戰爭所留下來的弊端並無平和的補救辦法，而人民選舉權則是一種溫和而安全的矯正手段；

——絕對服從多數人的決定，是共和政體的主要原則，如果訴諸武力，就變成了專制政治的主要原則和直接起源；

——維持訓練有素的後備軍人，使之成為和平時期和戰爭初期的最佳依靠，戰爭初期之後再由正規軍來接替；

——民權高於軍權；

——節省政府的開支，減輕人民的負擔；

——如實清償我們的債務，審慎地維護人民的信心；

——促進農業，並鼓勵商業扶植農業；

——普及知識，並依「公共理性」來糾舉一切弊端；

——保障宗教自由和媒體自由，並以人身保護令來保障人身自由，並以公正選出的陪審團來進行審判。

這些原則猶如明亮的星斗，在獨立戰爭和改革的期間，在我們的前方指引我們的腳步。我們聖哲們的智慧和英雄們的鮮血，都曾奉獻來實現這些原則。這些應當是我們政治信念的信條，是我們公民教育的課本，是人民所委託的政府的行事標準。我們要是因一時的錯誤或驚慌而走偏了，我們就應該趕快回頭，回到這條唯一能通往和平、自由和安全的大道上。

6. bulwark [ˈbʊlwərk] (n.) something that gives protection 堡壘

7. vigor [ˈvɪgər] (n.) an exertion of force 法律效力

8. sheet anchor: a person or thing that can be relied on if all else fails 最後的靠山

9. jealous [ˈdʒeləs] (a.) extremely careful in protecting somebody or something 小心守護的

10. acquiescence [ˌækwiˈesəns] (n.) acceptance without protest 默從

11. despotism [ˈdespətɪzəm] (n.) rule by a despot or tyrant 專制政治

12. militia [mɪˈlɪʃə] (n.) soldiers who are also civilians 後備軍人

13. arraignment [əˈreɪnmənt] (n.) the action of bringing somebody to court to answer a criminal charge 傳訊

14. public reason: the common reason of all citizens in a pluralist society 公共理性（在多元社會中，所有公民所共有的理性）

15. Habeas Corpus [ˌheɪbiəsˈkɔːrpəs]: a writ issued in order to bring somebody who has been detained into court 人身保護令

Abraham Lincoln:
Second Inaugural Address

林肯第二次就職演說：
我們禱告的是同一個上帝

在美國的歷任總統當中，華盛頓、林肯和小羅斯福被公認為三位最偉大的美國總統，其中華盛頓被歷史學家稱為國父，林肯則被譽為國家的拯救者。美國南北戰爭的爆發和結束，都在林肯的總統任期內。林肯在連任總統的一個多月之後，南北戰爭結束，但他卻在戰爭結束後的六天之後，遭到主張奴隸制度的分子所暗殺。這也讓他成為第一個遭到刺殺的美國總統。以下是林肯總統任期內的時間簡表：

1861 年 3 月 4 日	林肯第一任的總統任期開始
1861 年 4 月 12 日	南北戰爭爆發
1865 年 3 月 4 日	林肯第二任的總統任期開始
1865 年 4 月 9 日	南北戰爭結束
1865 年 4 月 15 日	林肯遇刺身亡

林肯出生於肯塔基州，21 歲時舉家搬到伊利諾州。林肯去世後被葬在伊利諾州春田市，因此伊利諾州的一個別稱就是「林肯之地」（Land of Lincoln）。1867 年 3 月，林肯遇刺後將屆滿兩年時，美國國會通過了興建林肯紀念堂的法案，並於 1922 年竣工。「林肯紀念堂」（Lincoln Memorial）位於華盛頓特區國家廣場（National Mall）的西側，與「國會大廈」（Capitol Building）和「華盛頓紀念碑」（Washington Monument）連成一直線，是美國著名的紀念性建築。

林肯紀念堂的中央有一座大理石雕成的林肯座像，其高達 5.8 公尺，在座像的左側牆壁上，刻著林肯第二次的就職演說，右側則刻著林肯另一篇著名的《蓋茨堡宣言》（Gettysburg Address）。另外，在知名的旅遊景點拉什莫爾山國家紀念公園（Mount Rushmore National Memorial，俗稱美國總統山）內，有四座高達 18 公尺左右的美國前總統頭像，其由左到右分別是華盛頓、傑弗遜、老羅斯福和林肯。

(L–R) Lincoln Memorial, Washington Monument, and United States Capitol Building

Speaker 美國第 16 任總統亞伯拉罕・林肯
（Abraham Lincoln, 1809–1865.4.15）

Time 1865 年 3 月 4 日

Place 美國華盛頓特區（Washington, D.C.）

▣ 錄音　▣ 擷錄

64

On the occasion corresponding to this four years ago, all thoughts were anxiously directed to an impending civil-war. All dreaded it—all sought to avert it.

While the inaugural address was being delivered from this place, devoted altogether to saving the Union without war, insurgent[1] agents were in the city seeking to destroy it without war—seeking to dissolve the Union, and divide effects, by negotiation. Both parties deprecated[2] war; but one of them would make war rather than let the nation survive; and the other would accept war rather than let it perish. And the war came.

One eighth of the whole population were colored slaves, not distributed generally over the Union, but localized in the Southern part of it. These slaves constituted a peculiar and powerful interest. All knew that this interest was, somehow, the cause of the war. To strengthen, perpetuate, and extend this interest was the object for which the insurgents would rend the Union, even by war; while the government claimed no right to do more than to restrict the territorial enlargement of it.

Neither party expected for the war, the magnitude, or the duration, which it has already attained. Neither anticipated that the cause of the conflict might cease with, or even before, the conflict itself should cease. Each looked for an easier triumph, and a result less fundamental and astounding.

Both read the same Bible, and pray to the same God; and each invokes His aid against the other. It may seem strange that any men should dare to ask a just God's assistance in wringing their bread from the sweat of other men's faces; but let us judge not that we be not judged[3].

The prayers of both could not be answered; that of neither has been answered fully. The Almighty has His own purposes. "Woe unto the world because of offences! for it must needs be that offences come; but woe to that man by whom the offence cometh![4]"

If we shall suppose that American Slavery is one of those offences which, in the providence[5] of God, must needs come, but which, having continued through His appointed time, He now wills to remove, and that He gives to both North and South, this terrible war, as the woe due to those by whom the offence came, shall we discern therein any departure from those divine attributes which the believers in a Living God always ascribe[6] to Him? →

在四年前這個同樣的場合裡，所有人所關注的都是即將爆發的內戰。那時大家都深感恐懼，想盡辦法要避免。

當時在這裡的就職演說，大家集思廣益，希望能在不發動戰爭的情況下拯救聯邦。然而城裡的反對分子卻處心積慮想在不發動戰爭的情況下，讓聯邦瓦解，以便在談判桌上分割聯邦。當時兩派人士都想避免戰爭，但其中一方寧願打仗，也不願讓國家繼續存在下去，而另一方則是寧可接受戰爭，也不願意讓國家滅亡。最後，戰爭於是爆發。

我們全國有八分之一的人口都是黑奴，他們不是遍布聯邦，而是集中在一些南方地區。大家都知道，這些黑奴代表了一種特殊且巨大的利益，而這也成為了導致戰爭的原因。因為政府主張限制黑奴區域的擴大，所以反對分子不惜發動戰爭以分裂聯邦，而其目的就是為了提高、保持和擴大這種利益。

當初雙方陣營都沒有預料到這場戰爭會蔓延得那麼廣，打得這麼久。大家也都沒有想到，早在戰爭結束，甚至尚未結束之前，戰爭的原因就不復存在了。雙方都希望想辦法盡快獲得勝利，並尋求一個比較中立、溫和的結果。

我們雙方都讀著同一本聖經，向同一個上帝做禱告，並祈求上帝幫助自己打敗對方。很不可思議的，人類竟敢祈求上帝幫助自己去搶奪別人辛苦掙來的麵包！然而，我們不要論斷別人，免得自己也被論斷。

我們雙方的祈禱是不可能同時如願的，而我們目前也沒有任何一方的祈求是完全被實現的。上帝行使他自己的旨意，「這世界有禍了，因為將人絆倒了；絆倒人的這種事，是免不了的，但那絆倒人的有禍了！」

如果美國的奴隸制度是屬於這種「絆倒人」的罪惡，而且按上帝的旨意而言是免不了的話，那在罪惡持續了上帝所指定的一段時間之後，上帝現在要消除罪惡了。上帝讓南北雙方掀起這場慘烈的戰爭，讓災難降臨到罪惡者的身上，這難道會有悖於信徒們心中所認定的上帝的聖德嗎？

---

1. insurgent [ɪnˈsɜːrdʒənt] (a.) in opposition to a civil authority or government 反對黨的

2. deprecate [ˈdeprɪkeɪt] (v.) to express strong disapproval of; deplore 企求避免

3. An extract from *Matthew* 7:1. "Judge not, that ye be not judged."
   出自《聖經・馬太福音》第 7 章第 1 節：「你們不要論斷人，免得你們被論斷。」

4. An extract from *Matthew* 18:7. 出自《聖經・馬太福音》第 18 章第 7 節

5. providence [ˈprɑːvɪdəns] (n.) a force which is believed by some people
   to control what happens in our lives and to protect us 天意；天命

6. ascribe [əˈskraɪb] (v.) attribute or credit to 歸屬於

Lincoln Memorial

65

Fondly do we hope—fervently do we pray—that this mighty scourge[7] of war may speedily pass away. Yet, if God wills that it continue, until all the wealth piled by the bond-man's two hundred and fifty years of unrequited[8] toil shall be sunk, and until every drop of blood drawn with the lash, shall be paid by another drawn with the sword, as was said three thousand years ago, so still it must be said "the judgments of the Lord, are true and righteous altogether."[9]

With malice toward none; with charity for all; with firmness in the right, as God gives us to see the right, let us strive on to finish the work we are in; to bind up the nation's wounds; to care for him who shall have borne the battle, and for his widow, and his orphan to do all which may achieve and cherish a just, and a lasting peace, among ourselves, and with all nations.

　　我們真誠懇切地祈禱，希望這場戰爭天譴能很快就結束。然而，如果上帝要讓這場戰爭繼續下去，直到黑奴們這兩百五十年來，無償的辛苦勞動所累積下來的財富付諸東流，直到鞭笞黑奴所流的每一滴血，用刀槍之下所流的血來血債血還，就像三千年前所宣示的那樣，那我們只能說「上帝的審判正確，全然公義。」

　　我們不對任何人懷有惡意，我們愛護所有的人。上帝讓我們看見正義，我們就應該堅守正義，為尚未完成的事業努力奮鬥，癒合國家分裂的傷口，照顧沙場上的戰士及其遺孀和遺孤，並盡一切力量來實現並維護國內外的正義與永久和平。

7. scourge [skɜːrdʒ] (n.) something that causes a lot of harm or suffering 災禍；天譴
8. unrequited [ˌʌnrɪˈkwaɪtɪd] (a.) not returned in kind 無報答的
9. An extract from *Psalm* 19:9. 出自《聖經·詩篇》第 19 章第 9 節

Franklin D. Roosevelt: First Inaugural Address

小羅斯福第一次就職演說： 我們唯一要害怕的，是恐懼本身

美國第 32 任總統富蘭克林・羅斯福又被稱為「小羅斯福」，他連續出任四屆總統（1933–1945 年），是美國歷史上唯一連任超過兩屆的總統。此後根據 1951 年通過的憲法第 22 條修正案，總統任期不得超過兩次。

從 1798 到 1933 年，美國總統的就職日都是在 3 月 4 日舉行，但這個傳統在小羅斯福總統的首次就職典禮後劃下句點。1933 年通過的《憲法第 20 條修正案》，規定總統宣誓就職的日期為 1 月 20 日中午時分。美國《憲法》第 2 條第 1 款規定了總統宣誓就職的誓詞：

I do solemnly swear (or affirm) that I will faithfully execute the Office of President of the United States, and will to the best of my ability, preserve, protect and defend the Constitution of the United States.
我謹莊嚴宣誓，我必忠實執行合眾國總統職務，竭盡全力，恪守、維護和捍衛合眾國憲法。

小羅斯福任內遭遇到了兩件歷史大事：1929–1940 年的經濟大蕭條危機，以及第二次世界大戰。在 1933 年，新當選的小羅斯福總統面臨的是經濟大蕭條的艱難處境。在這一哀鴻遍野的時刻，他在首任就職演說中敦促美國人不要屈服於恐懼與絕望。

在英國《每日電訊報》2008 年評選出的 20–21 世紀最重要的 25 場政治演說中，這一篇也被收錄其中。

ESTABLISH
NT BASED ON
OF ALL HUMAN
OF INDIVIDUAL
NEW ORDER.
S NOT ORDER.

Speaker 美國第 32 任總統富蘭克林・羅斯福
（Franklin Delano Roosevelt, 1882–1945）

Time 1933 年 3 月 4 日

Place 美國華盛頓特區（Washington, D.C.）

▣ 原音重現　▣ 擷錄

66

This is a day of national consecration[1]. And I am certain that on this day my fellow Americans expect that on my induction into the Presidency, I will address them with a candor[2] and a decision which the present situation of our people impels. This is pre-eminently[3] the time to speak the truth, the whole truth, frankly and boldly. Nor need we shrink from honestly facing conditions in our country today. This great Nation will endure, as it has endured, will revive and will prosper.

So, first of all, let me assert my firm belief that the only thing we have to fear is fear itself—nameless, unreasoning, unjustified terror which paralyzes needed efforts to convert retreat into advance.

In every dark hour of our national life, a leadership of frankness and of vigor has met with that understanding and support of the people themselves which is essential to victory. And I am convinced that you will again give that support to leadership in these critical days. In such a spirit on my part and on yours we face our common difficulties. They concern, thank God, only material things.

Happiness lies not in the mere possession of money; it lies in the joy of achievement, in the thrill of creative effort. The joy, the moral stimulation of work no longer must be forgotten in the mad chase of evanescent[4] profits. These dark days, my friends, will be worth all they cost us if they teach us that our true destiny is not to be ministered unto but to minister to ourselves, to our fellow men. →

31
我們唯一要害怕的，是恐懼本身

　　今天是國家授任典禮的日子，我相信在這一天，全國同胞們一定期待我能在總統就職典禮上，針對國家當前的局勢所需，做一個坦誠而明確的報告。這也的確是一個據實以告的最佳時機，我們不需要畏縮，我們可以坦然面對我們國家目前的情勢。這個偉大的國家一向經得起考驗，它會繼續存在下去，並且復甦、繁榮起來。

　　所以，首先容我先申明我的堅定信念：我們唯一要害怕的，就是恐懼本身——這意思是説，毫無理由、莫名其妙的恐懼，會阻礙我們從逆境中振作起來、繼續往前走。

　　在我們國家所經歷過的每一個黑暗時刻裡，一個坦誠、有魄力的領導人，都能獲得人民的體諒與支持，而這就是勝利的主要原因。我相信，在現在這個危急的時刻裡，你們也同樣會給予支持。不論是我個人還是你們各位，我們都要以這種精神來面對大家共同的困境。感謝上帝，我們面臨的還只是物質上的問題。

　　幸福，並不單單建立在金錢上。幸福也來自成就所帶來的喜悦，來自努力創造時所帶來的興奮感。我們不應該忘記工作本身所帶來的喜悦和鼓舞，而瘋狂地去追逐一時的利益。如果我們在這當中能夠學習到，我們真正的天命不是接受幫助，而是去幫助自己和同胞，那我們在這些黑暗日子裡所付出的代價都算是值得的了。

1. consecration [ˌkɑːnsɪˈkreɪʃən] (n.) the ceremony in which somebody or something is consecrated 授任儀式
2. candor [ˈkændər] (n.) the quality of being honest and telling the truth, even when the truth may be unpleasant or embarrassing 坦率；真誠
3. pre-eminently [ˌprɪˈemɪnəntli] (adv.) mainly, or to a very great degree 傑出地
4. evanescent [ˌevəˈnesənt] (a.) tending to vanish like vapor 逐漸消失的

67

Recognition of that falsity of material wealth as the standard of success goes hand in hand with the abandonment of the false belief that public office and high political position are to be valued only by the standards of pride of place and personal profit; and there must be an end to a conduct in banking and in business which too often has given to a sacred trust the likeness of callous[5] and selfish wrongdoing. Small wonder that confidence languishes[6], for it thrives only on honesty, on honor, on the sacredness of obligations, on faithful protection, and on unselfish performance; without them it cannot live. ◖

　　一旦體認到「用財富來衡量成功」是一種錯誤的觀念，自然也就不會用名和利來衡量官員。還有，銀行和企業常濫用神聖的委託信任，使之變成無情自私的錯誤行為，我們也必須遏阻這種惡風。這也難怪信心在崩盤，因為唯有誠實、信譽、恪盡義務、忠心維護和無私的行為，才能鼓舞信心，一旦少了這些，信心就不可能存在。

5. callous ['kæləs] (a.) unkind or cruel; without sympathy or feeling for other people 麻木不仁的
6. languish ['læŋgwɪʃ] (v.) to decline steadily, becoming less vital, strong, or successful 萎靡

John F. Kennedy:
Inaugural Address

甘迺迪就職演說：
火炬已經傳給新一代的美國人

美國第 35 任總統約翰・甘迺迪（慣稱 JFK）出身顯赫的甘迺迪政治家族，他是美國歷任總統中口才最好的一位，被視為新自由主義的代表。他在 1960 年的總統大選中，以些微的差距打贏尼克森，成為美國最年輕的總統之一，也是美國歷史上唯一信奉羅馬天主教的總統。

JFK 的任期從 1961 年 1 月 20 日開始，但在 1963 年 11 月 22 日於達拉斯遇刺身亡。在這兩年多的時間裡，他處理了一系列重大的危機事件，包括越南戰爭（1959–1975）、柏林圍牆的建立（1961）、古巴導彈危機（1962）、近代美國的民權運動（1955–1968）等等，並且和前蘇聯簽署了《核禁試條約》，緩和美蘇兩國的冷戰對峙。

當時候也是美蘇兩國太空競賽的巔峰時刻，美國的太空發展在 JFK 的任內獲得重大突破。成立於 1962 年 7 月的美國太空船發射操作中心，在 JFK 遇刺後將其更名為甘迺迪太空中心（Kennedy Space Center），以茲紀念。

JFK 在就職演説中，特別關注國際事務，並呼籲美國民眾承擔更多的義務。他疾呼全人類團結起來，共同反對極權、貧窮、疾病和戰爭，他在演說中最著名的一句話就是：

Ask not what your country can do for you;
ask what you can do for your country.
不要問你的國家能為你做些什麼，
而是要問你能為你的國家做些什麼。

President John F. Kennedy during his inauguration

Speaker 美國第 35 屆總統甘迺迪
（John Fitzgerald Kennedy, 1917–1963.11.22）

Time 1961 年 1 月 20 日

Place 美國華盛頓特區（Washington, D.C.）

▣ 原音重現　▣ 擷錄

68

We observe today not a victory of party, but a celebration of freedom—symbolizing an end, as well as a beginning—signifying renewal, as well as change. For I have sworn before you and Almighty God the same solemn oath our forebears prescribed nearly a century and three quarters ago.

The world is very different now. For man holds in his mortal hands the power to abolish all forms of human poverty and all forms of human life. And yet the same revolutionary beliefs for which our forebears fought are still at issue around the globe—the belief that the rights of man come not from the generosity of the state, but from the hand of God.

We dare not forget today that we are the heirs of that first revolution. Let the word go forth from this time and place, to friend and foe alike, that the torch has been passed to a new generation of Americans—born in this century, tempered by war, disciplined by a hard and bitter peace, proud of our ancient heritage, and unwilling to witness or permit the slow undoing of those human rights to which this nation has always been committed, and to which we are committed today at home and around the world.

Let every nation know, whether it wishes us well or ill, that we shall pay any price, bear any burden, meet any hardship, support any friend, oppose any foe, to assure the survival and the success of liberty.

Finally, to those nations who would make themselves our adversary, we offer not a pledge but a request: that both sides begin anew the quest for peace, before the dark powers of destruction unleashed[1] by science engulf[2] all humanity in planned or accidental self-destruction.

We dare not tempt them with weakness. For only when our arms are sufficient beyond doubt can we be certain beyond doubt that they will never be employed.

So let us begin anew—remembering on both sides that civility is not a sign of weakness, and sincerity is always subject to proof. Let us never negotiate out of fear, but let us never fear to negotiate.

Let both sides explore what problems unite us instead of belaboring[3] those problems which divide us. →

32

火炬已經傳給新一代的美國人

我們今天慶祝的，並不是一次政黨的勝利，而是一次自由的饗宴——它象徵著結束，也象徵著開始——它意味著復興，也意味著變革，因為我在你們和全能的上帝面前做出莊嚴的宣誓，那是我們祖先在一百七十多前所擬定的宣誓。

今日世界的面貌已經有很大的不同，我們人類的雙手，同時具有可以消除一切貧困，和足以毀滅一切生命的兩種力量。當初我們前人的革命信念，世界至今仍在議論中——這個信念是，人民的權利不是由政府所慷慨給予的，而是上帝本來就賦予給人類的。

至今，我們不敢忘記我們就是那一次革命的傳人。讓我們的朋友和敵人都聽見我在此時此地所講的話，那就是：火炬已經傳給新一代的美國人——我們出生在這個世紀，經歷過戰爭的洗禮，接受嚴酷、艱難的和平所調教，我們以前人留下的傳統為傲，我們不願看到，也不容許人權被踐踏。人權一向是我們這個國家所堅守的，當前在國內或是在全世界，我們都是力加維護的。

不論是友國還是敵國，我們要讓每一個國家都知道，為了確保自由的存在與實現，我們將不惜任何代價，願意背負任何的重擔，不畏任何艱辛，支援任何一個朋友，並與任何一個敵人抗戰到底。

最後，對於那些與我們敵對的國家，我們要提出的不是保證，而是要求：在科學釋放出可怕的毀滅力量，將全人類都捲入或是意外造成人類毀滅之前，我們雙方應該重新開始尋求和平。

我們不能示弱，以免對方蠢蠢欲動。我們唯有毫無疑問地擁有足夠的武力，我們才能毫無疑問地確保不會動用到武力。

因此讓我們重新開始——我們雙方都應該記住，客氣並不代表軟弱，而且誠意是要不斷地用行動展現出來。我們談判，從來不是出自於恐懼，而且我們也從來不害怕談判。

我們要探究的，是那些能讓我們雙方團結起來的問題，而不要耗費心神在那些讓彼此分化的問題上。

1. unleash [ʌnˈliːʃ] (v.) to release suddenly a strong, uncontrollable and usually destructive force 釋放；鬆開

2. engulf [ɪnˈgʌlf] (v.) to flow over or cover completely 吞沒；捲入

3. belabor [bɪˈleɪbər] (v.) to keep emphasizing a fact or idea in a way that is annoying 做過度的說明

69

All this will not be finished in the first one hundred days. Nor will it be finished in the first one thousand days; nor in the life of this Administration; nor even perhaps in our lifetime on this planet. But let us begin.

In your hands, my fellow citizens, more than mine, will rest the final success or failure of our course. Since this country was founded, each generation of Americans has been summoned to give testimony to its national loyalty. The graves of young Americans who answered the call to service surround the globe.

Now the trumpet summons us again—not as a call to bear arms, though arms we need—not as a call to battle, though embattled we are—but a call to bear the burden of a long twilight struggle, year in and year out, "rejoicing in hope; patient in tribulation,[4]" a struggle against the common enemies of man: tyranny, poverty, disease, and war itself.

Can we forge[5] against these enemies a grand and global alliance, North and South, East and West, that can assure a more fruitful life for all mankind? Will you join in that historic effort? →

　　所有的這一切，不會在百日內就達到，也不會在一千個日子裡就完成；在我的這個任期內，甚至在我們的有生之年裡，這一切也不會完成。然而，我們就動手開始吧！

　　同胞們，我們大業最終的成敗，不是掌握在我的手裡，而是掌握在你們大家的手中。這個國家自從開國以來，每一代的美國人都曾被召喚去展現他們對國家的忠誠。受到此召喚而從軍的年輕美國之子，他們的墳墓遍布全世界。

　　如今召喚的號角聲再度響起──雖然我們需要軍力，但這一次要號召的不是從軍──雖然我們嚴陣以待，但這一次要號召的也不是出征──我們這一次要號召的，是要肩負起迎接黎明來臨之前的漫長奮鬥，這是年復一年的奮鬥，我們「在指望中要喜樂，在患難中要忍耐」，這是一場對付人類公敵的奮鬥，它們是：暴政、貧窮、疾病，以及戰爭本身。

　　為了對付這些人類的公敵，全世界能否不分東南西北，結合成一個全球性的大聯盟，以確保全人類都能擁有一個更富裕的生活？你們是否願意加入這一場深具歷史性的奮鬥？

4. An extract from *Romans* 12:12. 出自《聖經‧羅馬書》第 12 章第 12 節：
「在指望中要喜樂，在患難中要忍耐。」

5. forge [fɔːrdʒ] (v.) to make or produce, especially with some difficulty
形成；製成；鍛造；打（鐵）

In the long history of the world, only a few generations have been granted the role of defending freedom in its hour of maximum danger. I do not shrink from this responsibility—I welcome it. I do not believe that any of us would exchange places with any other people or any other generation. The energy, the faith, the devotion which we bring to this endeavor will light our country and all who serve it. And the glow from that fire can truly light the world.

And so, my fellow Americans, ask not what your country can do for you; ask what you can do for your country.

My fellow citizens of the world, ask not what America will do for you, but what together we can do for the freedom of man.

Finally, whether you are citizens of America or citizens of the world, ask of us here the same high standards of strength and sacrifice which we ask of you. With a good conscience our only sure reward, with history the final judge of our deeds, let us go forth to lead the land we love, asking His blessing and His help, but knowing that here on earth God's work must truly be our own.

　　在漫長的世界歷史中，只有少數幾個世代的人們在自由岌岌可危的時刻裡，被賦予捍衛自由的任務。我決不會推諉這個責任——我毅然扛起這個責任。我不認為我們有誰會為了逃避，而寧可與別人交換角色，或是生在別的時代裡。我們為這場奮鬥所奉獻出的精力、信念和忠誠，將會照亮我們的國家，照亮所有為國服務的人民，而從這一火焰所發出的光芒，也必定會照亮全世界。

　　所以，同胞們，不要問國家能為你做什麼，而是要問你能為國家做什麼。

　　世界的公民們，不要問美國能為你做什麼，而是要問我們能一齊為人類的自由做出什麼貢獻。

　　最後，不論你是美國公民還是世界公民，讓我們在這裡對彼此做出相同的要求，一起努力奉獻出同等的力量，做出同等的犧牲。我們唯一能確定獲得的報酬，是求仁得仁。我們的行為，會由歷史來蓋棺論定。讓我們向前邁進，引領著我們深愛的國家，祈求上帝的賜福與幫助。我們知道，在這個塵世上，上帝的任務，就是我們必須自己肩負起來的工作。

We Shall Overcome

詹森總統：
我們終將克服難關

在美國，黑人要想爭取平權，首先必須獲得投票的平等權，然而 1964 年通過的《民權法案》（Civil Rights Act）並未達到此一目的。1964 年秋天，美國第三十六任總統詹森下令開始進行《投票權法案》（Voting Rights Act），並要求國會在隔年 1 月提出實施辦法，但國會予以拖延。

於是 1965 年 3 月，阿拉巴馬州的塞爾馬鎮（Selma）發生了黑人的遊行示威活動，並引發員警攻擊民眾的事件。此一事件在電視媒體上公開播放，立刻掀起全美的反彈，在四十八小時內，美國有八十幾座城市舉行了示威抗議，數以千計的宗教和民權領袖飛往塞爾馬鎮，其中包括美國黑人人權運動的精神領袖馬丁‧路德‧金恩。

就在這樣的危機之中，詹森總統在電視轉播的參眾兩院聯席會議中，面對全美民眾和參議員、眾議員發表了這場極獲佳評的演說。這場演講撼動人心，深具說服力，並且示範了總統帶領人走向民主與道德的典範。最後，在同年的 8 月 5 日，國會通過了《投票權法案》。

在這場演說中，詹森總統引用了《我們終將克服難關》（We Shall Overcome）這首歌的片段，這無異於是認同了黑人示威活動的合法性。這首歌原由黑人牧師丁德理（Charles Albert Tindley, 1851–1933）所創作，原名為《I'll Overcome Someday》。這首歌在六〇年代被選為美國民權運動主題歌，歌名並被更改為「We Shall Overcome」。

1963 年 8 月，在金恩博士領導眾人邁向華府之時，民歌手瓊‧拜雅（Joan Baez）曾於林肯紀念堂演唱過這首歌，而金恩博士也就是在這個時候發表了《我有一個夢想》這場著名的演講。此後，《我們終將克服難關》成為了民權運動的國歌，在全球各地的民權運動中廣被傳唱，下面是其歌詞。

Speaker	美國第三十六任總統詹森（Lyndon Baines Johnson, 1908–1973）
Time	1965 年 3 月 15 日
Place	美國華盛頓特區（Washington, D.C.）

☑ 原音重現　☑ 擷錄

Lyndon Baines Johnson, 1908–1973

We Shall Overcome ♫

We shall overcome, *	我們終將克服難關，
We shall overcome, some day.	我們終將克服難關，終有一天！
Oh, deep in my heart,	哦，在我內心深處，
I do believe	我堅信
We shall overcome, some day.	我們終將克服難關，終有一天！
We'll walk hand in hand, *	我們將會手牽著手站在一起，
We'll walk hand in hand, some day.	我們將會手牽著手站在一起，終有一天！
Oh, deep in my heart,	哦，在我內心深處，
We shall live in peace, *	我們將生活在和平之中，
We shall live in peace, some day.	我們將生活在和平之中，終有一天！
Oh, deep in my heart,	哦，在我內心深處，
We shall all be free, *	我們終將獲得自由，
We shall all be free, some day.	我們終將獲得自由，終有一天！
Oh, deep in my heart,	哦，在我內心深處，
We are not afraid, *	我們沒有恐懼，
We are not afraid, TODAY.	今天，我們沒有恐懼！
Oh, deep in my heart,	哦，在我內心深處，
We shall overcome, *	我們終將克服難關，
We shall overcome, some day.	我們終將克服難關，終有一天！
Oh, deep in my heart,	哦，在我內心深處，
I do believe	我堅信
We shall overcome, some day.	我們終將克服難關，終有一天！

* repeat two times

Our mission is at once the oldest and the most basic of this country: to right wrong, to do justice, to serve man.

In our time we have come to live with the moments of great crisis. Our lives have been marked with debate about great issues—issues of war and peace, issues of prosperity and depression. But rarely in any time does an issue lay bare the secret heart of America itself. Rarely are we met with a challenge, not to our growth or abundance, or our welfare or our security, but rather to the values, and the purposes, and the meaning of our beloved nation.

The issue of equal rights for American Negroes is such an issue.

And should we defeat every enemy, and should we double our wealth and conquer the stars, and still be unequal to this issue, then we will have failed as a people and as a nation. For with a country as with a person, "What is a man profited, if he shall gain the whole world, and lose his own soul?"[1]

There is no Negro problem. There is no Southern problem. There is no Northern problem. There is only an American problem. And we are met here tonight as Americans—not as Democrats or Republicans. We are met here as Americans to solve that problem.

This was the first nation in the history of the world to be founded with a purpose. The great phrases of that purpose still sound in every American heart, North and South: "All men are created equal," "government by consent of the governed," "give me liberty or give me death." Well, those are not just clever words, or those are not just empty theories. In their name Americans have fought and died for two centuries, and tonight around the world they stand there as guardians of our liberty, risking their lives.

Those words are a promise to every citizen that he shall share in the dignity of man. This dignity cannot be found in a man's possessions; it cannot be found in his power, or in his position. It really rests on his right to be treated as a man equal in opportunity to all others. It says that he shall share in freedom, he shall choose his leaders, educate his children, provide for his family according to his ability and his merits as a human being. →

我們當務之急要做的事，正是這個國家最基本的任務：糾正錯誤的事情、行使正義，以及服務人民。

我們這個時代經歷了許多重大的危機時刻，我們生活中常見各種重大議題的爭論——戰爭與和平的議題，繁榮與蕭條的議題，然而我們卻一直很少觸及能將美國內心祕密透露出來的議題。我們鮮少遭受挑戰，我指的不是成長與繁榮的挑戰，也不是福利與安全的挑戰，而是指我們所愛的這個國家，它的價值、目的和意義到底為何。

而美國黑人的平權問題，正凸顯出這樣一種議題。

假設我們戰勝了所有的敵人，民富國強，而且還征服了外太空，但我們卻仍然無法解決這個問題的話，那我們仍然是一個失敗的民族、一個失敗的國家。因為，不管是對國家還是對個人來說，「即使得到了全世界，卻失去了靈魂，何益之有？」

我們並沒有黑人的問題，也沒有南方的問題，也沒有北方的問題，而只有一個美國的問題。今晚，我們是以美國人的身分聚集在這裡，而不是以民主黨或共產黨的身分來到這裡。我們以美國人的身分來到這裡，就是為了決解這個問題。

在世界史上，我們是第一個以這樣一種目標而立國的國家，不管是在南方還是在北方，這個目標的偉大詞句仍在每一個美國人的心中迴盪著：「人人生而平等」，「政府是由人民所授權的」，「不自由，毋寧死」。這些不只是口頭上的標語，也不是空泛的理論，為了這些理想，美國人已經奮戰了兩百年，並為之犧牲性命。像今晚，在全世界都有美國人冒著性命的危險來捍衛我們的自由。

這些話是對每一位人民所做的承諾，讓大家都能擁有人類的尊嚴。這種尊嚴不是來自所擁有的財產，也不是來自權勢或地位，這種尊嚴是得自於平等權，人人都具有均等的機會。也就是說，享有同等的自由，具有選舉的權利，子女有平等的受教育權利，自己也有平等的機會，可以依照自己個人的能力與特長來養家活口。

1. An extract form *Matthew* 16:26. "For what is a man profited, if he shall gain the whole world, and lose his own soul? Or what shall a man give in exchange for his soul?"
出自《聖經‧馬太福音》第 16 章第 26 節

73

But even if we pass this bill[2], the battle will not be over. What happened in Selma[3] is part of a far larger movement which reaches into every section and State of America. It is the effort of American Negroes to secure for themselves the full blessings of American life. Their cause must be our cause too. Because it's not just Negroes, but really it's all of us, who must overcome the crippling legacy of bigotry[4] and injustice.

And we shall overcome.

As a man whose roots go deeply into Southern soil, I know how agonizing racial feelings are. I know how difficult it is to reshape the attitudes and the structure of our society. But a century has passed, more than a hundred years since the Negro was freed. And he is not fully free tonight.

It was more than a hundred years ago that Abraham Lincoln, a great President of another party, signed the Emancipation Proclamation[5]; but emancipation is a proclamation, and not a fact. A century has passed, more than a hundred years, since equality was promised. And yet the Negro is not equal. A century has passed since the day of promise. And the promise is un-kept.

The time of justice has now come. I tell you that I believe sincerely that no force can hold it back. It is right in the eyes of man and God that it should come. And when it does, I think that day will brighten the lives of every American. For Negroes are not the only victims. How many white children have gone uneducated? How many white families have lived in stark[6] poverty? How many white lives have been scarred by fear, because we've wasted our energy and our substance to maintain the barriers of hatred and terror?

And so I say to all of you here, and to all in the nation tonight, that those who appeal to you to hold on to the past do so at the cost of denying you your future.

This great, rich, restless country can offer opportunity and education and hope to all, all black and white, all North and South, sharecropper[7] and city dweller.

These are the enemies: poverty, ignorance, disease. They're our enemies, not our fellow man, not our neighbor. And these enemies too—poverty, disease, and ignorance: we shall overcome. ◖

即使我們通過了法案，這場奮鬥也還不會結束。今天發生在塞爾馬鎮的事件只是冰山一角，這場運動遍及了美國的每一個角落。這些美國黑人所做的努力，是為了保障自己能擁有一個真正美國人的生活。他們的理想，也應該是我們的理想。這不只是黑人的問題，也是我們所有人的切身問題，我們都必須去除這種偏狹、不公不義的遺毒。

而我們終將克服難關。

我是一個在南方長大的人，我很清楚種族情緒是如何的折磨人。我也很明白，要改變社會結構與人們的態度，會是如何的困難。都已經過了一個世紀，黑奴的解放都已經超過一百年了，但一直到今晚，黑人還是沒有獲得完全的自由。

代表共和黨的偉大的林肯總統，他簽署的《解放奴隸宣言》都已經有一百多年之久了，但時至今日，解放奴隸仍然只是一個宣言，而不是一個事實。一個世紀的時間都過去了，當初所承諾的平等權，至今整整超過一百年了，但黑人卻仍然沒有平等權。都已經過了一百年了，這個承諾都還沒有兌現。

如今，正義來臨的時刻到了。我要說，我認為這是勢不可擋的趨勢。就人類或就上帝來看，這都是必將來臨的正義之事。正義來臨的那一天，將會照亮每一位美國人的生活，因為蒙受傷害的並不只是黑人而已。我們有多少白人的小孩失學？我們有多少白人家庭為赤貧的生活所苦？我們有多少白人遭受恐懼的折磨，只因為我們把精神和資源拿來加強仇恨與恐怖的對立城池？

所以，今晚我要在這裡告訴大家，告訴全國的同胞們，如果我們緊緊抓住過去不放，那我們就是在犧牲我們的未來。

這個偉大、富裕、永遠不會停下腳步的國家，能夠給予所有人同樣的機會、教育和希望，包括所有的黑人和白人，所有的北方人和南方人，以及所有的農民和城市居民。

我們真正的敵人是貧窮、文盲和疾病。這些才是我們的敵人，而不是我們的親朋好友。貧窮、文盲和疾病，也是我們終將要征服的敵人。

2. bill (n.) a formal statement of a planned new law that is discussed before being voted on 法案

3. Selma: a town in central Alabama on the Alabama River; in 1965 it was the center of a drive to register Black voters 阿拉巴馬州的塞爾馬鎮

4. bigotry [ˈbɪɡətri] (n.) a person who has strong, unreasonable beliefs and who thinks that anyone who does not have the same beliefs is wrong 偏執的心態

5. Emancipation Proclamation: a declaration of freedom for enslaved people in Confederacy 美國《解放奴隸宣言》

6. stark [stɑːrk] (a.) empty, simple, or obvious 完全的；明顯的

7. sharecropper [ˈʃɛrkrɔːpər] (n.) small farmers and tenants 小佃農

Duty, Honor, Country

**General Douglas MacArthur's
Farewell Speech**

麥帥西點軍校告別演說：
責任、榮耀和國家

麥克阿瑟將軍出生於阿肯色州的軍人世家，他的父親曾因參加南北戰爭而獲頒國會勳章。1898 年，他考取西點軍校，並以百年來最佳的優異成績畢業。麥帥縱橫沙場有半世紀之久，戰功彪炳，獲頒美國最高的軍事榮銜「榮譽勳章」（Medal of Honor）。

1919 年，他被任命為西點軍校校長，成為西點軍校最年輕的校長，後於 1937 年退役。1941 年，第二次世界大戰爆發，他被徵召擔任遠東軍總司令。1944 年，升為五星上將。戰後 1945–1951 年間，擔任盟軍總司令，負責日本的重建工作。

1950 年 6 月 25 日，北韓領導人金日成進攻南韓，6 月 27 日杜魯門總統下令美軍參戰。10 月 15 日，杜魯門總統指示他只能打一場有限的戰爭，麥克阿瑟公開反對指示。1951 年 4 月 11 日，杜魯門以「未能全力支持美國和聯合國的政策」為由，將之撤職。

麥克阿瑟回到美國後，在華盛頓受到了萬人空巷的英雄式歡迎。1951 年 4 月 19 日，麥克阿瑟在國會大廈發表了著名的《老兵不死》的告別演說。

1962 年，麥克阿瑟最後一次回到西點軍校，並接受校方頒贈的勳章和獎狀。在閱兵慶典後，麥克阿瑟以西點軍校校訓為題──責任、榮譽、國家──發表了這篇著名的演講。

Speaker 美國名將麥克阿瑟將軍
（Douglas MacArthur, 1880–1964）

Time 1962 年 5 月 12 日

Place 美國紐約州西點軍校（West Point, New York）

▣ 原音重現　▣ 擷錄

74

Duty, Honor, Country: Those three hallowed words reverently dictate what you ought to be, what you can be, what you will be. They are your rallying points: to build courage when courage seems to fail; to regain faith when there seems to be little cause for faith; to create hope when hope becomes forlorn[1]. Unhappily, I possess neither that eloquence of diction, that poetry of imagination, nor that brilliance of metaphor[2] to tell you all that they mean.

The unbelievers will say they are but words, but a slogan, but a flamboyant[3] phrase. Every pedant[4], every demagogue[5], every cynic[6], every hypocrite, every troublemaker, and, I am sorry to say, some others of an entirely different character, will try to downgrade them even to the extent of mockery and ridicule.

But these are some of the things they do. They build your basic character. They mold you for your future roles as the custodians[7] of the nation's defense. They make you strong enough to know when you are weak, and brave enough to face yourself when you are afraid.

They teach you to be proud and unbending in honest failure, but humble and gentle in success; not to substitute words for action; not to seek the path of comfort, but to face the stress and spur of difficulty and challenge; to learn to stand up in the storm, but to have compassion on those who fall; to master yourself before you seek to master others; to have a heart that is clean, a goal that is high; to learn to laugh, yet never forget how to weep; to reach into the future, yet never neglect the past; to be serious, yet never take yourself too seriously; to be modest so that you will remember the simplicity of true greatness; the open mind of true wisdom, the meekness of true strength.

They give you a temperate will, a quality of imagination, a vigor of the emotions, a freshness of the deep springs of life, a temperamental predominance of courage over timidity, an appetite for adventure over love of ease.

They create in your heart the sense of wonder, the unfailing hope of what next, and the joy and inspiration of life. They teach you in this way to be an officer and a gentleman. ◀

「責任」、「榮譽」、「國家」——這三個神聖的字眼，虔敬地告誡著你們要成為什麼、能成為什麼，以及將會成為什麼。這也是可以用來激勵士氣的中心思想，在你眼看快要失去勇氣、信念和希望時，可以重新給予你勇氣、信念和希望。只可惜我沒有雄辯的口才和詩人的想像力，也不懂得如何透過精彩的比喻，來向各位闡述其完整的意義。

不相信的人會說，這不過是幾個字，只不過是一種口號，一種浮誇的空話罷了。一個迂腐的人，一個蠱惑人心的人，一個喜歡唱衰的人，一個假惺惺的人，一個唯恐天下不亂的好事分子，抱歉我還要加入一些性格迥然不同的人士，他們只會貶低這些字眼，甚至冷諷熱嘲。

但實則這幾個字眼能做到以下幾件事：它們會塑造你的基本人格，培養你日後能為這個國家擔任守護的工作。它們能讓你強壯到知道自己何時會感到軟弱，讓你勇敢到能夠在你感到害怕時去面對自己。

它們能教導你在面對光榮的失敗時，仍擁有尊嚴，不屈不撓；在面對成功時，能謙卑溫和；讓你付諸行動而不空談，不求得過且過，勇於面對困難和挑戰所帶來的壓力與鞭策；學習在暴風雨中屹立，能對失敗者懷有同理心；在你想帶領別人之前，你會先管好自己；讓自己思想單純，目標崇高；學習談笑以對，但從不會忘記如何哭泣；讓自己迎向未來，但不會忘記過去；態度認真，但不會過於嚴肅；保持虛心，這樣才能記得真正的偉大是如何的單純；具有真正的智慧，能敞開心胸；具有真正的力量，懂得順從。

它們能讓你懂得心平氣和，擁有良好的創造力，能讓你充滿熱情與活力，給予你一個源源不斷的生命源泉，並且能讓你培養出一個可以超越怯懦的勇敢性格，讓你寧願冒險犯難，也不願安於閒逸的生活。

它們能讓你心中產生驚奇的感受，永遠充滿好奇心，充滿生命的喜悅與感受。它們就是透過這樣的一個過程，把你調教成一個軍官、一個紳士。

---

1. forlorn [fərˈlɔːrn] (a.) sad and lonely because of isolation or desertion 幾乎無望的

2. metaphor [ˈmetəfɔːr] (n.) an implied comparison 隱喻；象徵

3. flamboyant [flæmˈbɔɪənt] (a.) behaving in a confident or exciting way that makes people notice you 浮誇的

4. pedant [ˈpednt] (n.) a person who is too interested in formal rules and small details that are not important 學究；迂腐的人

5. demagogue [ˈdeməgɑːg] (n.) an orator who appeals to the passions and prejudices of his audience 煽動者

6. cynic [ˈsɪnɪk] (n.) someone who is critical of the motives of others 犬儒

7. custodian [kʌˈstoʊdiən] (n.) one who has the care of something 守護者

Edward VIII: Farewell Address

只愛美人不愛江山：
愛德華八世退位宣言

英國國王愛德華八世，因為美人而放棄江山之後，換成了溫莎公爵（Duke of Windsor）這個頭銜。這篇演說便是他當時的退位宣言。

1930 年，愛德華八世認識了辛普森夫人（Wallis Simpson），因為這位婦女離過兩次婚，英國政府、民眾和教會都反對他們的婚事，因而爆發了憲政危機。最後，他選擇放棄王位，這也使他成為英國史上第一位自動退位的國王。

1936 年 1 月 20 日，英王喬治五世駕崩，愛德華八世繼任國王。然而在他登基 325 天後，他於同年 12 月 11 日宣布退位。在這篇演說裡，他以愛德華王子的名義，向不列顛和大英帝國的人民廣播，說明他退位的原因。

1937 年，被稱為「只愛美人、不愛江山」的溫莎公爵和辛普森夫人完成婚姻，女方獲得「溫莎公爵夫人」的頭銜。婚後，兩人一直旅居國外。

Speaker 英國愛德華八世，即後來的溫莎公爵
（Duke of Windsor, 1894–1972）

Time 1936 年 12 月 11 日

回 原音重現　回 全篇收錄

Prince Edward, Duke of Windsor (King Edward VIII)
By Solomon Joseph Solomon (1860–1927)

75

At long last I am able to say a few words of my own. I have never wanted to withhold anything, but until now it has not been constitutionally possible for me to speak.

A few hours ago I discharged my last duty as King and Emperor, and now that I have been succeeded by my brother, the Duke of York, my first words must be to declare my allegiance[1] to him. This I do with all my heart.

You all know the reasons which have impelled me to renounce the throne. But I want you to understand that in making up my mind I did not forget the country or the empire, which, as Prince of Wales and lately as King, I have for twenty-five years tried to serve.

But you must believe me when I tell you that I have found it impossible to carry the heavy burden of responsibility and to discharge my duties as King as I would wish to do without the help and support of the woman I love.

And I want you to know that the decision I have made has been mine and mine alone. This was a thing I had to judge entirely for myself. The other person most nearly concerned has tried up to the last to persuade me to take a different course.

I have made this, the most serious decision of my life, only upon the single thought of what would, in the end, be best for all.

This decision has been made less difficult to me by the sure knowledge that my brother, with his long training in the public affairs of this country and with his fine qualities, will be able to take my place forthwith[2] without interruption or injury to the life and progress of the empire. And he has one matchless blessing, enjoyed by so many of you, and not bestowed on me—a happy home with his wife and children. →

長久以來，我終於有機會能夠說說我心裡頭的話了。我向來就不想壓抑什麼，但一直到現在，在憲法上我才有這個機會可以說自己想說的話。

　　幾個小時以前，我卸下了國王和皇帝的最後職責，並且交由我的弟弟約克公爵來繼任。首先，我要宣誓效忠於他，忠誠地宣誓。

　　你們也都知道了我之所以放棄王位的原因。我希望你們能夠了解，這 25 年以來，我身為威爾斯王子，不久前繼任了國王，而當我在做出退位的決定時，我並不曾忘記這個國家和帝國。

　　但是，我要請你們相信的是，如果沒有我心愛的那位女子的幫助與支持，我是無法肩負起國家的重責大任、履行國王職責的。

　　還有，我希望你們能明白的是，這是我個人一個人所做出的決定，完全是我自己審度出的結果。與此事關係最密切的其他人，一直到最後還在勸我不要這樣做。

　　我只是想，要如何做才能在各方面達到最圓滿的結果，所以我就做出了這個我人生中最重大的決定。

　　當我確認了我弟弟足以立即接任國王時，我要做出退位的決定就不是那麼困難了。他長期以來就接受有關國家公共事務的磨練，並且擁有優秀的素質，國家的前景不會因為這件事而暫時停擺或是受到傷害。此外，他還擁有一種無與倫比的幸福——他和妻兒擁有一個美滿快樂的家庭——這也是你們許多人所擁有的幸福，但卻是我所沒有的。

1. allegiance [əˈliːdʒəns]
   (n.) the loyalty that
   citizens owe to their
   country 忠誠
2. forthwith [fɔːrθˈwɪð]
   (adv.) without delay or
   hesitation 立即

76

During these hard days I have been comforted by her majesty my mother and by my family. The ministers of the crown, and in particular, Mr. Baldwin, the Prime Minister, have always treated me with full consideration. There has never been any constitutional difference between me and them, and between me and Parliament. Bred in the constitutional tradition by my father, I should never have allowed any such issue to arise.

Ever since I was Prince of Wales, and later on when I occupied the throne, I have been treated with the greatest kindness by all classes of the people wherever I have lived or journeyed throughout the empire. For that I am very grateful.

I now quit altogether public affairs and I lay down my burden. It may be some time before I return to my native land, but I shall always follow the fortunes of the British race and empire with profound interest and if at any time in the future I can be found of service to his majesty in a private station, I shall not fail.

And now, we all have a new King. I wish him and you, his people, happiness and prosperity with all my heart. God bless you all! God save the King! ◖

35

愛德華八世退位宣言

the wedding portrait of
Duke of Windsor and Wallis Simpson (1937)

　　在這段煎熬的日子裡，我得到了母后和我家人們的安慰。王國的大臣們，尤其是首相鮑德溫先生，他一直非常地體諒我。我和大臣們或是和國會之間，在遵守憲法的問題上不曾產生過分歧。我的父親根據憲法傳統來教養我，所以我決不允許發生這種憲法上的問題。

　　從我當上威爾斯王子開始，後來又繼承了王位，期間不論我住在哪裡，我所到之處，都一直深受所有人民的愛戴。對於這一點，我深深感懷於心。

　　現在，我將完全退出公共事務，卸下職責。也許要好一段時間之後，我才會再回到我的國家故土，但對於英國人民和這個國家的未來，我永遠都會非常關心。將來不管任何時候，只要國王發現我能以個人的身分來貢獻些什麼，我將義不容辭。

　　現在，我們有了一個新的國王，我誠心祈願國王和人民都能夠安樂富庶。願上帝保佑你們大家！上帝保佑國王！

36

Appeal to American

甘地一生為印度的獨立而奮鬥，帶領國家脫離英國的殖民統治。聖雄（Mahatma），是印度詩人泰戈爾給予他的稱號，意思是「偉大的靈魂」。

甘地於 1888 年留學英國倫敦大學，修習法律。1893 年，甘地被一家印度公司派至南非，後來參與了南非的公民權利運動，並曾於 1913 年被捕。在南非的這段期間，甘地成了社會政治活動家，其不服從的「非暴力抵抗」也逐漸成形。

第一次世界大戰時，甘地返回印度。戰後，他參與國大黨的獨立運動，以不合作運動和絕食抗議等活動，受到國際關注。第二次世界大戰之後，甘地希望印度能夠獨立，成為一個完整的國家，但最後為了獨立，甘地接受讓印度與巴基斯坦分別獨立的方案，巴基斯坦於是成為一個獨立的穆斯林國家。

甘地的「非暴力」思想，影響後世極深，並成為許多民權鬥士的指導方針。像美國的金恩博士和南非的曼德拉，都受到甘地很大的啟發。

這篇演說是甘地在英國宣揚其政治理念時，透過英國電臺向美國所做的呼籲。

在 1937 年到 1948 年之間，甘地曾獲得過五次諾貝爾和平獎的提名，但始終沒有得名。多年以後，諾貝爾委員會曾對此公開表示過遺憾。在 20 世紀末時，《時代》雜誌曾評選 20 世紀的風雲人物，甘地名列前三名，其他兩名則分別是愛因斯坦和小羅斯福總統。

Speaker 印度聖雄甘地
（Mohandas Karamchand Gandhi, 1869–1948）

Time 1931 年 9 月 13 日

Place 英國電臺

◉ 錄音　◉ 擷錄

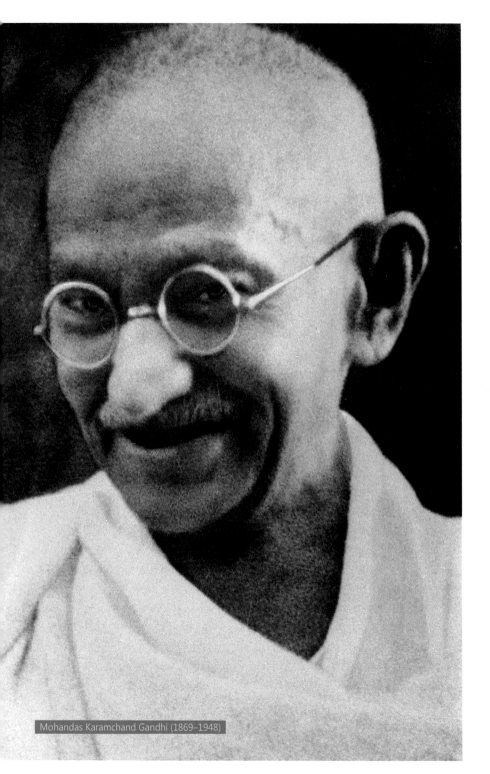
Mohandas Karamchand Gandhi (1869–1948)

In my opinion, the Indian struggle for freedom bears its consequence not only upon India and England but upon the whole world. It contains one-fifth of the human race. It represents one of the most ancient civilizations. It has traditions handed down from tens of thousands of years, some of which, to the astonishment of the world, remain intact[1]. No doubt the ravages[2] of time have affected the purity of that civilization as they have that of many other cultures and institutions[3].

If India is to revive the glory of her ancient past, she can only do so when she attains her freedom. The reason for the struggle having drawn the attention of the world I know does not lie in the fact that we Indians are fighting for our liberty, but in the fact the means adopted by us for attaining that liberty are unique and, as far as history shows us, have not been adopted by any other people of whom we have any record.

The means adopted are not violence, not bloodshed, not diplomacy as one understands it nowadays, but they are purely and simply truth and non-violence. No wonder that the attention of the world is directed toward this attempt to lead a successful bloodless revolution. Hitherto, nations have fought in the manner of the brute. They have wreaked[4] vengeance[5] upon those whom they have considered to be their enemies.

We find in searching national anthems adopted by great nations that they contain imprecations[6] upon the so-called enemy. They have vowed destruction and have not hesitated to take the name of God and seek divine assistance for the destruction of the enemy. We in India have endeavored to reverse the process. We feel that the law that governs brute creation is not the law that should guide the human race. That law is inconsistent with human dignity.

I, personally, would wait, if need be, for ages rather than seek to attain the freedom of my country through bloody means. I feel in the innermost of my heart, after a political extending, over an unbroken period of, close upon thirty-five years, that the world is sick unto death of blood spilling. The world is seeking a way out, and I flatter myself with the belief that perhaps it will be the privilege of the ancient land of India to show the way out to the hungering world. ◖

就我來看，印度為自由的奮鬥，其結果不只是影響印度和英國而已，也會影響到全世界。印度擁有全世界五分之一的人口，並且是全世界最古老的文明之一，其傳統延續了上萬年之久，有些至今仍保有最初的原貌，令世人驚嘆。當然，經過歲月的侵蝕，印度文明也和其他的文明或傳統一樣，失去了原初的風貌。

如果印度想要重振其過去的光榮，那首先就必須先獲得自由。印度的這一場奮鬥之所以受到世人的矚目，我知道並非是因為印度人在為自由而戰，而是因為我們爭取自由的方式是很獨特的，這是史上未見的，歷史上至今還沒有其他民族採取過這種方法。

我們採取的方法是非暴力的，是不流血的，也不是透過大家現在所熟知的外交途徑，而純粹是一種單純的理智與非暴力。難怪世人的眼光都等著在看這一場企圖不流血的革命能否成功。人類至今都是透過暴力的方式來進行革命，人們慣於對自己所認定的敵人施以報復。

查閱一些大國的國歌，我們可以發現，歌詞中都會含有對其敵人的詛咒，誓言毀滅對方，為了消滅敵人，會毫不猶豫地以上帝之名來祈求天助。在印度，我們現在採用了相反的方式。我們覺得，動物世界的野蠻法則不應該用來支配人類，這有悖於人類的尊嚴。

就我個人來説，如果有需要，我寧願長久靜靜等待下去，也不願意我的國家採用流血的方式來獲得自由。在我將近三十五年不間斷的政治生涯中，我深刻地感受到，人們對死亡流血是深惡痛絕的。人類在尋求一種新的方式，我深信，在這塊古老的印度大陸上，就有可能為這個渴望找到出路的世界，打開一條路。

1. intact [ɪnˈtækt] (a.) complete and in the original state 完整無缺的；原封不動的
2. ravage [ˈrævɪdʒ] (n.) the destruction, damaging, or plundering of something 荒蕪；蹂躪
3. institution [ˌɪnstɪˈtuːʃən] (n.) a custom that for a long time has been an important feature of some group or society 習俗
4. wreak [riːk] (v.) to do something unpleasant to someone to punish them for something they have done to you 施加（報復）
5. vengeance [ˈvɛndʒəns] (n.) punishment that is inflicted in return for a wrong 報復
6. imprecation [ˌɪmprɪˈkeɪʃən] (n.) a swear word 詛咒

I've Been to the Mountaintop

金恩博士最後的演講：
我已踏上山頂

馬丁・路德・金恩（Martin Luther King, 1929–1968.4.4）是美國史上最重要的黑人民權運動領袖，他的演講被喻為「充滿林肯和甘地精神的象徵，以及聖經的韻律」。1964 年，他獲得諾貝爾和平獎，世人常稱之為金恩博士或金恩牧師。

1968 年 4 月 4 日，金恩博士在支持田納西州孟菲斯市清潔工人的罷工活動中，被種族主義分子所暗殺，以下這篇是 4 月 3 日的演說，是金恩博士生前最後的演講。他在做這場演講的當時，已經預感到自己的命運，因為他收到了各種的死亡恐嚇。他在做完演講的隔天，便遭到暗殺。

〈我已踏上山頂〉（I've Been to the Mountaintop）這個演講題目，出自《聖經》以色列人出埃及的典故，摩西被上帝帶到山頂上，親眼目睹「應許之地」（Promised Land），但卻又被告知他無法抵達應許之地。金恩博士在演說中引用這個故事，表明自己可能到達不了應許之地，但人民終將到達。

2009 年，諾貝基金會評選出「諾貝爾獎百餘年來最受尊崇的三位獲獎者」，金恩博士名列首位，其餘兩人分別是 1921 年物理學獎得主愛因斯坦，以及 1979 年和平獎得主德蕾莎修女。

此篇演說中，金恩博士藉由好撒馬利亞人的比喻（Parable of the Good Samaritan：即「有一個人在路上遭遇強盜，受了傷。之後有三個人經過，其中兩個人不願多做停留，最後終於有一個人願意停下來幫助傷者。）來傳達此篇演講的重點：如果我不幫助這些清潔工人，他們會發生什麼事情？本書便擷取此一比喻作為開端。

Speaker　美國牧師兼黑人民權運動領袖馬丁・路德・金恩
　　　　　（Martin Luther King, 1929–1968.4.4）

Time　　　1968 年 4 月 3 日

Place　　　美國田納西州孟菲斯市梅森教堂（Mason Temple）
　　　　　（Church of God in Christ 基督神教會的總部）

▣ 原音重現　▣ 擷錄

Martin Luther King (1929–1968)

And so the first question that the priest asked—the first question that the Levite asked was, "If I stop to help this man, what will happen to me?"

But then the Good Samaritan[1] came by. And he reversed the question: "If I do not stop to help this man, what will happen to him?"

That's the question before you tonight. Not, "If I stop to help the sanitation[2] workers, what will happen to my job?" Not, "If I stop to help the sanitation workers what will happen to all of the hours that I usually spend in my office every day and every week as a pastor[3]?" The question is not, "If I stop to help this man in need, what will happen to me?"

The question is, "If I do not stop to help the sanitation workers, what will happen to them?" That's the question.

Let us rise up tonight with a greater readiness. Let us stand with a greater determination. And let us move on in these powerful days, these days of challenge to make America what it ought to be. We have an opportunity to make America a better nation. And I want to thank God, once more, for allowing me to be here with you.

You know, several years ago, I was in New York City autographing the first book that I had written. And while sitting there autographing books, a demented[4] black woman came up. The only question I heard from her was, "Are you Martin Luther King?"

And I was looking down writing, and I said, "Yes."

And the next minute I felt something beating on my chest. Before I knew it I had been stabbed by this demented woman.

I was rushed to Harlem Hospital. It was a dark Saturday afternoon. And that blade had gone through, and the X-rays revealed that the tip of the blade was on the edge of my aorta[5], the main artery[6]. And once that's punctured, your drowned in your own blood—that's the end of you. →

1. Good Samaritan: a person who voluntarily offers help or sympathy in times of trouble [the parable of the Good Samaritan (*Luke* 10:30–37), who helps a stranger beaten by robbers]
   好撒馬利亞人是基督教文化中一個著名的成語和口頭語，意為好心人、見義勇為者，出自《新約聖經・路加福音》（10:30–37）中耶穌基督講的故事：一個猶太人被強盜打劫，受了重傷，躺在路邊。先後有一位祭司和一位利未人路過，但他們不聞不問，惟有一個撒瑪利亞人路過，動了慈心照顧他。

那位祭司和那位利未人，他們第一個問的問題是：「如果我停下來幫助這個人，我會有什麼好處？」

然而，接下來經過的撒馬利亞人，他反過來問：「如果我沒有停下來幫助他，那他會發生什麼事？」

這也就是我們今晚所面對的問題，問題不在於「如果我停下來幫助這些清潔工人，我的工作會怎麼樣？」問題也不在於「如果我停下來幫助他們，我每天每週在教堂裡擔任牧師工作時，會怎麼樣？」問題更不在於「如果我停下來幫助了這個需要幫助的人，我會怎麼樣？」

真正的問題在於「如果我不停下來幫助這些清潔工人，他們會怎麼樣？」這才是問題的癥結。

就是今晚，讓我們為抗爭做好準備，讓我們以莫大的決心堅定我們的立場，趁現在這種關鍵的時刻繼續往前邁進，這是讓美國成為「真正的美國」的時刻。現在我們有這個機會把美國變成一個更好的國家。我要感謝上帝，讓我又能在這裡跟你們站在一起。

誠如你們所知，多年前我在紐約舉辦我第一本新書的簽名會。當時，我正坐在那裡簽名的時候，來了一名精神錯亂的黑人婦女，我聽見她問我說：「你是馬丁・路德・金恩嗎？」

我一邊埋著頭簽名，一邊回答她說：「是的。」

結果在下一刻，我就感到有東西往我的胸口搥打下去。在我還來不及反應，那個精神錯亂的婦女已經把刀刺進我的胸口了。

我被緊急送往哈林醫院，那是在一個陰暗的星期六下午。刀子刺進了我的胸部，根據 X 光顯示，刀尖就刺在主大動脈的旁邊。要是刺到了主大動脈，我就會被自己的鮮血給淹沒，一命嗚呼了。

---

2. sanitation [ˌsænɪˈteɪʃən] (n.) the protection of public health by removing and treating waste, dirty water etc. 公共衛生

3. pastor [ˈpæstər] (n.) a leader of a Christian group or church, especially one which is Protestant 基督教的本堂牧師

4. demented [dɪˈmɛntɪd] (a.) affected with madness or insanity 精神錯亂狀態的

5. aorta [eɪˈɔːrtə] (n.) the main artery leaving heart 主動脈

6. artery [ˈɑːrtəri] (n.) one of the tubes that carries blood from your heart to the rest of your body 動脈

79

It came out in the *New York Times* the next morning, that if I had merely sneezed, I would have died. Well, about four days later, they allowed me, after the operation, after my chest had been opened, and the blade had been taken out, to move around in the wheel chair in the hospital.

They allowed me to read some of the mail that came in, and from all over the states and the world, kind letters came in. I read a few, but one of them I will never forget.

I had received one from the President and the Vice-President. I've forgotten what those telegrams said. I'd received a visit and a letter from the Governor of New York, but I've forgotten what that letter said. But there was another letter that came from a little girl, a young girl who was a student at the White Plains High School. And I looked at that letter, and I'll never forget it. It said simply, "Dear Dr. King, I am a ninth-grade student at the White Plains High School." And she said,

While it should not matter, I would like to mention that I'm a white girl. I read in the paper of your misfortune, and of your suffering. And I read that if you had sneezed, you would have died. And I'm simply writing you to say that I'm so happy that you didn't sneeze.

And I want to say tonight—I want to say tonight that I too am happy that I didn't sneeze. Because if I had sneezed, I wouldn't have been around here in 1960, when students all over the South started sitting-in[7] at lunch counters. And I knew that as they were sitting in, they were really standing up for the best in the American dream, and taking the whole nation back to those great wells of democracy which were dug deep by the Founding Fathers in the *Declaration of Independence* and the *Constitution*.

If I had sneezed, I wouldn't have been around here in 1961, when we decided to take a ride for freedom and ended segregation[8] in inter-state travel.

If I had sneezed, I wouldn't have been around here in 1962, when Negroes in Albany, Georgia, decided to straighten their backs up. And whenever men and women straighten their backs up, they are going somewhere, because a man can't ride your back unless it is bent. →

　　這個消息隔天早上被登在《紐約時報》上。那時候，我是連打個噴嚏都不可以的，因為那會要了我的命。在做完胸腔手術、取出刀子之後，大約過了四天，院方才允許我可以坐著輪椅在醫院裡四處活動。

　　他們也讓我看了一些從國內及世界各地所捎來的問候信件。我讀了其中的一些信，有一封信的內容尤其讓我永遠也忘不了。

　　我看過總統和副總統打來的電報，不過我已經忘記信的內容了。紐約州州長來看過我，也寫信給我，但我也不記得信裡頭說了些什麼。然而，有一封紐約白原高中一位女學生寫來的信，卻讓我永遠也忘不了。信的內容很簡單，上面寫說：「親愛的金恩博士：我是白原高中一位九年級的學生。」接著她說：

> 　　這也許不重要，但我還是想告訴你，我是個白人女孩。我從報紙上得知你受傷的消息。我還看到報導說，你連打個噴嚏都不行，不然可能會死掉。我只是想寫信告訴你說，我好高興你沒有打噴嚏。

　　今晚我想告訴你們，我也很高興我那時候沒有打噴嚏。我那時候要是打了噴嚏，我就無法活到 1960 年，看到南方到處都有學生在餐廳裡靜坐抗議。我知道他們靜坐，是為了捍衛最美好的美國夢，他們要把整個美國帶回偉大的民主源泉，那是我們那些發表《獨立宣言》和《憲法》的開國祖先們所深深挖掘出的民主源泉。

　　如果我那時候打了噴嚏，我就無法活到 1961 年，和大家一起爭取乘坐國內交通工具的自由權，廢除種族隔離。

　　如果我那時候打了噴嚏，我就無法活到 1962 年，看到喬治亞州阿爾巴尼市的黑人，為自己的權利挺身而出。一旦人為自己的權利挺身而出，這就是一種進步，因為只要自己肯站起來，就沒有人可以騎到我們的頭上。

---

7. sit-in (v.) to participate in an act of civil disobedience 靜坐抗議

8. segregation [ˌsɛɡrɪˈɡeɪʃən] (n.) when people of different races, sexes, or religions are kept apart so that they live, work, or study separately 種族隔離

80

If I had sneezed—If I had sneezed I wouldn't have been here in 1963, when the black people of Birmingham, Alabama, aroused the conscience of this nation, and brought into being the Civil Rights Bill.

If I had sneezed, I wouldn't have had a chance later that year, in August, to try to tell America about a dream that I had had.

If I had sneezed, I wouldn't have been down in Selma, Alabama, to see the great Movement there.

If I had sneezed, I wouldn't have been in Memphis to see a community rally around those brothers and sisters who are suffering.

I'm so happy that I didn't sneeze. And they were telling me—Now, it doesn't matter, now. It really doesn't matter what happens now.

I left Atlanta this morning, and as we got started on the plane, there were six of us. The pilot said over the public address system, "We are sorry for the delay, but we have Dr. Martin Luther King on the plane. And to be sure that all of the bags were checked, and to be sure that nothing would be wrong with on the plane, we had to check out everything carefully. And we've had the plane protected and guarded all night."

And then I got into Memphis. And some began to say the threats, or talk about the threats that were out. What would happen to me from some of our sick white brothers?

Well, I don't know what will happen now. We've got some difficult days ahead. But it really doesn't matter with me now, because I've been to the mountaintop.

And I don't mind.

Like anybody, I would like to live a long life. Longevity has its place. But I'm not concerned about that now. I just want to do God's will. And He's allowed me to go up to the mountain. And I've looked over. And I've seen the Promised Land[9]. I may not get there with you. But I want you to know tonight, that we, as a people, will get to the promised land!

And so I'm happy, tonight. I'm not worried about anything. I'm not fearing any man!

Mine eyes have seen the glory of the coming of the Lord! ◀

如果我那時候打了噴嚏，我就無法活到 1963 年，看到阿拉巴馬州伯明罕市的黑人喚醒這個國家的良心，後來並促成了《民權法案》的通過。

　　如果我那時候打了噴嚏，我也無法在那一年的八月，向美國說出一直藏在我心裡頭的那個夢想。

　　如果我那時候打了噴嚏，我就無法去阿拉巴馬州的賽爾馬市，親眼目睹在那裡發生的偉大民權運動。

　　如果我那時候打了噴嚏，我也就不能來到孟菲斯市，目睹那些正遭受苦難的兄弟姊妹們所發動的集體抗爭活動。

　　我很高興我那時候並沒有打噴嚏。他們後來跟我說，現在沒事了，現在要怎麼樣打噴嚏都可以了。

　　今天早上，我從亞特蘭大飛過來，在我們上飛機時，一行共六個人。駕駛員透過廣播系統說：「很抱歉飛機延誤，因為馬丁‧路德‧金恩博士就在我們的飛機上，我們必須確認檢查過所有的行李，確認飛機上一切正常，並且要將所有的東西都做過詳細的檢查。我們昨晚徹夜都在對這架飛機進行保護和監視。」

　　不久，我抵達了孟菲斯市。有些人開始談到我受到了恐嚇，也有人說恐嚇已經排除了。我們一些生病的白人兄弟們，會對我做出什麼事呢？

　　我不知道這個時候會發生什麼事，我們未來還有艱苦的日子要奮鬥，但對我來說，我現在會怎麼樣已經都不重要了，因為我已經踏上山頂了！

　　所以，我都無所謂了。

　　我和任何人一樣，也希望長命百歲，這是人之常情，但我現在並不關心這個問題了，現在我只想行上帝的意旨，而祂已經讓我踏上山頂了！我仔細地張望，然後我看到了應許之地。我也許無法和你們一起走到那裡，但今晚我希望你們能夠明白，我們這個民族將會到達應許之地。

　　今晚，我非常的高興。我什麼事都不擔心，也不畏懼任何人！

　　我眼裡已經看到上帝即將到來的聖光。

---

9. Promised Land: in the *Bible*, the land of Canaan, promised by God to Abraham and his race 應許之地，是《聖經》中耶和華應允要給猶太人祖先亞伯拉罕及其後裔的地方（位於尼羅河至幼發拉底河之處）

38

On the Death of
Martin Luther King

羅伯特・甘迺迪：
金恩博士之死

羅伯特・甘迺迪（1925–1968, RFK）是美國第 35 任總
統約翰・甘迺迪（1917–1963, JFK）的胞弟，在 JFK 總
統任內擔任美國的司法部長，直至 1964 年。

1965 年，RFK 當選美國紐約州參議員，後來宣布投入美
國 1968 年民主黨總統候選人的黨內初選。在 JFK 遇刺
後，RFK 成為接班人，儼然是政壇的明日之星。甘迺迪
政治家族一向是自由主義的代表，RFK 更是投身於各種
人權運動，為民喉舌。

1968 年 4 月 4 日，美國史上最重要的黑人民權運動領袖
金恩博士在田納西州遭到暗殺身亡。當天晚上，RFK 為
爭取民主黨總統候選人的提名，計畫在印第安納州首府
一個貧窮的黑人區發表演說。當他來到印第安納州的機
場時，便被告知金恩博士遇刺的消息。

在印第安納州首府的演講會場上，臺下的聽眾尚未得知
金恩博士不幸去世的消息，RFK 於是在會場上宣布了這
個惡耗。RFK 在這篇演說中，也提及了兄長 JFK 於 1963
年 11 月 22 日的遇刺事件。

兩個月後，1968 年 6 月 5 日，RFK 在民主黨加州黨內
總統初選結束，於洛杉磯的大使飯店（Ambassador
Hotel）舉行記者會後，自己也不幸遭到激進分子席漢
（Sirhan Sirhan）槍擊重傷，隔天不治身亡。

Speaker 美國參議員羅伯特・甘迺迪
（Robert Francis Kennedy, 1925–1968.6.6）

Time 1968 年 4 月 4 日

Place 美國印第安納州首府（Indianapolis, Indiana）

▣ 原音重現　▣ 全篇收錄

Martin Luth

everend Martin Luther King, Jr.

⟨81⟩

Ladies and Gentlemen—I'm only going to talk to you just for a minute or so this evening. Because I have some very sad news for all of you, and I think sad news for all of our fellow citizens, and people who love peace all over the world, and that is that Martin Luther King was shot and was killed tonight in Memphis, Tennessee.

Martin Luther King dedicated his life to love and to justice between fellow human beings. He died in the cause of that effort.

In this difficult day, in this difficult time for the United States, it's perhaps well to ask what kind of a nation we are and what direction we want to move in.

For those of you who are black—considering the evidence evidently is that there were white people who were responsible—you can be filled with bitterness, and with hatred, and a desire for revenge. We can move in that direction as a country, in greater polarization—black people amongst blacks, and white amongst whites, filled with hatred toward one another.

Or we can make an effort, as Martin Luther King did, to understand and to comprehend, and replace that violence, that stain of bloodshed that has spread across our land, with an effort to understand, compassion and love.

For those of you who are black and are tempted to be filled with hatred and mistrust of the injustice of such an act, against all white people, I would only say that I can also feel in my own heart the same kind of feeling. I had a member of my family killed, but he was killed by a white man. But we have to make an effort in the United States, we have to make an effort to understand, to get beyond these rather difficult times. →

各位女士先生，今晚我只會發表一段簡短的談話。我有一個不幸的消息要告訴你們，要告訴我們所有的人民，告訴世界上所有愛好和平的人，那就是——馬丁‧路德‧金恩不幸在田納西州孟菲斯市遭到槍擊身亡了。

馬丁‧路德‧金恩將他的一生奉獻給愛與自由，他為了同胞而奮鬥，卻因此而失去了性命。

這是難熬的一天，對美國而言這是個艱難的時刻，我們或許應該要問，我們到底是什麼樣的一個國家？我們到底要我們的國家走向哪個方向？

對身為黑人的你們來說——想到刺殺現場的證據，白人顯然要為此事負責——你們可能會義憤填膺，極欲報仇。我們國家是可以走向黑白對立這個方向——黑人分一國，白人分一個，然後彼此互相仇視。

又或者，我們可以奮鬥，就像馬丁‧路德‧金恩那樣，我們可以嘗試互相了解、互相理解，努力用仁慈與愛來互相了解彼此，以代替已經到處血染這片國家土地的暴力。

對那些因為這個不正義事件，而對全體白人產生憤恨與仇視的黑人來說，我只能說，就我個人來講，我也產生了同樣的感受。我有一個家人也慘遭暗殺，而且刺殺他的兇手是個白人。然而，我們還是必須努力，在美國這塊土地上，我們必須努力互相了解，度過這個艱難的時期。

82

My favorite poet was Aeschylus.[1] He once wrote: "Even in our sleep, pain which cannot forget falls drop by drop upon the heart, until, in our own despair, against our will, comes wisdom through the awful grace of God."

What we need in the United States is not division; what we need in the United States is not hatred; what we need in the United States is not violence and lawlessness, but is love and wisdom, and compassion toward one another, and a feeling of justice toward those who still suffer within our country, whether they be white or whether they be black.

So I ask you tonight to return home, to say a prayer for the family of Martin Luther King, yeah that's true, but more importantly to say a prayer for our own country, which all of us love—a prayer for understanding and that compassion of which I spoke.

We can do well in this country. We will have difficult times. We've had difficult times in the past. And we will have difficult times in the future. It is not the end of violence; it is not the end of lawlessness; and it's not the end of disorder.

But the vast majority of white people and the vast majority of black people in this country want to improve the quality of our life, and want justice for all human beings that abide in our land.

Let us dedicate ourselves to what the Greeks wrote so many years ago: to tame the savageness of man and make gentle the life of this world.

Let us dedicate ourselves to that, and say a prayer for our country and for our people. Thank you very much. ◀

1. Aeschylus (525 BC–456 BC): the father of Greek tragic drama; the earliest of the three greatest Greek tragedians 古希臘悲劇詩人艾斯奇勒斯，被喻為「悲劇之父」

A memorial march in Pittsburg after the death of Dr. Martin Luther King, 1968

　　我最喜愛的詩人是希臘詩人艾斯奇勒斯。他寫道：「在我們入眠之時，無法消逝的痛苦，一點一滴地滴落心頭，直到在我們絕望的心底，透過上帝令人敬畏的恩寵，讓我們不再執著，因而流入了智慧。」

　　在美國，我們所需要的決不是分裂；在美國，我們所需要的決不是仇恨；在美國，我們所需要的決不是暴力或是無有法紀；我們需要的是愛與智慧，大家彼此相親相愛，我們對這個國家所有受苦的人們都應懷有仁愛之心，不管他們是白人還是黑人。

　　所以，我請求你們今晚趕快回家，為馬丁‧路德‧金恩的一家人做禱告，沒錯，更重要的是，也要為我們的這個國家做禱告。這是我們熱愛的國家，就像我剛剛講的，請為這個國家做祈求互相了解與相親相愛的禱告。

　　在這個國家，我們可以做得很好。我們將會遇到關卡，我們以前也有過難關，我們以後也還會遇到困難。暴力還沒結束，無法無天的情況還沒有結束，混亂的局面也還沒有結束。

　　但在這個國家裡，絕大部分的白人和黑人，他們想共同攜手生活，想改善我們的生活，想要讓居住在這塊土地上的人們都能夠得到公平的對待。

　　讓我們一起為希臘人很久以前所寫過的一句話而奮鬥：馴服人類的野蠻，讓這個世界的生活變得和樂安詳。

　　就讓我們一起來奮鬥，並為我們的國家和人民做禱告。謝謝大家。

Eulogy for John F. Kennedy

約翰‧甘迺迪總統哀悼文

這篇是美國政治家艾爾‧華倫（Earl Warren, 1891–1974）為約翰‧甘迺迪總統所作的哀悼文。JFK 遇刺後，艾爾‧華倫擔任調查委員會主席，故委員會又稱「華倫委員會」（Warren Commission）。

1963 年 11 月 22 日中午十二點半，美國第 35 任總統 JFK 和第一夫人及德州州長一起乘坐在一輛敞篷車上，就在車子駛過德州達拉斯市的迪利廣場（Dealey Plaza）時，JFK 遭到槍擊身亡。11 月 23 日清晨，甘迺迪的遺體從醫院移送回白宮。11 月 25 日，舉行葬禮。

JFK 是美國歷史上第四位遇刺身亡的總統，負責調查工作的華倫委員會在經過十個月的調查之後，發表官方報告指出行刺純屬個人行為，兇手李‧哈維‧奧斯辛（Lee Harvey Oswald）是美籍古巴人，他是教科書倉庫大樓的員工，在當時從大樓六樓的窗戶向敞篷車開槍。但一個後來成立的官方調查委員會再度對刺殺案進行調查之後，認為決非是個人行為。

到底是誰殺了甘迺迪？一直到今日，都還有人致力於調查甘迺迪遇刺案，但此案仍然疑點重重、撲朔迷離，成了歷史上永遠的懸案。

Three-year-old JFK Jr. saluting at his father's funeral

Speaker 美國政治家艾爾‧華倫
（Earl Warren, 1891–1974）

Time 1963 年 11 月 24 日

Place 美國國會大廈圓形大廳
（Rotunda, U.S. Capitol, Washington, D.C）

☑ 原音重現　☑ 全篇收錄

83

Mr. President, Mrs. Johnson, members of the Kennedy family, and my
fellow Americans:

There are few events in our national life that so unite Americans and so
touch the hearts of all of us as the passing of a President of the United
States. There is nothing that adds shock to our sadness more than the
assassination of our leader, chosen as he is to embody the ideals of
our people, the faith we have in our institutions and our belief in the
fatherhood of God and the brotherhood of man.

Such misfortunes have befallen the Nation on other occasions, but never
more shockingly than two days ago. We are saddened; we are stunned; we
are perplexed.

John Fitzgerald Kennedy, a great and good President, the friend of all
people of good will, a believer in the dignity and equality of all human
beings, a fighter for justice, an apostle of peace, has been snatched from
our midst by the bullet of an assassin.

What moved some misguided wretch to do this horrible deed may
be never be known to us, but we do know that such acts are commonly
stimulated by forces of hatred and malevolence, such as today are eating
their way into the bloodstream of American life.

What a price we pay for this fanaticism[1]. →

詹森總統、甘迺迪家族的朋友們、各位美國同胞們：

　　在我們國內，很少有什麼事件可以像美國總統的過世那樣，如此地將國人團結在一起，全國上下一心。再也沒有什麼事能比我們的總統遇刺來得更令我們痛心，我們選出的總統代表了我們人民的理念，代表了我們對政府的信念，也代表了我們對上帝的信仰、對人類四海之內皆兄弟這種理念的信仰。

　　這種不幸的事件，我們國家之前也發生過，但從來沒有像前兩天所發生的那樣令人震驚。我們感到悲傷，感到震驚，也感到迷惑。

　　約翰‧甘迺迪是一個偉大的好總統，是所有良善人民的好朋友，他相信人性的尊嚴，相信人人生而平等，他是一個正義的鬥士，他是和平的使徒，而現在刺客的子彈將他從我們身邊把他的性命給奪走。

　　是誰驅使兇手犯下這個可怕的惡行，這個答案可能永遠無法得知，但我們很清楚的是，這種行為是來自仇恨與惡意，而這種仇恨和惡意正在侵蝕著美國人的生活。

　　我們現在為了這種狂熱，付出了這樣大的代價。

---

1. fanaticism [fəˈnætɪsɪzəm] (n.) extreme political or religious beliefs—
   used to show disapproval 狂熱；盲信

(84)

It has been said that the only thing we learn from history is that we do not learn. But surely we can learn if we have the will to do so. Surely there is a lesson to be learned from this tragic event.

If we really love this country, if we truly love justice and mercy, if we fervently[2] want to make this Nation better for those who are to follow us, we can at least abjure[3] the hatred that consumes people, the false accusations that divide us, and the bitterness that begets[4] violence.

Is it too much to hope that the martyrdom of our beloved President might even soften the hearts of those who would themselves recoil[5] from assassination, but who do not shrink from spreading the venom[6] which kindles thoughts of it in others?

Our Nation is bereaved[7]. The whole world is poorer because of his loss. But we can all be better Americans because John Fitzgerald Kennedy has passed our way, because he has been our chosen leader at a time in history when his character, his vision, and his quiet courage have enabled him to chart a course for us—a safe course for us, through the shoals[8] of treacherous seas that encompass the world.

And now that he is relieved of the almost superhuman burden we imposed on him, may he rest in peace. ◖

人們說，我們從歷史中唯一能得知的就是——人們是學不會歷史的教訓的。然而，只要我們願意，我們就能記取教訓，而這也是我們要從這場悲劇中學習到的。

如果我們真的熱愛這個國家，真的熱愛正義和仁慈，如果我們強烈希望讓這個國家變得更好，為了那些跟隨我們信念的人，我們最起碼要放棄那些腐蝕人心的仇恨，放棄那些造成內閧的不實指責，放棄那些會導致暴力的痛苦。

我們敬愛的總統，對於那些傳播怨恨思想、煽動人心的人，他的殉身能否讓他們的心柔軟下來而放棄行刺？這樣的期待是否會不實際？

我們的國家遭受了很大的損失，而這也是全世界的損失。然而，約翰・甘迺迪的去世卻能激勵我們要成為一個更好的美國人，因為我們當初選他出任我們的總統時，就是因為他的性格、視野和沉著的勇氣能為我們指出一條路——一條能讓我們安全的路，能讓我們平安駛過世界這片汪洋中的詭譎暗礁。

如今，他卸下了這個我們加諸在他身上、不是常人所能負荷的重擔，願他安息！

---

2. fervently [ˈfɜːrvəntli] (adv.) with passionate fervor 強烈地

3. abjure [æbˈdʒʊr] (v.) to state publicly that you no longer agree with a belief or way of behaving 發誓棄絕

4. beget [bɪˈget] (v.) to cause something or make it happen 招致

5. recoil [rɪˈkɔɪl] (v.) to draw back, as with fear or pain 退卻

6. venom [ˈvenəm] (n.) great anger or hatred 怨恨

7. bereaved [bɪˈriːvd] (a.) having lost a loved one through death 失去所愛的人的

8. shoal [ʃoʊl] (n.) an underwater sandbank or sandbar that is visible at low water 淺灘；暗礁

Eulogy for
Robert F. Kennedy

羅伯特・甘迺迪哀悼文

甘迺迪家族是美國最顯赫政治家族，以下以約翰・甘迺迪為中心，簡列其世代：

- 祖先：約翰・甘迺迪（JFK, 1917–1963）的曾祖父 Patrick Kennedy（c. 1823–1858），由愛爾蘭移民到波士頓，是其第一代移民。
- 第一代政治世家：JFK 的爺爺 Patrick Joseph Kennedy（1858–1929），曾擔任麻州的眾議員和參議員。
- 第二代政治世家：JFK 的父親 Joseph Patrick Kennedy（1888–1969），曾任駐英大使。
- 第三代政治世家：JFK 和兩位弟弟羅伯特（Robert Francis Kennedy, RFK, 1925–1968）、愛德華（Edward Moore Kennedy, 1932–2009），為家族的第三代成員。（見右圖）

JFK 共有有三個兄弟、五個姊妹，其最大的兄長於第二次世界大戰中喪生，而剩下的三位兄弟後來都進入了政壇，其中 JFK 和 RFK 皆遇刺身亡，而家中最小的愛德華・甘迺迪則於 2009 年病逝，甘迺迪家族的傳奇也從此劃下了句點。

積極參與人權運動的 RFK，曾任美國司法部長、紐約州參議員。1968 年 6 月 5 日，他在加州為競選總統而奔走時，不幸遭到激進分子席漢（Sirhan Sirhan）槍擊重傷，隔天不治死亡。這篇哀悼文是由被參議院喻為「自由派雄獅」的胞弟愛德華所發表。

Speaker	愛德華・甘迺迪 （Edward M. Kennedy, 1932–2009）
Time	1968 年 6 月 8 日
Place	美國紐約聖派屈克教堂 （St. Patrick's Cathedral, New York）

▣ 原音重現　▣ 擷錄

The Kennedy brothers (L–R): John, Robert, and Edward

85

Your Eminences, Your Excellencies, Mr. President:

On behalf of Mrs. Kennedy, her children, the parents and sisters of Robert Kennedy, I want to express what we feel to those who mourn with us today in this Cathedral and around the world.

We loved him as a brother, and as a father, and as a son. From his parents, and from his older brothers and sisters—Joe and Kathleen and Jack—he received an inspiration which he passed on to all of us. He gave us strength in time of trouble, wisdom in time of uncertainty, and sharing in time of happiness. He will always be by our side.

Love is not an easy feeling to put into words. Nor is loyalty, or trust, or joy. But he was all of these. He loved life completely and he lived it intensely.

A few years back, Robert Kennedy wrote some words about his own father which expresses the way we in his family felt about him. He said of what his father meant to him, and I quote: "What it really all adds up to is love—not love as it is described with such facility in popular magazines, but the kind of love that is affection and respect, order and encouragement, and support. Our awareness of this was an incalculable source of strength, and because real love is something unselfish and involves sacrifice and giving, we could not help but profit from it." →

各位閣下：

　　今天我代表羅伯特・甘迺迪的夫人、子女、父母和姐妹，向教堂來賓和世界上所有與我們同悲的人們，表達我們內心裡的感受。

　　他是我們的兄長、父親和兒子，我們深愛著他。他將他從父母和兄姐身上所學習到的東西，傳給我們所有的家人。在艱難的時刻，他給予我們力量；在不安的時刻，他給予我們智慧；在快樂的時候，他與我們一起分享。他將會一直陪伴在我們的身邊。

　　我們對他的愛，很難用言語表達出來，那不是忠誠、信任和喜悅所能形容──儘管他帶給了我們這些感覺。他徹底地熱愛生命，對生活充滿了熱情。

　　幾年前，羅伯特・甘迺迪對家父所寫下的幾句話，正適合用來表達我們家人對羅伯特・甘迺迪的感覺，他在文中提到他對家父的感受，他寫道：「真正總歸來說，他代表了愛──不是暢銷雜誌上用流利文筆所寫出的那種愛，而是那種充滿情感與尊敬、秩序與勇氣，以及充滿支撐力量的愛。我們對他的這種感受，給予了我們無限的力量來源。真正的愛是無私且包含著犧牲奉獻的，我們就這樣一直從中受益著。」

RFK with his wife, Ethel Kennedy, and six children

86

And he continued, "Beneath it all, he has tried to engender a social conscience. There were wrongs which needed attention. There were people who were poor and needed help. And we have a responsibility to them and to this country. Through no virtues and accomplishments of our own, we have been fortunate enough to be born in the United States under the most comfortable conditions. We, therefore, have a responsibility to others who are less well off."

My brother need not be idealized, or enlarged in death beyond what he was in life; to be remembered simply as a good and decent man, who saw wrong and tried to right it, saw suffering and tried to heal it, saw war and tried to stop it.

Those of us who loved him and who take him to his rest today, pray that what he was to us and what he wished for others will some day come to pass for all the world. As he said many times, in many parts of this nation, to those he touched and who sought to touch him:

"Some men see things as they are and say why.
I dream things that never were and say why not." [1]

他繼續寫道：「此外，他努力在提升社會意識。不公義的事情是需要被關注的，社會上有貧窮和需要幫助的人們，而我們對這些人和這個國家都負有責任。我們很幸運能出生在美國這種良好的環境中，這完全不是得自我們自己的德性或功勞，因此我們有責任去幫助需要幫助的人。」

我哥哥不需要被理想化，或是在死時來誇大他的一生。我們單純地把他當做一個善良、正派的人來懷念他。他看到不義的事情時，他會努力去改善它；他看到有人受苦時，他會努力想去幫助他們走出來；他看到戰爭時，他會努力想去化解衝突。

我們這些深愛他的人，以及今天來送他最後一程的人，我們祈禱：他留給我們的，以及他對世人的願望，終有一日能傳送到整個世界上。他在這個國家的許多地方，曾多次對那些與他接觸的人說過以下的話：

「有人看到已經發生的事情，而問為什麼；
但我常夢想著尚未發生的事情，而問為什麼沒發生？」

1. A quote from George Bernard Shaw (1856–1950) 出自愛爾蘭劇作家蕭伯納之語

The Ballot or the Bullets

麥爾坎‧X：
是選票還是子彈？

麥爾坎‧X（Malcolm X），原名 Malcolm Little，他年少時是一個街頭混混，曾因為作奸犯科而鋃鐺入獄。入獄後，他開始自學各種知識，出獄後便投入黑人運動，成為聲望僅次於馬丁‧路德‧金恩的黑人運動領袖。他的自傳《麥爾坎‧X 的自傳》（*The Autobiography of Malcolm X*，Alex Haley 執筆）於 1965 年出版，1992 年被改拍成電影《黑潮：麥爾坎 X》（*Malcolm X*）。

他是一名美國非裔的伊斯蘭教教士，曾擔任美國激進黑人組織「伊斯蘭國」（Nation of Islam）的發言人。1964 年，他到麥加朝覲後改奉遜尼派，同年 3 月，他與「伊斯蘭國」決裂，呼籲和各種不同的宗教或組織合作，一起為黑人的人權奮鬥。

隨後在 4 月，他發表了此篇著名的演講。民主國家的政治，不是以子彈來決定政權，而是以選票來賦予政府的合法性，他在演講中鼓吹黑人用選票來決定自己的命運。三個月後，美國國會於 4 月 11 日通過了《民權法案》，宣布種族隔離和歧視政策為非法政策，而「Ballot or Bullet?」（是選票還是子彈？）也成為當時的風行的口號。

1965 年 2 月 21 日，他於另一場演講前被「伊斯蘭國」的三名殺手刺殺身亡。「是選票，還是子彈？」，他曾經自己下過註腳說道：

It'll be the ballot or it'll be the bullet. It'll be liberty or it'll be death. And if you're not ready to pay that price don't use the word freedom in your vocabulary.

不是選票，就是子彈；不是自由，就是死亡。
如果你沒有慷慨就義的準備，就不要輕言自由。

Speaker	美國黑人民權運動領袖麥爾坎・X
	（Malcolm X , 1925–1965）
Time	1964 年 4 月 3 日
Place	美國俄亥俄州克里夫蘭的柯瑞衛理公會
	（Cory Methodist Church, Ohio, USA）

▣ 錄音　▣ 擷錄

87

Mr. Moderator[1], Brother Lomax, brothers and sisters, friends and enemies:

I just can't believe everyone in here is a friend, and I don't want to leave anybody out. The question tonight, as I understand it, is "The Negro Revolt, and Where Do We Go From Here?" or "What Next?" In my little humble way of understanding it, it points toward either the ballot or the bullet.

Before we try and explain what is meant by the ballot or the bullet, I would like to clarify something concerning myself. I'm still a Muslim; my religion is still Islam. That's my personal belief. Just as Adam Clayton Powell[2] is a Christian minister who heads the Abyssinian Baptist Church in New York, but at the same time takes part in the political struggles to try and bring about rights to the black people in this country; and Dr. Martin Luther King is a Christian minister down in Atlanta, Georgia, who heads another organization fighting for the civil rights of black people in this country; and Reverend Galamison, I guess you've heard of him, is another Christian minister in New York who has been deeply involved in the school boycotts to eliminate segregated education; well, I myself am a minister, not a Christian minister, but a Muslim minister; and I believe in action on all fronts by whatever means necessary.

Although I'm still a Muslim, I'm not here tonight to discuss my religion. I'm not here to try and change your religion. I'm not here to argue or discuss anything that we differ about, because it's time for us to submerge our differences and realize that it is best for us to first see that we have the same problem, a common problem, a problem that will make you catch hell[3] whether you're a Baptist, or a Methodist, or a Muslim, or a nationalist. →

41
是選票還是子彈？

1. moderator ['mɑːdəreɪtər] (n.) someone who presides over a forum or debate
   會議主席
2. Adam Clayton Powell Jr. (1908–1972): a prominent African American congressman
   一位非裔的美國議員
3. catch hell: to be severely reprimanded, punished, or beaten 遭受訓斥或懲罰

主持人洛梅克斯弟兄、各位兄弟姊妹、朋友以及敵人們，你們好：

　　我不認為今晚每一個在場的人都是我的朋友，但我不希望任何一個人離開。就我所知，今晚的主題是「黑人起義，我們該何去何從？」或「下一步又是什麼？」我個人的小小看法是：不是選票，就是子彈！

　　在我開始之前，我想先澄清一些關於我個人的事情。我依然是個穆斯林，我的信仰仍是伊斯蘭教。這是我個人的信仰，就像亞當‧克萊德‧鮑威爾是個基督教牧師，他領導紐約的阿比西尼亞浸信會，但他同時也參與政治運動，爭取黑人在這個國家的權利。又如馬丁‧路德‧金恩博士，他是一名喬治亞州亞特蘭大的基督教牧師，但他也領導另一個組織，為黑人爭取公民權。再來，我想你應該也聽過，賈蘭米森牧師，他是另一個在紐約的基督教牧師，他積極抵制學校的種族隔離教育，想要消除它。而我呢？我也是個牧師，不過我不是基督教的牧師，而是伊斯蘭教的教士。我認為只要有需要，就應該全體動員起來。

　　雖然我仍是個穆斯林，但我今晚來這裡並不是要談論我的宗教信仰，或是要改變你們的信仰，更不是要來爭辯我們之間有什麼差異。今晚，讓我們消除對彼此的歧見，我們要了解到，不論你是浸禮宗的教徒、循道宗的教徒、穆斯林或是民族主義者，對我們大家最好的方式，就是首先明白到我們大家都面臨了相同的問題，這是一個很普遍的問題，而且是一個大家都飽受喝斥的問題。

88

Whether you're educated or illiterate, whether you live on the boulevard or in the alley, you're going to catch hell just like I am. We're all in the same boat and we all are going to catch the same hell from the same man. He just happens to be a white man. All of us have suffered here, in this country, political oppression at the hands of the white man, economic exploitation at the hands of the white man, and social degradation at the hands of the white man.

1964 threatens to be the most explosive year America has ever witnessed. The most explosive year. Why? It's also a political year. It's the year when all of the white politicians will be back in the so-called Negro community jiving[4] you and me for some votes. The year when all of the white political crooks[5] will be right back in your and my community with their false promises, building up our hopes for a letdown, with their trickery and their treachery, with their false promises which they don't intend to keep. As they nourish these dissatisfactions, it can only lead to one thing, an explosion; and now we have the type of black man on the scene in America today—I'm sorry, Brother Lomax—who just doesn't intend to turn the other cheek any longer.

Don't let anybody tell you anything about the odds are against you. If they draft you, they send you to Korea and make you face 800 million Chinese. If you can be brave over there, you can be brave right here. These odds aren't as great as those odds. And if you fight here, you will at least know what you're fighting for.

I'm not a politician, not even a student of politics; in fact, I'm not a student of much of anything. I'm not a Democrat. I'm not a Republican, and I don't even consider myself an American. If you and I were Americans, there'd be no problem. →

41
是選票還是子彈？

不管你是不是受過教育，不管你是住在大街還是小巷，你都跟我一樣會受到指責。我們大家都站在同一條船上，我們會遭受到同樣的人對我們的非難，而那個人恰巧就是一個白人。在這個國家裡，我們所有在場的人在政治上都飽受白人的迫害，在經濟上飽受白人的剝削，在社會上則飽受到白人的歧視。

1964 年（今年），大概是美國有史以來最具爆炸性的一年。為什麼說是最具爆炸性的一年？這也是充滿政治性的一年，所有的白人政客再次來到我們黑人社區，花言巧語地騙取我們選票。這些白人的政客騙子來到我們的社區，對我們亂開支票，他們用盡手段，給我們虛幻的希望，他們根本就不打算兌現他們的支票！他們的作為讓我們民怨沸騰，這必然只會導致一個爆炸性的後果。今天，在美國，我們現場就來了這樣的黑人——洛梅克斯弟兄，很抱歉——這些黑人再也不願意將另一邊的臉奉送給人挨打了。

不要去聽那些關於我們沒有勝算的話！如果你被徵召入伍，你會被送去韓國和八億的中國人打仗。你要是能在那裡英勇奮戰，你也就能在這裡為我們大家英勇奮鬥。在這裡奮鬥的勝算，並不比在韓國奮戰的勝算來得大，但在這裡你起碼知道你是為何而戰！

我不是一個政治家，甚至也不是政治系的學生，事實上，我根本沒念過太多書。我不是民主黨員，也不是共和黨員，我甚至不覺得自己是一位美國人。如果你和我都是名副其實的美國人，那今天就不會發生這些問題了。

4. jive [dʒaɪv] (v.) [US slang] to try to make someone believe something that is untrue
〔俚〕胡扯；花言巧語

5. crook [krʊk] (n.) [informal] a very dishonest person, especially a criminal or a cheat
〔口〕騙子

89

Those Honkies[6] that just got off the boat, they're already Americans; Polacks[7] are already Americans; the Italian refugees are already Americans. Everything that came out of Europe, every blue-eyed thing, is already an American. And as long as you and I have been over here, we aren't Americans yet.

Well, I am one who doesn't believe in deluding myself. I'm not going to sit at your table and watch you eat, with nothing on my plate, and call myself a diner. Sitting at the table doesn't make you a diner, unless you eat some of what's on that plate.

Being here in America doesn't make you an American. Being born here in America doesn't make you an American. Why, if birth made you American, you wouldn't need any legislation; you wouldn't need any amendments to the Constitution; you wouldn't be faced with civil-rights filibustering[8] in Washington, D.C., right now. They don't have to pass civil-rights legislation to make a Polack an American.

No, I'm not an American. I'm one of the 22 million black people who are the victims of Americanism. One of the 22 million black people who are the victims of democracy, nothing but disguised hypocrisy. So, I'm not standing here speaking to you as an American, or a patriot, or a flag-saluter, or a flag-waver[9]—no, not I. I'm speaking as a victim of this American system. And I see America through the eyes of the victim. I don't see any American dream; I see an American nightmare.

So, where do we go from here? First, we need some friends. We need some new allies. The entire civil-rights struggle needs a new interpretation, a broader interpretation. We need to look at this civil-rights thing from another angle—from the inside as well as from the outside. →

那些才剛下船的白人，已經是美國人，波蘭佬也當了美國人，義大利來的難民也已經變成美國人。每一個來自歐洲的人，每一個藍眼珠的人，都已經變成美國人了，而我們這些早就來到這裡的人，卻還不是美國人！

我不會自欺欺人。我不會坐在白人的餐桌上，看著他吃飯，而我的盤子裡空無一物，卻還說我自己也在用餐。坐在餐桌上，除非你吃了盤子裡的東西，否則不代表你就是在用餐。

你身處美國，並不代表你就是美國人；即使你是在美國出生的，也不代表你就是美國人。哦，如果說在美國出生就代表你是美國人，那根本就不用立法來保障，憲法也不用通過什麼修正案，現在在華盛頓特區也不會有公民權的抗爭活動了。他們也不需要通過什麼公民權立法，來讓波蘭佬成為合法的美國人。

沒錯，我不是個真正的美國人。我只是兩千兩百萬個黑人當中，其中一個美國主義底下的受害者。我也只是那兩千兩百萬個黑人當中，被民主的偽善所蒙蔽的其中一人。所以，我今天並不是以美國人、愛國者，或是一位激進的國家主義者，來站在這裡跟你說話——不是的，並不是的。我是以美國體制下受害者的身分，來站在這裡講話的。我從一位受害者的角度來看美國，我看到的不是美國夢，而是美國的夢魘。

那麼，我們何去何從？首先，我們需要一些朋友，需要一些新的夥伴。整個公民權的運動需要做一個新的詮釋，需要一個更廣泛的定義。不論是從內部或外部來看，我們需要從不同的觀點去看待公民權。

6. honky [ˈhɑːŋki] (n.) offensive names for a White man 〔蔑〕白人

7. Polack [ˈpoʊlæk] (n.) [Offensive slang] a person of Polish descent 〔蔑〕波蘭佬

8. filibustering [ˈfɪlɪbʌstərɪŋ] (n.) to act as a filibuster, or military freebooter 暴民行為；義勇軍行為

9. flag-waver: an extreme bellicose nationalist 狂熱的國家主義者

90

And I love my Brother Lomax, the way he pointed out we're right back where we were in 1954. We're not even as far up as we were in 1954. We're behind where we were in 1954. There's more segregation now than there was in 1954. There's more racial animosity[10], more racial hatred, more racial violence today in 1964, than there was in 1954. Where is the progress?

And now you're facing a situation where the young Negro's coming up. They don't want to hear that "turn the-other-cheek" stuff, no. In Jacksonville, those were teenagers, they were throwing Molotov cocktails[11]. Negroes have never done that before. But it shows you there's a new deal coming in. There's new thinking coming in. There's new strategy coming in.

It'll be Molotov cocktails this month, hand grenades[12] next month, and something else next month. It'll be ballots, or it'll be bullets. It'll be liberty, or it will be death. The only difference about this kind of death—it'll be reciprocal[13].

Well, we're justified in seeking civil rights, if it means equality of opportunity, because all we're doing there is trying to collect for our investment. Our mothers and fathers invested sweat and blood. Three hundred and ten years we worked in this country without a dime in return—I mean without a dime in return. You let the white man walk around here talking about how rich this country is, but you never stop to think how it got rich so quick. It got rich because you made it rich.

Not only did we give of our free labor, we gave of our blood. Every time he had a call to arms, we were the first ones in uniform. We died on every battlefield the white man had. We have made a greater sacrifice than anybody who's standing up in America today. We have made a greater contribution and have collected less. Civil rights, for those of us whose philosophy is black nationalism, means: "Give it to us now. Don't wait for next year. Give it to us yesterday, and that's not fast enough." ◀

我親愛的洛梅克斯弟兄指出，我們退回到了 1954 年的那個時候，甚至我們現在的處境還不比當時，我們今不如昔，現在種族隔離的情況比當時還嚴重。在 1964 年的今天，充斥著更多種的種族仇恨、敵意和暴力，試問比起當年，我們有什麼進步嗎？

我們現在還面臨了新一代黑人的問題。他們不信「打不還手、罵不還口」這一套。在傑克遜維，有年輕人在丟擲汽油瓶，以前從來沒有黑人會做這種事，這顯示一種新的局面在形成，一種新的想法在產生，一種新的對策在發展。

這個月是汽油彈，下個月有可能是手榴彈或是其他東西。不是選票，就是子彈；不是自由，就是死亡。這種死亡唯一的差別在於它是有回報的。

假如公民權是指每個人都擁有平等的機會，那麼我們就有正當的理由來追求它。我們所做的一切，只是想討回我們所投入的心血。過去我們的先祖父母流血流汗地工作，整整的三百一十年，我們付諸所有的心血在這塊土地上，而我們卻半毛錢都沒有拿到！你們讓白人四處高談闊論這個國家有多富有，但你們卻沒有想過這個國家怎麼會如此快速地致富。它之所以致富，正是你們所賜的。

我們不只提供了免費的勞動力，也獻出了我們的性命。每次要開戰前，我們總是第一個穿上軍服的。我們在每一個白人的戰場上貢獻出我們的生命，我們比今天每一個美國人所做的犧牲都還要大。我們做出了很多的貢獻，但卻鮮為人知。公民權，對我們這些黑人民族主義的擁護者來說，意思是說：「此刻就給我們！不要叫我們再等到明年！即使是昨天就給我們，也都嫌晚了！」

10. animosity [ˌænɪˈmɑːsɪti] (n.) strong dislike, opposition, or anger 仇恨

11. Molotov cocktail: a simple gasoline bomb 用來攻擊戰車的汽油瓶

12. grenade [grɪˈneɪd] (n.) a hand-thrown bomb 手榴彈

13. reciprocal [rɪˈsɪprəkəl] (a.) given or done in return for something else 有所回報的

Nelson Mandela: Inaugural Address

曼德拉總統就職演說

南非的民族鬥士曼德拉出生於一個部落酋長家庭，他是個長子，為酋長繼承人，但他卻選擇為人權而戰，終生奉獻於人類的自由與和平。26 歲時，他參與創建了南非非洲人國民大會（非國大）青年聯盟，以和平方式爭取黑人人權為訴求。

1962 年 8 月，曼德拉被捕入獄，囚禁在大西洋羅本島（Robben Island）近 20 年，接著數次移監，總共被囚長達 27 年。

1990 年，南非當局在國內外強大輿論壓力下，被迫釋放已經 72 歲的曼德拉。南非自 1940 年代開始實施的種族隔離政策，也於 1990 年廢除。

1994 年 4 月，非國大在南非首次不分種族的大選中獲勝，曼德拉於同年 5 月成為南非第一位黑人總統，而且也是透過全面代議制的民主選舉所選出的首任南非元首。1997 年 12 月，曼德拉辭去非國大主席一職，並表示不再參加 1999 年 6 月的總統競選。

曼德拉四十年來獲得的榮譽和獎項不計其數，並於 1993 年獲得諾貝爾和平獎。2009 年 7 月 18 日，在曼德拉 91 歲生日這一天，南非將 7 月 18 日訂定為「曼德拉日」（Mandela Day），呼籲人們在這一天至少花 67 分鐘參與社會公益活動，以紀念曼德拉為人權運動奮鬥的 67 年。

在英國《每日電訊報》2008 年評選出 20–21 世紀最重要的 25 場政治演說中，這篇也被收錄其中。

Nelson Mandela Statue in Nelson Mandela Square,
Johannesburg, South Africa

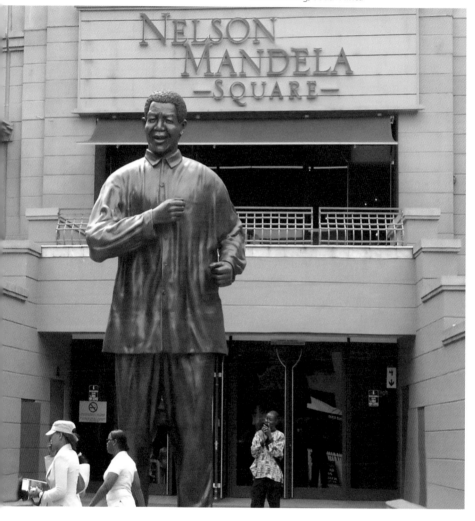

Speaker 南非的民族鬥士曼德拉
（Nelson Mandela, 1918–2013）

Time 1994 年 5 月 10 日

Place 南非行政首都普利托里亞之聯合大廈
（Union Buildings, Pretoria）

☑ 錄音　☑ 擷錄

To my compatriots, I have no hesitation in saying that each one of us is as intimately attached to the soil of this beautiful country as are the famous jacaranda[1] trees of Pretoria[2] and the mimosa trees[3] of the bushveld[4]. Each time one of us touches the soil of this land, we feel a sense of personal renewal. The national mood changes as the seasons change. We are moved by a sense of joy and exhilaration[5] when the grass turns green and the flowers bloom.

That spiritual and physical oneness we all share with this common homeland explains the depth of the pain we all carried in our hearts as we saw our country tear itself apart in a terrible conflict, and as we saw it spurned[6], outlawed and isolated by the peoples of the world, precisely because it has become the universal base of the pernicious[7] ideology and practice of racism and racial oppression.

We, the people of South Africa, feel fulfilled that humanity has taken us back into its bosom, that we, who were outlaws not so long ago, have today been given the rare privilege to be host to the nations of the world on our own soil. We thank all our distinguished international guests for having come to take possession with the people of our country of what is, after all, a common victory for justice, for peace, for human dignity. We trust that you will continue to stand by us as we tackle the challenges of building peace, prosperity, non-sexism, non-racialism, and democracy.

We deeply appreciate the role that the masses of our people and their political mass democratic, religious, women, youth, business, traditional, and other leaders have played to bring about this conclusion. Not least among them is my Second Deputy President, the Honorable F.W. de Klerk[8].

We would also like to pay tribute to our security forces, in all their ranks, for the distinguished role they have played in securing our first democratic elections and the transition to democracy, from blood-thirsty forces which still refuse to see the light.

The time for the healing of the wounds has come. The moment to bridge the chasms[9] that divide us has come. The time to build is upon us. →

1. jacaranda [ˌdʒækəˈrændər] (n.) an important Brazilian timber tree yielding a heavy hard dark-colored wood streaked with black 藍花楹（俗名非洲紫薇、巴西紫薇、紫雲木）

42
曼德拉總統就職演說

對我們同胞來說，我大可以這麼說，我們每一個人都和這個美麗的國家緊緊相繫在一起，這種關係就好像普利托里亞和有名的非洲紫薇的關係，好像合歡和南非灌木林區的關係一樣。我們每一個人，只要我們每次一觸摸到這塊土地，我們就會感覺到像充了電一樣。四季的變化，也讓我們國人的感受隨之變化，當大地變綠、百花盛開時，我們會被喜悅和愉快的感覺所觸動。

我們和我們的這一塊土地，在情感上和生活上都密不可分，於是乎，當我們看到我們的國家因為可怕的衝突而四分五裂，尤其成了萬夫所指的邪惡的意識型態和種族歧視與種族迫害的代表，而被世界上的其他民族所摒棄、放逐和孤立時，我們的內心裡就感到異常的沉痛。

我們南非的人民今天感到很欣慰，我們又重回了世界的懷抱。不久前，我們還是被世界所驅逐的，而現在卻有這個榮幸能在自己的土地上，招待來自世界各國的嘉賓。我們感謝所有這些國外來的傑出貴賓，他們來和我們的人民一起分享這個國家在正義、和平和人類尊嚴上的全面勝利。我們堅信，在我們面臨各種挑戰，以建立一個和平、繁榮、沒有性別歧視和種族歧視的民主國家時，世界各國會繼續與我們並肩站在一起。

我們非常感謝我們廣大的人民，以及各方在民主政治、宗教信仰、婦幼、商業和傳統等各方面所扮演的角色，才讓我們有了今天的結果。其中功不可沒的，是我的第二副總統戴克拉克先生。

我們還要感謝我們的國安警力，他們全員動員，在我們第一次的民主選舉中做了一次出色的維安工作，在民主化的過程中，防止冥頑不靈的反對分子暴力滋事。

撫平國家傷口的時候到了，化解嫌隙的時候到了，創造的時機就在我們眼前。

---

2. Pretoria: the seat of the executive branch of the government of South Africa
   南非行政首都普利托里亞

3. mimosa tree: a species of legume in the genus Albizia 合歡

4. bushveld: a sub-tropical woodland ecoregion of Southern Africa 南非灌木林區

5. exhilaration [ɪɡˌzɪləˈreɪʃən] (n.) a feeling of being happy, excited, and full of energy
   愉快的心情

6. spurn [spɜːrn] (v.) to reject with contempt 摒棄；唾棄

7. pernicious [pərˈnɪʃəs] (a.) having a very harmful effect or influence 邪惡的；有害的

8. Frederik Willem de Klerk (1936–): the last State President of apartheid-era South Africa, engineering the end of apartheid, South Africa's racial segregation policy, and supporting the transformation of South Africa into a multi-racial democracy
   弗雷德里克‧威廉‧戴克拉克（南非種族隔離時代的最後一任白人總統）

9. chasm [ˈkæzəm] (n.) a big difference between two people, groups, or things 隔閡；分歧

We have, at last, achieved our political emancipation. We pledge ourselves to liberate all our people from the continuing bondage of poverty, deprivation, suffering, gender, and other discrimination.

We succeeded to take our last steps to freedom in conditions of relative peace. We commit ourselves to the construction of a complete, just and lasting peace.

We have triumphed in the effort to implant hope in the breasts of the millions of our people. We enter into a covenant[10] that we shall build the society in which all South Africans, both black and white, will be able to walk tall, without any fear in their hearts, assured of their inalienable right to human dignity—a rainbow nation at peace with itself and the world.

As a token of its commitment to the renewal of our country, the new Interim[11] Government of National Unity will, as a matter of urgency, address the issue of amnesty[12] for various categories of our people who are currently serving terms of imprisonment.

We dedicate this day to all the heroes and heroines in this country and the rest of the world who sacrificed in many ways and surrendered their lives so that we could be free.

Their dreams have become reality. Freedom is their reward.

We are both humbled and elevated by the honor and privilege that you, the people of South Africa, have bestowed on us, as the first President of a united, democratic, non-racial and non-sexist South Africa, to lead our country out of the valley of darkness.

We understand it still that there is no easy road to freedom. We know it well that none of us acting alone can achieve success. We must therefore act together as a united people, for national reconciliation, for nation building, for the birth of a new world.

Let there be justice for all. Let there be peace for all. Let there be work, bread, water and salt for all. Let each know that for each the body, the mind and the soul have been freed to fulfil themselves.

Never, never and never again shall it be that this beautiful land will again experience the oppression of one by another and suffer the indignity of being the skunk[13] of the world. Let freedom reign. The sun shall never set on so glorious a human achievement!

God bless Africa! ◖

42

曼德拉總統就職演説

我們目前至少已經完成了政治上解放。我們誓言，我們還要把陷於貧困、剝削、痛苦和性別歧視等各種不公平待遇之中的所有人民解放出來。

我們在還算和平的過程中，成功地踏出了邁向自由的最後幾步，我們要肩負起責任去建設一個全面的、正義的、持續性的和平。

我們成功地讓我們數百萬人民的心中都燃起了希望，我們立下誓約，要建立一個讓所有南非人，不論是黑人還是白人，都可以昂首闊步的社會，讓人們不會再心存恐懼，而是確定自己擁有不可剝奪的人類尊嚴——我們要建立這樣一個四海昇平的美好國度。

要證明我們這個國家已獲得重生，新成立的全國團結臨時政府的當務之急，是處理目前在獄中服刑的各類囚犯的特赦問題。

我們要把今天這一天，獻給這個國家和世界各地的所有英雄們，他們為了人類的自由，做了很多的犧牲奉獻，甚至失去了性命。

如今他們的夢想實現了，而用來報答他們的就是自由。

身為一個統一、自由、沒有種族和性別歧視的南非首任總統，我們懷著戰戰兢兢又欣喜的心情，接受南非人民所給予我們的這份榮譽和權利，來帶領我們國家走出黑暗的幽谷。

我們深知，我們邁向自由的道路仍然崎嶇。我們很清楚，我們誰都沒辦法靠單打獨鬥來達到這個目的。為了國內的和解，為了建立我們這個國家，為了打造一個新的世界，我們必須團結奮鬥。

讓所有人都享有正義，讓所有人都享有和平，讓所有人都有工作權，可以得到溫飽。讓每一個人都知道，我們每一個人的身體、心靈和靈魂，都可以自由地去自我實現。

我們永永遠遠都不要讓這塊美麗的土地，再發生人類互相迫害的事情，或是再被全世界所唾棄，遭受屈辱。讓自由戰勝一切吧！今天對於人類的這項成就，陽光照耀得格外燦爛。

願上帝保佑南非！

10. covenant [ˈkʌvənənt] (n.) a formal agreement between two or more people; a promise 盟約

11. interim [ˈɪntərɪm] (n.) the time between one event, process, or period and another 過渡期間

12. amnesty [ˈæmnəsti] (n.) an official order by a government that allows a particular group of prisoners to go free 大赦；特赦

13. skunk [skʌnk] (n.) a black-and-white animal that ejects a foul-smelling liquid as a defensive action 臭鼬；卑鄙的人

Who Will Speak for the Common Good?

女性黑人議員基調演說：
誰能代表共同的利益？

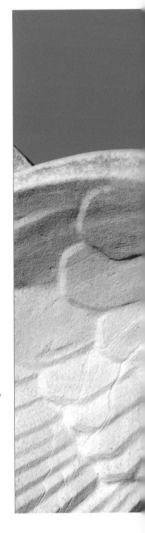

芭芭拉·喬丹（Barbara Charline Jordan, 1936–1996），美國女性政治家。1966 年，成為美國第一位非裔女性黑人的州議員；1973–1979 年間，擔任美國眾議院國會議員。

1976 年，芭芭拉·喬丹成為第一位在民主黨全國大會上發表基調演說的非裔女性黑人。她這一場演講，在美國 20 世紀最偉大的百篇演說中，被評選為第五名，也是公認在歐巴馬 2004 年民主黨全國大會上基調演說之前，最優秀的一篇基調演說。

1973 年，芭芭拉·喬丹不幸得到硬化症；1979 年，她退出政壇，擔任教職，1992 年，她再度授命在民主黨全國大會上發表基調演說，主題設定為「改變：從哪裡改變？要改變成什麼樣子？」（Change: From What to What?）

芭芭拉·喬丹的貢獻，使她獲頒過不計其數的榮譽和獎項，並於 1994 年榮獲「總統自由勳章」。在她去世後，她的故事曾以《美好希望之聲》（Voice of Good Hope）的劇名搬上百老匯舞臺。2009 年，德州的奧斯汀大學在校園裡豎立了一座她的雕像。

Speaker 美國前女性黑人議員芭芭拉‧喬丹
（Barbara Charline Jordan, 1936–1996）

Time 1976 年 7 月 12 日

Place 美國紐約市，1976 年民主黨全國大會基調演說
（Democratic National Convention Keynote Address）

▣ 原音重現　▣ 擷錄

93

Thank you ladies and gentlemen for a very warm reception.

It was one hundred and forty-four years ago that members of the Democratic Party first met in convention to select a Presidential candidate. Since that time, Democrats have continued to convene once every four years and draft a party platform and nominate a Presidential candidate. And our meeting this week is a continuation of that tradition. But there is something different about tonight. There is something special about tonight. What is different? What is special?

I, Barbara Jordan, am a keynote speaker.

When—A lot of years passed since 1832, and during that time it would have been most unusual for any national political party to ask a Barbara Jordan to deliver a keynote address. But tonight, here I am. And I feel—I feel that notwithstanding the past that my presence here is one additional bit of evidence that the American Dream need not forever be deferred.

Now—Now that I have this grand distinction, what in the world am I supposed to say?

I could easily spend this time praising the accomplishments of this party and attacking the Republicans—but I don't choose to do that. I could list the many problems which Americans have. I could list the problems which cause people to feel cynical, angry, frustrated: problems which include lack of integrity in government; the feeling that the individual no longer counts; the reality of material and spiritual poverty; the feeling that the grand American experiment[1] is failing or has failed. I could recite these problems, and then I could sit down and offer no solutions. But I don't choose to do that either. The citizens of America expect more. They deserve and they want more than a recital of problems.

We are a people in a quandary[2] about the present. We are a people in search of our future. We are a people in search of a national community. We are a people trying not only to solve the problems of the present, unemployment, inflation, but we are attempting on a larger scale to fulfill the promise of America. We are attempting to fulfill our national purpose, to create and sustain a society in which all of us are equal.

And now—now we must look to the future. Let us heed the voice of the people and recognize their common sense. If we do not, we not only blaspheme[3] our political heritage, we ignore the common ties that bind all Americans. →

感謝你們各位先生女士的熱情迎接。

　　一百四十四年前，民主黨的黨員們第一次召開全國代表大會，以便選出總統候選人。從那時候起，民主黨每四年都會召開一次全國代表大會，制定黨的綱領，並提名總統及副總統候選人。我們這個星期的會議，就是在延續這個傳統。然而，今晚與以往有些許的不同，今晚特別的不一樣。不一樣的地方在哪裡？到底是哪裡特別了？

　　我，芭芭拉‧喬丹，竟然是這場基調演說的演講者！

　　從 1832 年到現在，已經過了很長的時間了，在當時，要是有任何政黨來叫芭芭拉‧喬丹做基調演說的發表人，那是很匪夷所思的。然而，就在今晚，我竟然站上這裡了！我感到，不管過去如何，我今晚站在這裡，就是另一個證明：證明美國夢並非是永遠遙不可及的。

　　現在，我有這無比的榮幸站在這裡，我到底應該要說什麼？

　　我可以拍拍黨的馬屁，罵罵共和黨，很容易就可以混過這場演講──但我不會這樣做。我也可以列出一大堆美國的問題，大談那些讓人民感到悲觀、憤怒或沮喪的問題：像是政府不夠清廉，人民失去信心，民生物質匱乏，人們心靈感到空虛，或是感到美國企圖達到真正自由的努力並不會成功。我可以把這些問題唸出來，然後坐回位子上，對於解決辦法隻字不提──但我也不會這麼做，美國人民要的不只是這些，他們要的不是把問題唸一唸就好，他們應得到的收穫也應該要比這個多。

　　我們是一個陷入眼前困境的國家。我們在尋找我們的未來，在尋找一個整體的國家社會。我們不只是要解決眼前的問題，像是失業或通膨的問題，我們還要更廣泛地去兌現美國的承諾。我們在努力實現國家的目標，創造和維持一個人人生而平等的社會。

　　現在，就是現在，我們必須往前看，我們必須傾聽人民的聲音，了解主流民意，不然我們不只會褻瀆先人所留下來的政治遺產，也會忽略了將全體美國人相繫在一起的關係。

---

1. grand American experiment: American revolution toward freedom
   指美國企圖成為一個真正自由之國家的革命與努力
2. quandary [ˈkwɑːndəri] (n.) a state of hesitation or doubt; dilemma 進退兩難的困境
3. blaspheme [blæsˈfiːm] (v.) to treat sacred things disrespectfully through words or action
   褻瀆

94

Many fear the future. Many are distrustful of their leaders, and believe that their voices are never heard. Many seek only to satisfy their private work—wants; to satisfy their private interests. But this is the great danger America faces—that we will cease to be one nation and become instead a collection of interest groups: city against suburb, region against region, individual against individual; each seeking to satisfy private wants. If that happens, who then will speak for America? Who then will speak for the common good?

This is the question which must be answered in 1976: Are we to be one people bound together by common spirit, sharing in a common endeavor; or will we become a divided nation? For all of its uncertainty, we cannot flee the future. We must not become the "New Puritans" and reject our society. We must address and master the future together. It can be done if we restore the belief that we share a sense of national community, that we share a common national endeavor. It can be done.

There is no executive order[4]; there is no law that can require the American people to form a national community. This we must do as individuals, and if we do it as individuals, there is no President of the United States who can veto[5] that decision.

As a first step—As a first step, we must restore our belief in ourselves. We are a generous people, so why can't we be generous with each other? We need to take to heart the words spoken by Thomas Jefferson:

Let us restore the social intercourse—"Let us restore to social intercourse that harmony and that affection without which liberty and even life are but dreary things."

A nation is formed by the willingness of each of us to share in the responsibility for upholding the common good. A government is invigorated when each one of us is willing to participate in shaping the future of this nation. In this election year, we must define the "common good" and begin again to shape a common future. Let each person do his or her part. If one citizen is unwilling to participate, all of us are going to suffer. For the American idea, though it is shared by all of us, is realized in each one of us. →

許多人對未來感到不安。許多人都不相信領導者，也不認為人民的聲音會被聽到。許多人只追求個人工作與需求的滿足，只關心自己個人的事情。這是美國所面臨的重大危機——我們這個國家可能會分崩離析，變成只是各種利益團體的組合：市區與郊區對立，各個地區互相對立，人與人互相對立，只求能夠滿足個人的需求就好。一旦演變成這樣，那麼，到時候誰講的話可以代表美國？誰講的話又可以代表大家共同的利益？

這是今年應該要被回答的問題：我們是一個基於共同精神和共同努力所形成的民族，還是我們要變成一個四分五裂的國家？眼前有這麼多不確定的因素，讓我們無法不面對未來。我們不應該變成「新清教徒」，而離棄我們的社會。我們必須一起來討論和創造未來，如果我們重拾信念，認為我們是一個整體的國家和社會，大家都在為這個國家打拚，那我們就能一起來討論未來、創造未來。

沒有什麼總統的行政命令或是法律規定，可以要求美國人民來創造一個整體的國家社會。這是我們每一個人所必須做的，而且只要我們每一個人都肯做，那就算是美國總統也無法否決這項決議。

第一步，我們要踏出的第一步，就是重拾我們自己的信念。我們是一個寬宏大量的民族，難道我們就不能也對自己人寬大嗎？我們應該要把傑佛遜的話聽進我們的心裡頭：

讓我們恢復社會的交流——「讓我們恢復和諧溫馨的社會交流，否則自由——甚至連生活本身——都會變成是一種惡夢。」

一個國家之所以形成，是基於每一個人的意願，願意為增進大家共同的利益，而共同分擔責任。當我們每一個人都願意參與、一起打造這個國家的未來，那這個國家的政府就會顯得生氣勃勃。在今年這個選舉年裡，我們需要定義什麼是「共同利益」，然後重新打造一個共同的未來。讓我們每一個人都盡自己的一份責任，只要有任何一個人民不想參與，我們所有人就都會受到影響。我們所有人都分享了「美國」這個概念，但這個概念需要在我們每一個人的身上實現出來。

---

4. executive order: an order having the force of law issued by the president of the U.S. to the army, navy, or other part of the executive branch of the government 美國總統的行政命令

5. veto [ˈviːtoʊ] (v.) to vote against; refuse to endorse 否決

95

And now, what are those of us who are elected public officials supposed to do? We call ourselves "public servants" but I'll tell you this: We as public servants must set an example for the rest of the nation. It is hypocritical for the public official to admonish[6] and exhort[7] the people to uphold the common good if we are derelict[8] in upholding the common good. More is required—More is required of public officials than slogans and handshakes and press releases. More is required. We must hold ourselves strictly accountable. We must provide the people with a vision of the future.

If we promise as public officials, we must deliver. If—If we as public officials propose, we must produce. If we say to the American people, "It is time for you to be sacrificial"—sacrifice. If the public official says that, we [public officials] must be the first to give. We must be. And again, if we make mistakes, we must be willing to admit them. We have to do that. What we have to do is strike a balance[9] between the idea that government should do everything and the idea, the belief, that government ought to do nothing. Strike a balance.

Let there be no illusions about the difficulty of forming this kind of a national community. It's tough, difficult, not easy. But a spirit of harmony will survive in America only if each of us remembers that we share a common destiny; if each of us remembers, when self-interest and bitterness seem to prevail, that we share a common destiny.

I have confidence that we can form this kind of national community. I have confidence that the Democratic Party can lead the way. I have that confidence.

We cannot improve on the system of government handed down to us by the founders of the Republic. There is no way to improve upon that. But what we can do is to find new ways to implement that system and realize our destiny.

Now I began this speech by commenting to you on the uniqueness of a Barbara Jordan making a keynote address. Well I am going to close my speech by quoting a Republican President and I ask you that as you listen to these words of Abraham Lincoln, relate them to the concept of a national community in which every last one of us participates:

"As I would not be a slave, so I would not be a master." This—This—"This expresses my idea of Democracy. Whatever differs from this, to the extent of the difference, is no Democracy." Thank you. ◖

現在，我們這些由人民所選出來的政務官，我們到底應該做什麼？我們自稱是「公僕」，但我要跟各位說：我們這些公僕必須要率先做國家人民的典範。如果政府官員只規勸和敦促人民要為共同的利益而努力，自己卻不努力，那就很假惺惺了。政府官員要做的，決非只是喊喊口號、握握手和上上媒體而已。政府官員要做的事很多，我們必須嚴格要求自己負責，並為人民提出一個願景。

我們政府官員要是開出了支票，就一定要兌現。我們要是做出了什麼計畫，就一定要去完成它。如果我們跟美國人民說：「這是你們要做出犧牲奉獻的時候了。」如果政府官員說出了這種話，那我們就必須先自行做到。我們務必做到這一點。還有，我們要是做錯了，我們就必須願意坦誠認錯，非這樣做不可。我們還一定要做到的，是在政府凡事有為與凡事無為之間，找到一個折衷的辦法，找到一個兩全的辦法。

建設這樣一個整體的國家社會，我們也不用假裝說這其實並不難。這並不是一件容易的事，這是一項艱鉅困難的工作。然而，只要我們大家都牢記著我們是同舟共濟的，那麼美國就會產生和諧的精神。在面臨個人的利害關係時，只要我們大家都牢記著，我們是同舟共濟的就可以了。

我有信心我們一定可以建立這樣一個整體的國家社會，我也有信心民主黨能夠帶領我們去完成這件事，我對此深具信心。

我們無法靠美國的締造者們來改進政府的體制，這是不可能的事，但我們可以找出新的出路來改善體制，創造我們的命運。

今天我用芭芭拉‧喬丹成為基調演說一事來做為演講的開場白，現在我要引用一位美國總統的話來做結尾，並且請求你們在聆聽林肯的話時，能夠將他的話和整體國家社會這個概念連結起來，在其中我們每一個人都參與在裡頭的：

「我不要成為奴隸，所以我也不要成為奴隸主──這表達了我的民主概念。只要違反這個原則，不管是違反的程度如何，就都不是民主。」

謝謝各位！

6. admonish [əd'mɑːnɪʃ] (v.) to tell someone severely that they have done something wrong 勸告
7. exhort [ɪg'zɔːrt] (v.) to try very hard to persuade someone to do something 敦促
8. derelict ['derɪlɪkt] (a.) failing in what duty requires 怠忽職守的
9. strike a balance: an expression alludes to accounting, where it signifies finding a profit or loss by weighing income versus outlay 找到折衷辦法；權衡利害得失

Science and Art

生物學家赫胥黎：
科學與藝術

赫胥黎（Thomas Henry Huxley, 1825–1895）是英國著名的博物學家，他學識廣博，而且才華橫溢，具有文學稟賦，其科普文章簡潔易懂，清末學者嚴復還曾翻譯過他的作品《天演論》（Evolution and Ethics）。

赫胥黎是達爾文演化論最傑出的代表，在達爾文發表《物種起源》（On the Origin of Species: By Means of Natural Selection）一書後，他力倡演化論，是第一個提出人類起源問題的學者。

赫胥黎在科學研究上的成就，使他在 1850 年被選為皇家學會院士，並且至少獲得 53 個海外科學團體授予的榮譽稱號。晚年，他主要致力於哲學和神學的寫作，並且曾用「不可知論」（agnostic）來描述自己的哲學觀點。

在赫胥黎的後代中，有幾個人也有很傑出的表現，因此形成了知名的赫胥黎家族。這個人才輩出的家族簡例如下：

1. 著名的反烏托邦小說《美麗新世界》（Brave New World），就是其孫子阿道斯（Aldous Huxley, 1894–1963）的名作。

2. 生理學家安德魯（Andrew Huxley, 1917–2012）是 1963 年的諾貝爾獎得主。

3. 朱利安（Julian Huxley, 1887–1975）則是第一屆聯合國教育科學文化組織首長（1946–1948 年），也是世界自然基金會創始成員之一。

Speaker 英國生物學家赫胥黎
（Thomas Henry Huxley, 1825–1895）

Time 1883 年 5 月 5 日

Place 倫敦皇家學院某一宴會（Royal Academy, London）

◉ 錄音　◉ 全篇收錄

Perseus, Andromeda, and the Dragon

I beg leave to thank you for the extremely kind and appreciative manner in which you have received the toast of Science. It is the more grateful to me to hear that toast proposed in an assembly of this kind, because I have noticed of late years a great and growing tendency among those who were once jestingly said to have been born in a pre-scientific age to look upon science as an invading and aggressive force, which if it had its own way would oust from the universe all other pursuit.

I think there are many persons who look upon this new birth of our times as a sort of monster rising out of the sea of modern thought with the purpose of devouring the Andromeda[1] of art. And now and then a Perseus, equipped with the shoes of swiftness of the ready writer, with the cap of invisibility of the editorial article, and it may be with the Medusa head of vituperation[2], shows himself ready to try conclusions with the scientific dragon. →

請允許我感謝各位的友好和賞光，聆聽了這篇關於「科學」的祝酒辭。讓我更感動的是，想不到能在今天這樣的聚會上聽到這樣的祝酒辭，因為我發現在最近這幾年，有一種愈來愈明顯的趨勢——那就是那些被笑稱生於前科學時代的人，他們把「科學」視為洪水猛獸，認為要是任科學這樣為所欲為，就會把其他行業都趕出宇宙之外。

我想有很多人把當代這個新誕生的東西，看成是在現代思潮海洋中冒出來的一頭怪物，準備一口把「藝術女神安朵美達」吞噬掉。於是，一位「柏修斯」就會不時出現，他配備著「才思敏捷之作家的飛鞋」，和一頂「重要評論的隱形帽」，抓著滿口謾罵的「梅杜莎的蛇髮頭顱」，準備和這隻科學惡龍一決勝負。

---

1. In Greek mythology, Andromeda was an Ethiopian princess, who was rescued from a monster by her future husband Perseus. Medusa was a woman transformed into a Gorgon by Athena; she was slain by Perseus. Then, Perseus used Medusa's head to destroy the dragon.
在古希臘神話中，安朵美達是一位衣索匹亞的公主，她母親因為觸怒海中女神，她因此被俘來準備獻給海怪。這時，才剛解決蛇髮女妖梅杜莎的英雄柏修斯，他恰巧騎著飛馬，持著梅杜莎的頭顱飛過，使用梅杜莎的頭顱殺掉惡龍，救出安朵美達。兩人後來成了夫妻。

2. vituperation [vaɪˌtuːpəˈreɪʃən] (n.) an outburst of violently abusive or harshly critical language 謾罵

Sir, I hope that Perseus will think better of it; first, for his own sake, because the creature is hard of head, strong of jaw, and for some time past has shown a great capacity for going over and through whatever comes in his way; and secondly, for the sake of justice, for I assure you, of my own personal knowledge that if left alone, the creature is a very debonair[3] and gentle monster.

As for the Andromeda of art, he has the tenderest respect for that lady, and desires nothing more than to see her happily settled and annually producing a flock of such charming children as those we see about us.

But putting parables aside, I am unable to understand how any one with a knowledge of mankind can imagine that the growth of science can threaten the development of art in any of its forms. If I understand the matter at all, science and art are the obverse and reverse of Nature's medal; the one expressing the eternal order of things, in terms of feeling, the other in terms of thought.

When men no longer love nor hate; when suffering causes no pity, and the tale of great deeds ceases to thrill, when the lily of the field shall seem no longer more beautifully arrayed than Solomon[4] in all his glory, and the awe has vanished from the snow-capped peak and deep ravine[5], then indeed science may have the world to itself, but it will not be because the monster has devoured art, but because one side of human nature is dead, and because men have lost the half of their ancient and present attributes.

3. debonair [ˌdebəˈner] (a.) having a cheerful, lively, and self-confident air 和藹親切的

4. Solomon: (Old Testament) son of David and king of Israel noted for his wisdom (10th century BC) 所羅門王，在舊約聖經中以智慧著稱

5. ravine [rəˈviːn] (n.) a deep narrow steep-sided valley (especially one formed by running water) 深谷

Perseus used Medusa's head to destroy the dragon

　　各位，但願柏修斯能三思。首先，這是為了柏修斯自己的安危，因為這隻怪物的頭很堅硬，下顎非常有力，而且過去這一段時間以來已經顯示出，誰要是擋牠的路，牠都有能力把他解決掉。再者，這是基於公平的原因來考量，我敢跟你們打包票，依我的個人之見，只要不要去招惹牠，牠就會是一隻很乖、很溫馴的怪物。

　　至於那位藝術女神安朵美達，這隻怪物可是很敬愛她的。牠別無所求，只期盼她能過得幸福快樂，每年生出一群可愛的兒女，就像我們凡夫一樣。

　　而以上這個譬喻就講到這裡。我無法了解的是，凡具有人類知識的人，怎麼會認為科學的發展會對任何形式的藝術造成威脅。如果我還是略有所懂的話，我想科學和藝術是大自然的一體兩面，一面是用「感受」來表達出萬物永恆的秩序，另一面則是透過「思維」來表達。

　　當人類不再有愛有恨，對苦難無動於衷；當偉大事跡不再感動人心；當田野上的百合花，不能再與「智慧之王所羅門」一身的榮耀相媲美；當雪峰和深谷不再令人屏息──如果到時候科學果真獨霸了天下，那並不是因為科學怪物把藝術吞噬掉了，而是因為人類喪失了某些天性，喪失了自古以來的大半天性。

The Road to Business Success
A Talk to Young Men

卡內基給年輕人的話：
事業成功之道

美國鋼鐵大王安德魯・卡內基（Andrew Carnegie, 1835–1919）出生於蘇格蘭，父親當時是紡織工人，因為生活很苦，在卡內基 12 歲時舉家移居美國。

卡內基白手起家，他從小就開始打工，閒暇時喜歡閱讀。美國內戰之前，他就已經是一個成功的企業投資者，之後他不斷地擴大投資，財富也不斷地增加。在人類近代歷史上，卡內基被認為是世界第二富豪，僅次於與他同時代的石油大王洛克斐勒。1900 年，他在《財富的福音》（The Gospel of Wealth）一書中宣布：「我將不再汲於賺取更多的財富」。

卡內基也是一名慈善家。他以前常去圖書館借書，所以他特別喜歡捐贈圖書館。1881 年他捐贈了第一座圖書館，之後 16 年內，他興辦了將近三千間的圖書館，而且遍及世界各地。

1900 年，他在匹茲堡創辦了卡內基技術學校（Carnegie Technical Schools）。這個學校於 1967 年與梅隆工業研究所合併，改為卡內基梅隆大學（Carnegie Mellon University）。

1911 年，他以 1.5 億美元創立了「紐約卡內基基金會」（Carnegie Corporation of New York）。這個基金會旨在促進提升教育和傳播知識，這也是美國成立最久且最具影響力的基金會之一。

在 1919 年去世之前，卡內基一共捐出三億五千多萬美元。卡內基認為財富不應該留給自己的後代，他臨終前囑咐要將剩餘的財富全部捐出。

Speaker 美國鋼鐵大王卡內基（Andrew Carnegie, 1835–1919）

Time 1885 年 6 月 23 日

Place 美國匹茲堡克里商業學院
（Curry Commercial College, Pittsburgh）

☑ 錄音　☑ 擷錄

Andrew Carnegie (1835–1919)

It is well that young men should begin at the beginning and occupy the most subordinate[1] positions. Many of the leading businessmen of Pittsburgh had a serious responsibility thrust upon them at the very threshold of their career. They were introduced to the broom, and spent the first hours of their business lives sweeping out the office.

I notice we have janitors and janitresses now in offices, and our young men unfortunately miss that salutary[2] branch of business education. But if by chance the professional sweeper is absent any morning, the boy who has the genius of the future partner in him will not hesitate to try his hand at the broom. It does not hurt the newest comer to sweep out the office if necessary. I was one of those sweepers myself.

And here is the prime condition of success, the great secret: concentrate your energy, thought, and capital exclusively upon the business in which you are engaged. Having begun in one line, resolve to fight it out on that line, to lead in it, adopt every improvement, have the best machinery, and know the most about it.

The concerns which fail are those which have scattered their capital, which means that they have scattered their brains also. They have investments in this, or that, or the other, here there, and everywhere. "Don't put all your eggs in one basket." is all wrong. I tell you to "put all your eggs in one basket, and then watch that basket."

Look round you and take notice, men who do that not often fail. It is easy to watch and carry the one basket. It is trying to carry too many baskets that breaks most eggs in this country. He who carries three baskets must put one on his head, which is apt to tumble and trip him up. One fault of the American businessman is lack of concentration.

To summarize what I have said: aim for the highest; never enter a bar room; do not touch liquor, or if at all only at meals; never speculate; never indorse beyond your surplus cash fund; make the firm's interest yours; break orders always to save owners; concentrate; put all your eggs in one basket, and watch that basket; expenditure always within revenue; lastly, be not impatient, for as Emerson says, "no one can cheat you out of ultimate success but yourselves."

年輕人應該從最基礎的開始，從最基層的工作開始做起。匹茲堡的很多大企業家，他們在創業之初，都肩負過需要認真對待的重任：他們從灑掃庭除開始，這是他們事業最初的起步。

我看到我們公司現在有專門的清潔人員，這使我們的年輕人不幸地錯過了這個可以讓人獲益良多的職業訓練。如果碰巧哪天早上清潔人員請假了，一個具有潛力成為企業家的年輕人，會二話不說地拿起掃把來打掃。如果有需要，讓新來的員工去打掃辦公室的外面，這並不會傷到他們的自尊心，因為我自己就是一個過來人。

成功的首要條件和最大祕訣是：把你全部的精力、心思和資本，都投入在你目前的事業上。一旦開始了那一行，就要拿出決心拚出一個名堂，要走在別人的前頭，一點一滴不斷地改善，要進最優良的機器，而且要通曉這一行。

一些公司的失敗就在於他們分散了資金，這也意謂著他們分散了他們的精力。他們這裡投資一些，那裡投資一些，東投資西投資，什麼都要摻一腳。「不要把所有的雞蛋放在同一個籃子裡」，這句話是大錯特錯的。我會跟你說：「把你所有的雞蛋都裝進同一個籃子裡，然後好好照顧好那個籃子。」

看看你四周的人，你會發現，採取這種作法的人通常不會失敗。只有一個籃子要看管，是比較容易的事。在這個國家，人們因為想要提很多的籃子，結果把大部分的蛋都打破了。想要提三個籃子的人，只得把其中一個籃子放在頭頂上，這樣籃子就容易掉下來，把自己絆到。美國企業家的一個缺點，就是不夠專注。

我把我的話做個總結，那就是：要胸懷大志，不要涉足酒吧，不要沾酒，頂多只能在用餐時喝一點；不要做投機買賣，不要寅吃卯糧；要把公司的利益當作是自己的利益；以業主的利益，為自己工作的準則；要集中精力，要把所有的雞蛋放在同一個籃子裡，然後小心地看好它；要量入為出；最後，要有耐心，就像愛默生所說的：「除了你自己，沒有人能把你拉離開最終的成功。」

---

1. subordinate [sə'bɔːrdɪnət] (a.) having a lower or less important position 下級的；次要的
2. salutary ['sæljuteri] (a.) causing improvement of behavior or character 有益健康的

Seventieth Birthday

馬克・吐溫：
七十大壽謝辭

馬克・吐溫被譽為美國文學之父、美國文學界的林肯，是美國文學中最具代表性的作家。他來自密蘇里州一個貧窮的家庭，所以他的學識與文筆都是靠自學而來的。他年輕時，特別喜歡閱讀莎士比亞、狄更斯和西班牙文學家塞凡提斯等人的作品。

當時密蘇里州是奴隸州，而黑奴的故事也成為馬克・吐溫小說中常見的主題，像是《湯姆歷險記》（ *The Adventures of Tom Sawyer* ）和《頑童流浪記》（ *Adventures of Huckleberry Finn* ）。《湯姆歷險記》是全世界最家喻戶曉的一本名著。而《頑童流浪記》則是公認最偉大的美國小說之一，它是美國文學史上具劃時代意義的寫實主義作品，被喻為「美國版的魯賓遜漂流記」，也是馬克・吐溫登峰造極之作，作家海明威甚至說：

All modern American literature comes from one
book by Mark Twain called *Huckleberry Finn.*
美國所有的現代文學，都濫觴於馬克・吐溫的
一本書《頑童流浪記》。

馬克・吐溫的作品以幽默諷刺著稱，這篇演說是他在 70 歲生日祝壽會上所發表的，保持其詼諧逗趣的一貫風格。

Speaker	美國大文豪馬克・吐溫 （Mark Twain, 1835–1910)
Time	1905 年 12 月 5 日
Place	紐約 Delmonico's 餐廳 （Delmonico's, New York, USA）

回 錄音　回 摘錄

I have had a great many birthdays in my time. I remember the first one very well, and I always think of it with indignation[1]; everything was so crude, unaesthetic, primeval. Nothing like this at all. No proper appreciative preparation made; nothing really ready. Now, for a person born with high and delicate instincts—why, even the cradle wasn't whitewashed—nothing ready at all. I hadn't any hair, I hadn't any teeth, I hadn't any clothes, I had to go to my first banquet just like that.

Well, everybody came swarming in. It was the merest little bit of a village—hardly that, just a little hamlet, in the backwoods of Missouri, where nothing ever happened, and the people were all interested, and they all came; they looked me over to see if there was anything fresh in my line. Why, nothing ever happened in that village—I—why, I was the only thing that had really happened there for months and months and months; and although I say it myself that shouldn't, I came the nearest to being a real event that had happened in that village in more than, two years.

Well, those people came, they came with that curiosity which is so provincial, with that frankness which also is so provincial, and they examined me all around and gave their opinion. Nobody asked them, and I shouldn't have minded if anybody had paid me a compliment, but nobody did. Their opinions were all just green with prejudice, and I feel those opinions to this day.

Well, I stood that as long as—well, you know I was born courteous, and I stood it to the limit. I stood it an hour, and then the worm turned[2]. I was the worm; it was my turn to turn, and I turned. I knew very well the strength of my position; I knew that I was the only spotlessly pure and innocent person in that whole town, and I came out and said so: And they could not say a word. It was so true: They blushed; they were embarrassed. Well, that was the first after-dinner speech I ever made: I think it was after dinner.

It's a long stretch between that first birthday speech and this one. That was my cradle-song; and this is my swan-song[3], I suppose. I am used to swan-songs; I have sung them several, times. ◖

我這一生，已經過了很多次的生日。我的第一個生日，我還記得很清楚，而且我一想到它就義憤填膺，因為所有的一切都顯得那麼粗糙、醜陋、野蠻，跟今晚完全不一樣。那時連個什麼都沒有，什麼東西都沒有準備。對一個生來就具有高強本領而且又細膩的人來說——哎，竟然連個搖籃也不粉刷一下——什麼都沒準備：我頭上一根毛也沒有，也沒有牙齒，還一絲不掛，我竟然不得不用這副德性出席我第一次的生日派對。

哎呀，村民們蜂擁而至，那是密蘇里州一個偏遠的小村落，一個彈丸之地，那裡從來不曾發生過什麼大事情，所以村民們都跑來看熱鬧。他們很仔細地觀察我，想看看我會不會有哪裡長得不一樣，哦，那個村子裡沒有什麼新鮮事——我的出生，是村子裡這麼多個月以來唯一的大事。雖然我自己會說這根本算不上是什麼事，但村子已經整整兩年多沒有發生過事情了。

所以那些村民們就來囉，他們滿懷好奇心，而且很俗氣，講話又白又俗，他們一直在那邊檢查我，而且品頭論足。又沒有人詢問他們的意見，如果有人跟我講句好話，那我也就算了不計較，但偏偏就是沒有。他們的意見都充滿了酸溜溜的偏見，我到現在還覺得很不是滋味。

我當時就這樣忍下來——你也知道的，我生來就是一個很懂得禮貌的人，所以一直忍到忍無可忍。弱小不堪的我忍了一個鐘頭之後，開始反抗了。我像條蠕蟲，我開始東扭西扭，奮力反抗。我很清楚我當時所處的地位具有何等的力量，我知道我那時是整個村子裡唯一潔白無瑕、天真無邪的人，所以我就挺身而出，直言不諱，眾人們也只能默默地接受。真實不虛的是，他們臉紅了，窘大了。這就是我生平第一次所做的餐後演講，我想那是餐後的時間沒錯。

從第一次生日演講到現在，是一段漫漫的歲月了。那一次是我的搖籃曲，現在呢，差不多是我的垂死之歌了，我常常在唱垂死之歌，我已經唱過好幾個回合了。

1. indignation [ˌɪndɪɡˈneɪʃən] (n.) feelings of anger and surprise because you feel insulted or unfairly treated 憤怒；憤慨
2. the worm will turn: from a proverb, "Tread on a worm and it will turn." 出自俗諺，指「忍無可忍時，弱小者也會反抗。」
3. swan-song: an ancient belief that the Mute Swan is completely mute during its lifetime until the moment just before it dies, when it sings one beautiful song 垂死之歌

Mother Teresa: Nobel Lecture

德蕾莎修女諾貝爾獎謝辭：
毀滅和平的最大兇手

德蕾莎修女（Blessed Teresa of Calcutta, 1910–1997）出生於現今為馬其頓共和國的首都史高比耶（Skopje），是阿爾巴尼亞裔人。她在 1931 年正式成為修女，1937 年成為終身職的修女，並改名為德蕾莎修女。2003 年 10 月，教宗若望・保祿二世把她列入天主教的真福名單。

1929 年，年紀輕輕的德蕾莎修女來到了印度。1940 年代初期，德蕾莎修女在加爾各答聖瑪莉中學擔任校長。1948 年，教宗庇護十二世准予她以自由修女身分行善，並撥給她一個社區和住所。德蕾莎修女隨即接受醫療訓練，1950 年 10 月，她與其他 11 位修女成立仁愛會（the Missionaries of Charity）。

1960 年代，德蕾莎修女的收容所急速成長，並且開始招募世界各地的義工。她在印度和其他國家創辦了五十多所學校、醫院、濟貧院、青年中心和孤兒院。

2009 年，在諾貝爾獎各獎項即將揭曉之際，諾貝爾基金會評出了諾貝爾獎百餘年以來最受尊崇的三位獲獎者。他們分別是：1964 年和平獎得主金恩博士、1921 年物理學獎得主愛因斯坦，以及 1979 年和平獎得主德蕾莎修女。以下這篇便是德蕾莎修女的和平獎謝辭。

Speaker 天主教慈善工作家真福德蕾莎修女
（Blessed Teresa of Calcutta, 1910–1997）

Time 1979 年 12 月 11 日

Place 挪威首都奧斯陸市政廳（Oslo City Hall）

☑ 錄音　☑ 擷錄

Copyright © The Nobel Foundation

(100)

I never forget an opportunity I had in visiting a home where they had all these old parents of sons and daughters who had just put them in an institution and forgotten maybe. And I went there, and I saw in that home they had everything, beautiful things, but everybody was looking towards the door. And I did not see a single one with their smile on their face.

And I turned to the Sister and I asked: How is that? How is it that the people they have everything here, why are they all looking towards the door, why are they not smiling?

I am so used to see the smile on our people, even the dying one smile, and she said: This is nearly every day, they are expecting, they are hoping that a son or daughter will come to visit them. They are hurt because they are forgotten, and see—this is where love comes.

That poverty comes right there in our own home, even neglect to love. Maybe in our own family we have somebody who is feeling lonely, who is feeling sick, who is feeling worried, and these are difficult days for everybody. Are we there, are we there to receive them, is the mother there to receive the child?

I was surprised in the West to see so many young boys and girls given into drugs, and I tried to find out why—why is it like that, and the answer was: Because there is no one in the family to receive them. Father and mother are so busy they have no time. Young parents are in some institution and the child takes back to the street and gets involved in something. →

Kalighat Temple, one of Mother Teresa's place to help the poor, India

　　我永遠也不會忘記那一次我去拜訪一間老人之家，那裡的老人都是被自己的兒女送過來的，他們可能從此就留在機構裡，被兒女所遺忘。我到了那裡，看到那裡的設備一應俱全，布置得還不錯，但每個老人卻都望著門口，我沒有看到任何一個老人的臉上是掛著笑容的。

　　我轉身問修女說：這是怎麼一回事？這裡什麼都有，可是為什麼每個人都看著門口，而且一點笑容也沒有？

　　我一向是習慣看到人們的臉上掛著笑容的，甚至是臨終的笑容。修女回答我說：他們每天差不多都是這樣的，都在滿心期盼看到兒女來探望他們。他們很難過，因為兒女忘記他們了。瞧，那道門就是愛會進來的地方。

　　在我們自己的家裡頭，貧窮就這樣降臨了，連愛都被忽略了。在自己的家裡，可能就有人感到孤獨，或是很不快樂，或是內心裡很不安，而這對每一個人來說都是很難熬的。在這種時刻，我們是否就在他們身邊接納著他們？做母親的是否在孩子旁邊迎接著他們？

　　看到西方世界有那麼多年輕的孩子吸毒，讓我很驚訝，我一直想找出其中的原因，我找到的答案是：因為他們回到家裡時，沒有人迎接他們。父母親忙於工作，無暇照顧孩子，年輕的父母在為工作打拚，孩子就在街頭遊蕩，甚至染上惡習。

Blessed Teresa of Calcutta (1910–1997)

We are talking of peace. These are things that break peace, but I feel the greatest destroyer of peace today is abortion, because it is a direct war, a direct killing—direct murder by the mother herself. We would not be here if our parents would do that to us. Our children, we want them, we love them, but what of the millions?

Many people are very, very concerned with the children in India, with the children in Africa where quite a number die, maybe of malnutrition, of hunger and so on, but millions are dying deliberately by the will of the mother. And this is what is the greatest destroyer of peace today.

Because if a mother can kill her own child—what is left for me to kill you and you kill me—there is nothing between. And this I appeal in India, I appeal everywhere: Let us bring the child back, and this year being the child's year: What have we done for the child? At the beginning of the year I told, I spoke everywhere and I said: Let us make this year that we make every single child born, and unborn, wanted.

And today is the end of the year, have we really made the children wanted? I will give you something terrifying. We are fighting abortion by adoption, we have saved thousands of lives, we have sent words to all the clinics, to the hospitals, police stations—please don't destroy the child, we will take the child. →

我們今天在談論和平，而這些事情恰恰都在破壞和平，其中我認為和平的最大破壞者就是墮胎，這是一種直接的戰爭和謀殺——由母親自己來親自下手執行。如果當初我們的父母親這樣對待我們，我們今天就都不會在這裡了。我們自己的孩子，我們想要他，我們愛護他，但那些無數的沒人要、沒人疼的孩子呢？

有很多人都非常關心在印度的兒童，還有非洲的兒童，他們有很多人死於營養不良或是饑餓等等的，然而，卻有更多無數的孩子死於母親蓄意的謀殺之下，而這就是今天毀滅和平的最大兇手。

如果連母親都可以殺掉自己的孩子——那我殺你、你殺我又算什麼？所以我在印度呼籲，在世界各地呼籲：把我們的孩子帶回來吧！今年是兒童年，我們為兒童做了些什麼？今年年初時我就說過，我在每個地方都呼籲：讓我們在這一年裡，保證每一個孩子都能順利出生，讓每個未出生的孩子都能在被期待下出生。

今天，已經到了年底了，我們是否確實做到了這一點？我要告訴你們一件令人震撼的事，我們用領養的方式來對抗墮胎，而且已經挽救了成千上萬的小生命。我們向所有的診所、醫院和警察局發送文件——請求他們不要奪走孩子的性命，我們會負責來收養。

The poor are very wonderful people. One evening we went out and we picked up four people from the street. And one of them was in a most terrible condition—and I told the Sisters: You take care of the other three, I take of this one that looked worse. So I did for her all that my love can do. I put her in bed, and there was such a beautiful smile on her face. She took hold of my hand, as she said one word only: Thank you—and she died.

I could not help but examine my conscience before her, and I asked what would I say if I was in her place. And my answer was very simple. I would have tried to draw a little attention to myself, I would have said I am hungry, that I am dying, I am cold, I am in pain, or something, but she gave me much more—she gave me her grateful love. And she died with a smile on her face.

And I think that we in our family don't need bombs and guns, to destroy to bring peace—just get together, love one another, bring that peace, that joy, that strength of presence of each other in the home. And we will be able to overcome all the evil that is in the world.

There is so much suffering, so much hatred, so much misery, and we with our prayer, with our sacrifice are beginning at home. Love begins at home, and it is not how much we do, but how much love we put in the action that we do.

And so here I am talking with you—I want you to find the poor here, right in your own home first. And begin love there. Be that good news to your own people. And find out about your next-door neighbor—do you know who they are?

You must come to know the poor, maybe our people here have material things, everything, but I think that if we all look into our own homes, how difficult we find it sometimes to smile at each other, and that the smile is the beginning of love.

And so let us always meet each other with a smile, for the smile is the beginning of love, and once we begin to love each other naturally we want to do something. ◖

窮人是很可愛的。有一天傍晚，我們去街上接回來四個遊民，其中有一個人情況很嚴重──我就跟修女們説：你們去照顧其他三個人，這個看起來最嚴重的人由我來照顧。我盡我所能給的一切來照顧她，我把她扶上床後，她的臉上露出無比動人的笑容，接著她握住我的手，説了一句謝謝，然後就斷氣了。

　　我不禁在她面前反思著，我自問：如果我是她，我會説什麼？我得到了一個很簡單的答案：我大概會盡可能吸引別人的注意，然後説我很餓，説我快死了，説我很痛，諸如此類的。而那個人教了我一種感恩的愛，這讓她在臨終時含笑而走。

　　我想在我們的家裡頭，是不需要用炸彈和槍枝來爭取和平的──我們所要做的，就只是大家聚在一起，彼此相親相愛，為家裡帶來和平、喜悦，還有家中每一分子凝聚在一起的力量。這樣，我們就能夠克服這世界上所有的惡。

　　我們要用祈禱，用我們的犧牲奉獻，從家裡開始，來消除世上這麼多的苦難、仇恨和不幸的事情。愛，要從家裡開始。重點不在於我們做了多少，而是在於我們用了多少的愛心在付諸行動。

　　所以我在這裡要跟大家説──我希望你們能從這裡來尋找貧窮，首先就從你們自己的家庭裡頭找起。然後，讓愛也從家裡開始，讓你自己成為家人的佳音，接著再從鄰居那裡去尋找貧窮──你認識你的鄰居嗎？

　　你一定要去認識那些窮人，我們在場的人也許衣食無憂，應有盡有，但我想如果我們大家都去觀察一下我們自己的家庭，我們會發現，有時要在家人身上看到笑容是何等的困難，而這個笑容就是愛的起點。

　　所以，讓我們永遠笑容迎人吧，微笑是愛的起點，而一旦我們能夠這樣養成自然地去愛別人時，我們就能開始做出貢獻了。

Helen Keller:
Knights of the Blind

海倫‧凱勒：
盲人的騎士

海倫‧凱勒在出生後 19 個月，因為染上猩紅熱而喪失視力與聽力。後來在老師蘇利文（Anne Sullivan）不懈的教導下，開始學習手語、點字和說話。海倫‧凱勒後來畢業於雷德克利夫學院（Radcliffe College），成為一位教育家，並且終其一生都在為失能人士奔走。1955 年，她榮獲哈佛大學頒發的榮譽學位，成為歷史上第一個受此殊榮的女性。

海倫‧凱勒從童年時起，就會被每一任美國總統邀請至白宮做客。1964 年，詹森總統並頒發給她「總統自由勳章」（Presidential Medal of Freedom）。「總統自由勳章」與「國會金質獎章」（Congressional Gold Medal），並列為美國最高的平民榮譽。

1924 年，她發起海倫凱勒基金會（Helen Keller Endowment Fund），同年並加入美國盲人基金會（American Foundation for the Blind）。1925 年，她在國際獅子會的年會上發表了以下這篇演說，呼籲獅子會成為「盲者的武士，出征對抗黑暗」。

這次的演講極為成功，國際獅子會接受了她的要求，遂將視力保健和盲人福利列入主要的服務宗旨之一。1960 年，在海倫八十歲生日那天，美國海外盲人基金會（American Foundation for Overseas Blind）宣布頒發「國際海倫‧凱勒獎」，以獎勵為盲人公共事業做出傑出貢獻的人士。1971 年，國際獅子會的國際理事宣布將海倫‧凱勒逝世這一天——6 月 1 日——訂為全球的「海倫凱勒紀念日」，在這一天，全球的獅子會都會舉辦視力相關的服務活動。

她一生出版過 14 本著作，還有其他一些文章。1903 年，她出版自傳《我的生活》（The Story of My Life）。1954 年發行的電影《海倫凱勒傳》（The Unconquered），由她自己擔任主演，這部片子並獲得奧斯卡最佳紀錄片獎。

Helen Keller (right) and Anne Mansfield Sullivan

Speaker 美國知名盲聾人士海倫・凱勒
（Helen Adams Keller, 1880–1968）

Time 1925 年 6 月 30 日

Place 美國俄亥俄州 Cedar Point，1925 年國際獅子會年會
（Lions Clubs International Convention at Cedar Point, Ohio, USA）

▣ 錄音　▣ 全篇收錄

Dear Lions and Ladies:

I suppose you have heard the legend that represents opportunity as a capricious lady, who knocks at every door but once, and if the door isn't opened quickly, she passes on, never to return. And that is as it should be. Lovely, desirable ladies won't wait. You have to go out and grab 'em.

I am your opportunity. I am knocking at your door. I want to be adopted. The legend doesn't say what you are to do when several beautiful opportunities present themselves at the same door. I guess you have to choose the one you love best. I hope you will adopt me. I am the youngest here, and what I offer you is full of splendid opportunities for service.

The American Foundation for the Blind is only four years old. It grew out of the imperative needs of the blind, and was called into existence by the sightless themselves. It is national and international in scope and in importance. It represents the best and most enlightened thought on our subject that has been reached so far. Its object is to make the lives of the blind more worthwhile everywhere by increasing their economic value and giving them the joy of normal activity.

Try to imagine how you would feel if you were suddenly stricken blind today. Picture yourself stumbling and groping at noonday as in the night; your work, your independence, gone.

In that dark world wouldn't you be glad if a friend took you by the hand and said, "Come with me and I will teach you how to do some of the things you used to do when you could see?" That is just the kind of friend the American Foundation is going to be to all the blind in this country if seeing people will give it the support it must have. →

親愛的獅友與女士：

　　我想你們都聽過這樣的說法：機會猶如一位善變的女子，她會去敲每一扇門，但不會多做停留，只要門沒有很快打開，她就會倏然離去，永遠不會再來。事情似乎就是這樣，美麗可愛的女子是不會等待的，你必須積極去爭取。

　　現在，我就是你們的機會，來敲你們的門，並期待你們的回應。剛剛那個說法並沒有告訴我們，要是有好幾個機會同時敲著一扇門時，我們應該要怎麼做。我猜是選擇自己最喜歡的那個機會吧，而我但願你們選擇的是我。我所提出來的訴求是最新穎的，能為各位帶來服務人類的大好機會。

　　「美國盲人基金會」成立到現在只有四年的歷史，它的成立是基於盲人朋友們的迫切需要，是由盲胞們自己所創立的。其服務範圍涵蓋海內外，對國家或對全球的重要性都不容忽視。這個基金會是啟蒙大眾思想的最佳代表，就其成立的宗旨做了很成功的推廣。基金會的目標是要透過經濟收入的增加，以及使之享受能正常活動的喜悅，以改善全世界盲人朋友們的生活。

　　你可以想像一下，要是今天你突然失明了，你會有什麼樣的感受。想像一下，在大白天裡，你卻像在半夜裡摸黑走路，身體東撞西撞的樣子。你的工作、你的獨立性，都不見了。

　　在黑暗的世界裡，如果有個朋友握著你的手，對你說：「跟我來，我會教你如何做到你在失明之前所能做的事。」你不會因此感到高興嗎？「美國盲人基金會」就是想要當這樣一個朋友，成為這個國家所有盲胞們的朋友──只要健視人士能夠給予所需支援的話。

Helen Keller and her dog

104

You have heard how through a little word dropped from the fingers of another, a ray of light from another soul touched the darkness of my mind and I found myself, found the world, found God. It is because my teacher learned about me and broke through the dark, silent imprisonment which held me that I am able to work for myself and for others.

It is the caring we want more than money. The gift without the sympathy and interest of the giver is empty. If you care, if we can make the people of this great country care, the blind will indeed triumph over blindness.

The opportunity I bring to you, Lions, is this: To foster and sponsor the work of the American Foundation for the Blind. Will you not help me hasten the day when there shall be no preventable blindness; no little deaf, blind child untaught; no blind man or woman unaided?

I appeal to you Lions, you who have your sight, your hearing, you who are strong and brave and kind. Will you not constitute yourselves Knights of the Blind in this crusade against darkness?

I thank you.

你們都聽過這件事:透過某個人指尖所寫出來的一個小小的字,那個人的靈魂所投射出來的光芒照進了我黑暗的心靈世界;然後,我找到了自己,發現了這個世界,也找到了上帝——這都是因為我的恩師聽說了我的事,她勇闖進幽禁我的那個黑暗無聲的監牢裡,讓我獲得了可以為自己、也為別人工作的能力。

我們對於關懷的渴求,更勝於對金錢的需求。缺少了贈與者的同情與關懷,所收到的禮盒裡面猶如空無一物。如果你們關心我們,如果我們能夠讓這個偉大國家的人民都付出關心,盲人同胞就能真正戰勝黑暗。

獅友們,我為你們帶來的機會是:請支持並贊助「美國盲人基金會」的工作。如果有那麼一天,可預防性的失明都被預防了,而且所有的盲聾孩子都能夠上學,所有的盲人同胞都獲得了幫助——你們願意幫助我盡快達到這個理想嗎?

獅友們,我懇請你們,你們耳聰目明,強壯、勇敢又仁慈,你們能不自命為「盲人的騎士」,為擊退黑暗而出征嗎?

在此致上無盡的謝意。

49

Show Me What You're Doing on HIV
Elizabeth Glaser's DNC Speech

民主黨全國大會演說：為愛滋請命

美國各政黨在總統大選之前，須先經歷政黨初選（2–6 月分舉行）、「政黨全國代表大會」的提名（7–8 月分舉行）、競選活動、全民投票、選舉人團投票等階段。在 5–6 月間，「政黨全國代表大會」的大部分成員已經產生，總統候選人也已提名底定，因此全國代表大會是認可提名的最後一道程序，此外在大會上會聽取各委員會報告，並且制定黨綱。

以下這篇演說是在 1992 年民主黨全國大會上所發表的，主講人是伊莉莎白‧葛雷瑟（Elizabeth Glaser, 1947–1994），她是美國知名的愛滋病運動人士，她在此次的演說上為愛滋防治請命，痛斥政府對愛滋病的漠視。

葛雷瑟的丈夫保羅‧麥可‧葛雷瑟（Paul Michael Glaser）是一位導演兼演員。1981 年，世界公布首例愛滋病，就在同年，她在生產接受輸血時，她和新生的女兒不幸感染愛滋病。她於 1984 年出生的兒子，亦遭到垂直感染。

然而，一直到 1985 年女兒發生一系列疾病，送到醫院做愛滋病篩檢時，才發現這一家有三口感染了愛滋病。1988 年，女兒病逝後，同年成立了「伊莉莎白‧葛雷瑟兒童愛滋病基金會」，這是致力於愛滋病防治工作的重要代表機構。

Stir HIV/AIDS Poster from STIR
(funded through World Vision of Australia)

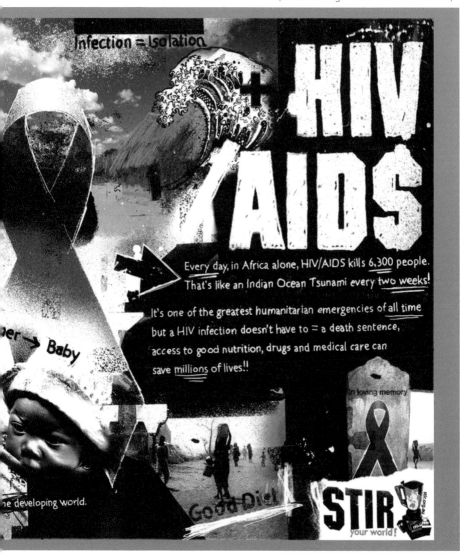

Speaker 美國知名的愛滋病運動人士伊莉莎白‧葛雷瑟
（Elizabeth Glaser, 1947–1994）

Time 1992 年 7 月 14 日

Place 紐約麥迪遜花園廣場， 1992 年民主黨全國
大會（Madison Square Garden, New York,
1992 Democratic National Convention Speech）

▣ 原音重現　▣ 全篇收錄

105

I'm Elizabeth Glaser. Eleven years ago, while giving birth to my first child, I hemorrhaged[1] and was transfused with seven pints[2] of blood. Four years later, I found out that I had been infected with the AIDS virus and had unknowingly passed it to my daughter, Ariel, through my breast milk, and my son, Jake, in utero[3].

Twenty years ago I wanted to be at the Democratic Convention because it was a way to participate in my country. Today, I am here because it's a matter of life and death. Exactly—Exactly four years ago my daughter died of AIDS. She did not survive the Reagan Administration. I am here because my son and I may not survive four more years of leaders who say they care, but do nothing. I—I am in a race with the clock. This is not about being a Republican or an Independent or a Democrat. It's about the future—for each and every one of us.

I started out just a mom—fighting for the life of her child. But along the way I learned how unfair America can be today, not just for people who have HIV, but for many, many people—poor people, gay people, people of color, children. A strange spokesperson for such a group: a well-to-do white woman. But I have learned my lesson the hard way, and I know that America has lost her path and is at risk of losing her soul. America wake up: We are all in a struggle between life and death.

I understand—I understand the sense of frustration and despair in our country, because I know firsthand about shouting for help and getting no answer. I went to Washington to tell Presidents Reagan and Bush that much, much more had to be done for AIDS research and care, and that children couldn't be forgotten. The first time, when nothing happened, I thought, "They just didn't hear me." The second time, when nothing happened, I thought, "Maybe I didn't shout loud enough." But now I realize they don't hear because they don't want to listen.

When you cry for help and no one listens, you start to lose your hope. I began to lose faith in America. I felt my country was letting me down— and it was. This is not the America I was raised to be proud of. I was raised to believe that other's problems were my problems as well. But when I tell most people about HIV, in hopes that they will help and care, I see the look in their eyes: "It's not my problem," they're thinking. →

我是伊莉莎白‧葛雷瑟。十一年前，我在生第一個小孩時因為大量出血，所以輸了三千多 C.C. 的血。四年後，我才發現我感染了愛滋病毒，期間我在不知情的情況下，在哺乳女兒艾莉兒時將病毒傳染給她，而我的兒子傑克則遭到垂直感染。

二十年前，我就想要參加民主黨全國大會，因為這是個參與國家事務的方式。今天，我站在這裡，因為這是個攸關生死的議題。就在四年前，我的女兒被愛滋病奪走了性命，當時還是雷根政府的執政。而我現在會站在這裡，是因為如果政府領導者光說不練的話，我和我的兒子很可能撐不過下一任總統的四年任期。我正在和時間賽跑，這無關乎你是共和黨員、無黨籍人士，還是民主黨員，這是攸關著未來前途的事──關係著我們每一個人的未來。

我是以身為一個母親為出發點，我要為搶救我孩子的性命而奮鬥。然而在這個過程中，我才知道現在的美國社會是如何的不平等，不只是愛滋病患，還有其他很多人都遭受著不公平的待遇，像是窮人、同性戀者、有色人種和兒童等等。我是一個富裕的白人婦女，要為這些族群發聲，似乎顯得格格不入，但這是我吃過苦頭才學到的一課，我了解到：美國已經迷失方向，它正處在失去靈魂的危險當中。美國，請快醒過來！我們全部的人都陷於生與死的掙扎之中。

我深深了解到，在我們這個國家裡求助無門的感覺，因為我自己就曾這樣大聲疾呼、懇求幫助，卻得不到任何的回應。我跑到華府向雷根和布希總統陳情，請求投入更多、更多的愛滋病研究和醫療照顧，而且決不能忽視愛滋病童。在我第一次陳情後，什麼措施反應都沒有，我就想：「他們只是沒有聽到我的請求。」在我第二次陳情之後，政府還是沒有任何的動作，我就又想：「大概是我講得不夠清楚。」但一直到現在我才知道，他們沒聽到，是因為他們根本不想聽。

當你大聲求救卻沒有人理會時，你會開始喪失希望。那時我開始失去對美國的信念，我覺得我的國家讓我失望透頂，真的是失望透頂。這個美國，不是我從小被教導要引以為傲的那個美國。我從小被教導，要感同身受地看待別人的問題；然而，當我跟別人提到愛滋病，盼望他們能夠幫忙和照顧時，我在大部分人眼裡所看到的心理反應是：「這又不是我的問題。」

1. hemorrhage ['hemərɪdʒ] (n.) a medical condition in which there is severe loss of blood from inside a person's body 出血

2. pint [paɪnt] (n.) a unit for measuring an amount of liquid, in the US it is equal to 0.473 liters, and in Britain a pint is equal to 0.568 liters
品脫（在美國，一品脫等於 0.473 公升，7 品脫約等於 3.311 公升，也就是 3,311 cc.）

3. in utero: in the uterus 〔拉丁語〕在子宮內；出胎之前

106

Well, it's everyone's problem and we need a leader who will tell us that. We need a visionary to guide us—to say it wasn't all right for Ryan White[4] to be banned from school because he had AIDS, to say it wasn't alright for a man or a woman to be denied a job because they're infected with this virus. We need a leader who is truly committed to educating us.

I believe in America, but not with a leadership of selfishness and greed—where the wealthy get health care and insurance and the poor don't. Do you know—Do you know how much my AIDS care costs? Over 40,000 dollars a year. Someone without insurance can't afford this. Even the drugs that I hope will keep me alive are out of reach for others.

Is their life any less valuable? Of course not. This is not the America I was raised to be proud of—where rich people get care and drugs that poor people can't. We need health care for all. We need a leader who will say this and do something about it.

I believe in America, but not a leadership that talks about problems but is incapable of solving them—two HIV commission reports with recommendations about what to do to solve this crisis sitting on shelves, gathering dust. We need a leader who will not only listen to these recommendations, but implement them.

I believe in America, but not with a leadership that doesn't hold government accountable. I go to Washington to the National Institutes of Health and say, "Show me what you're doing on HIV." They hate it when I come because I try to tell them how to do it better. But that's why I love being a taxpayer, because it's my money and they must feel accountable.

I believe in an America where our leaders talk straight. When anyone tells President Bush that the battle against AIDS is seriously under-funded, he juggles[5] the numbers to mislead the public into thinking we're spending twice as much as we really are. While they play games with numbers, people are dying. →

為愛滋請命

4. Ryan White: a teenage hemophiliac who became a national poster child for HIV/AIDS in the United States after being expelled from school because of his infection from a contaminated blood treatment
美國印第安納州的一位血友病患，12 歲時被診斷出因為輸血而感染愛滋病，並且因此被學校開除，後來成為美國宣傳對抗愛滋病的象徵性人物。

5. juggle [ˈdʒʌɡəl] (v.) to change things or arrange them in the way you want, or in a way that makes it possible for you to do something 耍花招；歪曲；竄改

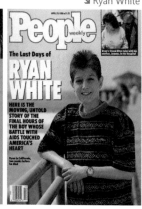

其實，這是每一個人的問題——我們需要一個能夠這樣告訴我們的領袖。我們需要一個具有遠見的領袖來帶領我們，告訴我們——不能因為萊恩・懷特感染愛滋病，就將他退學；也不能因為人們感染了愛滋病，就不准他們工作，這不是正確的做法。我們需要的領袖，是一個真正可以教育我們的領袖。

我是相信美國的，但我不相信一個自私貪婪的政府——在這樣的美國，只有有錢人才能享有醫療照顧和醫療保險，窮人就沒辦法。你們知道我的愛滋病治療要花費多少錢嗎？一年最少要四萬美元以上！沒有醫療保險的人，根本支付不起這筆費用。甚至那些我指望能讓我活得久一點的藥物，有許多人根本是拿不到的。

他們的命難道就比較不值錢嗎？當然不是！這不是我被教導要引以為傲的那個美國，在這個國家裡只有有錢人才獲得醫療和藥物，窮人是沒有份的。我們需要的是一個可以照顧所有人的醫療體系，我們需要的是一個會做這種聲明的領袖，並且付諸行動。

我相信美國，但我不相信一個只會談論問題，卻不拿出解決辦法的政府——有兩個愛滋委員會的研究報告，它們提出解決問題的方法，可是這兩份報告卻被束之高閣、封塵在架子上。我們需要的領袖，不只要能聆聽這些建議，也要能夠付諸實現。

我相信美國，但我不相信一個不負責任的政府。我跑去華府的國家衛生研究院，對他們說：「告訴我，你們為愛滋病做了什麼？」他們很討厭看到我，因為我一直想告訴他們要如何才能做得更好。但這就是我喜歡當一個納稅人的原因，因為那是我繳的稅，他們有義務要為我解說。

有一個直言不諱的總統，才是我所相信的美國。當有人向布希總統陳情說，對抗愛滋病的經費嚴重不足時，布希總統卻操弄數字，誤導民眾，讓人們誤以為花在愛滋病上的經費要比實際上多了兩倍。當他們在玩弄數字遊戲的同時，人們也在一步步走向死亡。

107

I believe in America, but an America where there is a light in every home. A thousand points of light just wasn't enough: My house has been dark for too long.

Once every generation, history brings us to an important crossroads. Sometimes in life there is that moment when it's possible to make a change for the better. This is one of those moments. For me, this is not politics. This is a crisis of caring.

In this hall is the future—women, men of all colors saying, "Take America back." We are—We are just real people wanting a more hopeful life. But words and ideas are not enough. Good thoughts won't save my family. What's the point of caring if we don't do something about it?

A President and a Congress that can work together so we can get out of this gridlock[6] and move ahead, because I don't win my war if the President cares and the Congress doesn't, or if the Congress cares and the President doesn't support the ideas. The people in this hall this week, the Democratic Party, all of us can begin to deliver that partnership, and in November we can all bring it home.

My daughter lived seven years, and in her last year, when she couldn't walk or talk, her wisdom shone through. She taught me to love, when all I wanted to do was hate. She taught me to help others, when all I wanted to do was help myself. She taught me to be brave, when all I felt was fear. My daughter and I loved each other with simplicity. America, we can do the same.

This was the country that offered hope. This was the place where dreams could come true, not just economic dreams, but dreams of freedom, justice, and equality. We all need to hope that our dreams can come true. I challenge you to make it happen, because all our lives, not just mine, depend on it.

Thank you. ◀

49
為
愛
滋
請
命

| 6. gridlock ['grɪdlɑːk] (n.) a traffic jam which is so bad that no movement is possible 僵局

我相信美國，但我相信的是一個能讓每一個家庭都擁有光明的美國。只有一千個光明的家庭是不夠的，像我自己的家庭，我們已經活在黑暗之中很久了。

在每一個世代裡，歷史都會將我們帶到一個命運的十字路口上。在人生中，有時就會遇到那種可以變得更好的時刻，而此時此刻就是這樣一個大好時機。對我來說，這不是政治問題，而是一個人性關懷的危機。

這個大會就是我們的未來──人們不分膚色，一齊喊道：「讓我們把美國找回來！」我們只想尋求更有希望的人生，單單只有空談和想法是不夠的，好的見解不足以拯救我們的家人。如果我們不付諸行動，只在一旁關切又有何用？

如果總統和國會能攜手合作，我們就能突破困境、向前邁進。如果總統和國會只有單一方關心，另一方卻不予支持，那我的奮鬥就還沒有成功。這個星期來參與大會的民主黨人們，我們所有的人可以開始來訴求這種總統和國會的合作，到了十一月（總統大選）結束，我們就可以付諸實行了。

我的女兒只活了七歲，在她人生的最後一年，她已經無法走路和說話，但她卻顯露出她的智慧。當我只想恨這個世界的時候，她教我如何去愛；當我一心只想救我自己時，她教我如何去幫助別人；當我內心充滿恐懼時，她教我要勇敢起來。我和女兒，我們彼此真誠相愛。美國！我們也可以達到這種關係！

這裡本來應該是一個給予希望的國家，一個能讓夢想成真的地方，不只是經濟上的夢想，還有自由、正義和平等的夢想。我們每一個人都希望能夠如願以償，我請求你們讓夢想成真，不只是我，這也是所有人們賴以生存的信念。

謝謝你們！

50

For America

Patriotic 9–11 Poem

911 恐怖攻擊追悼詩：
給美國

2001 年 9 月 11 日，美國爆發有史以來在美國境內最嚴重的恐怖分子攻擊事件，死亡人數近三千人，其中紐約「世界貿易中心」雙子星大樓遭受客機衝撞後雙雙倒塌，災情最為慘重。如今，在原雙子星大樓的遺址，已重建世界貿易中心一號大樓（One World Trade Center）。

在 911 事件發生之後，全美國的各大體育活動和賽事紛紛停賽。6 天之後，美國職棒大聯盟決定於 9 月 17 日率先開打，爾後，其他的體育競技賽也陸續開始恢復運作。

在大聯盟重新開打的第一天晚上，約翰・巴克（Jack Buck, 1924–2002）在比賽開始之前，朗誦了自己所寫的 911 事件追悼詩〈給美國〉（For America），接著鳴起 21 聲禮炮的儀式，這個儀式代表了給予烈士最高的致意和榮譽。

約翰・巴克在第二次世界大戰時曾入伍從軍，後來負傷。1954 年，他開始擔任美國大聯盟球隊紅雀隊（St. Louis Cardinals）的主播報員，一直擔任到 1990 年代後期，這個工作後來由他的兒子喬（Joe）接手。2002 年，約翰・巴克不幸病逝。

1987 年，約翰・巴克獲得棒球名人堂頒給廣播人的「福特・弗立克獎」（Ford C. Frick Award）；1995 年，獲選進入國家廣播名人堂。於 2006 年啟用的紅雀新球場布希體育場（Busch Stadium），則在球場的四號門外安置了他的紀念銅像。

Speaker 美國職棒大聯盟紅雀之聲約翰·巴克
（Jack Buck, 1924–2002）

Time 2001 年 9 月 17 日

Place 美國密蘇里州聖路易市紅雀球場
（Busch Memorial Stadium）

▣ 原音重現　▣ 全篇收錄

108

Since this nation was founded under God,
More than 200 years ago,
We have been the bastion of freedom,
The light that keeps the free world aglow.

We do not covet the possessions of others;
We are blessed with the bounty we share.
We have rushed to help other nations;
Anything . . . anytime . . . anywhere.

War is just not our nature,
We won't start but we will end the fight.
If we are involved,
We shall be resolved,
To protect what we know is right.

We have been challenged by a cowardly foe,
Who strikes and then hides from our view.
With one voice we say,
"We have no choice today,
There is only one thing to do."

Everyone is saying the same thing and praying,
That we end these senseless moments we are living.
As our fathers did before,
We shall win this unwanted war,
And our children will enjoy the future we'll be giving. ◀

蒙上帝之恩，誕生了這個國家，
兩百多年以來，
我們一直是自由的堡壘，
灼灼煌煌地照亮著自由世界。

我們一向不覬覦別人的領土；
我們分享所被賜予的富庶。
我們勇於對異邦伸出援手；
不管是何事、何時、何地。

我們天生就不愛動干戈，
我們不會挑釁，但我們會奮戰到底。
在我們身陷其中時，我們會堅毅不屈，
捍衛我們心中的正義。

卑劣的敵人對我們下了戰帖，
他們只敢在我們背後做攻擊。
我們同聲說道：
「今日，我們已經退無可退，
我們只有一條路可以走。」

人人都在說著同樣的事，做著同樣的祈禱，
我們將不再麻木過日。
一如祖先們所奮鬥過的，
我們要打贏這場不受歡迎的戰爭，
給我們後代一個幸福的未來。

The BioTech Century

生物科技的世紀：
生命的大哉問

傑若米・雷夫金（Jeremy Rifkin, 1945–）是美國知名
的經濟學家及作家，他是「經濟趨勢基金會」的創辦
人，並提出了「第三次工業革命」（Third Industrial
Revolution）的理論。他也是一位反戰人士，積極推動世
界和平。

他提出有名的「氫經濟」（hydrogen economy），企圖
利用氫氣化學反應後所產生的能量，來取代目前的石油
經濟體系。這種替代性能源不會造成廢氣污染，也可以
儲存能量。

傑若米・雷夫金的著作豐富，目前已經出版 17 本著作，
主要在談論科學與科技的改變所會造成的衝擊。他有多
本著作皆譯有中文版，例如《歐洲夢：21 世紀人類發展
的新夢想》、《第二個創世紀》、《付費體驗的時代》等。

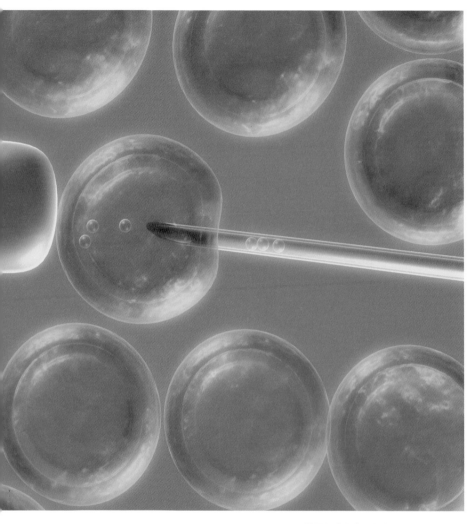

Speaker 美國經濟學家及作家傑若米・雷夫金
（Jeremy Rifkin, 1945–）

Time 1998 年 5 月

Place 美國俄亥俄州克里夫蘭會所
（City Club of Cleveland, Ohio, USA）

◉ 原音重現　◉ 擷錄

109

We are in the midst of a fundamental transformation, one of the great changes in history. We're moving out of the industrial revolution and into the BioTech Century.

For the last 40 years, two technology revolutions have been operating essentially on parallel tracks: computers and gene splicing[1]; the information sciences, the life sciences. In the last few years, they've begun to fuse together to create a powerful new technological and commercial revolution that's going to remake our entire civilization.

The computer is merely a prelude[2] to the new economic era, and the new economic era is based on genetic commerce. The computer is the language, the organizing tool to decipher, download, organize and manipulate genes. And genes are the raw resource of the Biotech Century, just as metals, minerals, and fossil fuels were the raw resource of the industrial century just passing from view.

Let me try and place this tremendous change in an anthropological context. This shift in the next 50 years will be as fundamental as the shift from medieval agriculture to the industrial way of life. It's going to force all of us to rethink the social contract[3].

And now companies are scouting the planet in search of rare genes in microorganisms, plants, animals, and indigenous human populations, because genes are the raw resource for the next century. Whoever controls the genes, controls genetic commerce. When they locate these genes they patent them. The mergers and acquisitions and consolidations going on in the giant life science industries dwarf the mergers going on telecommunications, entertainment, and software industries. Does that surprise you?

It's just we hear very little about it and here's why. Our futurists have done us a disservice[4]. For fifteen years our futurists have written books preparing us for the information age, so that's where we're focusing our debates. Calling the next century the information age is like calling the modern age the print press age. Neither are resources; both are forms of communication. The print press was essential as a new form of communication to organize a society based on steam power and coal. The computer is not a resource either; it's a form of communication to organize a new economy based on the raw resource of genes.

So what I'm suggesting here is that we're woefully behind, we in the public, where this whole revolution's moving. We have not been prepared by our media, by our academic institutions, and by our politicians. →

我們正處於一個非常重要的轉變當中，這是歷史上非常重大的一個轉變。我們正在從工業革命走向生物科技的時代。

　　過去的四十年來，有兩波科技革命在平行發展著，那就是「電腦」和「基因重組」，它們一個是資訊科學，一個是生命科學。在過去的幾年裡，這兩種革命開始匯合，創造出一種強大的新科技與商業革命，這股力量將會讓我們整個文明改觀。

　　電腦只是這個新經濟時代的前奏，而新經濟時代的基礎則是建立在基因商業。在這當中電腦是語言工具、組織工具，用來破解、轉植、組織和修改基因；基因則是生物科技時代的原物料，就像在過去金屬、礦物和化石燃料是工業時代的原物料一樣。

　　我就用人類學的角度來說明這種劇烈的轉變。在未來的五十年，這種轉變會好比從中世紀的農業時代進入到工業革命的時代一樣，它會迫使我們重新思考「社會契約論」這種問題。

　　現在有許多公司正在尋找地球上的罕見基因，他們在微生物、植物、動物和原住民身上找，因為基因將成為下個世紀（21 世紀）的原物料。誰要是能控制基因，誰就能掌控基因交易。當他們找到罕見基因時，他們會申請專利。在龐大的生命科學產業中，現代通訊業、娛樂業和軟體產業的結合，跟基因的合併、增添和強化比起來，根本是小巫見大巫。我這樣說有沒有嚇到你們？

　　這些訊息我們很少聽到，其原因是：未來學的學家幫了個倒忙。過去這十五年來，未來學的學家已經寫了許多書要我們做好準備迎接資訊時代——而這就是我現在要論述的重點——把下一個世紀（21 世紀）說成是資訊時代，那就好比是把我們目前這個時代（這一篇演說的時間是 1998 年）說成是印刷時代一樣！不管是資訊還是印刷，它們都不是原物料，而是一種傳播的方式。在蒸汽動力和燃煤時代裡，印刷業是一種新的主要傳播方式，用以組織社會；而電腦也不是原物料，它是一種傳播方式，用來組織以基因為原物料的新經濟。

　　所以我要在此提出，相對於這整個革命的腳步，我們的社會大眾是遠遠落於其後的。我們的媒體、學術機構或是政治人物，都沒有讓我們準備好要來面對這個新的時代。

---

1. gene splicing: the process of preparing recombinant DNA 基因重組技術
2. prelude [ˈprɛljuːd] (n.) something done to prepare the way for something more important 前奏；序幕
3. social contract: an agreement among individual people in a society or between the people and their government that outlines the rights and duties of each party. It derives from the ideas of Hobbes, Locke, and Rousseau and involves people giving up freedoms in return for benefits such as state protection
   社會契約論（指政府與人民之間的契約，明列雙方的權利與義務）
4. disservice [dɪsˈsɜːrvɪs] (n.) an act intended to help that turns out badly 幫倒忙的行為

110

Yet this technology revolution will more intimately affect our lives than any in the history of humanity. How we date, who we marry, how we have our children, the foods we eat, the kind of work we do, even our perception of life will be dramatically affected by this revolution. Let's look at a few of the issues.

You're going to hear a new term, genetic pollution. In the next twenty years, the Life Science companies are going to be introducing thousands and thousands of genetically engineered, laboratory conceived organisms into our biosphere, mass propagated[5] over all the ecosystems in the world. We're already introducing thousands now. Microorganisms to eat up toxic wastes, new genetically engineered plants in our fields, millions of acres this year are grown with the first genetically engineered plants, all in the last year.

Now when you introduce a genetically engineered organism into the environment it's not like introducing a chemical product. These products are alive. They're more unpredictable. They reproduce. Chemical and nuclear products, for all their problems, do not reproduce.

And genetically engineered organisms migrate; they proliferate. How do you recall to the laboratory a genetically engineered microorganism, bacteria, virus, or plant if it runs amuck[6] and causes damage. How do you get it back? Imagine the scale here, thousands and thousands of introductions all over the world of genetically engineered life forms reseeding the earth with a second genesis[7], all in the next twenty years.

Genetic pollution is just one issue. We also have to introduce the social implications. There's a word here that no one in the industry wants to talk about; it's called "eugenics[8]." You older people here will be very familiar with this term. Eugenics is the philosophy of using genetic manipulation to improve an organism or to create a perfect species.

Eugenics is inseparable from the new genetic technology, because the whole point of genetic engineering is to improve an organism, to improve a species. Well, who decides what is a good gene and what is a bad gene?

Right now thousands of laboratories, corporate, government, academic, around the world are changing around the genetic code of life from the lowliest microorganisms to human beings. Who decides what is a good and bad gene? →

這一次的科技革命，將比人類歷史上的任何一次革命，都要來得更徹底影響人類的生活，包括人類約會的方式、結婚的對象、生育，還有食物、工作的種類，甚至是我們對生命的看法等等，這一次的革命都將對我們產生極大的影響。我們就來看一下其中的幾個議題。

你將會聽到一個新的字眼：基因污染。在未來的二十年內，生命科學產業的公司會推出無數種由實驗室培養出來的基因改造生物，它們會加入我們這個生物圈，在世界上的所有生態系中大量繁殖。目前像這樣的生物就有數千種了，像是能吞噬毒廢料的微生物，或是農田上生產的基因改造植物。在去年一年裡，就有幾百萬英畝的田地在生產第一批的基因改造植物。

而今，把基因改造生物投放到大自然中，跟出產新的化學產品是不一樣的——這些生物是活的，是不可預測的，它們會繁殖——像化學或核能產品儘管有那麼多問題，但它們不會繁殖。

然而基因改造生物會遷移、會繁衍，當這些基因改造的微生物、細菌、病毒或植物在外面蔓延，造成傷害，你要怎麼把它們叫回實驗室？你要怎麼把它們帶回來？你現在可以想像一下這種大規模的情況：在未來的二十年內，無數的基因改造物種遍布全世界，它們在地球上大量繁衍，造成第二個創世紀的出現，你想這會是什麼樣的一種光景？

基因污染只是其中的一個議題，我們還得來談談其所會涉及的社會問題。接下來的這個字眼，是生命科學產業閉口不提的——那就是「優生學」。在座老一輩的人，一定都很熟悉這個字眼。優生學就是透過基因的控制以改善後代的遺傳，或是培育出完美的物種。

優生學是無法和新的基因科技做分割的。基因工程的全部目的，就在於改良生物或物種。那麼，要由誰來決定什麼是好基因、什麼是壞基因？

此時此刻，世界各地數以千計的實驗室、企業、政府和學術單位，他們正在著手改變生物的基因密碼，其對象從最低等的微生物，到最高等的人類都有。那麼，到底是誰在決定基因的好壞的？

---

5. propagate [ˈprɑːpəgeɪt] (v.) to reproduce a plant or animal, or cause one to reproduce 繁殖；增殖

6. amuck [əˈmʌk] (adv.) wildly; without self-control 殺氣騰騰地；狂暴地

7. genesis [ˈdʒenɪsɪs] (n.) the origin of something, when it is begun or starts to exist (*Genesis*: the first book of the *Bible*, which describes how God made the world) 創始；起源

8. eugenics [juːˈdʒenɪks] (n.) the study of methods of improving humans by allowing only carefully chosen people to reproduce 優生學

111

So what I'm suggesting to you is that the new eugenics is not social eugenics. We don't have an evil cabal[9] of political ideologues trying to force us into brave new worlds[10]. The new eugenics is banal[11]; it's market driven. It's based on consumer desires. We've met the enemy and it is us. What parent wouldn't want the best for their child?

Let me deal with one more social issue, which already may have affected somebody in this room. You're going to hear another term in the next few years: "genetic discrimination." It's already here. In *the BioTech Century*, in the book, I have a survey by Harvard University.

They've already seen widespread genetic discrimination by employers, insurance companies, adoption agencies, and schools. Employers screen you with blood tests for their health insurance plan. Do you know everything they're screening for? Employers may want to screen you to see if you have a genetic predisposition for cancer. They may not want to hire you; if you get cancer on their watch, it's going to be more health costs for their company. A company might want to know if you have a genetic predisposition for diabetes. They may not want to put you on the corporate fast track and spend a lot of money on you if you will be disabled and can't work to full capacity.

Well let's get this one step removed. What if you were hiring for an air traffic controller? Do you want to know if he or she has the genetic predisposition for manic depression or alcoholism?

Here's where the discrimination comes in. Even if you have these predispositions, you may not manifest the disease, and even if you manifest it, it may be controllable. And there may be others who become manic depressed, or alcoholic, or get cancer because of environmental triggers. The gene is not all powerful.

The last thought. I wrote this book, *the BioTech Century*, on the eve of this new century, because I wanted to encourage a robust debate, a great public debate. The greatest contribution of this new genetic science, it's going to force our generation and our children's generation to ask the big questions once again:

生命的大哉問

What is life? What does it mean to be a human being? Is life just genetic codes and blueprints that can be patented? Or does life has intrinsic value, not just utility value? What's our responsibility to future generations? What are our obligations to our fellow creatures that we coexist with? Should we play God in the laboratory? Or are there other ways to use this genetic science that are more humane and civilized and create opportunities rather than foreclose options for those not yet here?

我想跟各位說的是，這種新的優生學並不是社會優生學，它的背後並沒有一個邪惡的政治組織，密謀要逼我們走進「美麗新世界」。但這種新的優生學是很腐敗的，它會被市場因素所主宰，以消費者的需求為基礎──因此其中的敵人就是我們自己──因為有哪個父母不想生出最優秀的子女？

我接下來要談另一個社會問題，在場的人可能有人已經遇到這種情況了。在接下來的幾年內，你們就會聽到另一個新的字眼「基因歧視」。這個問題實際上已經存在了，我在《生物科技的世紀》一書中就曾提過一個哈佛大學所做的調查研究。

基因歧視已經普遍存在於雇主、保險業、收養機構和學校之中。雇主會檢查你的血液，看你是否符合其健康保險方案，但你知道他們到底檢查了哪些嗎？雇主們想知道你是否可能有癌症的遺傳，如果是，他們可能就不會雇用你。如果你在工作期間罹患癌症，公司就得為你支付更多的醫療成本。雇主也想知道你是否有糖尿病的遺傳體質，如果你有失能之虞、無法全力工作，他們就不會讓你得到升遷的管道，或是花大錢來投資你。

我們再來說另外一種情況：如果你想雇用一名航空管制員，你會不會想知道他是否有躁鬱症或酗酒傾向的基因？

這也就是會產生歧視的地方了。就算一個人有這些傾向，並不代表他就會得到這些疾病，而且就算是得了，也不是不可治療的。人會爆發躁鬱症、酗酒或是得到癌症，也可能是環境所造成的，基因並不能決定一切。

最後，在這個新世紀的前夕，我之所以寫了《生物科技的世紀》這本書，是因為我想引發社會大眾的廣泛討論。這場基因科學最大的貢獻，就是迫使我們這一代和下一代的人，再一次去面對這些大哉問：

> 生命究竟是什麼？人類存在的意義為何？生命僅僅是由那些能夠申請專利的基因密碼和基因藍圖所形成嗎？還是說，生命不只是具有功能上的價值，生命本身就應該是一種價值？我們對未來的子孫，應該負有什麼樣的責任？對於現在與我們一起共存的生物，我們又具有哪些義務？我們可否在實驗室裡扮演上帝的角色？還是說，還有其他更人性、更文明的方法可以來善用基因科學，創造出更多的機會，而不是讓後代子孫連選擇的機會都沒有？

---

9. cabal [kə'bæl] (n.) a small group of people who make secret plans, especially in order to have political power 陰謀集團

10. brave new world: the world of the future, usually either a technology-based utopia or a sinister totalitarian world devoid of human values, from the dystopian novel *Brave New World* (1932) by Aldous Huxley 美麗新世界（出自同名的反烏托邦小說，小說中諷刺科學技術為人類帶來的文化與人性災難）

11. banal [bə'næl] (a.) boring, ordinary and not original 陳腐的

Barack Obama:
Inaugural Address

歐巴馬就職演說：
這一代的美國人也要這樣走下去

歐巴馬出生於美國夏威夷州檀香山，父親是肯亞的黑人。歐巴馬年幼時父母便離異，他 10 歲之後與祖父母同住。21 歲時，父親在肯亞車禍去世，1995 年，母親亦撒手人寰。

2008 年，歐巴馬當選美國第 44 任總統。身為美國的第一位黑人總統，他的就職演說受到全美國和全世界的關注，一方面當時全球正陷入經濟風暴之中，另一方面美國人期待他能承續金恩博士的精神。

歐巴馬從少年時代就很尊崇林肯總統，他稱林肯為導師，深受其思想與言行的感召。歐巴馬在就職典禮上，特地選擇林肯宣誓所用的聖經，而且就職演說一開始還使用了林肯《蓋茲堡演說》（The Gettysburg Address）的口吻。歐巴馬在就職演說中，以承續美國的傳統精神開始，呼籲美國人要繼續為實現美國崇高的理想而努力。

歐巴馬在進入政壇之前，於 1995 年就出版過《歐巴馬的夢想之路：以父之名》（*Dreams from My Father: A Story of Race and Inheritance*）。該書於 2004 年再版，新版加入了他在 2004 年民主黨全國代表大會上的演說，並且將演說的主題「無畏的希望」作為下一本書的書名，於 2006 年出版《無畏的希望：重申美國夢》（*The Audacity of Hope: Thoughts on Reclaiming the American Dream*）。2009 年，歐巴馬獲得諾貝爾和平獎。

Speaker　美國第 44 任總統歐巴馬
（Barack Hussein Obama II, 1961-）

Time　　2009 年 1 月 20 日

Place　　美國國會大廈（US Capitol）

◉ 原音重現　◉ 擷錄

112

My fellow citizens:

I stand here today humbled by the task before us, grateful for the trust you've bestowed, mindful of the sacrifices borne by our ancestors. I thank President Bush for his service to our nation, as well as the generosity and cooperation he has shown throughout this transition.

Forty-four Americans have now taken the presidential Oath. The words have been spoken during rising tides of prosperity and the still waters of peace. Yet, every so often the Oath is taken amidst gathering clouds and raging storms. At these moments, America has carried on not simply because of the skill or vision of those in high office, but because We the People have remained faithful to the ideals of our forbearers, and true to our founding documents.

So it has been. So it must be with this generation of Americans.

Today I say to you that the challenges we face are real. They are serious and they are many. They will not be met easily or in a short span of time. But know this, America: They will be met.

On this day, we gather because we have chosen hope over fear, unity of purpose over conflict and discord. On this day, we come to proclaim an end to the petty grievances[1] and false promises, the recriminations[2] and worn out dogmas, that for far too long have strangled[3] our politics.

We remain a young nation, but in the words of Scripture, the time has come to "set aside childish things."[4] The time has come to reaffirm our enduring spirit; to choose our better history; to carry forward that precious gift, that noble idea, passed on from generation to generation: the God-given promise that all are equal, all are free, and all deserve a chance to pursue their full measure of happiness.

What is required of us now is a new era of responsibility—a recognition, on the part of every American, that we have duties to ourselves, our nation, and the world, duties that we do not grudgingly accept but rather seize gladly, firm in the knowledge that there is nothing so satisfying to the spirit, so defining of our character, than giving our all to a difficult task. →

各位親愛的同胞：

　　今天我站在這裡，我懷著謙卑的心來面對我們未來的工作，並感謝你們託付於我的信任，我心裡頭牢記著祖先們的犧牲奉獻。我感謝前總統布希對國家的效命，並感謝他在整個交接的過程中所給予的慷慨與配合。

　　至今已經有四十四位美國人發表過總統宣誓。這些誓詞的宣讀，有時在國泰民安之際，有時則是在國家風雨欲來之際。在這樣的時刻裡，美國可以繼續屹立下去，並不單單是靠政府高層的能力和洞見，也是因為美國人民深信我們先人們的理念，並且忠於建國法統。

　　美國就是這樣走過來的，我們這一代的美國人也要這樣走下去。

　　今天，我要跟各位說的是，我們所面對的都是真真實實的挑戰，這些挑戰又大又多。這些問題雖然無法在短時間內輕鬆解決，但美國人要知道的是，它們終將迎刃而解。

　　在今天，我們聚在這裡，是因為我們選擇希望而非恐懼，選擇有決心的團結，而非衝突或歧異。在今天，我們大聲宣告，我們要終結那些無用的牢騷和虛偽的承諾，終結交相指責和陳腐的教條，這些把我們的政治綑綁得太久、太久了。

　　我們仍是一個年輕的國家，用《聖經》的話來說，是該「脫去稚氣」的時候了。這個時候我們應該要重申我們堅忍的精神，選擇一個更好的歷史，將前人的崇高理想、將這個珍貴的禮物繼續代代傳承下去：上帝允諾人人生而平等、生而自由，並且人人都具有追求個人完整幸福的平等機會。

　　現在，眼前要求我們要肩負起一個新時代的責任——每一個美國人都要體認到，我們對自己、對國家、對世界是負有責任的，對於這份責任我們毫無怨言，我們欣然接受。我們堅信，沒有什麼會比全力解決艱難任務，更能帶來精神上的滿足，更能確立我們的骨氣。

1. grievance [ˈgriːvəns] (n.) a complaint about a (real or imaginary) wrong that causes resentment and is grounds for action 抱怨；牢騷
2. recrimination [rɪˌkrɪmɪˈneɪʃən] (n.) arguments between people who are blaming each other 互相指責
3. strangle [ˈstræŋgəl] (v.) to limit or prevent the growth or development of something 使窒息；抑制
4. A quote from *Corinthians* 13:11. "When I was a child, I spake as a child, I understood as a child, I thought as a child: but when I became a man, I put away childish things." 出自《聖經・歌林多前書》第 13 章第 11 節：「當我還是個孩子時，說話像孩子，心思像孩子，想法像孩子：當我是個成人了，我要脫去稚氣。」

113

This is the price and the promise of citizenship. This is the source of our confidence—the knowledge that God calls on us to shape an uncertain destiny.

This is the meaning of our liberty and our creed—why men and women and children of every race and every faith can join in celebration across this magnificent mall, and why a man whose father less than sixty years ago might not have been served at a local restaurant can now stand before you to take a most sacred Oath. So let us mark this day with remembrance, of who we are and how far we have traveled.

In the year of America's birth, in the coldest of months, a small band of patriots huddled by dying campfires on the shores of an icy river. The Capitol was abandoned. The enemy was advancing. The snow was stained with blood. At a moment when the outcome of our revolution was most in doubt, the father of our nation ordered these words be read to the people:

Let it be told to the future world . . . that in the depth of winter, when nothing but hope and virtue could survive . . . that the city and the country, alarmed at one common danger, came forth to meet [it].

America: In the face of our common dangers, in this winter of our hardship, let us remember these timeless words. With hope and virtue, let us brave once more the icy currents, and endure what storms may come. Let it be said by our children's children that when we were tested we refused to let this journey end, that we did not turn back nor did we falter[5]; and with eyes fixed on the horizon and God's grace upon us, we carried forth that great gift of freedom and delivered it safely to future generations.

Thank you, God bless you, and God bless the United States of America. ◖

　　這是公民的代價和承諾，這也是我們信心的來源──我們知道上帝召喚我們來創造一個不確定的命運。

　　這也就是我們自由和信念的意義所在──因而，不分種族，不分信仰，所有的男女老少都能來到這個廣場參加典禮。某位父親，他在六十年前還不能在一般餐館裡吃飯，而現在，他的兒子卻能站在你們前面，做出最神聖的宣誓。所以，讓我們特別記住這一天，記住我們是誰，記住我們走過了多少的路。

　　在美國誕生的那一年，在最寒冷的幾個月分裡，一小群愛國的人們，他們在結冰的河川邊，互相依偎在快要熄滅的火堆旁。當時國會大廈被棄守了，敵軍已經逼近，白雪上紅血斑斑。就在革命最令人失去信心的時候，我們的國父向人民宣讀了以下這段話：

　　　　讓它流傳萬世吧……在隆冬裡，在唯有希望與美德能倖存下來之際……這座城市和這個國家因遭受同一個危險，而站出來迎戰。

　　美國──在面對我們共同的危險時，在這樣一個艱辛的冬天裡，讓我們記住這些不朽的話！帶著希望和美德，讓我們再次勇敢地去面對逆境，不管是什麼樣的風雪都能堅持下去！讓後世傳頌下去，在我們受到試煉時，我們不願中途放棄，我們既不折返，也不躊躇。我們望著前方，上帝的恩典降臨我們身上，我們要把「自由」這份偉大的禮物，安全地交到我們後代子孫的手裡。

　　謝謝，上帝保佑你，天佑美國。

5. falter ['fɑːltər] (v.) to move hesitatingly, as if about to give way 猶豫；畏縮

Aung San Suu Kyi: Nobel Lecture

翁山蘇姬諾貝爾獎謝辭：
我們不會被遺忘

翁山蘇姬（Aung San Suu Kyi, 1945–），緬甸非暴力政治家、人權鬥士，深受聖雄甘地的非暴力理論影響，並致力於推行民主制度。

翁山蘇姬出生於緬甸的舊首都仰光，父親是緬甸獨立運動的領袖翁山將軍（Aung San, 1915–1947），他帶領緬甸脫離英國。然而，他在翁山蘇姬兩歲時，遭政敵暗殺，後來被緬甸人民尊稱為國父。

翁山蘇姬 15 歲時，隨著出任印度大使的母親前往印度。後來，進入英國牛津大學就學，主修經濟、哲學和政治，並在此結識了後來的丈夫邁克·阿里斯（Michael Vaillancourt Aris），兩人育有兩子。

1988 年，為照顧生病的母親，43 歲的翁山蘇姬返回緬甸。1990 年，她帶領全國民主聯盟贏得大選的勝利，卻遭到軍政府的軟禁，一直到 2010 年，緬甸大選後，才終於獲釋。

在遭軟禁的 20 年之間，軍政府開出條件，只要她永遠離開緬甸，就釋放她，但是她始終拒絕以被驅逐出境的方式，來重獲個人的自由。2010 年，美國《時代》雜誌（Time）歸結出「史上十大政治犯」，並將翁山蘇姬列於首位。

1991 年，被軟禁中的翁山蘇姬獲得了諾貝爾和平獎，卻無法親自前往領獎，由她的兒子代為發表答辭。一直到 21 年之後，挪威奧斯陸為她補辦了頒獎儀式。這篇所收錄的，就是她在 2012 年所發表的諾貝爾和平獎得獎感言。

Speaker 緬甸非暴力政治家翁山蘇姬
（Aung San Suu Kyi, 1945–）

Time 2012 年 6 月 16 日

Place 挪威首都奧斯陸市政廳（Oslo City Hall）

◉ 原音重現 ◉ 擷錄

Copyright © The Nobel Foundation 2012
Audio copyright to © Nobel Media AB

Often during my days of house arrest[1] it felt as though I were no longer a part of the real world. There was the house which was my world, there was the world of others who also were not free but who were together in prison as a community, and there was the world of the free; each was a different planet pursuing its own separate course in an indifferent universe. What the Nobel Peace Prize did was to draw me once again into the world of other human beings outside the isolated area in which I lived, to restore a sense of reality to me. This did not happen instantly, of course, but as the days and months went by and news of reactions to the award came over the airwaves, I began to understand the significance of the Nobel Prize. It had made me real once again; it had drawn me back into the wider human community. And what was more important, the Nobel Prize had drawn the attention of the world to the struggle for democracy and human rights in Burma. We were not going to be forgotten.

To be forgotten. The French say that to part is to die a little. To be forgotten too is to die a little. It is to lose some of the links that anchor us to the rest of humanity. When I met Burmese migrant workers[2] and refugees during my recent visit to Thailand, many cried out: "Don't forget us!" They meant: "don't forget our plight, don't forget to do what you can to help us, don't forget we also belong to your world." When the Nobel Committee awarded the Peace Prize to me they were recognizing that the oppressed and the isolated in Burma were also a part of the world, they were recognizing the oneness of humanity. So for me receiving the Nobel Peace Prize means personally extending my concerns for democracy and human rights beyond national borders. The Nobel Peace Prize opened up a door in my heart. →

Aung San Suu Kyi (1945–)

　　在我被軟禁的期間，我常常感到自己不再屬於真實世界的一部分。房子就是我的世界，那些同樣不自由的人也有他們的世界，但是他們在監獄裡可以互相陪伴，而自由的人們又有他們的世界。每個世界各是不同的星球，在漠然的宇宙中，各自循著不同的軌道。而諾貝爾和平獎所做的，是將我從孤立的獨居世界，又拉回到人們的世界，喚回了我的現實感。當然，這不是一下子就回復的，而是隨著日子一天天地過，幾個月過去了，回應獲獎的各種新聞報導，透過電波傳到我這裡，我才開始了解到諾貝爾獎的意義。這讓我又再次回到了真實，帶我回到廣闊的人類社會。更重要的是，諾貝爾獎讓全世界關注了緬甸的民主和人權奮鬥，我們不會被遺忘。

　　被人們所遺忘。法國人說，分離，意謂著生命被奪去了一部分。被人們所遺忘，亦是如此，這會讓我們失去和其他人類的一些連結。我最近訪問泰國時，會見了緬甸的外勞和難民，許多人喊道：「不要忘了我們！」他們是說：「不要忘了我們困苦的處境，不要忘記盡你的一切力量來幫助我們，不要忘記我們也同樣屬於你的世界。」當諾貝爾獎委員會授予我和平獎，他們體認到，受到壓迫和被孤立的緬甸，也是世界的一部分，他們意識到了人類的一體性。因此，對我來講，接受諾貝爾和平獎，意謂擴展了我個人對民主與人權的關懷，它超越了國界。諾貝爾和平獎打開了我心中的一扇門。

1. house arrest: the state of being kept as a prisoner in one's own house, rather than in a prison 軟禁

2. migrant worker: a worker who moves from place to place to do seasonal work 移住勞工；外勞

The Burmese concept of peace can be explained as the happiness arising from the cessation of factors that militate[3] against the harmonious and the wholesome. The word nyein-chan translates literally as the beneficial coolness that comes when a fire is extinguished. Fires of suffering and strife are raging around the world. In my own country, hostilities have not ceased in the far north; to the west, communal violence resulting in arson[4] and murder were taking place just several days before I started out on the journey that has brought me here today. News of atrocities[5] in other reaches of the earth abound. Reports of hunger, disease, displacement, joblessness, poverty, injustice, discrimination, prejudice, bigotry[6]; these are our daily fare. Everywhere there are negative forces eating away at the foundations of peace. Everywhere can be found thoughtless dissipation[7] of material and human resources that are necessary for the conservation of harmony and happiness in our world.

The First World War represented a terrifying waste of youth and potential, a cruel squandering[8] of the positive forces of our planet. The poetry of that era has a special significance for me because I first read it at a time when I was the same age as many of those young men who had to face the prospect of withering before they had barely blossomed. A young American fighting with the French Foreign Legion[9] wrote before he was killed in action in 1916 that he would meet his death: "at some disputed barricade;" "on some scarred slope of battered hill;" "at midnight in some flaming town." Youth and love and life perishing forever in senseless attempts to capture nameless, unremembered places. And for what? Nearly a century on, we have yet to find a satisfactory answer.

Are we not still guilty, if to a less violent degree, of recklessness, of improvidence with regard to our future and our humanity? War is not the only arena[10] where peace is done to death. Wherever suffering is ignored, there will be the seeds of conflict, for suffering degrades and embitters and enrages. →

53
我們不會被遺忘

3. militate [ˈmɪlɪˌteɪt] (v.) have force or influence 起作用；有影響
4. arson [ˈɑːrsən] (n.) the criminal act of deliberately setting fire to property 縱火
5. atrocity [əˈtrɑsətɪ] (n.) behavior or an action that is wicked or ruthless 殘暴的行為
6. bigotry [ˈbɪɡətrɪ] (n.) the practice of having very strong and unreasonable opinions, especially about politics, race, or religion, and refusing to consider other people's opinions 偏執

　　對緬甸來說，和平的概念可以解釋為終止那些阻礙和諧與福祉的因素，以增進福祉。「nyein-chan」這個字，它字面上的意思是「當火被撲滅後的裨益清涼」。苦難和衝突之火，在世界上熊熊延燒著。在我的祖國，最北部的戰爭仍未歇息；在西部，就在我啟程準備今天來到這裡的幾天前，才發生了因族群暴力衝突而導致的縱火與殺害。世界各地充滿暴行的新聞。饑餓、疾病、被迫離家、失業、貧窮、不公、歧視、偏見、偏執，充斥了我們每天的生活。到處都有負面的力量，在蠶食著和平的基石；到處都能看到對物質和人力資源的輕率浪費，而這卻是保有世界和諧與福祉所必要的。

　　第一次世界大戰顯示了對青春和潛能的可怕虛擲，是對我們地球上正面力量的殘酷揮霍。那個年代的詩篇對我別具意義，因為當我初次吟讀時，我正和那些年輕人年齡相仿，而他們卻在生命尚未盛開之際，就不得不迎接凋萎。1916 年，一名在法國外籍軍團中參戰的美國年輕人，他在戰死沙場前夕，寫到自己即將迎接死神，「在某個爭奪的壁壘前」，「滿目瘡痍的山丘，在某個傷痕累累的斜坡上」，「深夜，在某個火焰熾然的城鎮裡」。為了佔領那些既湮沒無聞也不會被記住的地方，在毫無意義的攻佔中，青春、愛和生命，永遠地消逝了。這究竟是為了什麼？快一個世紀過去了，我們還在尋找一個令人滿意的答案。

　　如此罔顧和漠視人類的未來與人道，就算暴力程度輕一點，就能因此脫罪嗎？戰爭，不是扼殺和平的唯一競技場；凡是漠視苦難的地方，必有衝突的種子，因為苦難激起屈辱、怨恨和憤怒。

7. dissipation [ˌdɪsɪˈpeɪʃən] (n.) the act of wasting something such as time, money, or supplies by not using it in a sensible way 耗散；浪費

8. squander [ˈskwɑndər] (v.) to spend wastefully or extravagantly 浪費；揮霍

9. French Foreign Legion: a former foreign legion in the French army that was used for military duties outside of France 法國外籍兵團

10. arena [əˈriːnə] (n.) an enclosed area for the presentation of sports events and spectacles（古羅馬圓形劇場中央的）競技場

A positive aspect of living in isolation was that I had ample time in which to ruminate[11] over the meaning of words and precepts[12] that I had known and accepted all my life. As a Buddhist, I had heard about dukha, generally translated as suffering, since I was a small child. Almost on a daily basis elderly, and sometimes not so elderly, people around me would murmur "dukha, dukha" when they suffered from aches and pains or when they met with some small, annoying mishaps.

However, it was only during my years of house arrest that I got around to investigating the nature of the six great dukha. These are: to be conceived, to age, to sicken, to die, to be parted from those one loves, to be forced to live in propinquity[13] with those one does not love. I examined each of the six great sufferings, not in a religious context but in the context of our ordinary, everyday lives. If suffering were an unavoidable part of our existence, we should try to alleviate it as far as possible in practical, earthly ways. I mulled over the effectiveness of ante- and post-natal[14] programmes and mother and childcare; of adequate facilities for the aging population; of comprehensive health services; of compassionate nursing and hospices[15].

I was particularly intrigued by the last two kinds of suffering: to be parted from those one loves and to be forced to live in propinquity with those one does not love. What experiences might our Lord Buddha have undergone in his own life that he had included these two states among the great sufferings? I thought of prisoners and refugees, of migrant workers and victims of human trafficking[16], of that great mass of the uprooted of the earth who have been torn away from their homes, parted from families and friends, forced to live out their lives among strangers who are not always welcoming. →

53

我們不會被遺忘

隔離的生活，倒有一個好處，這讓我有很多的時間，可以去沉思我一生所信奉的教法和戒律。身為一個佛教徒，我自幼便得知「dukha」（苦諦），這一般翻譯為「苦」。可以說在我的日常生活中，我身邊的長者，或者有時年紀沒那麼大的人，當他們遭受病痛，或是遇到一些瑣碎惱人的不幸時，他們嘴裡會唸著「苦諦，苦諦」。

　　而一直到我被軟禁的那些年裡，我才有機會去深究六大苦之相：生、老、病、死、愛別離、怨憎會。我細細審視這六大苦，不是從宗教脈絡中去看，而是從日常生活中去體察。如果苦是生活中無可避免的一部分，我們就應該在世俗活動中盡量去減輕這些苦。我仔細思考過產前和產後的母子照護的有效性，還有給予老年人口足夠設施、全面的公共醫療衛生服務、慈善看護和臨終安養等問題。

　　我對後面這種兩種苦尤感興趣：愛別離和怨憎會。我們的佛陀世尊在他自己的生活中經歷了什麼，讓他要將這兩種苦從諸多大苦中總結出來？我想到了囚犯、難民、外勞和人口販賣的受害者，這麼多的人被從故土上被連根拔起，離開家園，和親友分離，被迫在永遠不歡迎他們的陌生人之中討生活。

11. ruminate [ˈruːməˌneɪt] (v.) think deeply about something 沉思

12. precept [ˈpriːsɛpt] (n.) a rule, instruction, or principle that teaches correct behavior 戒律

13. propinquity [prəˈpɪŋkwɪtɪ] (n.) nearness in place or time 接近

14. ante- and post-natal: antenatal and postnatal 產前和產後的

15. hospice [ˈhɑspɪs] (n.) a hospital that looks after people who are dying 臨終安養院

16. trafficking [ˈtræfɪkɪŋ] (n.) deal or trade in something illegal 非法交易

The peace of our world is indivisible. As long as negative forces are getting the better of positive forces anywhere, we are all at risk. It may be questioned whether all negative forces could ever be removed. The simple answer is: "No!" It is in human nature to contain both the positive and the negative. However, it is also within human capability to work to reinforce the positive and to minimize or neutralize the negative. Absolute peace in our world is an unattainable goal. But it is one towards which we must continue to journey, our eyes fixed on it as a traveler in a desert fixes his eyes on the one guiding star that will lead him to salvation. Even if we do not achieve perfect peace on earth, because perfect peace is not of this earth, common endeavors to gain peace will unite individuals and nations in trust and friendship and help to make our human community safer and kinder.

I used the word "kinder" after careful deliberation; I might say the careful deliberation of many years. Of the sweets of adversity, and let me say that these are not numerous, I have found the sweetest, the most precious of all, is the lesson I learnt on the value of kindness. Every kindness I received, small or big, convinced me that there could never be enough of it in our world. To be kind is to respond with sensitivity and human warmth to the hopes and needs of others. Even the briefest touch of kindness can lighten a heavy heart. Kindness can change the lives of people. Norway has shown exemplary kindness in providing a home for the displaced of the earth, offering sanctuary[17] to those who have been cut loose from the moorings of security and freedom in their native lands.

Ultimately our aim should be to create a world free from the displaced, the homeless and the hopeless, a world of which each and every corner is a true sanctuary where the inhabitants will have the freedom and the capacity to live in peace. Every thought, every word, and every action that adds to the positive and the wholesome is a contribution to peace. Each and every one of us is capable of making such a contribution. Let us join hands to try to create a peaceful world where we can sleep in security and wake in happiness. ◀

我們這個世界的和平，是不可分割的。只要有一個地方的負面力量大於正面力量，我們就都處於危險之中。也許，有人會質疑負面力量是否能夠消除殆盡，答案很簡單：不會！人性原本就善惡並存，不過人類同樣也具有強化正面力量的能力，將負面力量削弱，或是消除其負面性。絕對的世界和平，是無法企及的目標，但這是我們要繼續朝向的目標。我們抬眼望著目標，猶如沙漠旅人望著指引方向的星辰，引領他最終獲救一樣。即使完的和平不存在於這個塵世間，終究無法實現，但是，為和平所做的共同努力，將團結個人與國家，在相互的信任和友誼之下，有助於將我們的人類社會建設得更安全、更具仁慈。

我使用「更具仁慈」一詞，是經過琢磨的，應該說，我仔細推敲了好些年。逆境中的快樂，並不多見；而我所找到最甜美、最寶貴的東西，就是我所學到的仁慈的價值。我所得到的每一份仁慈，不論大小，都使我確信在我們這個人間裡，仁慈永遠都不嫌多。仁慈待人，是用理解和溫暖的心，去回應他人的期望與需求。即使是最短暫的仁慈接觸，也能夠照亮沉重的心靈。仁慈可以改變人們的生活。挪威已經做出了仁慈的表率，為世上流離失所的人們提供家園，為那些在自己國家得不到安全與自由保障的人們提供庇護所。

我們最終的目標，是創造一個沒有被迫遷徙、沒有無家可歸、沒有絕望的世界，每個角落都是真正的聖堂，每個居民都生活在自由與和平之中。能夠提升正面力量和福祉的每一個想法、每一句話、每一個動作，都能裨益於和平，而我們每一個人都有能力做出這樣的貢獻。讓我們攜起手來，努力創造一個和平的世界，讓我們可以在安心中入睡，在幸福中醒來。

17. sanctuary [ˋsæŋktʃuəri] (n.) official protection given to someone by a place that is safe for them 庇護所

Malala Yousafzai's Speech to the UN General Assembly

馬拉拉聯合國大會演說：
書本和筆才是最強大的武器

馬拉拉（1997–），出生於巴基斯坦西北部，投身於教育權和婦女權等運動。

馬拉拉在年少時就開始發表教育權的演說。2008 年底，11 歲的馬拉拉開始在英國廣播公司 BBC 烏爾都語網站的部落格發表文章，談及軍事行動對女學童和學校的影響。

2009 年初，塔利班頒布禁令，禁止女童上學，並破壞當地的學校。值此之際，馬拉拉參與了一部紀錄片的拍攝。紀錄片上映後，馬拉拉開始在電視上公開主張女性教育。隨著知名度的增加，馬拉拉收到的死亡威脅也愈來愈多。

2012 年 10 月 9 日，馬拉拉坐在校車上，於放學途中，遭到塔利班分子暗殺，她受到三次槍擊，其中一顆子彈穿過大腦。傷重的馬拉拉，受到許多國家的醫療幫助，後來前往英國接受進一步治療。

2014 年，馬拉拉獲得諾貝爾和平獎，年僅 17 歲，成為諾貝爾獎史上最年輕的獲獎者。聯合國並將馬拉拉的生日（7 月 12 日）訂為「馬拉拉日」，藉此呼籲女童的教育權。

本書所收錄的這篇聯合國大會演說，是馬拉拉知名的演講，而其中一句名言就是：

「一個孩子、一位老師、一本書、一枝筆，就能改變世界。」

Speaker 巴基斯坦改革活動家馬拉拉
（Malalah Yusafzay, 1997–）

Time 2013 年 7 月 12 日

Place 紐約市聯合國總部大樓
（United Nations Headquarters）

▣ 原音重現　▣ 擷錄

Dear brothers and sisters, do remember one thing: Malala Day[1] is not my day. Today is the day of every woman, every boy and every girl who have raised their voice for their rights.

There are hundreds of human rights activists and social workers who are not only speaking for their rights, but who are struggling to achieve their goal of peace, education and equality. Thousands of people have been killed by the terrorists and millions have been injured. I am just one of them. So here I stand, one girl among many. I speak not for myself, but so those without a voice can be heard. Those who have fought for their rights. Their right to live in peace. Their right to be treated with dignity. Their right to equality of opportunity. Their right to be educated.

Dear friends, on 9 October 2012, the Taliban shot me on the left side of my forehead. They shot my friends, too. They thought that the bullets would silence us, but they failed. And out of that silence came thousands of voices. The terrorists thought they would change my aims and stop my ambitions. But nothing changed in my life except this: weakness, fear and hopelessness died. Strength, power and courage was born. I am the same Malala. My ambitions are the same. My hopes are the same. And my dreams are the same.

Dear sisters and brothers, I am not against anyone. Neither am I here to speak in terms of personal revenge against the Taliban[2] or any other terrorist group. I am here to speak for the right of education for every child. I want education for the sons and daughters of the Taliban and all the terrorists and extremists[3].

I do not even hate the Talib who shot me. Even if there was a gun in my hand and he was standing in front of me, I would not shoot him. This is the compassion I have learned from Mohamed, the prophet of mercy, Jesus Christ and Lord Buddha. This the legacy of change I have inherited from Martin Luther King, Nelson Mandela and Mohammed Ali Jinnah[4]. This is the philosophy of nonviolence that I have learned from Gandhi, Bacha Khan[5] and Mother Teresa. And this is the forgiveness that I have learned from my father and from my mother. This is what my soul is telling me: be peaceful and love everyone. →

54
書本和筆才是最強大的武器

親愛的兄弟姐妹們，請記得一件事：馬拉日，並非是我的日子。今天這個日子，屬於每一位為自己的權利發聲的女性、男孩和女孩。

有數以百計的人權活動人士和社會工作者，他們不只是為自己的權利發聲，也為了達成和平、教育和平權的目標而奮鬥。成千上萬的人死在恐怖分子的手上，數以百萬的人受到傷害，而我只是其中的一位。為此，我站在這裡，是那些諸多女孩中的一位。我不是為自己而發聲，而是為了那些無法發聲的人而說話。他們為自己的權利而抗爭，那是太平生活的權利、被尊嚴對待的權利、機會平等的權利，以及接受教育的權利。

Malalah Yusafzay (1997–)

親愛的朋友們，2012 年 10 月 9 日，塔利班開槍打中我的前額左側，他們也射殺我的朋友們。他們以為，子彈能夠讓我們閉嘴，但是他們並沒有得逞。從這一沉默之中，響起成千上萬的聲音。恐怖分子以為，他們能夠改變我的目標，阻遏我的抱負。然而，除了使怯弱、恐懼和絕望從我的生命中消失之外，我一無所改。堅定、力量和勇氣，於焉而生。我依然是那個馬拉拉，仍抱持同樣的志向、同樣的願望，夢想依舊。

新愛的兄弟姐妹們，我不與任何人對立。我在這裡發言，不是挾帶私怨，要報復塔利班或任何恐怖分子團體。我在這裡發言，是為每一個孩子的教育權利而發聲。我希望塔利班分子和所有恐怖分子、極端主義者的兒子和女兒，都能夠接受教育。

我甚至不怨恨射殺我的那名塔利班分子。即使我手中握有槍，而他就站在我前面，我也不會對他開槍。這樣的仁慈，是我從仁愛先知穆罕默德、耶穌基督和佛陀世尊那裡所學到的。這種變革的遺澤，是我從馬丁·路德·金、納爾遜·曼德拉和穆罕默德·阿里·真納的身上所學到的。這樣的非暴力哲學，是我從甘地、巴夏汗和德蕾莎修女的身上所學到的。這樣的寬恕，是我從家父和家母身上所學到的。我的靈魂是這樣的告訴我：心存和平，用愛對待每一個人。

1. Malala Day: is celebrated on July 12, to raise awareness and to help girls get their right to education
   聯合國以馬拉拉的生日（7月 12 日）為「馬拉拉日」，以此特別呼籲女童的教育權

2. Taliban [ˈtælɪbæn] (n.) an Islamic political and military organization, active in Afghanistan and Pakistan 塔利班

3. extremist [ɪkˈstriːmɪst] (n.) someone who has beliefs or opinions that are considered to be extremely unreasonable by most people 極端主義分子

4. Mohammed Ali Jinnah (1876–1948): founder and first governor-general (1947–1948) of Pakistan 巴基斯坦第一位總督，被擁為巴基斯坦的國父

5. Bacha Khan (1890–1988): a Pashtun political and spiritual leader 巴基斯坦第二大民族普什圖人（與馬拉拉同族）的政治和精神領袖

Dear sisters and brothers, we realize the importance of light when we see darkness. We realize the importance of our voice when we are silenced. In the same way, when we were in Swat[6], the north of Pakistan, we realized the importance of pens and books when we saw the guns. The wise saying, "The pen is mightier than the sword." It is true. The extremists are afraid of books and pens.

The power of education frightens them. They are afraid of women. The power of the voice of women frightens them. This is why they killed 14 innocent students in the recent attack in Quetta. And that is why they kill female teachers. That is why they are blasting schools every day because they were and they are afraid of change and equality that we will bring to our society.

And I remember that there was a boy in our school who was asked by a journalist: "Why are the Taliban against education?" He answered very simply by pointing to his book, he said: "A Talib doesn't know what is written inside this book."

They think that God is a tiny, little conservative being who would point guns at people's heads just for going to school. These terrorists are misusing the name of Islam for their own personal benefit. Pakistan is a peace-loving, democratic country. Pashtuns[7] want education for their daughters and sons. Islam is a religion of peace, humanity and brotherhood. It is the duty and responsibility to get education for each child, that is what it says.

Peace is a necessity for education. In many parts of the world, especially Pakistan and Afghanistan, terrorism, war and conflicts stop children from going to schools. We are really tired of these wars. Women and children are suffering in many ways in many parts of the world. →

54
書本和筆才是最強大的武器

6. Swat: a river valley and an administrative district in the Khyber Pakhtunkhwa Province of Pakistan 馬拉拉的故鄉，景色秀麗，有「巴基斯坦的瑞士」之稱
7. Pashtun: an ethnic minority speaking Pashto and living in northwestern Pakistan and southeastern Afghanistan
普什圖族（主要居住於巴基斯坦西北部和阿富汗的東南部，馬拉拉即普什圖族人）

親愛的兄弟姐妹們，當眼前一片黑暗，我們能了解到光明的重要；當我們一片靜默時，我們能知道發聲的重要。同樣地，以前我們在巴基斯坦北部的斯瓦特，當映入眼前的是槍枝的時候，我們明白到筆和書本的重要性。智者說：「筆誅勝於劍伐。」的確，極端分子害怕書本和筆。

教育的力量，震懾他們。他們害怕婦女，女性發聲力量，令他們顫慄。這就是為什麼他們在最近的奎達攻擊中，殺害了十四名無辜的學生。也因為如此，他們殺害女教師。也因為如此，他們每天炸襲學校，因為他們一直以來都害怕我們會給社會帶來改變與平等。

我記得，以前有一個記者訪問我們學校的一個男孩說：「為什麼塔利班反對教育？」男孩指著自己的書，簡潔地回答道：「因為塔利班分子不知道這本書裡頭在寫什麼。」

他們以為，真主是一個微小的保守主義者，會對著人的頭顱開槍，只因為人們要去上學。這些恐怖分子濫用伊斯蘭教之名，以圖謀私利。巴基斯坦是一個愛好和平的民主國家，普什圖人希望自己的兒女可以接受教育。伊斯蘭教是一個重視和平、慈愛和兄弟情誼的宗教。它主張，讓每一個孩子接受教育，是責任與義務。

對於教育，和平是不可或缺的。在世界諸多地方，特別是在巴基斯坦和阿富汗，恐怖主義、戰爭和衝突，讓孩子們失學。我們對這些戰爭感到疲倦不堪。在世界許許多多的地方，婦女和兒童飽受各種折磨。

120

In India, innocent and poor children are victims of child labor. Many schools have been destroyed in Nigeria. People in Afghanistan have been affected by extremism. Young girls have to do domestic child labor and are forced to get married at an early age. Poverty, ignorance, injustice, racism and the deprivation of basic rights are the main problems, faced by both men and women.

Dear brothers and sisters, we want schools and education for every child's bright future. We will continue our journey to our destination of peace and education. No one can stop us. We will speak up for our rights and we will bring change to our voice. We believe in the power and the strength of our words. Our words can change the whole world because we are all together, united for the cause of education. And if we want to achieve our goal, then let us empower ourselves with the weapon of knowledge and let us shield ourselves with unity and togetherness.

Dear brothers and sisters, we must not forget that millions of people are suffering from poverty and injustice and ignorance. We must not forget that millions of children are out of their schools. We must not forget that our sisters and brothers are waiting for a bright, peaceful future.

So let us wage a glorious struggle against illiteracy, poverty and terrorism, let us pick up our books and our pens, they are the most powerful weapons. One child, one teacher, one book and one pen can change the world. Education is the only solution. Education first. Thank you. ◀

54

書本和筆才是最強大的武器

在印度，無辜的貧童，是童工的受害者；在奈及利亞，許多學校被摧毀；在阿富汗，極端主義影響了人們。年幼的女孩要做家務，年幼之時就被迫嫁人。貧窮、無知、不公不義、種族主義、基本權利被剝奪，這是主要的問題，男性和女性都面臨了這樣的問題。

親愛的兄弟姐妹們，為了每一個孩子前途的光明，我們要求要有學校和教育。我們會繼續我們的旅程，向和平和教育的目的地邁進。沒有人可以阻止我們，我們會為我們的權利發聲，也會為我們的聲音帶來改變。我相信我們這些發聲的力量與作用，當我們為教育而團結在一起，我們的發聲就能改變整個世界。如果我們想要達成目標，就讓我們透過知識的武器，來強化我們的力量；透過團結一致，來捍衛我們自己。

親愛的兄弟姐妹們，我們不可忘記，有數以百萬計的人們正遭受著貧窮、不公不義和無知的苦難；我們不可忘記，有數以百萬計的兒童失學；我們不可忘記，我們的兄弟姐妹正等待著一個光明、和平的未來。

所以，讓我們展開一場輝煌的奮鬥，為打擊文盲、貧困和恐怖主義而努力。讓我們拾起我們的書本和筆，這是威力最強大的武器。一個孩子、一位老師、一本書、一枝筆，就能改變世界。教育，是唯一的解決之道。教育優先。謝謝大家。

Haruki Murakami's Jerusalem Prize Acceptance Speech

村上春樹耶路撒冷獎得獎感言：牆與蛋

村上春樹（Murakami Haruki, 1949–），日本享譽國際的小說家。生於京都，父母都是中學的日文教師，村上春樹自幼便喜愛閱讀，深受西方文學的影響。

29 歲時，村上春樹立志開始寫小說，六個月後，初試啼聲的小說《聽風的歌》，立即奪得日本群像新人獎。

1986 年，他和妻子旅居歐洲，並於隔年完成了《挪威的森林》，這是日本近代文學史上銷售量第一的長篇小說。這部作品讓他的名氣如日中天，並因此被譽為日本 1980 年代的文學旗手。

1990 年代，村上春樹的作品的英譯本陸續問世，此後他便成為國際各項文學獎項的常客，也是日本最有希望獲得下一個諾貝爾文學獎的作家。他從 2009 年起，便開始獲諾貝爾文學獎提名。然而，他年年入圍，持續八年，卻始終失之交臂。

本篇收錄的，是村上春樹於 2009 年獲頒耶路撒冷文學獎的得獎感言。他在迦薩烽火四起的敏感時刻，前往以色列領獎。他對此直言不諱，並揭露他未曾表白過的內心世界：

「在一道堅硬的高牆，和一顆撞牆即破的蛋之間，
我會一直站在蛋的那一邊。」

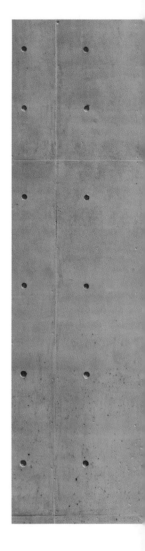

Speaker	日本文學家村上春樹
	（Murakami Haruki, 1949–）
Time	2009 年 2 月 15 日
Place	以色列首都耶路撒冷
	（Jerusalem, the capital of Israel）

▣ 錄音　▣ 全篇收錄

121

I have come to Jerusalem today as a novelist, which is to say as a professional spinner of lies. Of course, novelists are not the only ones who tell lies. Politicians do it, too, as we all know. Diplomats and military men tell their own kinds of lies on occasion, as do used car salesmen, butchers and builders. The lies of novelists differ from others, however, in that no one criticizes the novelist as immoral for telling them. Indeed, the bigger and better his lies and the more ingeniously he creates them, the more he is likely to be praised by the public and the critics. Why should that be?

My answer would be this: Namely, that by telling skillful lies—which is to say, by making up fictions that appear to be true—the novelist can bring a truth out to a new location and shine a new light on it. In most cases, it is virtually impossible to grasp a truth in its original form and depict it accurately. This is why we try to grab its tail by luring the truth from its hiding place, transferring it to a fictional location, and replacing it with a fictional form. In order to accomplish this, however, we first have to clarify where the truth lies within us. This is an important qualification for making up good lies.

Today, however, I have no intention of lying. I will try to be as honest as I can. There are a few days in the year when I do not engage in telling lies, and today happens to be one of them.

So let me tell you the truth. A fair number of people advised me not to come here to accept the Jerusalem Prize. Some even warned me they would instigate a boycott of my books if I came.

The reason for this, of course, was the fierce battle that was raging in Gaza[1]. The UN reported that more than a thousand people had lost their lives in the blockaded Gaza City, many of them unarmed citizens—children and old people. →

今天，我來到耶路撒冷，以一個小說家的身分，也就是說，是一位職業的織謊者。當然，會說謊的，並不是只有小說家。像我們知道的，政治家也是，而外交官和軍方人士，他們在必要時也會編織自己的謊言，一如中古車的業務員、肉販或建築商，亦是同然。不過，不同的是，倒沒有人會非難小說家滿口的謊言很缺德。尤有甚者，謊言扯得愈大、愈好、愈巧妙，社會大眾和評論家就愈可能褒揚他。怎麼會這樣呢？

Murakami Haruki (1949~)

我的答案是這樣的：那就是，編織技巧高超的謊言——也就是說，捏造故事，弄假似真——小說家能夠在一個新的場景，投射出一道新的光，將真正的實情帶出來。在大多數的情況下，要在原貌上抓出事實，然後準確地描繪出來，幾乎是不可能的。也因為這樣，我們要試著去抓住實情的尾巴，從隱蔽之處把實情引誘出來，然後將實情變換成一個虛構的場景，用杜撰的方式來替代。而為了完成這個任務，我們首先要弄清楚，實情究竟是隱匿在我們當中的何處。這是編織優秀謊言的重要條件。

不過，今天，我無意撒謊。我盡量誠實以告。一年之中，有幾天的時間我不埋頭於說謊，今天碰巧就是這樣一個日子。

所以，容我向諸位講述實情。有不少人勸我不要來這裡受頒耶路撒冷獎，有一些人甚至警告我，如果我來了，就要發動杯葛我的書。

1. Gaza [ˈgɑːzə] (n.) a city in the Gaza Strip (It was under Egyptian administration from 1949 until occupied by Israel.) 迦薩城

當然，其中的原因，是因為迦薩激烈的戰火。聯合國的報導說，在迦薩城的封鎖區，已有上千人喪生，而且當中有很多是非武裝市民——兒童和老人。

Any number of times after receiving notice of the award, I asked myself whether traveling to Israel at a time like this and accepting a literary prize was the proper thing to do, whether this would create the impression that I supported one side in the conflict, that I endorsed the policies of a nation that chose to unleash its overwhelming military power. This is an impression, of course, that I would not wish to give. I do not approve of any war, and I do not support any nation. Neither, of course, do I wish to see my books subjected to a boycott.

Finally, however, after careful consideration, I made up my mind to come here. One reason for my decision was that all too many people advised me not to do it. Perhaps, like many other novelists, I tend to do the exact opposite of what I am told. If people are telling me—and especially if they are warning me—"don't go there," "don't do that," I tend to want to "go there" and "do that." It's in my nature, you might say, as a novelist. Novelists are a special breed. They cannot genuinely trust anything they have not seen with their own eyes or touched with their own hands.

And that is why I am here. I chose to come here rather than stay away. I chose to see for myself rather than not to see. I chose to speak to you rather than to say nothing.

This is not to say that I am here to deliver a political message. To make judgments about right and wrong is one of the novelist's most important duties, of course. It is left to each writer, however, to decide upon the form in which he or she will convey those judgments to others. I myself prefer to transform them into stories—stories that tend toward the surreal. Which is why I do not intend to stand before you today delivering a direct political message.

Please do, however, allow me to deliver one very personal message. It is something that I always keep in mind while I am writing fiction. I have never gone so far as to write it on a piece of paper and paste it to the wall: Rather, it is carved into the wall of my mind, and it goes something like this: →

收到得獎通知之後，我問過自己無數次，在這樣的時刻，我前來以色列領文學獎，是否恰當；或者，此舉會造成一個印象，認為我在這個衝突中選邊站，以為我在為一個選擇發動優勢武力的國家政策背書。當然，我並不想給人這樣的印象。我不贊成任何戰爭，也不支持任一國家。當然，我也不樂見自己的書受到抵制。

而最後，經過審慎思考之後，我下定決心來到這裡。我作出這個決定的一個原因，是因為有太多人勸我不要來。或許，就跟很多其他的小說家一樣，別人叫我不要做的事，我就偏偏要去做。人們要是告訴我——尤其如果是帶上警告的語氣——「別去那裡」、「不要做那種事」，我就會想「要去那裡」、「要去做那種事」。身為一個小說家，你可能可以說這是我的天性。小說家是特殊物種，非親眼所見、非親手所摸，他們無法打從心底去相信任何事情。

這就是我來到這裡的原因。我選擇前來此地，而非保持距離；我選擇親眼目睹，而非撇眼不見；我選擇跟諸君談話，而非閉口不言。

這並不是說我來到此地，是要傳達政治訊息。當然，評斷對與錯，是小說家最重要的天職之一。不過，這要留給每一個寫作者，任由他們去決定要透過何種形式，來向人們傳達這些判斷。而我自己偏好將這些判斷改造成故事的形式——而且傾向於超寫實的故事。是故，今天站在大家的面前，我不打算傳達直接的政治訊息。

然而，請容許我表達非常個人的事。當我在寫小說時，有一件事情我一直放在心頭上。至今為止，我未曾將之付諸文字，貼在牆上，而是將之刻在吾心的牆上，此事如下：

123

*"Between a high, solid wall and an egg that breaks against it,
I will always stand on the side of the egg."*

Yes, no matter how right the wall may be and how wrong the egg, I will
stand with the egg. Someone else will have to decide what is right and
what is wrong; perhaps time or history will decide. If there were a novelist
who, for whatever reason, wrote works standing with the wall, of what
value would such works be?

What is the meaning of this metaphor? In some cases, it is all too simple
and clear. Bombers and tanks and rockets and white phosphorus shells[2] are
that high, solid wall. The eggs are the unarmed civilians who are crushed
and burned and shot by them. This is one meaning of the metaphor.

This is not all, though. It carries a deeper meaning. Think of it this way.
Each of us is, more or less, an egg. Each of us is a unique, irreplaceable
soul enclosed in a fragile shell. This is true of me, and it is true of each of
you. And each of us, to a greater or lesser degree, is confronting a high,
solid wall. The wall has a name: It is The System. The System is supposed to
protect us, but sometimes it takes on a life of its own[3], and then it begins
to kill us and cause us to kill others—coldly, efficiently, systematically.

I have only one reason to write novels, and that is to bring the dignity
of the individual soul to the surface and shine a light upon it. The purpose
of a story is to sound an alarm, to keep a light trained on The System in
order to prevent it from tangling our souls in its web and demeaning them.
I fully believe it is the novelist's job to keep trying to clarify the uniqueness
of each individual soul by writing stories—stories of life and death, stories
of love, stories that make people cry and quake with fear and shake with
laughter. This is why we go on, day after day, concocting fictions with utter
seriousness. →

「在一道堅硬的高牆，和一顆撞牆即破的蛋之間，
我會一直站在蛋的那一邊。」

是的，不論那道牆如何的對、那顆蛋如何的錯，我會跟蛋站在同一邊。對與錯，由別人裁斷；或許時間或歷史會做出定奪。如果有一位小說家，不管是基於什麼樣的理由，他要是站在牆的那一邊來寫作品，作品會有何價值？

這個隱喻是在說什麼？在某些情況，這個隱喻就顯得太清楚不過了。轟炸機、戰車、火箭炮、白磷彈，就是那堵堅固的高牆；手無寸鐵的平民，因此被輾壓、燒灼、射殺，這就是蛋。這是這個隱喻的一層意思。

但這不是全部的喻意，它有更深層的意義。試想，我們每一個人都差不多是那顆蛋。我們每一個人都是一個獨特、無可取代的靈魂，被包覆在一層脆弱的蛋殼裡。這是真實的我，諸君亦是。我們每一個人，或多或少，都面對著一堵堅固的高牆。這道牆有個名字，叫作「體制」。體制，照理說應該是要用來保護我們的，但有時卻變得不再受到任何人的控制，然後開始來殺害我們，或是令我們去殺害別人——無情地、有效地、系統性地。

我寫小說，只有一個原因，那就是帶出個人靈魂的尊嚴，令之浮現，清楚顯露出來。一篇故事的目的，是要敲響警鐘，讓體制無所遁形，以防我們的靈魂被纏捲進體制的網裡，失去了尊嚴。我著實相信，小說家的工作是盡量去清楚顯現出每一個靈魂個體的獨特性，透過寫故事的方式——生與死的故事、愛的故事，令人們落淚、顫慄或笑不可仰。這也就是為什麼我們不斷日復一日、嚴肅地撰寫故事的原因。

2. white phosphorus shell: an incendiary and toxic chemical substance used as a
  filler in a number of different munitions that can be employed for a variety of
  military purposes 白磷彈（攻擊型燃燒武器，含大量黏稠劑，能黏在人體和裝備上燃
  燒，殺傷效果極大，《聯合國常規武器公約》列為違禁武器，不允許對平民或在平民區
  使用。美英曾在伊拉克戰爭中使用白磷彈，遭到國際輿論指責。

3. take on a life of its own: to no longer be controlled by anyone 不受任何人的支配

124

My father died last year at the age of 90. He was a retired teacher and a part-time Buddhist priest[4]. When he was in graduate school, he was drafted into the army and sent to fight in China. As a child born after the war, I used to see him every morning before breakfast offering up long, deeply-felt prayers at the Buddhist altar in our house. One time I asked him why he did this, and he told me he was praying for the people who had died in the war. He was praying for all the people who died, he said, both ally and enemy alike. Staring at his back as he knelt at the altar, I seemed to feel the shadow of death hovering around him.

My father died, and with him he took his memories, memories that I can never know. But the presence of death that lurked about him remains in my own memory. It is one of the few things I carry on from him, and one of the most important.

I have only one thing I hope to convey to you today. We are all human beings, individuals transcending nationality and race and religion, fragile eggs faced with a solid wall called The System. To all appearances, we have no hope of winning. The wall is too high, too strong—and too cold. If we have any hope of victory at all, it will have to come from our believing in the utter uniqueness and irreplaceability of our own and others' souls and from the warmth we gain by joining souls together.

Take a moment to think about this. Each of us possesses a tangible, living soul. The System has no such thing. We must not allow The System to exploit us. We must not allow The System to take on a life of its own. The System did not make us: We made The System.

That is all I have to say to you. I am grateful to have been awarded the Jerusalem Prize. I am grateful that my books are being read by people in many parts of the world. And I am glad to have had the opportunity to speak to you here today. ◀

去年，家父過世，得年九十。他是一位退休教師，有時也會兼做佛教僧侶。他在讀研究所的時候，被徵召進入陸軍，被送到中國去打仗。我是戰後出生的小孩，每天早上，在早餐之前，我都會看到他在家中的佛龕前，做情感深沉的冗長課誦。有一次，我問他為什麼課誦，他跟我說，是為在戰爭中喪生的人念經。他說，他為一切死於戰爭中的人誦經，不管是敵方還是我方的人。望著他跪在佛龕前的背影，我彷彿感受到死亡的陰影在他身邊縈繞不去。

家父去世了，帶著他的回憶一起走了，那是我永遠無法知曉的回憶。不過，潛行在他周遭的死亡之相，留在我自己的記憶裡。這是少數我從他身上所繼承到的東西，而且是最重要的東西。

今天，我只想跟諸君傳達一件事。我們都是人類，是超越國籍、種族、宗教的個體，是一顆脆弱的蛋卵，對一堵名為「體制」的硬牆。不管怎麼看，我們都毫無勝算。這堵牆太高、太堅固，也太冷酷。如果我們有那麼一絲絲勝算，那是來自於我們深信自己和他人的靈魂具有絕對的獨特性和不可取代性，來自於靈魂結合在一起所獲取到的溫暖。

請片刻思索一下，我們每一個人都擁有可觸及、活生生的靈魂。這是體制所沒有的，我們不能容許體制來剝削我們，不能允許體制自行其道。不是體制來塑造我們，是我們創造體制。

我要對諸君說的，就是這些了。我很感謝能獲得耶路撒冷獎，我也很感謝世界許多地方的人們讀了我的書。我很高興今天能有機會在這裡和各位談話。

4. Murakami's father,
   Chiaki, is a Kyoto
   Buddhist priest
   村上春樹的父親叫
   作村上千秋（Chiaki
   Murakami），為京都
   西山淨土宗安養寺之
   僧侶

Gerhard Schröder Speech: I Express My Shame

德國總理施羅德道歉演說： 我深表羞愧

1970 年 12 月 7 日，當時的西德總理威利·布蘭特（Willy Brandt, 1913–1992）來到波蘭華沙猶太區的殉難紀念碑前，他獻上花圈時，突然下跪，為在納粹德國侵略期間被殺害的受難者默哀。他這一跪，不但驚動全世界，也讓他在隔年（1971 年）獲得了諾貝爾和平獎。

1995 年 6 月，另一位德國總理赫爾穆特·柯爾（Helmut Kohl, 1930–），再次在以色列的猶太人受難者紀念碑前，下跪道歉。事實上，德國歷任總理都在各種場合中，針對納粹罪行，代表德國向受難者道歉和懺悔。

德國不僅不斷致歉，也致力於透過各種方式來贖罪和斷絕前惡，包括賠償、立法、教育等。在德國國內，反納粹教育成為法律，嚴格規定反猶太行為的非法性。

位於波蘭的奧斯威辛（Auschwitz）集中營，是納粹德國時期最主要的死亡集中營，建於 1940 年。1945 年 1 月 27 日，蘇聯紅軍進入奧斯威辛，解放了集中營。後來，聯合國將 1 月 27 日訂為「國際大屠殺紀念日」，以提醒人類記取教訓。

此篇演說，是位於德國柏林的「國際奧斯威辛委員會」（International Auschwitz Committee），邀德國第 33 任總理格哈特·施羅德（Gerhard Schröder, 1944–）所作的道歉演說。

Speaker 德國第 33 任總理格哈特·施羅德
（Gerhard Schröder, 1944–）

Time 2005 年 1 月 25 日

Place 德國首都柏林
（Berlin, the capital of Germany）

▣ 錄音　▣ 全篇收錄

125

Ladies and gentlemen,

I would like to thank the International Auschwitz Committee for the invitation to speak to you here today. In my estimation an invitation of this kind is still not something that can be taken for granted.

It would be fitting for us Germans to remain silent in the face of what was the greatest crime in the history of mankind. Words by government leaders are inadequate when confronted with the absolute immorality and senselessness of the murder of millions.

We look for rational understanding of something that is beyond human comprehension. We seek definitive answers, but in vain.

What is left is the testimony of those few who survived and their descendants.

What is left are the remains of the sites of these murders and the historical record.

What is left also is the certainty that these extermination camps[1] were a manifestation of absolute evil.

Evil is not a political or scientific category. But, after Auschwitz, who could doubt that it exists, and that it manifested itself in the hate-driven genocide[2] carried out by the Nazi regime? However, noting this fact does not permit us to circumvent[3] our responsibility by blaming everything on a demonic Hitler. The evil manifested in the Nazi ideology was not without its precursors[4]. There was a tradition behind the rise of this brutal ideology and the accompanying loss of moral inhibition. Above all, it needs to be said that the Nazi ideology was something that people supported at the time and that they took part in putting into effect.

Now, sixty years after the liberation of Auschwitz by the Red Army[5], I stand before you as the representative of a democratic Germany. I express my shame for the deaths of those who were murdered and for the fact that you, the survivors, were forced to go through the hell of a concentration camp. →

56

我深表羞愧

各位女士先生：

　　我要感謝國際奧斯威辛委員會邀請我今天來這裡向各位發言。就我個人來看，這樣的邀請，尚未被認為是天經地義之事。

　　在人類史上最大的罪行面前，我們德國人民保持靜默，這是合宜的。面對此一絕對的不道德和屠殺數百萬人的愚蠢，政府領導人的發言都是嫌不夠的。

　　我們尋找能夠超越人類理解的理性認知，尋求最終的答案，但是徒勞無功。

　　留下來的，是少數倖存者和其後代子孫的證詞。

　　留下來的，是這些殺戮的遺跡和歷史文件。

　　留下來的，罪證確鑿，這些死亡集中營是絕對邪惡的顯現。

　　邪惡，不是政治或科學的範疇。但是，經過了奧斯維辛集中營，由納粹政權所進行仇恨的種族滅絕，昭然若揭，誰會懷疑其存在？不過，注意到此一事實，並非就允許我們將一切怪罪於邪惡的希特勒，然後就可以迴避責任。納粹意識形態中顯現出的邪惡，並非沒有前兆。這個野蠻的意識形態背後有一個傳統，當中伴隨著道德的淪喪。首先，要說的是，納粹的意識形態受到當時人們的支持，會付諸實行也有他們的一份。

　　今日，在紅軍解放奧斯維辛集中營的六十年後，我代表一個民主的德國，站在諸位的面前。我向被殺害的亡者，向被強制進入集中營煉獄的各位倖存者，深表羞愧。

Gerhard Schröder (1944–)

1. extermination camp: a camp where people are imprisoned and killed 死亡集中營

2. genocide [ˋdʒɛnəˏsaɪd] (n.) 種族滅絕

3. circumvent [ˏsɝːkəmˋvɛnt] (v.) to evade or go around 規避

4. precursor [prɪˋkɝːrsər] (n.) a person or thing that precedes and shows or announces someone or something to come 前兆

5. Red Army: the army of the former Soviet Union, formed after the revolution of 1917 (The name was officially dropped in 1946.) 蘇聯紅軍

126

Chelmno, Belzec, Sobibor, Treblinka, Maidanek, and Auschwitz-Birkenau are names that will forever be associated with the history of the victims as well as with German and European history. We know that. We bear this burden with sadness, but also with a serious sense of responsibility.

Millions of men, women, and children were gassed, starved, or shot by German SS troops[6] and their helpers. Jews, gypsies, homosexuals, political prisoners, POWs[7], and resistance fighters from across Europe were exterminated with cold industrial perfection or were enslaved and worked to death.

Never before had there been a worse breakdown of thousands of years of European culture and civilization. After the war it took some time before the full extent of this breakdown was realized. We are aware of it, but I doubt that we will ever be able to understand it. The past cannot be "overcome." It is the past. But its traces and, above all, the lessons to be learned from it extend to the present.

There will never be anything that can make up for the horror, the torment, and the agony that took place in the concentration camps. It is only possible to provide the families of those who died and the survivors a certain amount of compensation. Germany has faced this responsibility for a long period of time now with its government policies and court decisions, supported by a sense of justice on the part of the people.

The young men and women in the photo we see here were freed in the summer of 1945. Most survivors went in different directions after their liberation: to Israel, to North and South America, to neighboring European countries, or back to their countries of origin. However, some of them stayed in or returned to Germany, the country where the so-called "Final Solution[8]" originated.

It was an extraordinarily difficult decision for them, and often enough it was not a voluntary decision, but rather the result of total desperation. However, hope did return to their disrupted lives, and many did remain in Germany, and we are grateful for that. →

我們深知，徹姆諾、巴札茨、索比堡、特布林卡、邁登涅克、還有奧斯威辛集中營，這些名字，將與這段受害者的歷史，以及與德國歷史、歐洲歷史，永永遠遠地連在一起。我們用沉痛的心，扛起這個重擔，但也帶著一種嚴肅的責任感。

數以百萬計的男性、婦女、兒童，他們被德國黨衛軍部隊和其共犯，或被用毒氣毒死，或被餓死，或被槍殺而死。猶太人、吉普賽人、同性戀者、政治犯、戰俘，以及來自歐洲各地的反抗戰士，他們死於冷酷的極致工業之下，或是被奴役而勞動至死。

在此之前，數千年的歐洲文化和文明，未曾崩壞至此。戰爭結束後，經過了一些時間，才認知到這個崩壞的全貌。我們有所驚覺，但是我懷疑為我們是否真正能有所了解。我們無法「克服」過去，那是過去的歷史。不過歷史的足跡可循，最重要的是，我們從中所得到的教訓，能夠延續到今日。

集中營裡那些所發生的恐怖、折磨和劇烈的痛苦，永遠沒有任何東西可以彌補。只有盡可能為亡者和倖存者的家屬，提供相當數量的賠償。如今，德國以國家政策和法院決策來面對此一責任，已有好一段時間，並且受到我們人民這一方的正義感所支持。

我們在這張相片上所看到的這些青年男女，他們在 1945 年的夏天被釋放。被釋放的倖存者，大都被遣至各個不同的地方，有的去以色列，去北美和南美，去鄰近的歐洲國家，或回到原來的國家。不過，當中也有一些人留在德國，或是返回德國，而這個國家正是所謂「最終解決方案」的始作俑者。

對他們來說，這是一個非常困難的決定，而且往往不是一個出於自願的決定，反而是完全絕望所造成的結果。然而，「希望」回到了他們破碎的生活裡，有許多人留在了德國，對此我們很感激。

6. German SS troops: Schutzstaffel, special police force in Nazi Germany, founded as a personal body-guard for Adolf Hitler 黨衛隊；親衛隊（負責集中營）

7. POWs: prisoner of war 戰俘

8. Final Solution: the Nazi program of exterminating Jews under Hitler 納粹德國針對歐洲猶太人的系統性種族滅絕計畫

Today the Jewish community in Germany is the third-largest in Europe. It is full of vitality and growing rapidly. New synagogues are being built. The Jewish community is and will remain an irreplaceable part of our society and culture. Its brilliant as well as painful history will continue to be both an obligation and a promise for the future.

We will use the powers of government to protect it against the anti-Semitism[9] of those who refuse to learn the lessons of the past. There is no denying that anti-Semitism continues to exist. It is the task of society as a whole to fight it. It must never again become possible for anti-Semites to attack and cause injury to Jewish citizens in our country or any other country and in doing so bring disgrace upon our nation.

Right-wing extremists, with their spray-painted slogans, have the special attention of our law enforcement and justice authorities. But the process of dealing politically with neo-Nazis[10] and former Nazis is something we all need to do together. It is the duty of all democrats to provide a strong response to neo-Nazi incitement[11] and recurrent attempts on their part to play down the importance of the crimes perpetrated by the Nazi regime. For the enemies of democracy and tolerance there can be no tolerance.

The survivors of Auschwitz have called upon us to be vigilant, not to look away, and not to pretend we don't hear things. They have called upon us to acknowledge human rights violations and to do something about them. They are being heard, particularly by young people, for instance by those who are looking at the Auschwitz memorial today with their own eyes. They are speaking with former prisoners. They are helping to maintain and preserve the memorial. They will also help to inform future generations of the crimes committed by the Nazi regime.

The vast majority of the Germans living today bear no guilt for the Holocaust[12]. But they do bear a special responsibility. Remembrance of the war and the genocide perpetrated by the Nazi regime has become part of our living constitution[13]. For some this is a difficult burden to bear. →

56
我深表羞愧

今天，德國的猶太社區在歐洲是第三大的。它充滿活力，成長迅速。新的猶太會堂一間間蓋起來，在我們的社會和文化裡，猶太社區是不可取代的一部分，而且將一直是如此。其輝煌和痛苦的歷史，將繼續是展望未來的義務與承諾。

對於那些不肯從歷史中學到教訓的反猶太主義分子，我們會動用國家力量來進行保護。不可否認的，反猶太主義還繼續存在著，而對之加以打擊，是整體社會的任務。不管是在我們國家，還是在任何其他的國家，我們決不可能再讓反猶太分子去攻擊、傷害猶太公民。如果發生了這種事，就是為我們國家帶來恥辱。

噴漆寫標語的右翼極端分子，都受到我們執法部門和司法單位的特別關注。而新納粹和前納粹的政治處理過程，是我們所有人都要齊心努力的。對於新納粹的煽動，以及一再企圖淡化納粹政權所犯下的罪行的重大性，我們所有的民主黨人，都有職責要對此做出強烈回應。決不能包容的，是與民主和包容為敵的人。

奧斯維辛倖存者呼籲我們，要提高警覺，切莫視而不見，也不要假裝什麼都沒聽到。他們呼籲我們，要承認這是侵犯人權，應該加以制止。他們的呼籲被聽到了，特別是被年輕人聽到了，譬如今天親眼來見證奧斯威辛紀念館那些人。他們和以前被囚禁的人談話，這有助於紀念館的維護和存續。他們也有助於將於納粹政權犯下的罪行，告知給代代的後世知道。

今天，絕大部分在世的德國人，他們對大屠殺雖沒有負罪感，但是他們的確負一種有特殊的責任。納粹政權所發動的戰爭和種族屠殺，其悼念已經成為我們現有法規的一部分。對一些人來說，這是難以承受的重擔。

New Synagogue, Berlin

9. anti-Semitism [ˌæntiˈsemɪtɪzəm] (n.) the intense dislike for and prejudice against Jewish people 反猶太主義

10. neo-Nazi [ˌniːoʊˈnɑːtsɪ] (n.) a person of extreme racist or nationalist views 新納粹分子

11. incitement [ɪnˈsaɪtmənt] (n.) something that encourages people to be violent or commit crimes 煽動

12. Holocaust [ˈhɑləˌkɔːst] (n.) a war in which many ordinary people are killed 大屠殺

13. constitution [ˌkɑnstɪˈtjuːʃən] (n.) the fundamental political principles on which a state is governed, especially when considered as embodying the rights of the subjects of that state 憲法；法規

Nonetheless this remembrance is part of our national identity. Remembrance of the Nazi era and its crimes is a moral obligation. We owe it to the victims, we owe it to the survivors and their families, and we owe it to ourselves.

It is true, the temptation to forget is very great. But we will not succumb to this temptation. The Holocaust memorial in the center of Berlin cannot restore the lives or the dignity of the victims. It can perhaps serve survivors and their descendants as a symbol of their suffering. It serves us all as a reminder of the past.

We know one thing for sure. There would be no freedom, no human dignity, and no justice if we were to forget what happened when freedom, justice, and human dignity were desecrated by government power. Exemplary efforts are being undertaken in many German schools, in companies, in labor unions, and in the churches. Germany is facing up to its past.

From the Shoa and Nazi terror a certainty has arisen for us all that can best be expressed by the words "never again." We want to preserve this certainty. All Germans, but also all Europeans, and the entire international community need to continue to learn to live together with respect, humanity, and in peace.

The Convention on the Prevention and Punishment of the Crime of Genocide[14] was a direct effect of the Holocaust on international law. It requires people of different cultural, religious, and racial origins to respect and protect life and human dignity throughout the world. You in the International Auschwitz Committee support this with the exemplary work you are doing in the interest of all people.

Together with you I bow my head before the victims of the death camps. Even if one day the names of the victims should fade in the memory of mankind, their fate will not be forgotten. They will remain in the heart of history. ◀

56

我深表羞愧

14. The Convention on the Prevention and Punishment of the Crime of Genocide
《聯合國防止及懲治種族屠殺罪公約》

不過，此悼念是我們國家認同的一部分。悼念納粹時代及其罪行，是一種道德上的義務。我們愧對受害者，愧對倖存者及其家屬，也愧對我們自己。

的確，「忘記」的誘惑很大，但我們不會屈服於這種誘惑。柏林市中心的大屠殺紀念館，無法讓受害者重獲生命或是重拾尊嚴。也許，這會是倖存者及其後代的一種苦痛象徵，會提醒我們所有人過去所發生的事。

我們確知一件事，當用政府的力量褻瀆了自由、人性尊嚴、正義，如果我們忘記其所造成的後果，那自由、正義和人性尊嚴就不會存在。在德國的許多學校、公司行號、工會、教堂裡，正進行著示範性的努力。德國正在面對自己的過去。

從大屠殺和納粹暴行當中，對我們所有人來說，可確定的是，最能表達的字眼是「千萬不要再發生了」。我們要保持這種確定性。所有的德國人，而且還有所有的歐洲人，整個國際社會都需要繼續學習在尊重、人性和和平中共存。

《聯合國防止及懲治種族屠殺罪公約》是國際法中對於大屠殺的一個直接法律效力，其要求不同文化、宗教和種族淵源的人們，要尊重和保護世界各地的生命與人類尊嚴。在國際奧斯威辛委員會的你們，以示範性工作來支持這一點，亦即是在謀全人類的福祉。

在你們面前，我向死亡集中營的受害者，鞠躬致意。就算有那麼一天，受害者的名字會在人類的記憶中褪去，但是他們的命運不會被遺忘。他們會一直存留在歷史的核心裡。

國家圖書館出版品預行編目資料

聚焦英語演說（新增二版）/ Cosmos Language
Workshop 編著；一二版. 一
[臺北市]：寂天文化, 2019.2 面；公分

ISBN　978-986-318-458-4 (20K平裝附光碟片)
ISBN　978-986-318-548-2 (25K精裝附光碟片)
ISBN　978-986-318-656-4 (32K平裝附光碟片)
ISBN　978-986-318-778-3 (25K平裝附光碟片)
　　　1. 英語　2. 讀本

805.18　　　　　　　　　　108001316

編者 _ Cosmos Language Workshop
校對 _ 陳慧莉
製程管理 _ 洪巧玲
出版者 _ 寂天文化事業股份有限公司
電話 _ +886-2-2365-9739
傳真 _ +886-2-2365-9835
網址 _ www.icosmos.com.tw
讀者服務 _ onlineservice@icosmos.com.tw
出版日期 _ 2019年2月 二版四刷（250201）
郵撥帳號 _ 1998620-0 寂天文化事業股份有限公司

本書為《遇見偉大的聲音》和《感動世界的聲音》
兩本書之合輯